"Stayed in from recess to read it . . . **CAN'T WAIT FOR NEXT ONE!**"
—Zac A., age 9, Hood River, Ore.

I **LOVE** this book because it is **EXCITING** and **FUNNY.**"
—Nate A., age 8, Brooklyn

"**GINA WAS MY FAVORITE** character because she's into science and soccer like me! I also liked D.J.'s family because it looks like mine!"
—Kiran M., age 7, Carlsbad, Calif.

"*Hilo* is **REALLY, REALLY FUNNY.** It has a **LOT OF LAUGHS.** The raccoon is the funniest."
—Theo M., age 7, Miami, Fla.

"**HIGH ENERGY** and **HILARIOUS**!"
—Gene Luen Yang, National Ambassador for Young People's Literature

"**FANTASTIC. EVERY SINGLE THING ABOUT THIS . . . IS TERRIFIC.**"
—Boingboing.net

"My students are obsessed with this series. **OBSESSED!**"
—Colby Sharp, teacher, blogger, and co-founder of the Nerdy Book Club

"More **GIANT ROBOTIC ANTS . . .** than in the complete works of Jane Austen."
—Neil Gaiman, author of *Coraline*

"My big brother and I **FIGHT OVER THIS BOOK.**"
—Nory V., age 8, Montclair, N.J.

"*Hilo* is loads of **SLAPSTICK FUN!**"
—Dan Santat, winner of the Caldecott Medal

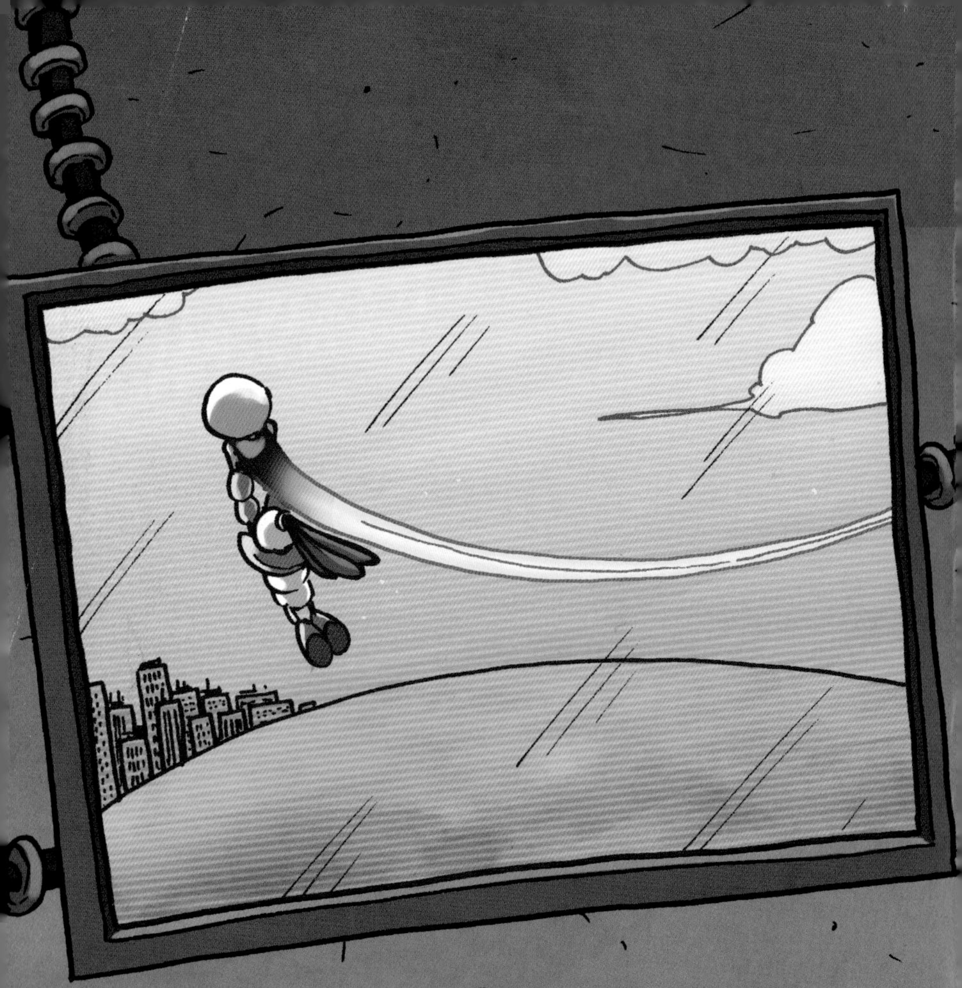

READ ALL THE HILO BOOKS!

HILO #1 THE BOY WHO CRASHED TO EARTH

HILO #2 SAVING THE WHOLE WIDE WORLD

HILO #3 THE GREAT BIG BOOM

HILO #4 WAKING THE MONSTERS

HiLo

BOOK 4

WAKING THE MONSTERS

BY JUDD WINICK

COLOR BY
STEVE HAMAKER

RANDOM HOUSE 🏠 NEW YORK

Copyright © 2018 by Judd Winick

All rights reserved. Published in the United States by Random House Children's Books, a division of Penguin Random House LLC, New York.

Random House and the colophon are registered trademarks of Penguin Random House LLC.

Visit us on the Web! rhcbooks.com

Educators and librarians, for a variety of teaching tools, visit us at RHTeachersLibrarians.com

Library of Congress Cataloging-in-Publication Data

Names: Winick, Judd, author.

Title: Hilo. Book 4, waking the monsters / by Judd Winick.

Description: First edition. | New York : Random House, [2018] | Summary: Hilo and his friends learn more about Hilo's past while they battle robots that were buried underground on Earth a thousand years ago.

Identifiers: LCCN 2016052236 | ISBN 978-1-5247-1493-2 (hardcover) | ISBN 978-1-5247-1494-9 (hardcover library binding) | ISBN 978-1-5247-1495-6 (ebook)

Subjects: LCSH: Graphic novels. | CYAC: Graphic novels. | Robots—Fiction. | Extraterrestrial beings—Fiction. | Friendship—Fiction. | Identity—Fiction. | Science fiction.

Classification: LCC PZ7.7.W57 Wl 2018 | DDC 741.5/973—dc23

MANUFACTURED IN CHINA

10 9 8 7 6 5 4 3 2 1

Book design by Bob Bianchini

First Edition

FOR MY BIG BROTHER,
ORIN

CHAPTER 1

WHOA

WHOA.
FEEL THAT?

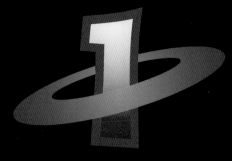

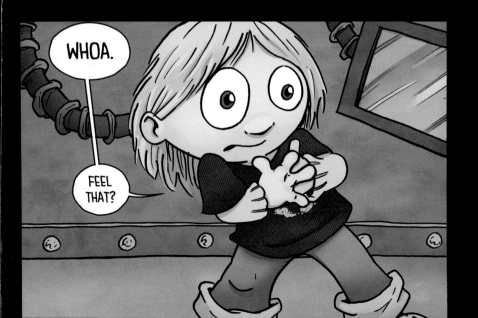

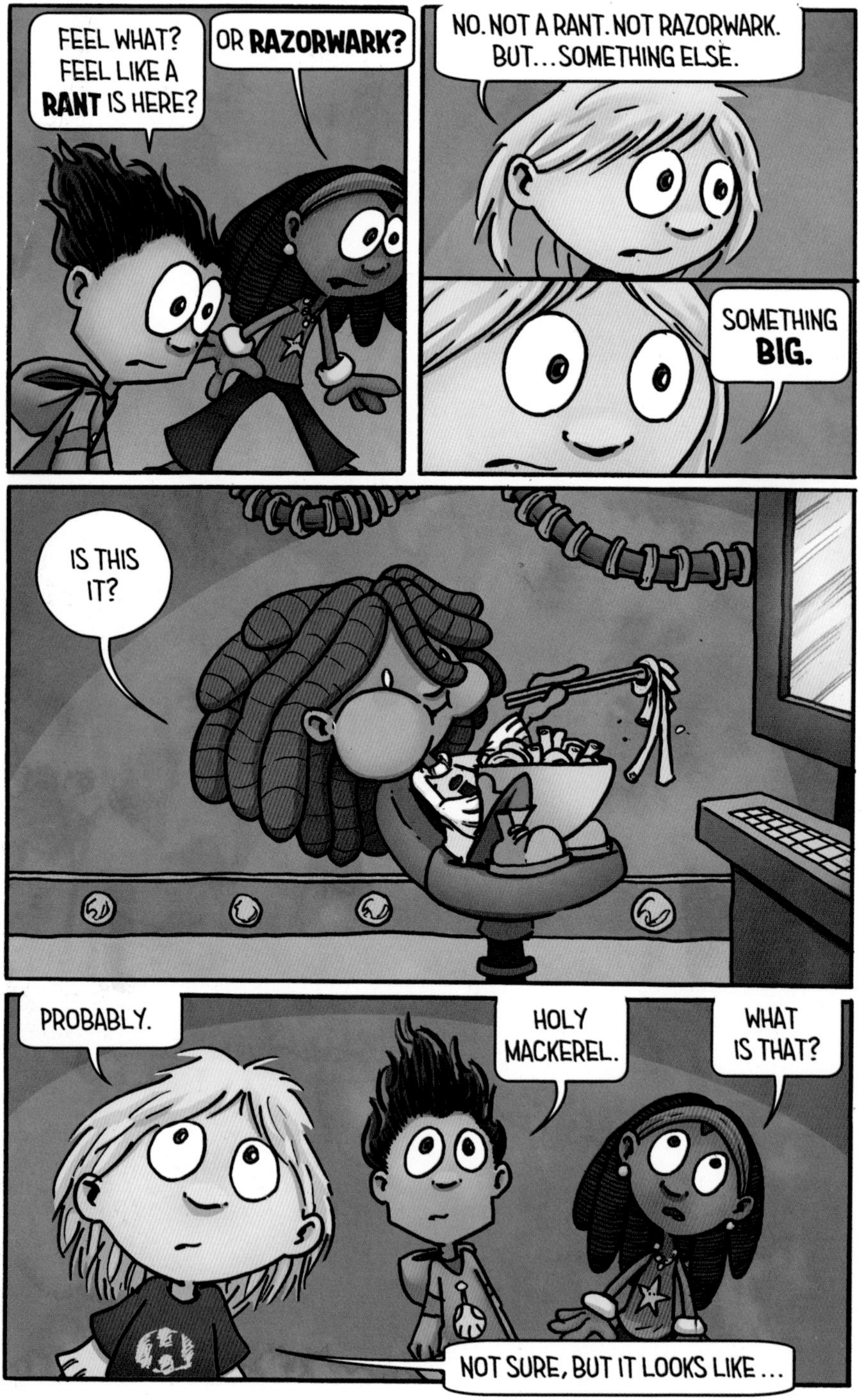
FEEL WHAT? FEEL LIKE A **RANT** IS HERE?
OR **RAZORWARK?**
NO. NOT A RANT. NOT RAZORWARK. BUT... SOMETHING ELSE.
SOMETHING **BIG.**
IS THIS IT?
PROBABLY.
HOLY MACKEREL.
WHAT IS THAT?
NOT SURE, BUT IT LOOKS LIKE ...

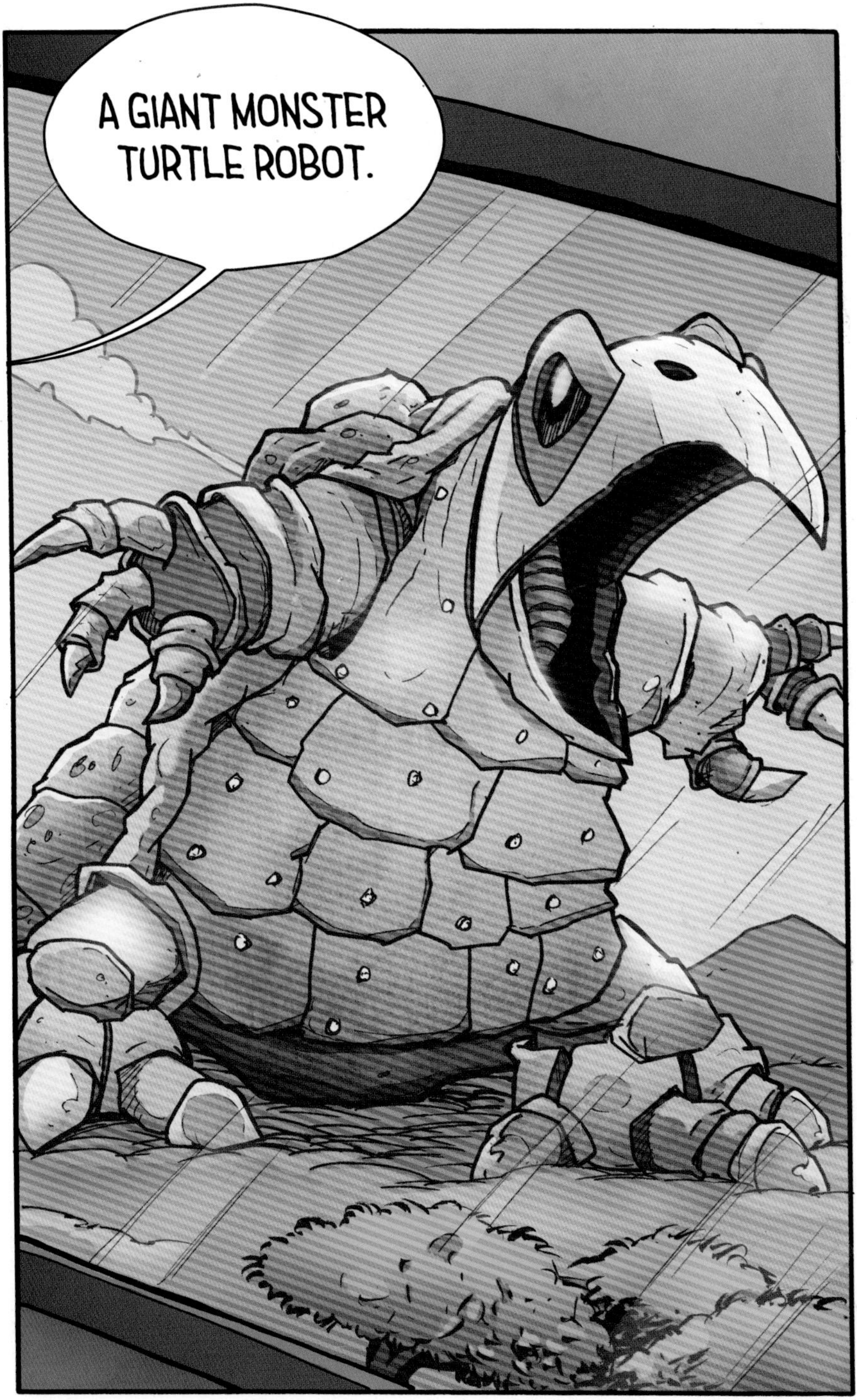
A GIANT MONSTER TURTLE ROBOT.

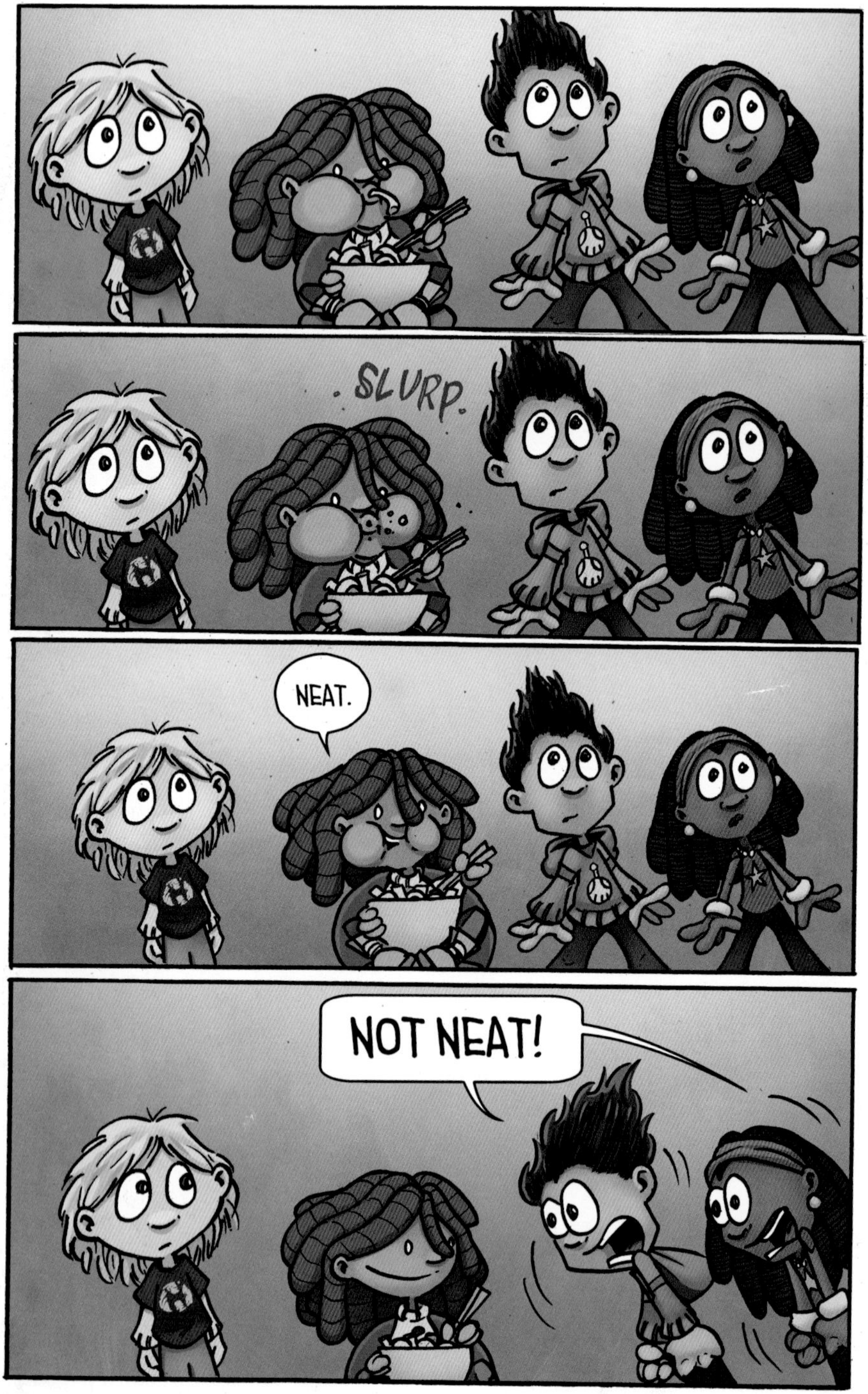
SLURP
NEAT.
NOT NEAT!

CHAPTER 2

HERE TO HELP

TWO MONTHS EARLIER.

MY NAME IS **DANIEL JACKSON LIM.** BUT EVERYONE CALLS ME **D.J.**

THIS IS MY BEST FRIEND, **HILO.**

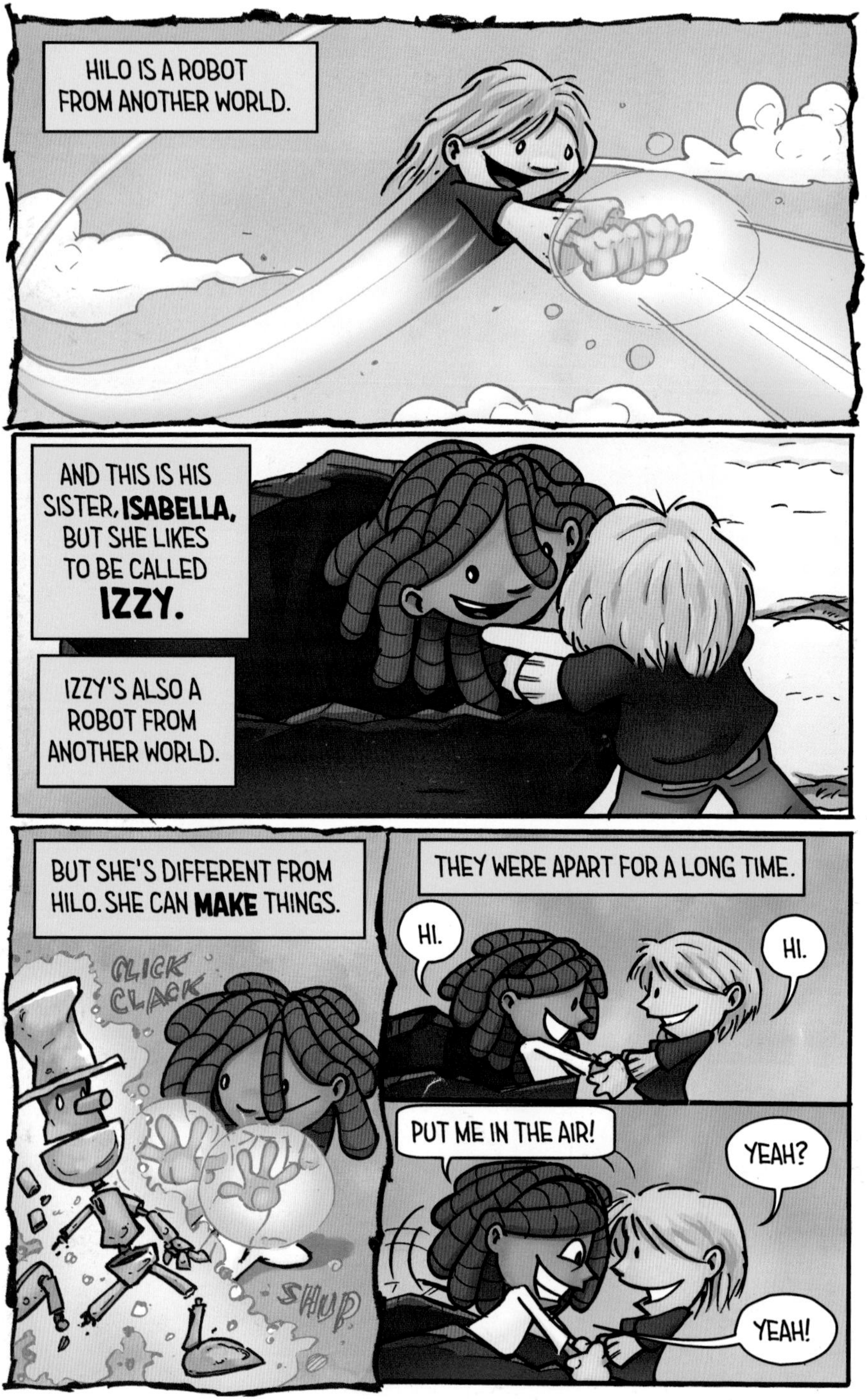
HILO IS A ROBOT FROM ANOTHER WORLD.
AND THIS IS HIS SISTER, **ISABELLA,** BUT SHE LIKES TO BE CALLED **IZZY.**
IZZY'S ALSO A ROBOT FROM ANOTHER WORLD.
BUT SHE'S DIFFERENT FROM HILO. SHE CAN **MAKE** THINGS.
CLICK CLACK
SHUP
THEY WERE APART FOR A LONG TIME.
HI.
HI.
PUT ME IN THE AIR!
YEAH?
YEAH!

ZIIIP

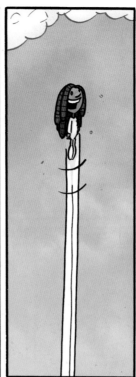

Poof

AAAAH!

I STILL CAN'T BELIEVE SHE'S HERE. IT'S SO WEIRD -- SO **WRONG** -- THAT I DIDN'T REMEMBER HER.

HILO!

THERE'S JUST NOTHING ...

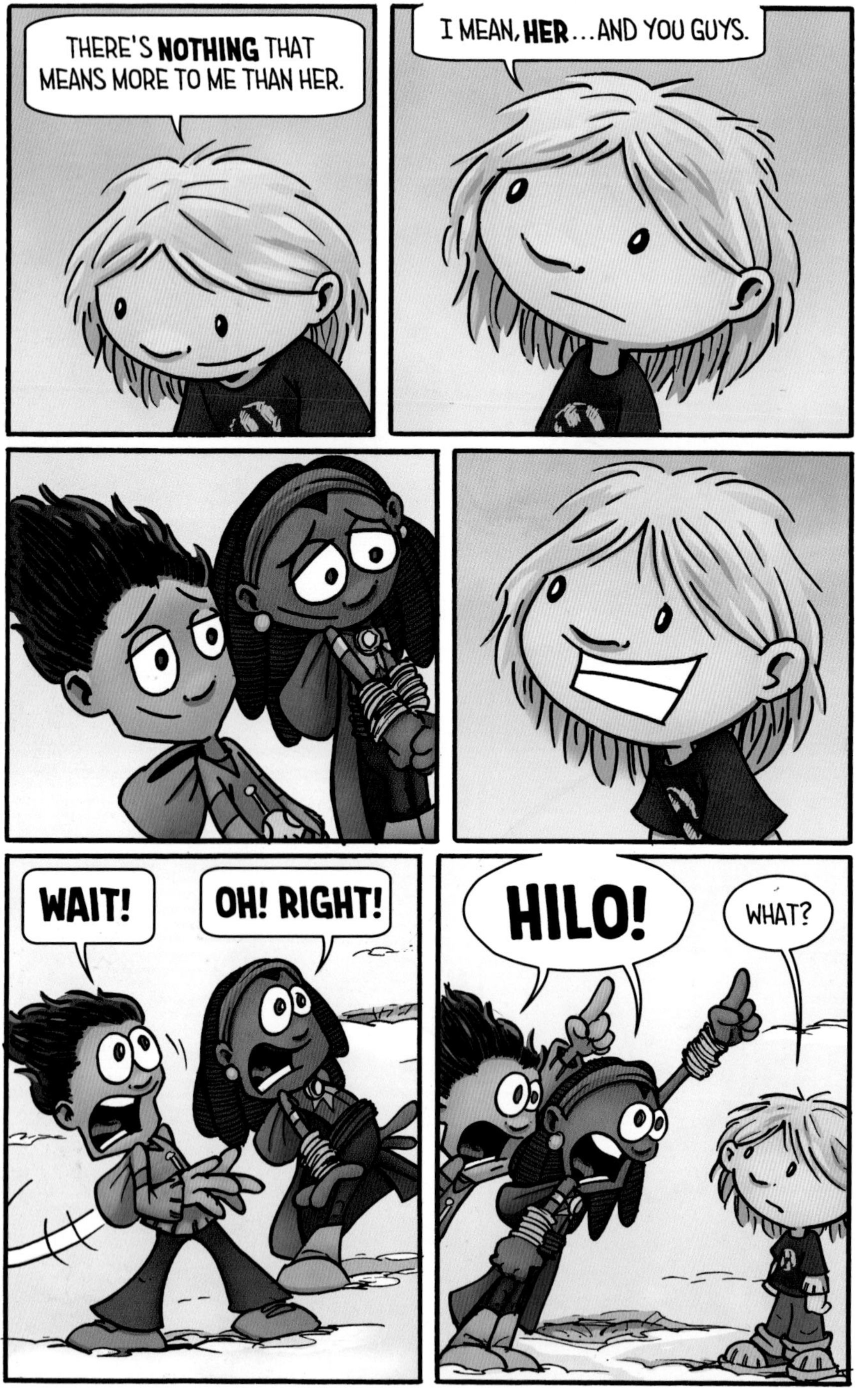
THERE'S **NOTHING** THAT MEANS MORE TO ME THAN HER.
I MEAN, **HER**...AND YOU GUYS.
WAIT!
OH! RIGHT!
HILO!
WHAT?

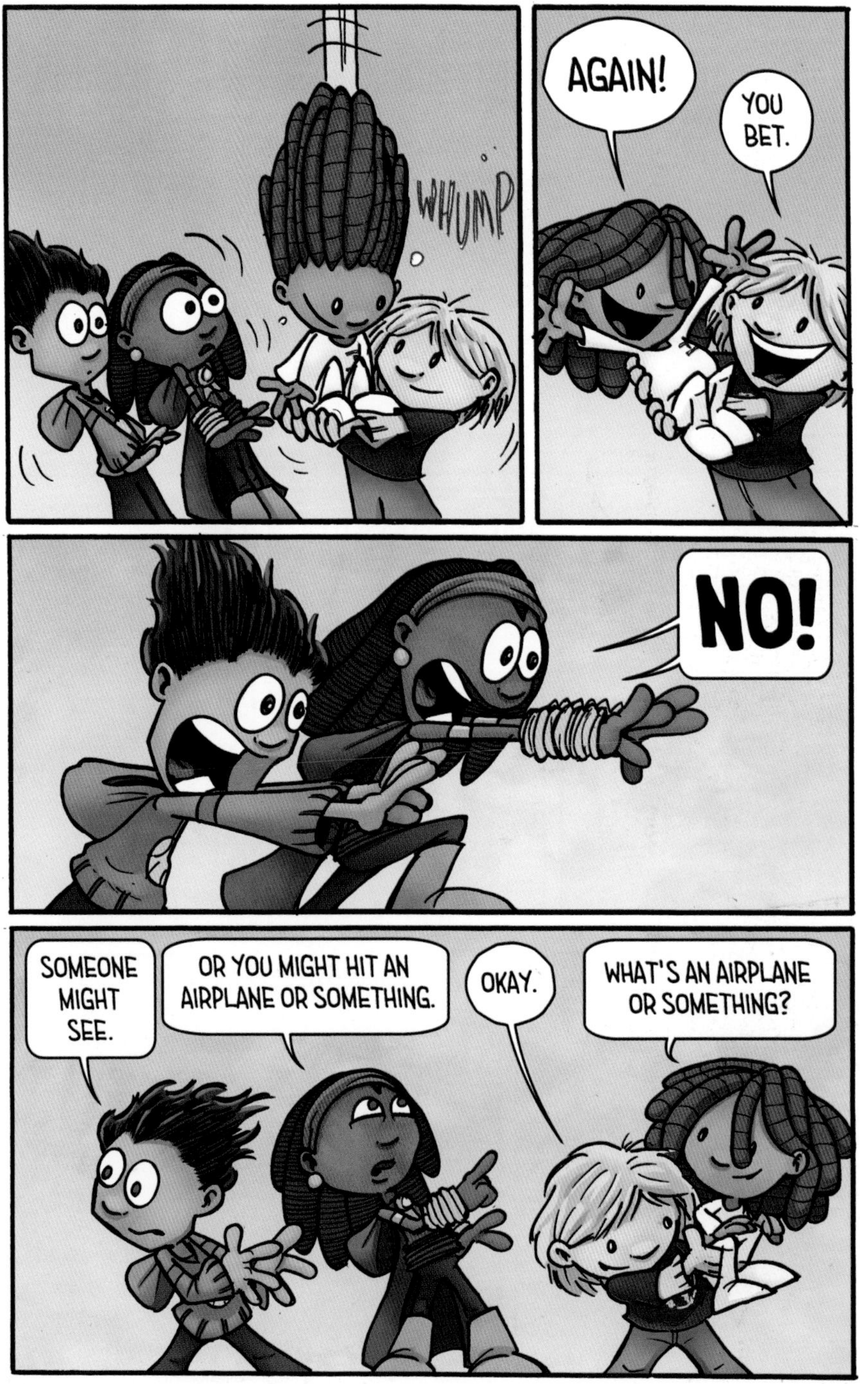
WHUMP
AGAIN!
YOU BET.
NO!
SOMEONE MIGHT SEE.
OR YOU MIGHT HIT AN AIRPLANE OR SOMETHING.
OKAY.
WHAT'S AN AIRPLANE OR SOMETHING?

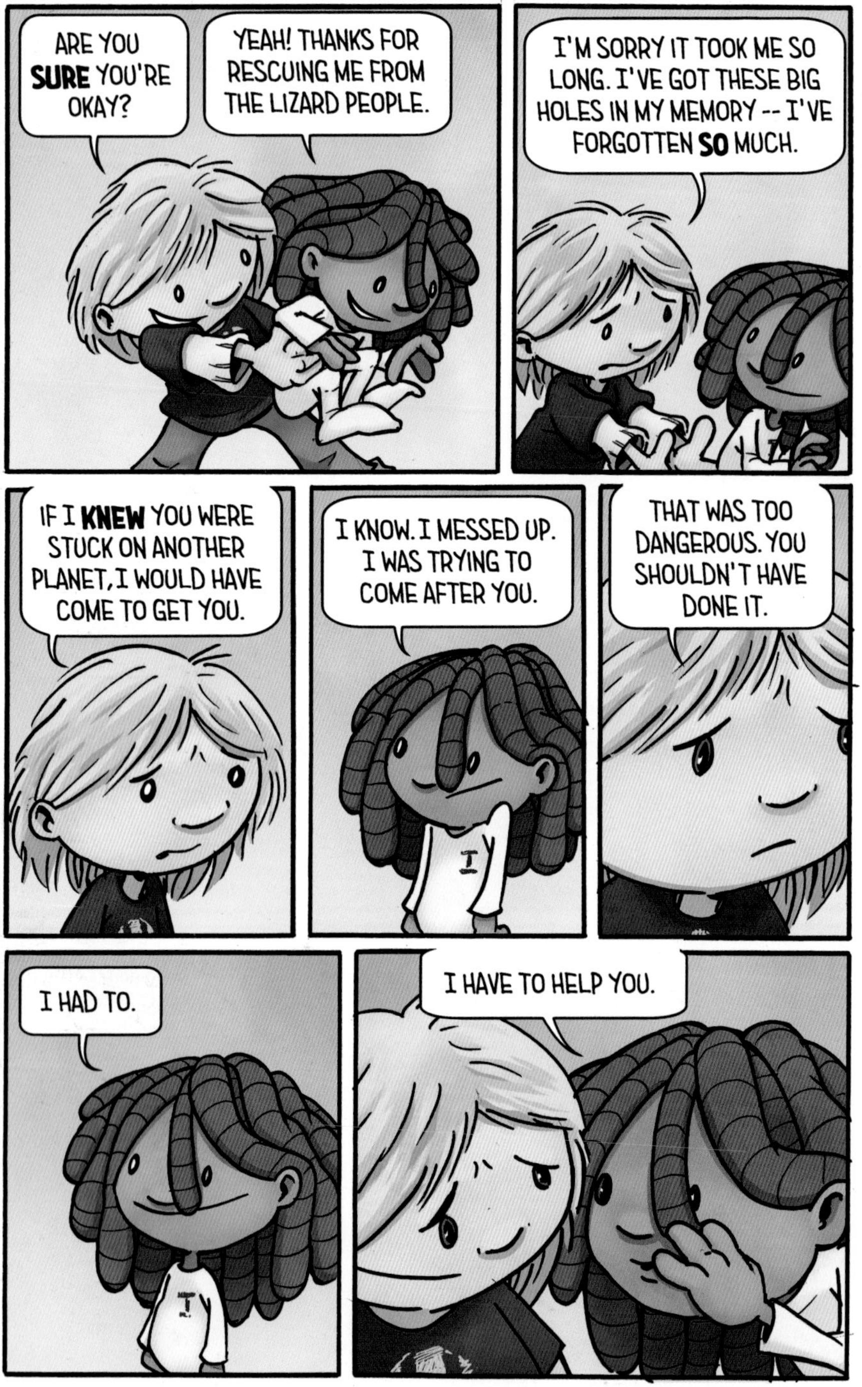
ARE YOU SURE YOU'RE OKAY?
YEAH! THANKS FOR RESCUING ME FROM THE LIZARD PEOPLE.
I'M SORRY IT TOOK ME SO LONG. I'VE GOT THESE BIG HOLES IN MY MEMORY -- I'VE FORGOTTEN SO MUCH.
IF I KNEW YOU WERE STUCK ON ANOTHER PLANET, I WOULD HAVE COME TO GET YOU.
I KNOW. I MESSED UP. I WAS TRYING TO COME AFTER YOU.
THAT WAS TOO DANGEROUS. YOU SHOULDN'T HAVE DONE IT.
I HAD TO.
I HAVE TO HELP YOU.

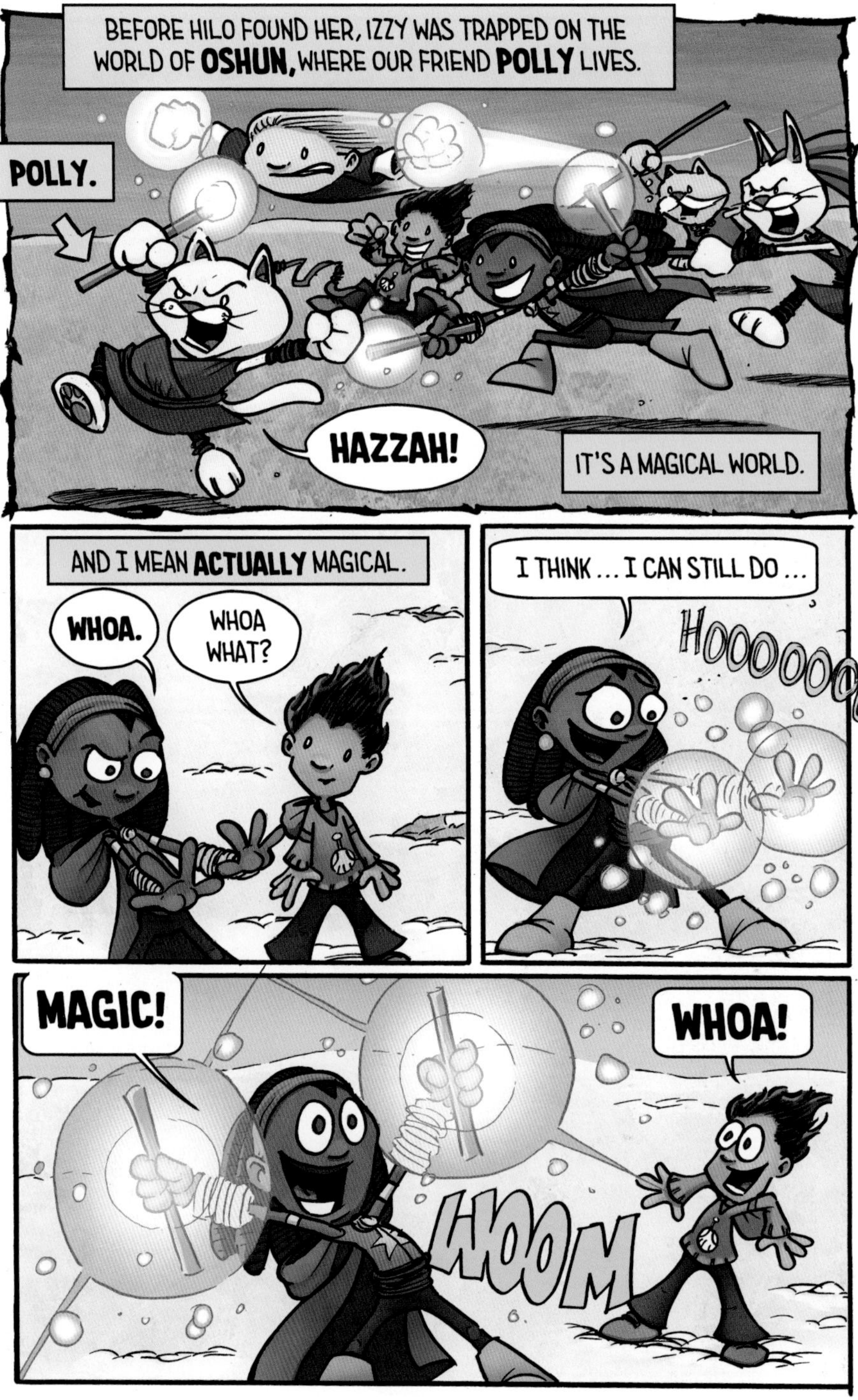
BEFORE HILO FOUND HER, IZZY WAS TRAPPED ON THE WORLD OF **OSHUN,** WHERE OUR FRIEND **POLLY** LIVES.
POLLY.
HAZZAH!
IT'S A MAGICAL WORLD.
AND I MEAN **ACTUALLY** MAGICAL.
WHOA.
WHOA WHAT?
I THINK . . . I CAN STILL DO . . .
HOOOOOOOO
MAGIC!
WHOA!
WOOM

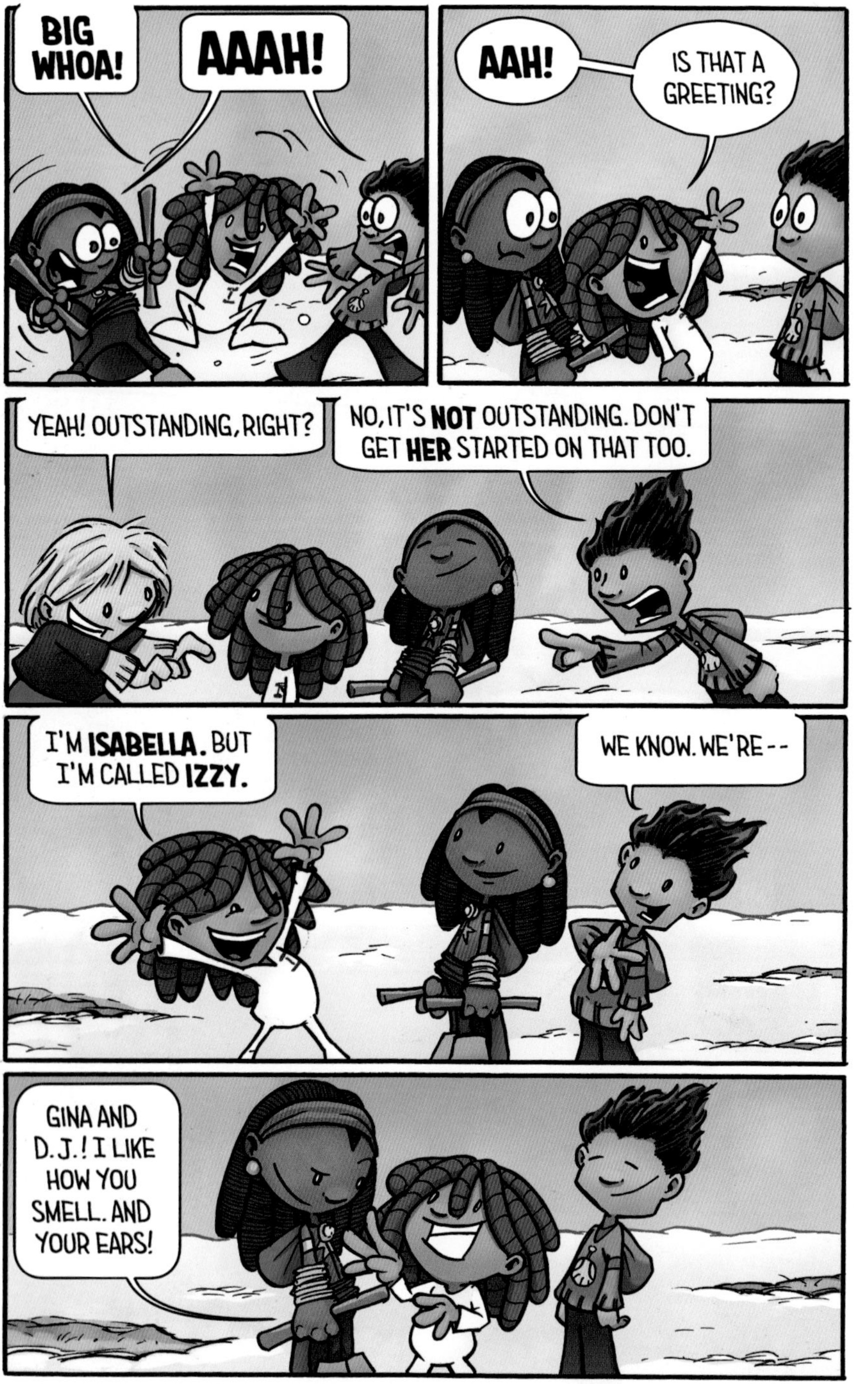
BIG WHOA!
AAAH!
AAH!
IS THAT A GREETING?
YEAH! OUTSTANDING, RIGHT?
NO, IT'S **NOT** OUTSTANDING. DON'T GET **HER** STARTED ON THAT TOO.
I'M **ISABELLA.** BUT I'M CALLED **IZZY.**
WE KNOW. WE'RE--
GINA AND D.J.! I LIKE HOW YOU SMELL. AND YOUR EARS!

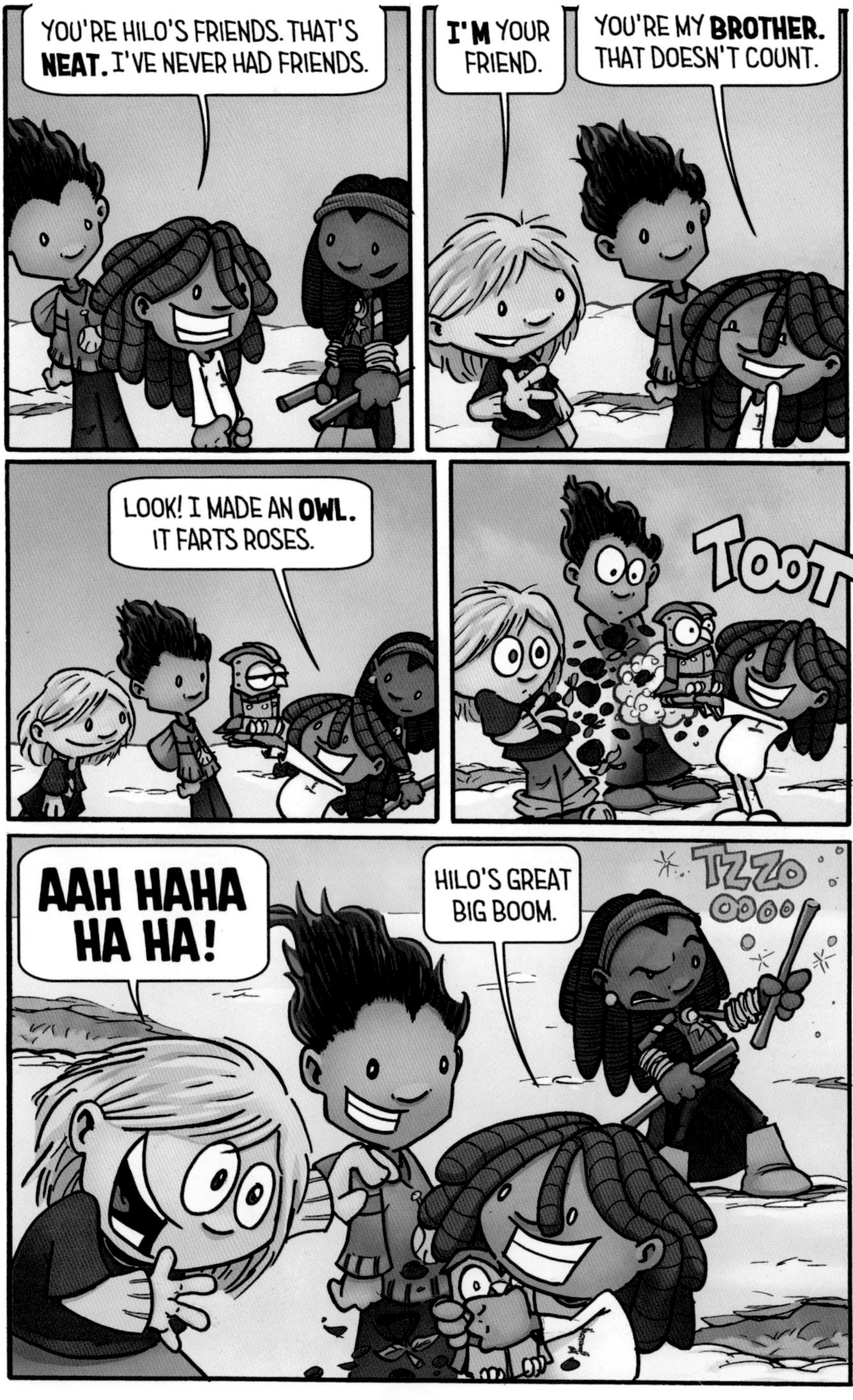
YOU'RE HILO'S FRIENDS. THAT'S **NEAT.** I'VE NEVER HAD FRIENDS.
I'M YOUR FRIEND.
YOU'RE MY **BROTHER.** THAT DOESN'T COUNT.
LOOK! I MADE AN **OWL.** IT FARTS ROSES.
TOOT
AAH HAHA HA HA!
HILO'S GREAT BIG BOOM.
TZZOOOOO

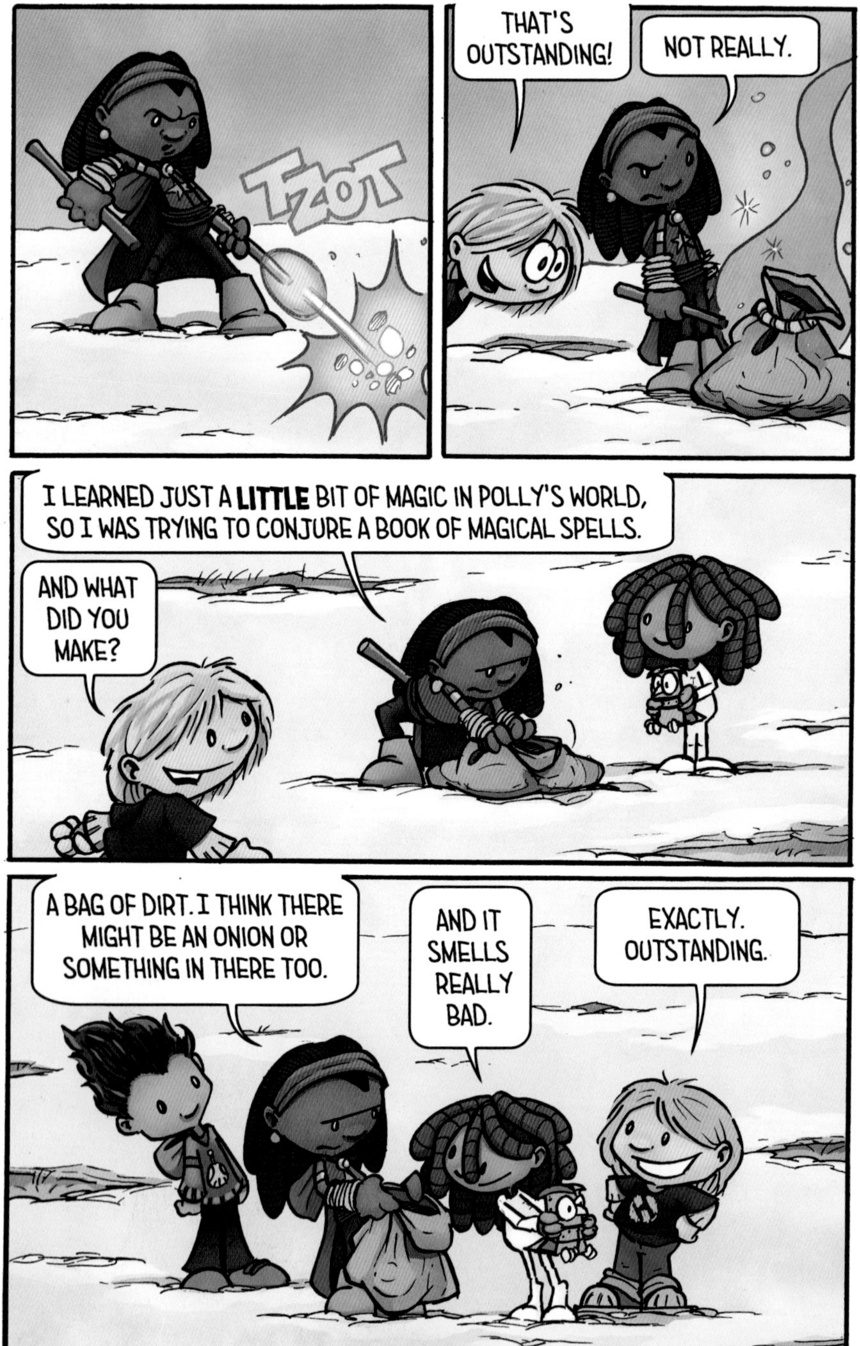
TZOT
THAT'S OUTSTANDING!
NOT REALLY.
I LEARNED JUST A **LITTLE** BIT OF MAGIC IN POLLY'S WORLD, SO I WAS TRYING TO CONJURE A BOOK OF MAGICAL SPELLS.
AND WHAT DID YOU MAKE?
A BAG OF DIRT. I THINK THERE MIGHT BE AN ONION OR SOMETHING IN THERE TOO.
AND IT SMELLS REALLY BAD.
EXACTLY. OUTSTANDING.

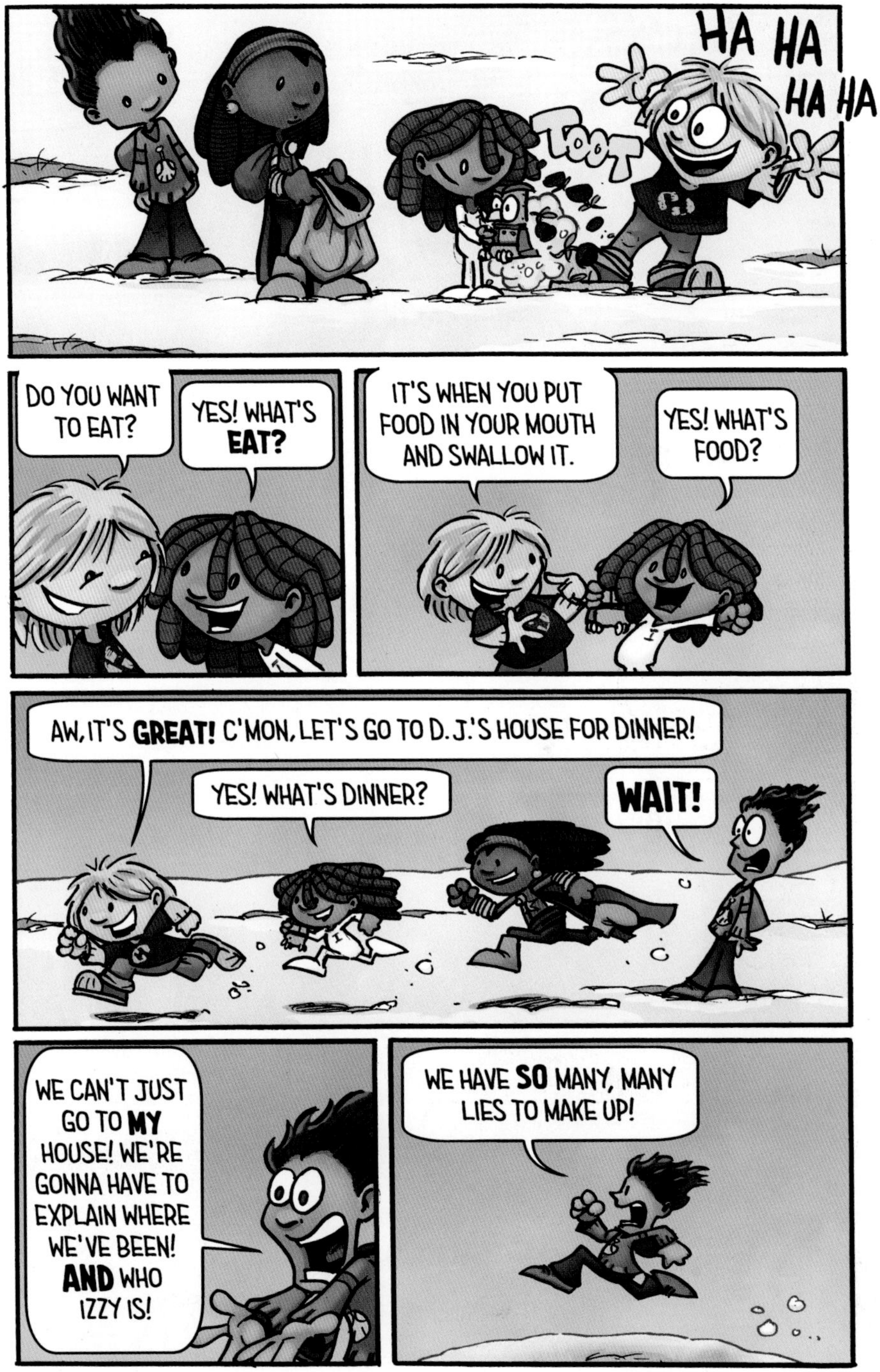
HA HA HA HA
TOOT
DO YOU WANT TO EAT?
YES! WHAT'S **EAT?**
IT'S WHEN YOU PUT FOOD IN YOUR MOUTH AND SWALLOW IT.
YES! WHAT'S FOOD?
AW, IT'S **GREAT!** C'MON, LET'S GO TO D. J.'S HOUSE FOR DINNER!
YES! WHAT'S DINNER?
WAIT!
WE CAN'T JUST GO TO **MY** HOUSE! WE'RE GONNA HAVE TO EXPLAIN WHERE WE'VE BEEN! **AND** WHO IZZY IS!
WE HAVE **SO** MANY, MANY LIES TO MAKE UP!

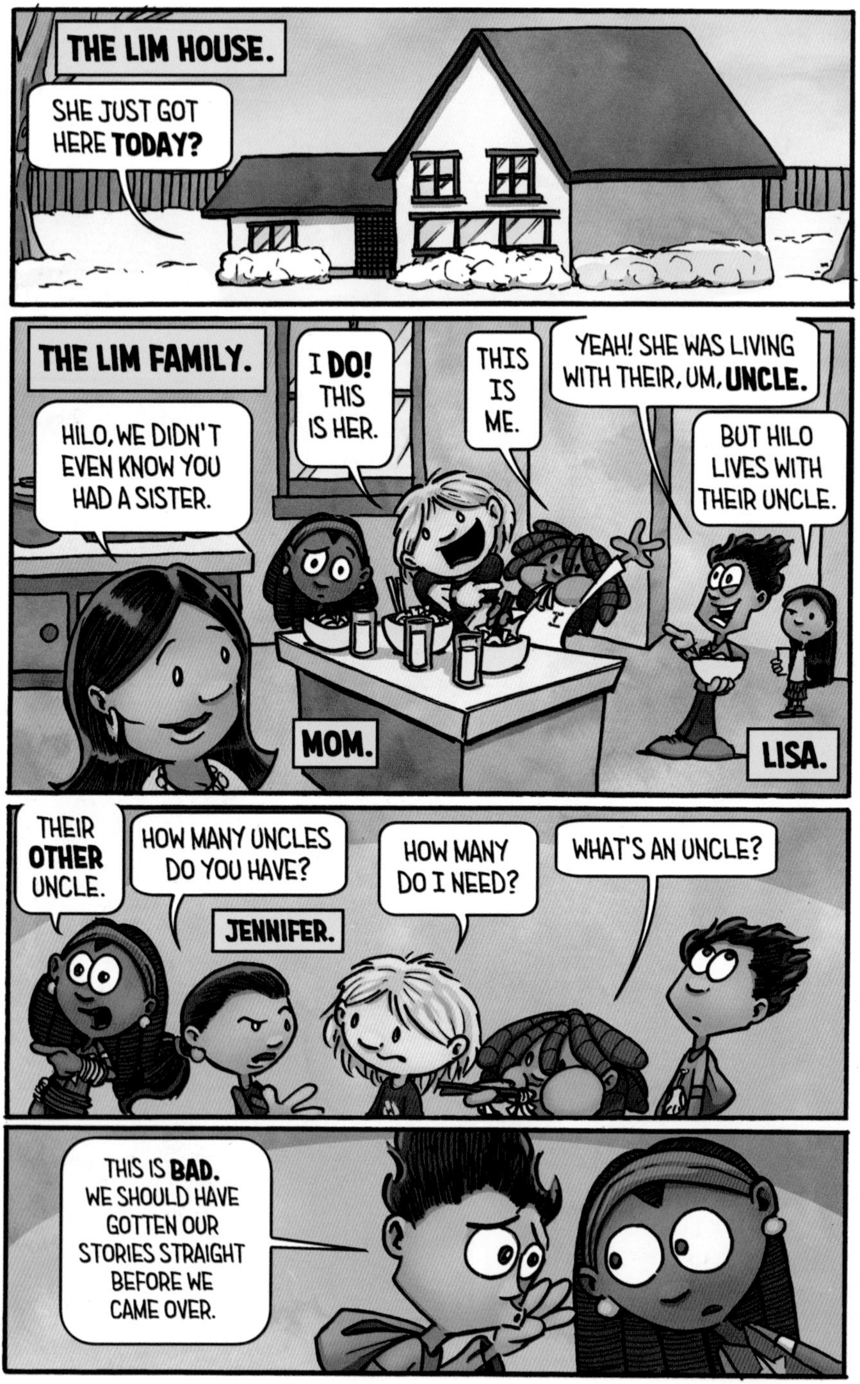
THE LIM HOUSE.
SHE JUST GOT HERE **TODAY?**
THE LIM FAMILY.
HILO, WE DIDN'T EVEN KNOW YOU HAD A SISTER.
I **DO!** THIS IS HER.
THIS IS ME.
YEAH! SHE WAS LIVING WITH THEIR, UM, **UNCLE.**
BUT HILO LIVES WITH THEIR UNCLE.
MOM.
LISA.
THEIR **OTHER** UNCLE.
HOW MANY UNCLES DO YOU HAVE?
JENNIFER.
HOW MANY DO I NEED?
WHAT'S AN UNCLE?
THIS IS **BAD.** WE SHOULD HAVE GOTTEN OUR STORIES STRAIGHT BEFORE WE CAME OVER.

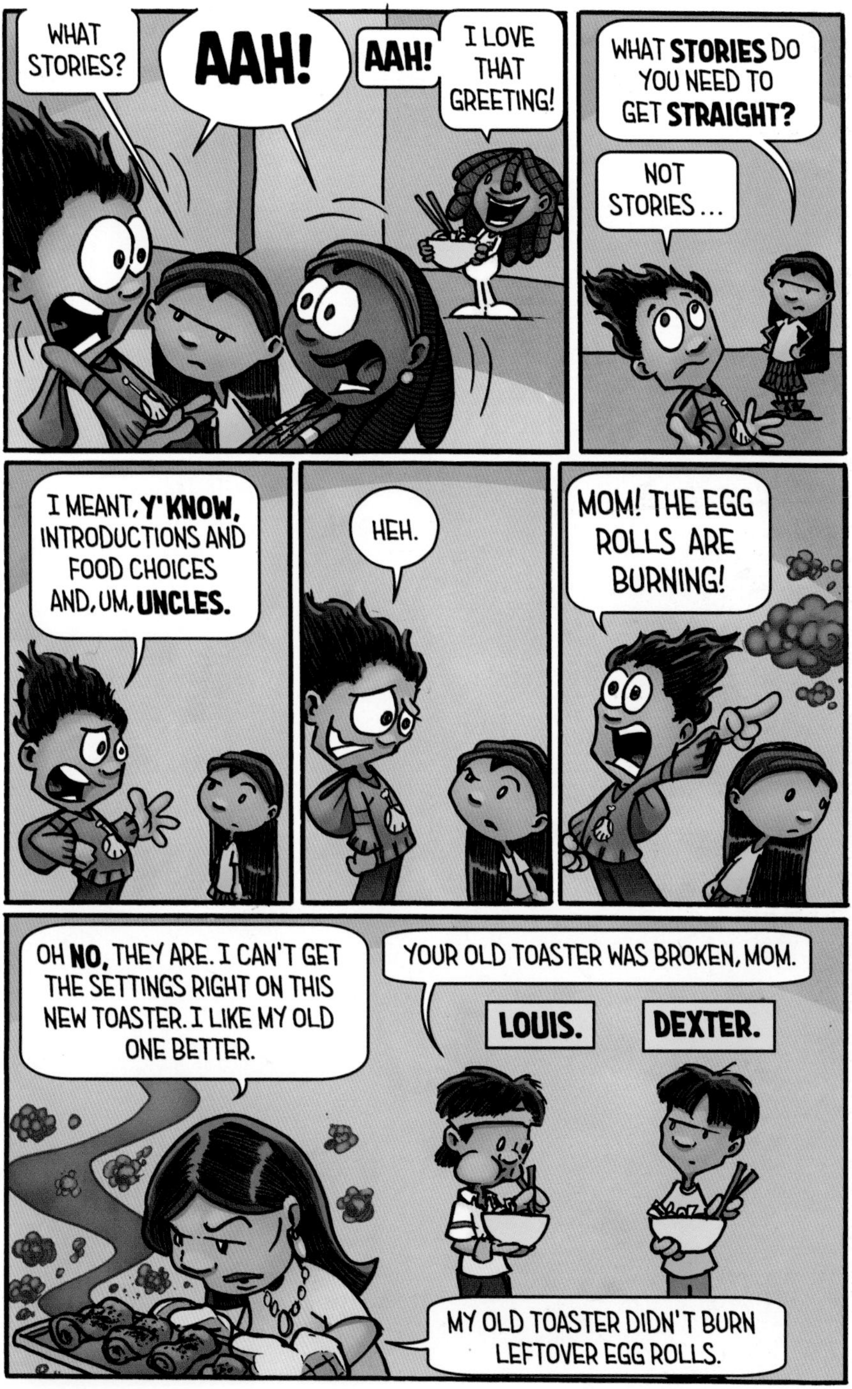
WHAT STORIES?
AAH!
AAH!
I LOVE THAT GREETING!
WHAT STORIES DO YOU NEED TO GET STRAIGHT?
NOT STORIES . . .
I MEANT, Y'KNOW, INTRODUCTIONS AND FOOD CHOICES AND, UM, UNCLES.
HEH.
MOM! THE EGG ROLLS ARE BURNING!
OH NO, THEY ARE. I CAN'T GET THE SETTINGS RIGHT ON THIS NEW TOASTER. I LIKE MY OLD ONE BETTER.
YOUR OLD TOASTER WAS BROKEN, MOM.
LOUIS.
DEXTER.
MY OLD TOASTER DIDN'T BURN LEFTOVER EGG ROLLS.

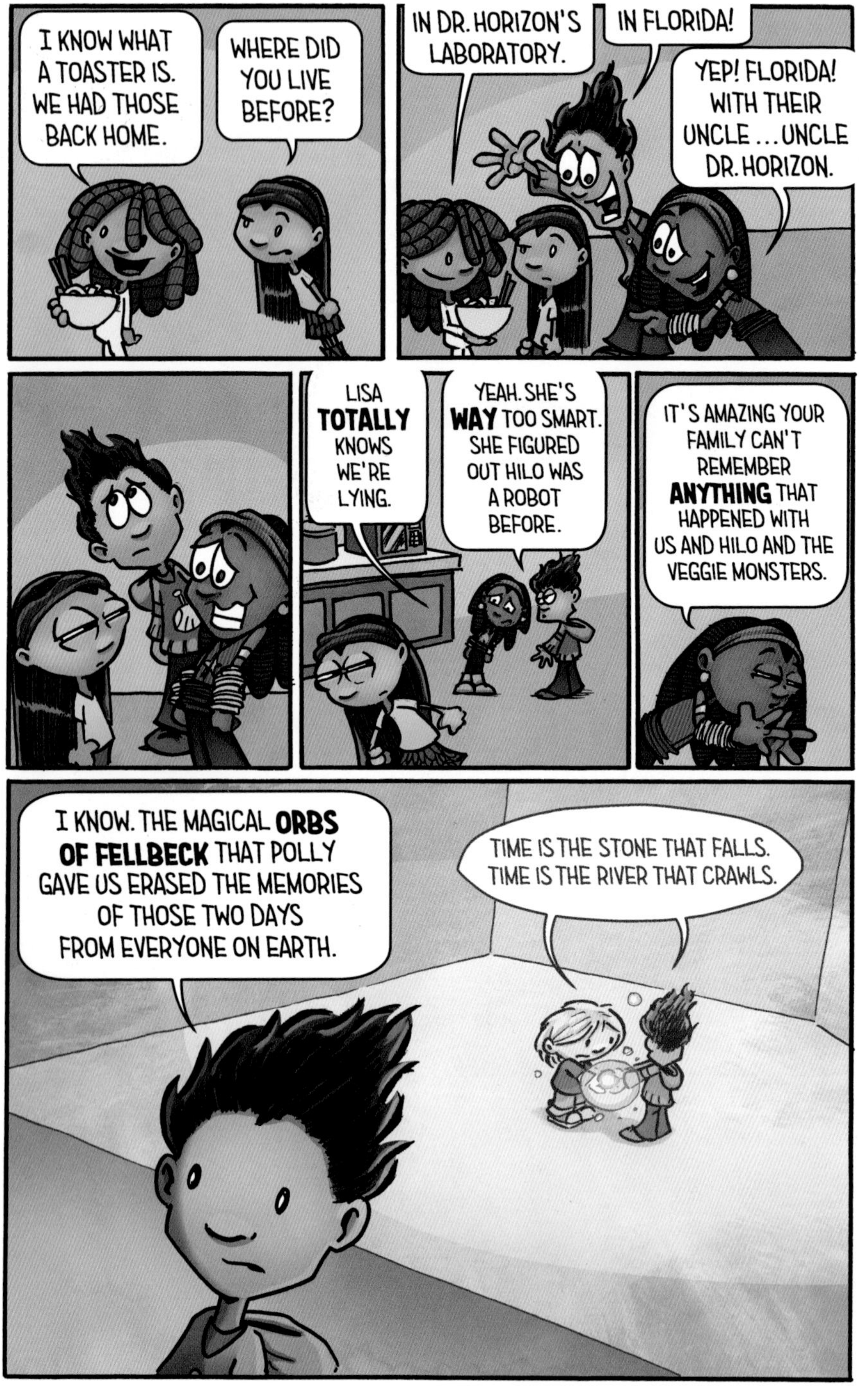
I KNOW WHAT A TOASTER IS. WE HAD THOSE BACK HOME.
WHERE DID YOU LIVE BEFORE?
IN DR. HORIZON'S LABORATORY.
IN FLORIDA!
YEP! FLORIDA! WITH THEIR UNCLE ... UNCLE DR. HORIZON.
LISA **TOTALLY** KNOWS WE'RE LYING.
YEAH. SHE'S **WAY** TOO SMART. SHE FIGURED OUT HILO WAS A ROBOT BEFORE.
IT'S AMAZING YOUR FAMILY CAN'T REMEMBER **ANYTHING** THAT HAPPENED WITH US AND HILO AND THE VEGGIE MONSTERS.
I KNOW. THE MAGICAL **ORBS OF FELLBECK** THAT POLLY GAVE US ERASED THE MEMORIES OF THOSE TWO DAYS FROM EVERYONE ON EARTH.
TIME IS THE STONE THAT FALLS. TIME IS THE RIVER THAT CRAWLS.

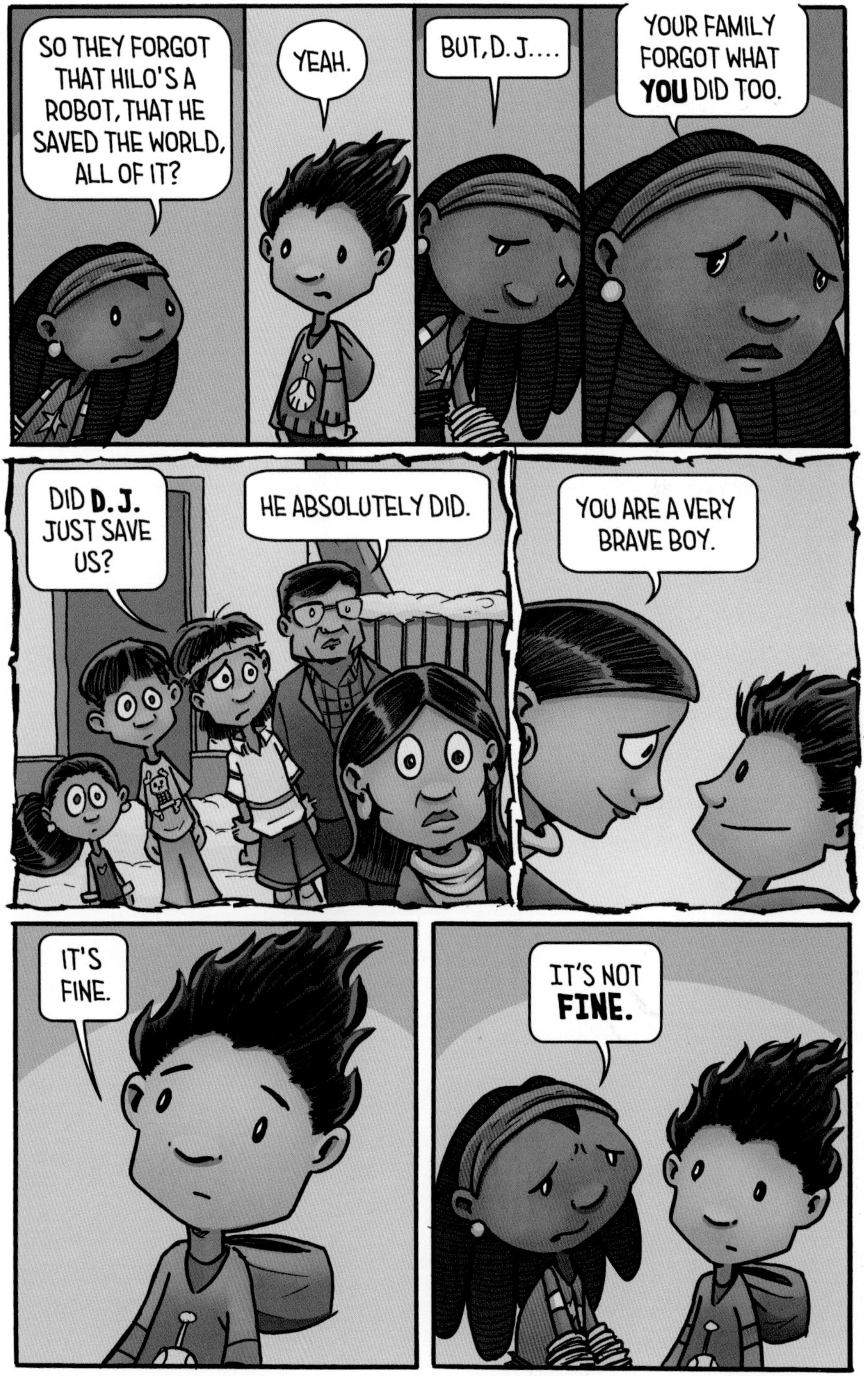

SO THEY FORGOT THAT HILO'S A ROBOT, THAT HE SAVED THE WORLD, ALL OF IT?
YEAH.
BUT, D. J....
YOUR FAMILY FORGOT WHAT **YOU** DID TOO.
DID **D. J.** JUST SAVE US?
HE ABSOLUTELY DID.
YOU ARE A VERY BRAVE BOY.
IT'S FINE.
IT'S NOT **FINE.**

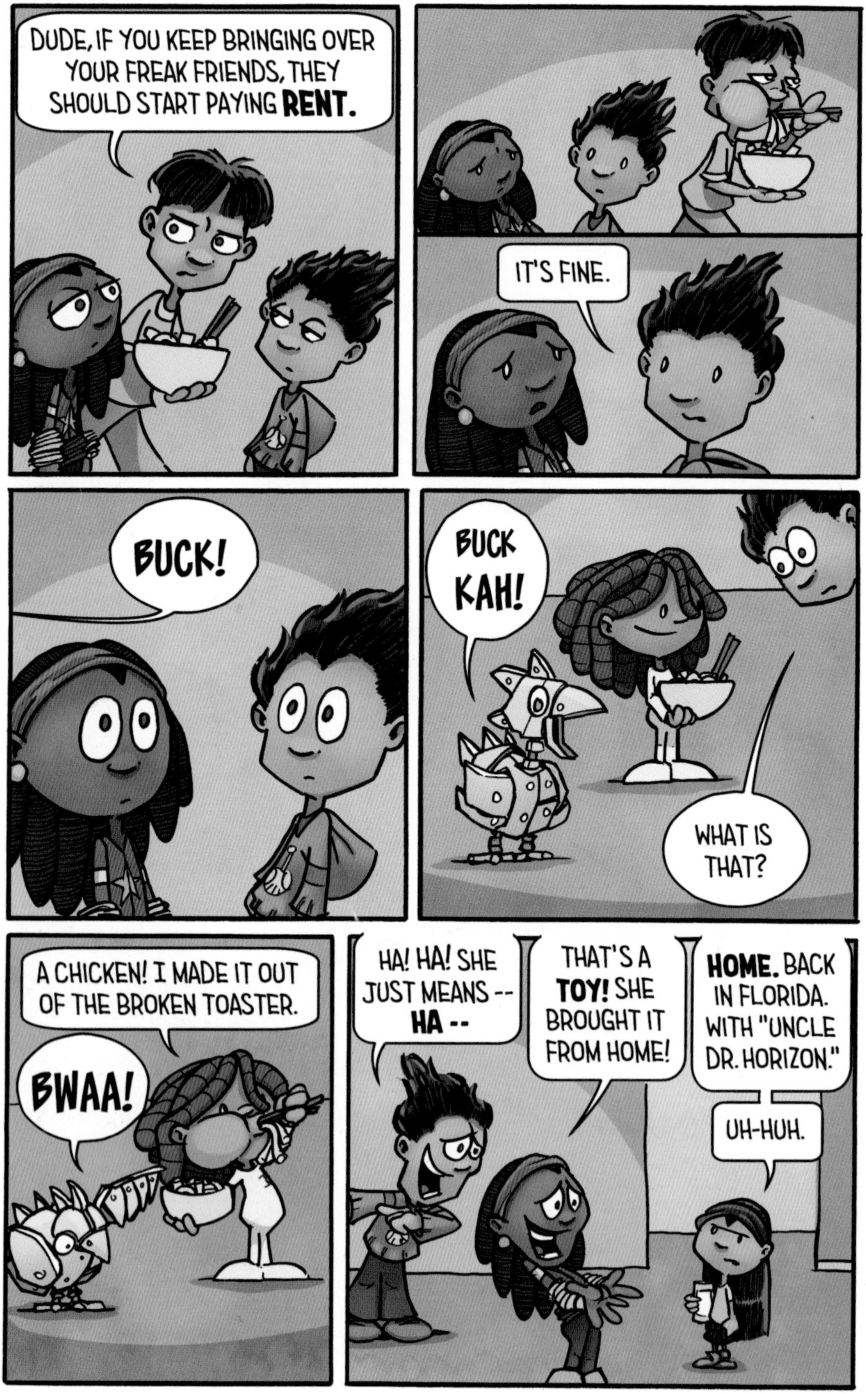
DUDE, IF YOU KEEP BRINGING OVER YOUR FREAK FRIENDS, THEY SHOULD START PAYING **RENT.**
IT'S FINE.
BUCK!
BUCK KAH!
WHAT IS THAT?
A CHICKEN! I MADE IT OUT OF THE BROKEN TOASTER.
BWAA!
HA! HA! SHE JUST MEANS -- **HA** --
THAT'S A **TOY!** SHE BROUGHT IT FROM HOME!
HOME. BACK IN FLORIDA. WITH "UNCLE DR. HORIZON."
UH-HUH.

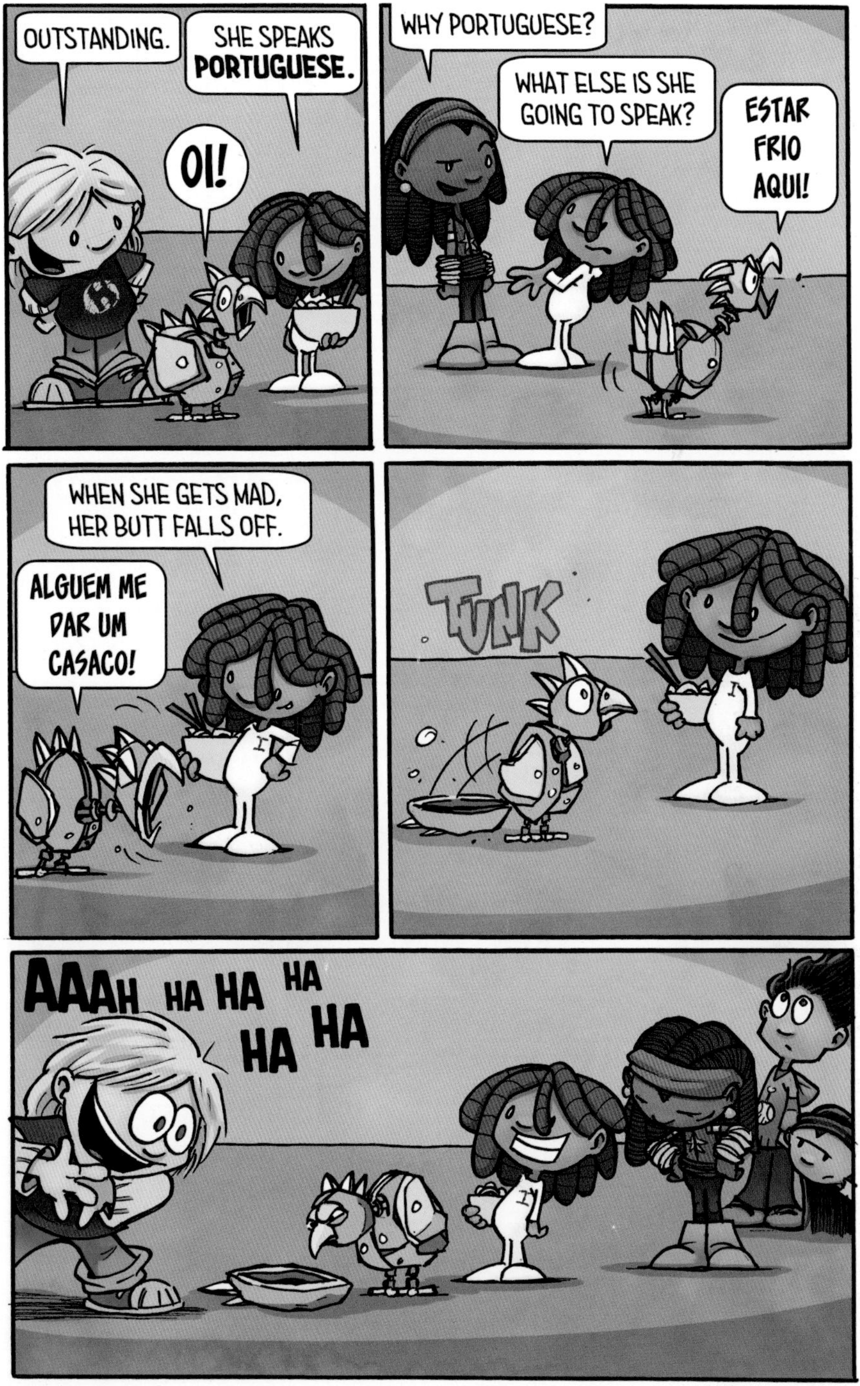
OUTSTANDING.
SHE SPEAKS **PORTUGUESE.**
OI!
WHY PORTUGUESE?
WHAT ELSE IS SHE GOING TO SPEAK?
ESTAR FRIO AQUI!
WHEN SHE GETS MAD, HER BUTT FALLS OFF.
ALGUEM ME DAR UM CASACO!
TUNK
AAAH HA HA HA HA HA

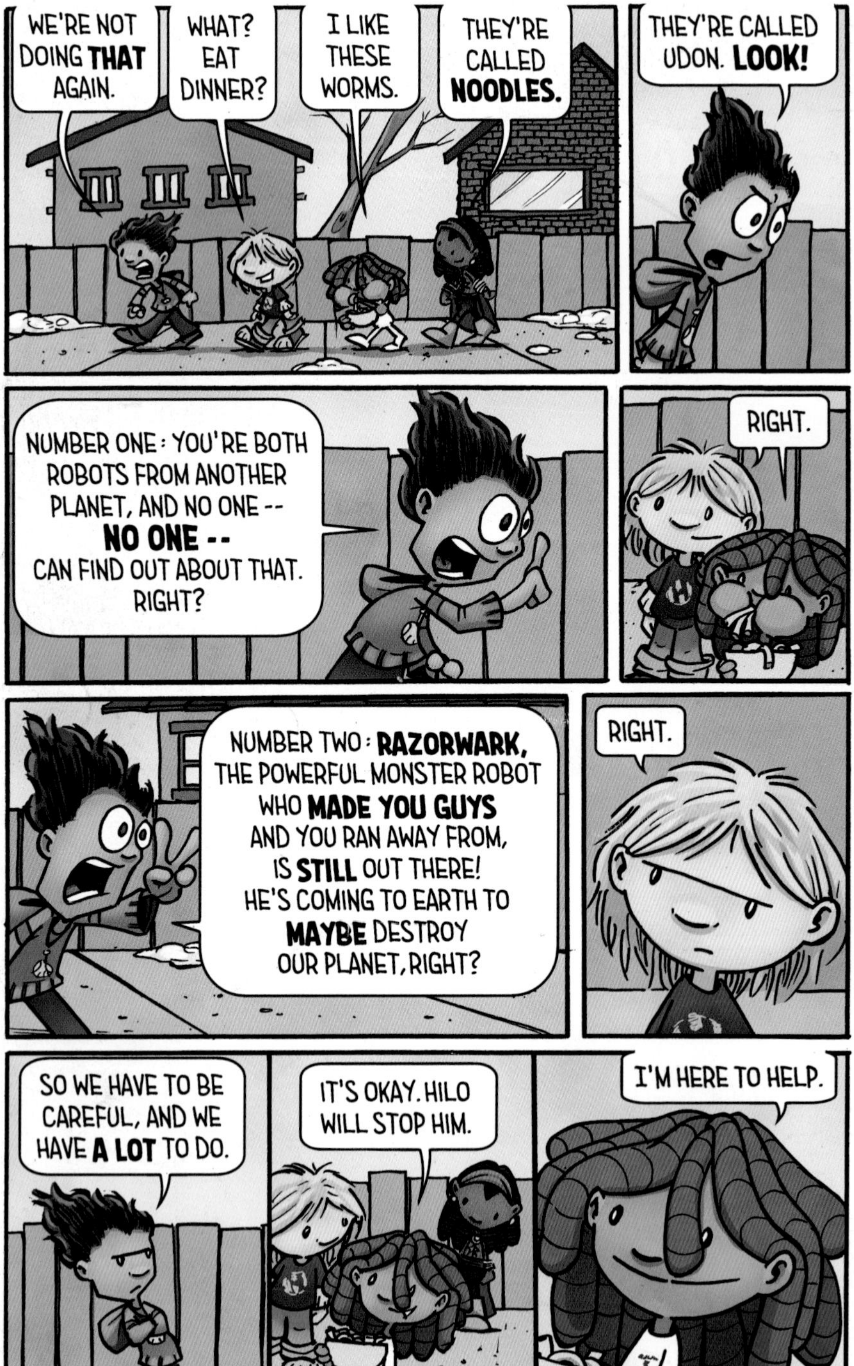
WE'RE NOT DOING THAT AGAIN.
WHAT? EAT DINNER?
I LIKE THESE WORMS.
THEY'RE CALLED NOODLES.
THEY'RE CALLED UDON. LOOK!
NUMBER ONE: YOU'RE BOTH ROBOTS FROM ANOTHER PLANET, AND NO ONE -- NO ONE -- CAN FIND OUT ABOUT THAT. RIGHT?
RIGHT.
NUMBER TWO: RAZORWARK, THE POWERFUL MONSTER ROBOT WHO MADE YOU GUYS AND YOU RAN AWAY FROM, IS STILL OUT THERE! HE'S COMING TO EARTH TO MAYBE DESTROY OUR PLANET, RIGHT?
RIGHT.
SO WE HAVE TO BE CAREFUL, AND WE HAVE A LOT TO DO.
IT'S OKAY. HILO WILL STOP HIM.
I'M HERE TO HELP.

CHAPTER 3

A LOT TO DO

JUST LIKE HILO, NOBODY CAN KNOW IZZY'S A ROBOT. SO WE HAD A LOT TO DO. LIKE, HER **CLOTHES.**

WHAT WAS WRONG WITH MY OLD CLOTHES?

THEY LOOKED LIKE PAJAMAS.

GOTCHA. WHAT'S PAJAMAS?

SHE LOOKS SO CUTE, I'M GONNA EXPLODE!

I KNOW, RIGHT?

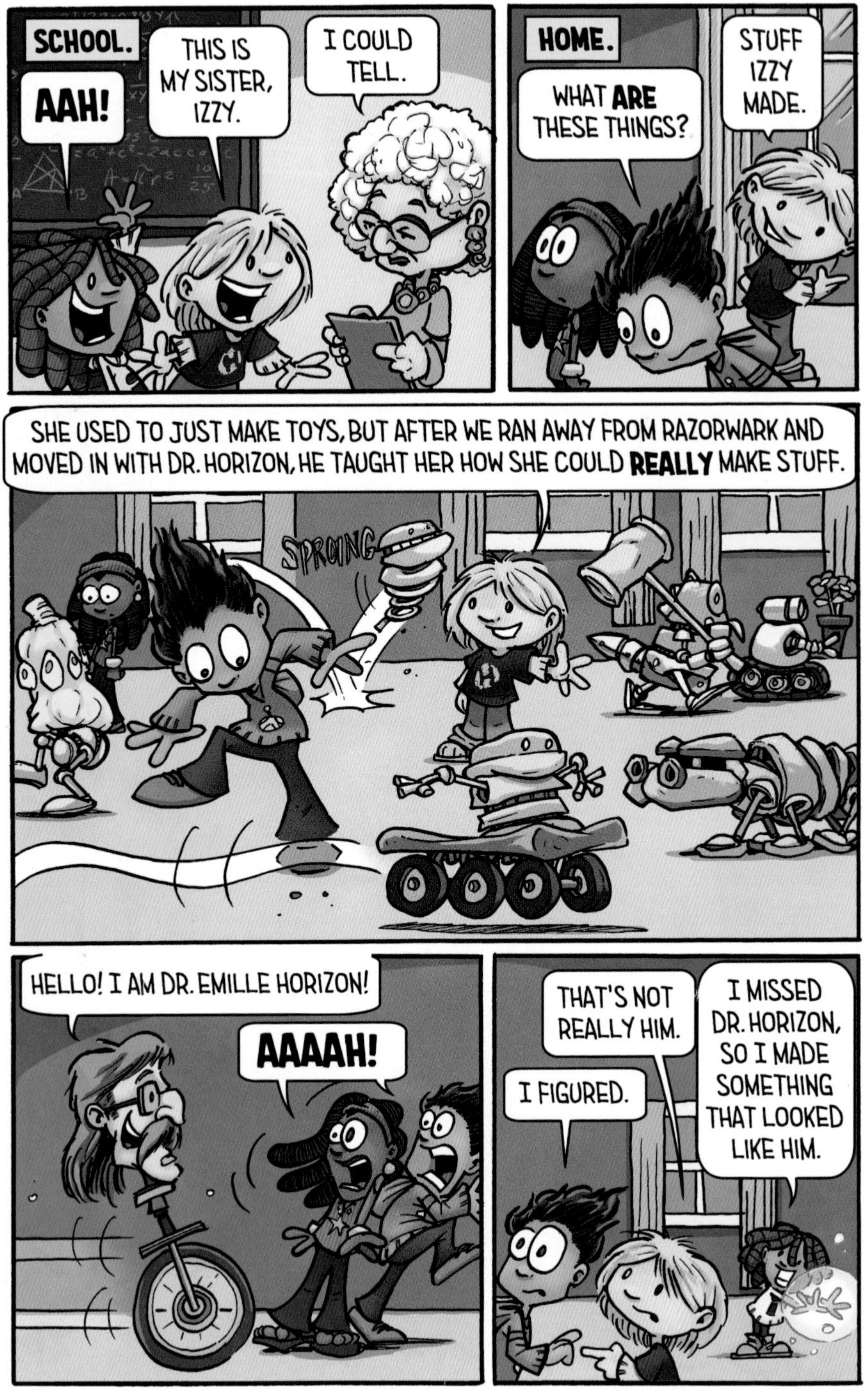
SCHOOL.
AAH!
THIS IS MY SISTER, IZZY.
I COULD TELL.
HOME.
WHAT ARE THESE THINGS?
STUFF IZZY MADE.
SHE USED TO JUST MAKE TOYS, BUT AFTER WE RAN AWAY FROM RAZORWARK AND MOVED IN WITH DR. HORIZON, HE TAUGHT HER HOW SHE COULD REALLY MAKE STUFF.
SPROING
HELLO! I AM DR. EMILLE HORIZON!
AAAAH!
THAT'S NOT REALLY HIM.
I FIGURED.
I MISSED DR. HORIZON, SO I MADE SOMETHING THAT LOOKED LIKE HIM.

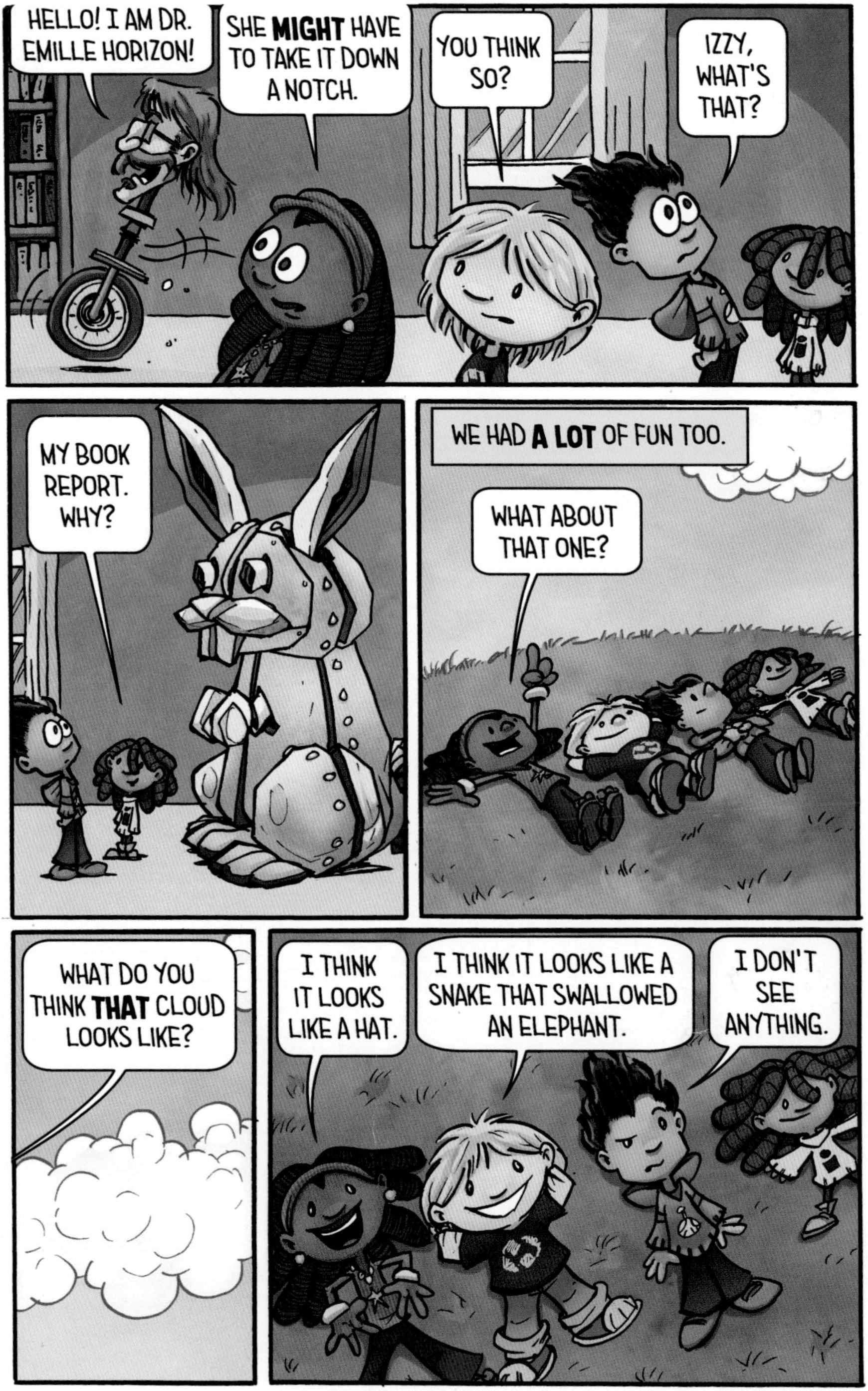
HELLO! I AM DR. EMILLE HORIZON!
SHE **MIGHT** HAVE TO TAKE IT DOWN A NOTCH.
YOU THINK SO?
IZZY, WHAT'S THAT?
MY BOOK REPORT. WHY?
WE HAD **A LOT** OF FUN TOO.
WHAT ABOUT THAT ONE?
WHAT DO YOU THINK **THAT** CLOUD LOOKS LIKE?
I THINK IT LOOKS LIKE A HAT.
I THINK IT LOOKS LIKE A SNAKE THAT SWALLOWED AN ELEPHANT.
I DON'T SEE ANYTHING.

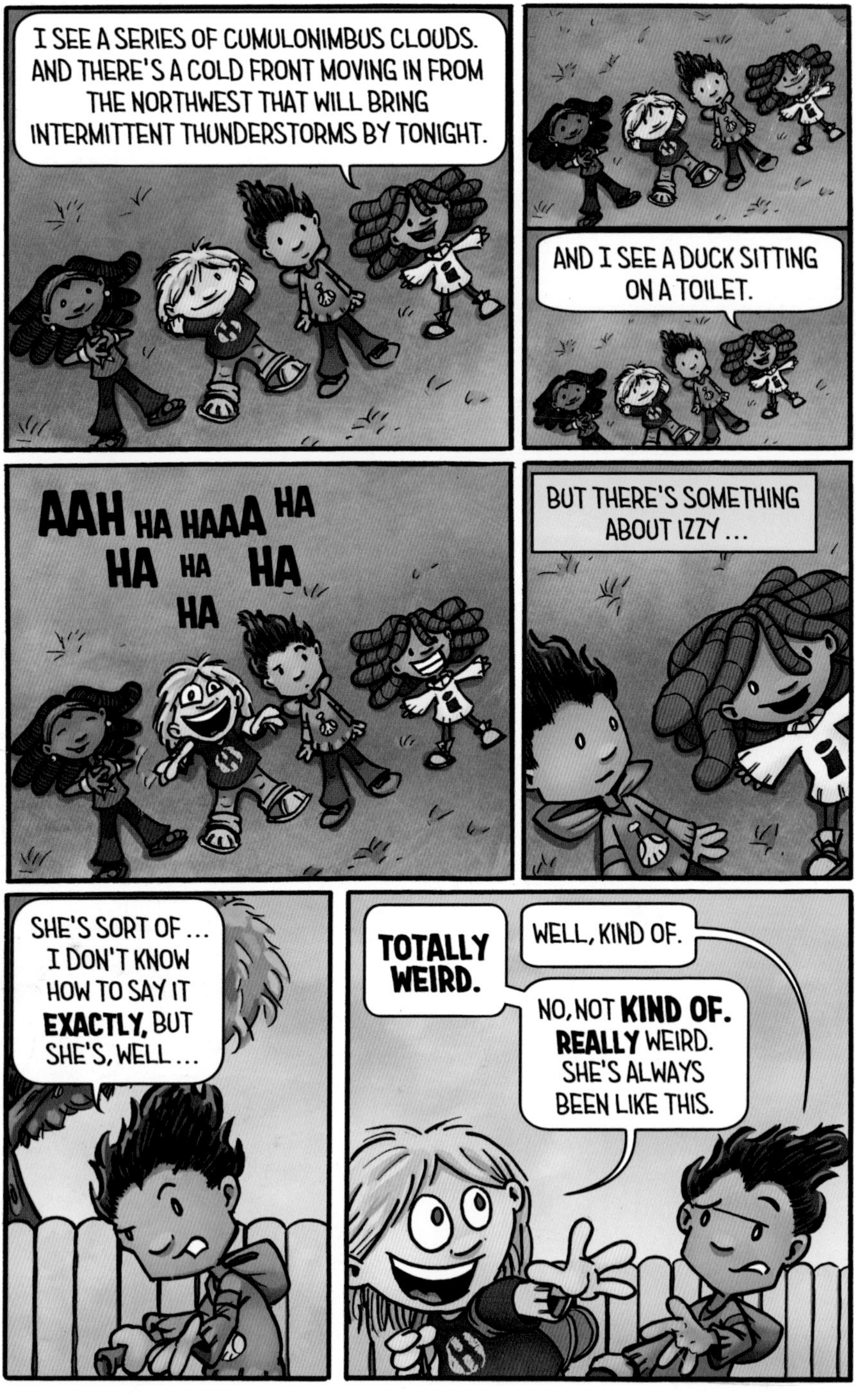
I SEE A SERIES OF CUMULONIMBUS CLOUDS. AND THERE'S A COLD FRONT MOVING IN FROM THE NORTHWEST THAT WILL BRING INTERMITTENT THUNDERSTORMS BY TONIGHT.
AND I SEE A DUCK SITTING ON A TOILET.
AAH HA HAAA HA HA HA HA HA
BUT THERE'S SOMETHING ABOUT IZZY ...
SHE'S SORT OF ... I DON'T KNOW HOW TO SAY IT EXACTLY, BUT SHE'S, WELL ...
TOTALLY WEIRD.
WELL, KIND OF.
NO, NOT KIND OF. REALLY WEIRD. SHE'S ALWAYS BEEN LIKE THIS.

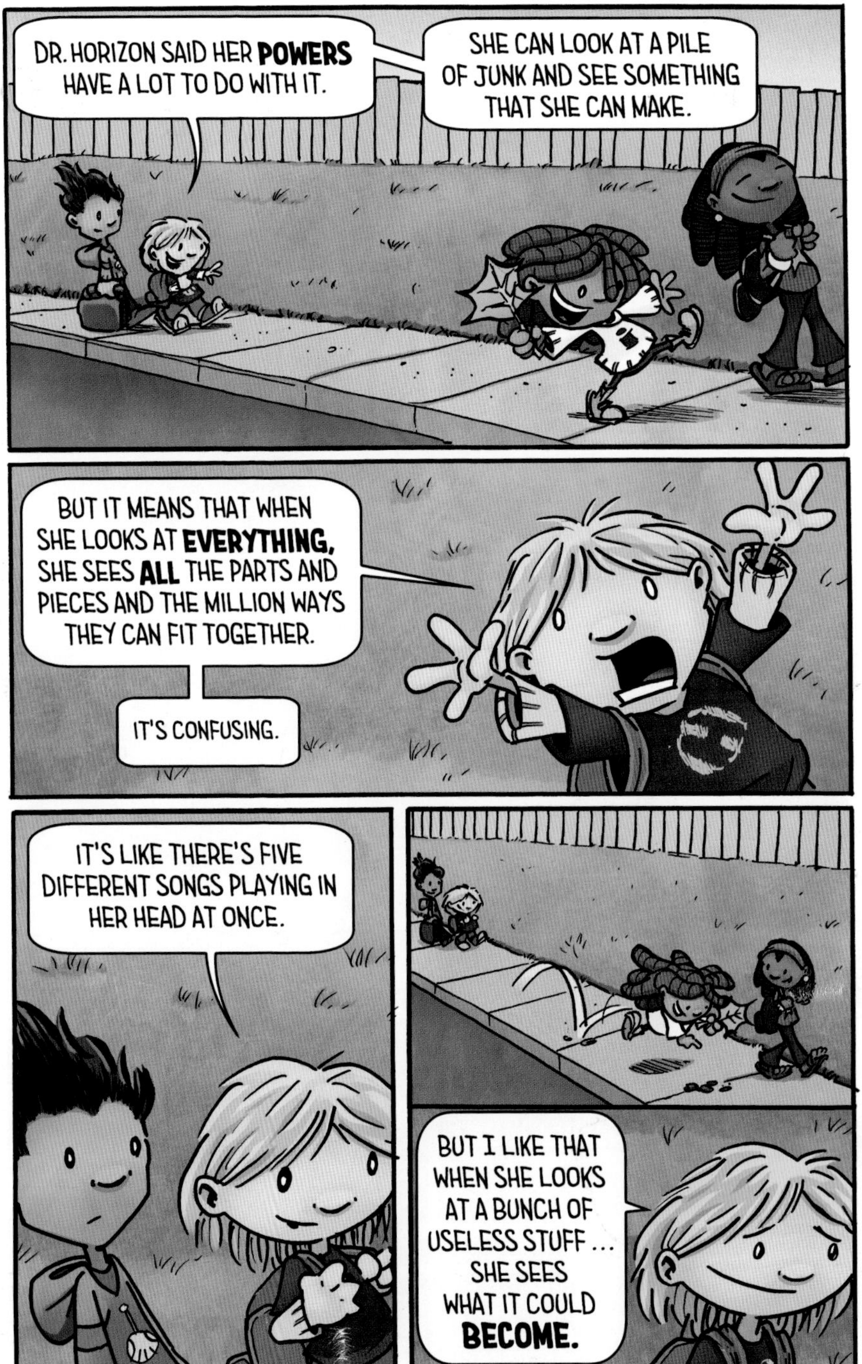
DR. HORIZON SAID HER POWERS HAVE A LOT TO DO WITH IT.
SHE CAN LOOK AT A PILE OF JUNK AND SEE SOMETHING THAT SHE CAN MAKE.
BUT IT MEANS THAT WHEN SHE LOOKS AT EVERYTHING, SHE SEES ALL THE PARTS AND PIECES AND THE MILLION WAYS THEY CAN FIT TOGETHER.
IT'S CONFUSING.
IT'S LIKE THERE'S FIVE DIFFERENT SONGS PLAYING IN HER HEAD AT ONCE.
BUT I LIKE THAT WHEN SHE LOOKS AT A BUNCH OF USELESS STUFF ... SHE SEES WHAT IT COULD BECOME.

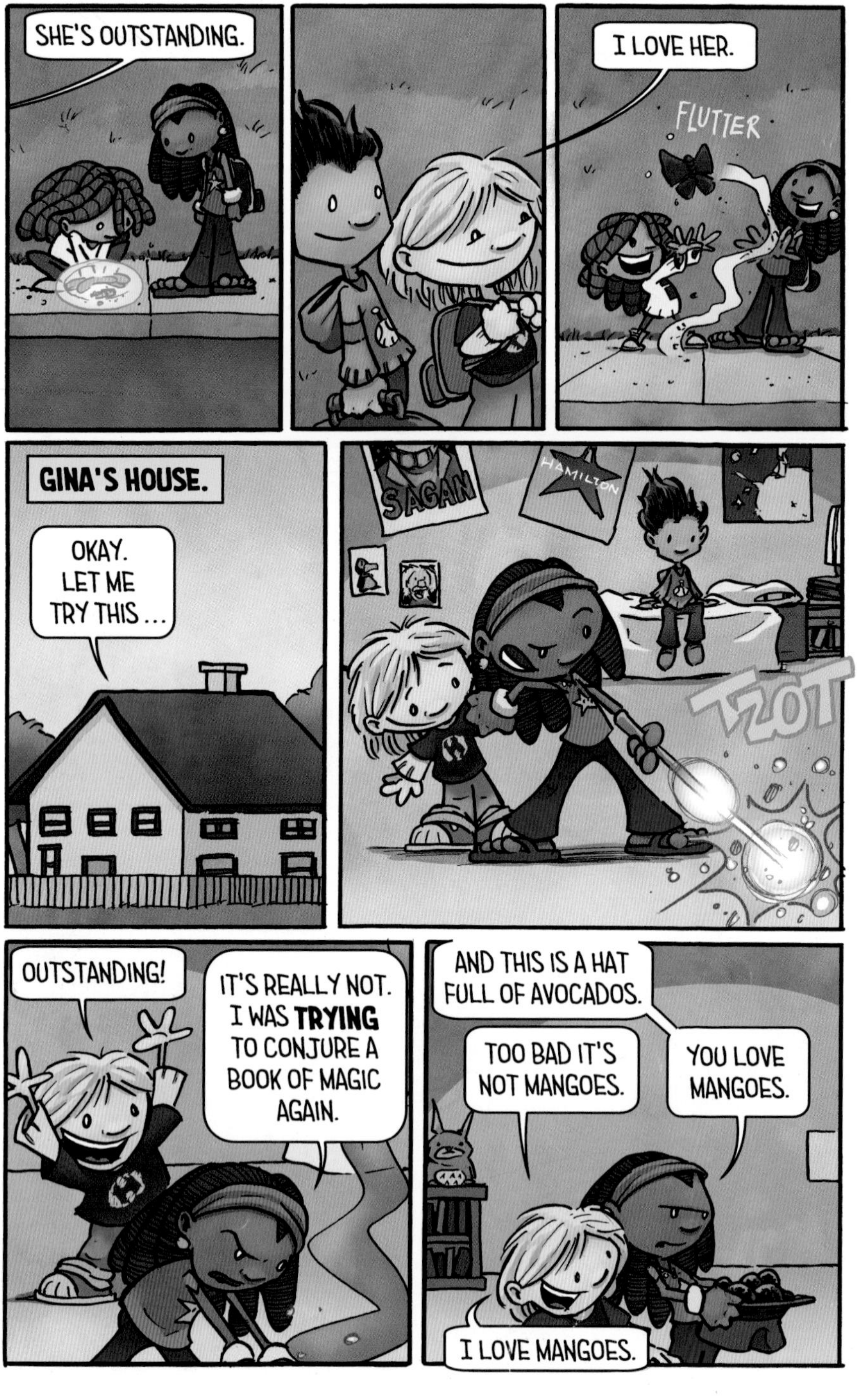
SHE'S OUTSTANDING.
I LOVE HER.
FLUTTER
GINA'S HOUSE.
OKAY. LET ME TRY THIS . . .
SAGAN
HAMILTON
TZOT
OUTSTANDING!
IT'S REALLY NOT. I WAS **TRYING** TO CONJURE A BOOK OF MAGIC AGAIN.
AND THIS IS A HAT FULL OF AVOCADOS.
TOO BAD IT'S NOT MANGOES.
YOU LOVE MANGOES.
I LOVE MANGOES.

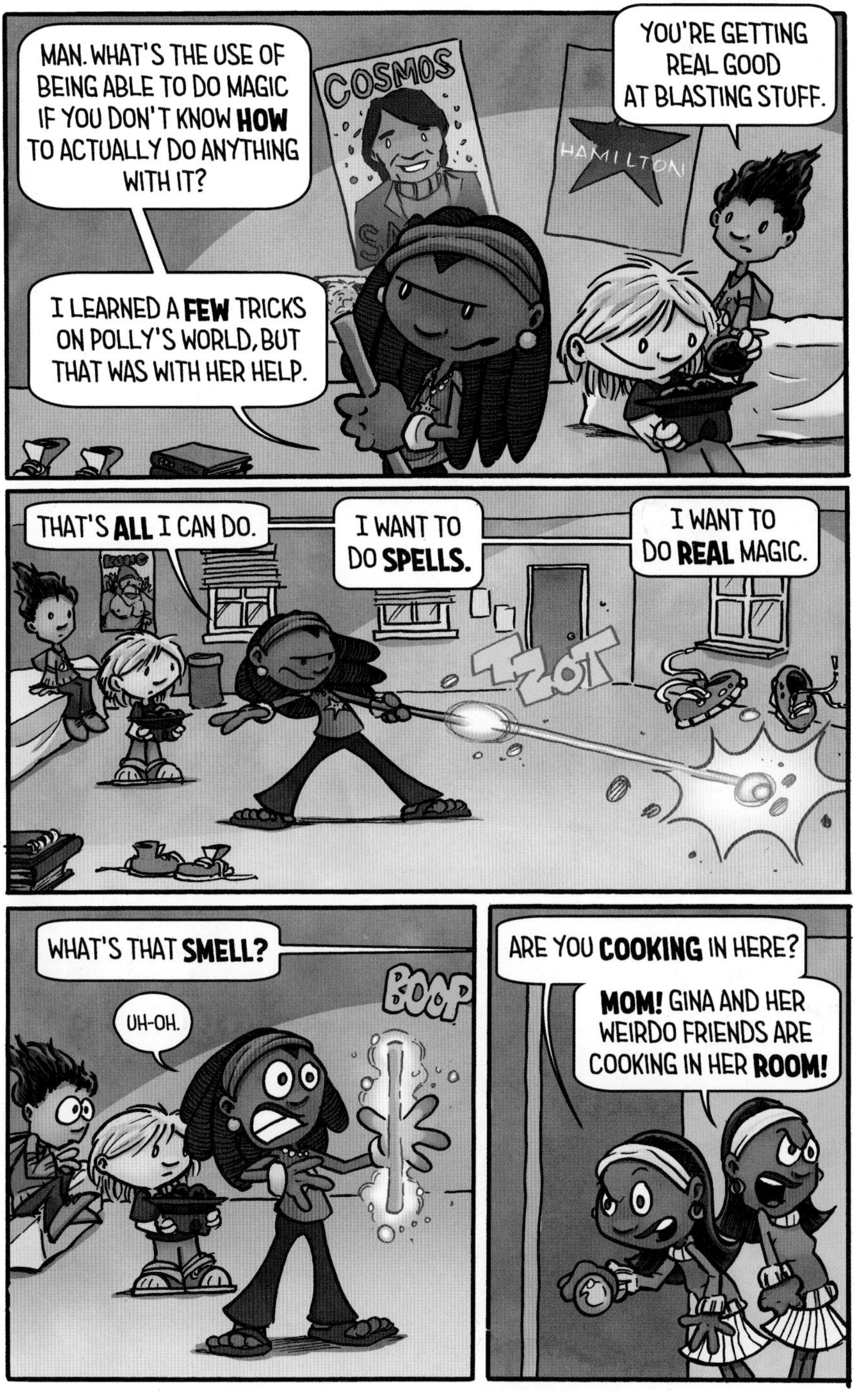
MAN. WHAT'S THE USE OF BEING ABLE TO DO MAGIC IF YOU DON'T KNOW **HOW** TO ACTUALLY DO ANYTHING WITH IT?
COSMOS
HAMILTON
YOU'RE GETTING REAL GOOD AT BLASTING STUFF.
I LEARNED A **FEW** TRICKS ON POLLY'S WORLD, BUT THAT WAS WITH HER HELP.
THAT'S **ALL** I CAN DO.
I WANT TO DO **SPELLS.**
I WANT TO DO **REAL** MAGIC.
TZOT
WHAT'S THAT **SMELL?**
BOOP
UH-OH.
ARE YOU **COOKING** IN HERE?
MOM! GINA AND HER WEIRDO FRIENDS ARE COOKING IN HER **ROOM!**

HEY, CONNIE! HEY, BONNIE!

WHAT-EVER.

WHAT. EVER.

SNIFF

WHAT **IS** THAT SMELL?

BRIMSTONE.

HILO.

WE'RE NOT COOKING! THESE AVOCADOS JUST... **SMELL.**

WHERE'D YOU GET THOSE AVOCADOS?

UH, **ME!** I BROUGHT THEM! I THOUGHT THEY SMELLED AAAALL KINDS OF **FUNKY.** SO I WANTED TO SHOW GINA.

YOU BROUGHT THEM IN A **HAT?**

HE **IS** A LITTLE WEIRD.

YOU SHOULD SMELL THE HAT!

ANYWAY ...

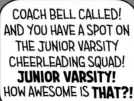

COACH BELL CALLED! AND YOU HAVE A SPOT ON THE JUNIOR VARSITY CHEERLEADING SQUAD! **JUNIOR VARSITY!** HOW AWESOME IS **THAT?!**

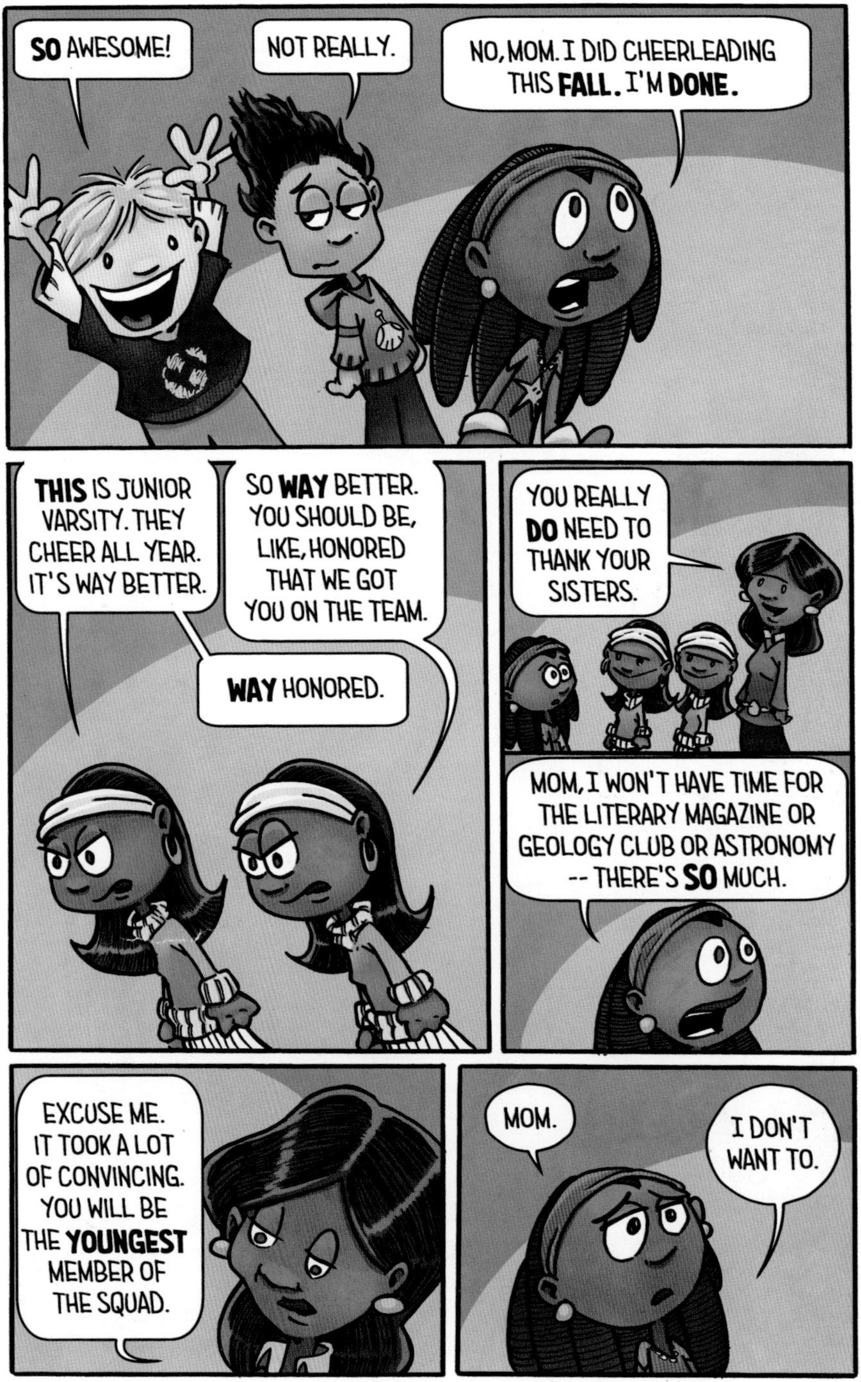

SO AWESOME!
NOT REALLY.
NO, MOM. I DID CHEERLEADING THIS FALL. I'M DONE.
THIS IS JUNIOR VARSITY. THEY CHEER ALL YEAR. IT'S WAY BETTER.
SO WAY BETTER. YOU SHOULD BE, LIKE, HONORED THAT WE GOT YOU ON THE TEAM.
WAY HONORED.
YOU REALLY DO NEED TO THANK YOUR SISTERS.
MOM, I WON'T HAVE TIME FOR THE LITERARY MAGAZINE OR GEOLOGY CLUB OR ASTRONOMY -- THERE'S SO MUCH.
EXCUSE ME. IT TOOK A LOT OF CONVINCING. YOU WILL BE THE YOUNGEST MEMBER OF THE SQUAD.
MOM.
I DON'T WANT TO.

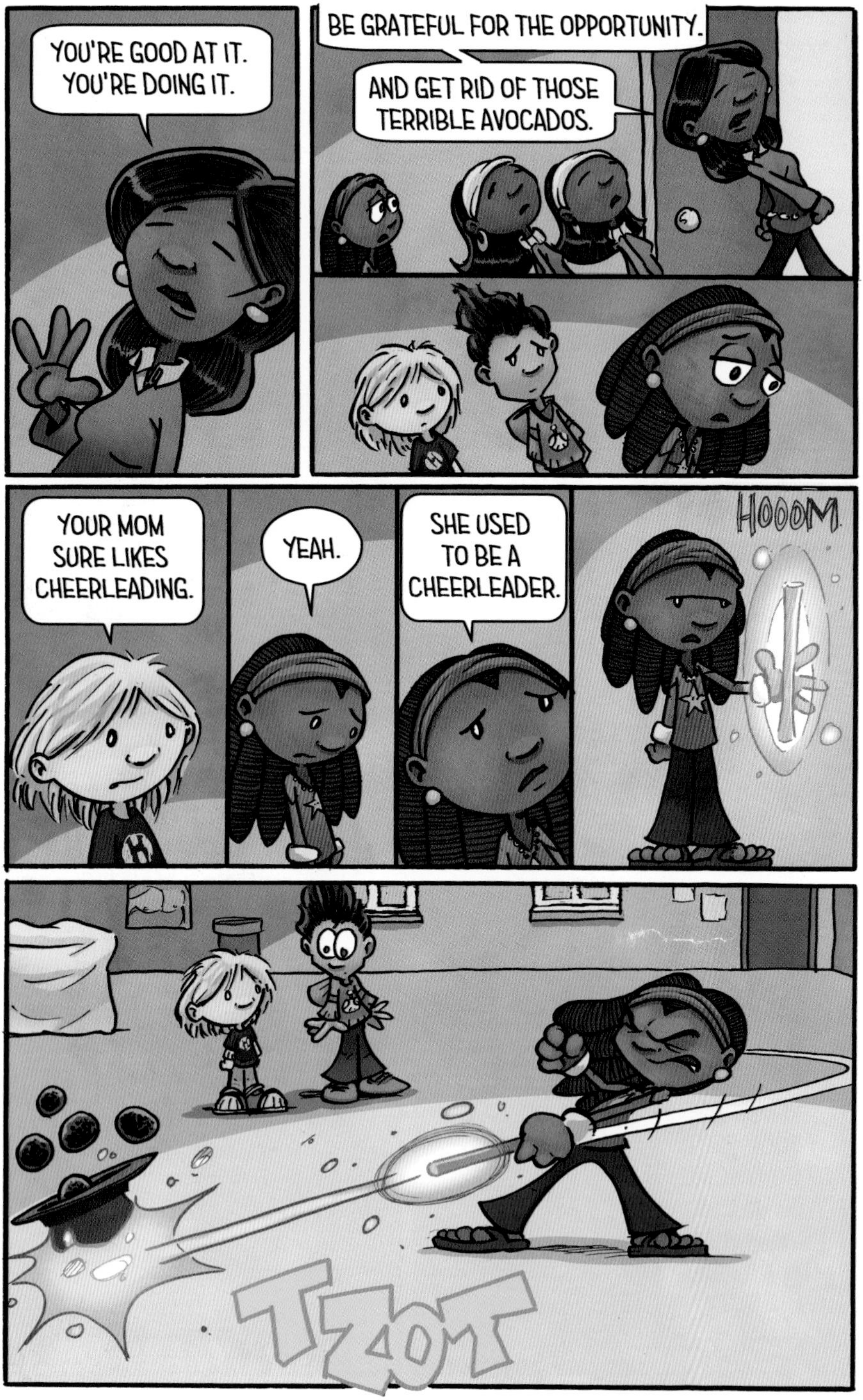
YOU'RE GOOD AT IT. YOU'RE DOING IT.
BE GRATEFUL FOR THE OPPORTUNITY.
AND GET RID OF THOSE TERRIBLE AVOCADOS.
YOUR MOM SURE LIKES CHEERLEADING.
YEAH.
SHE USED TO BE A CHEERLEADER.
HOOOM
TZOT

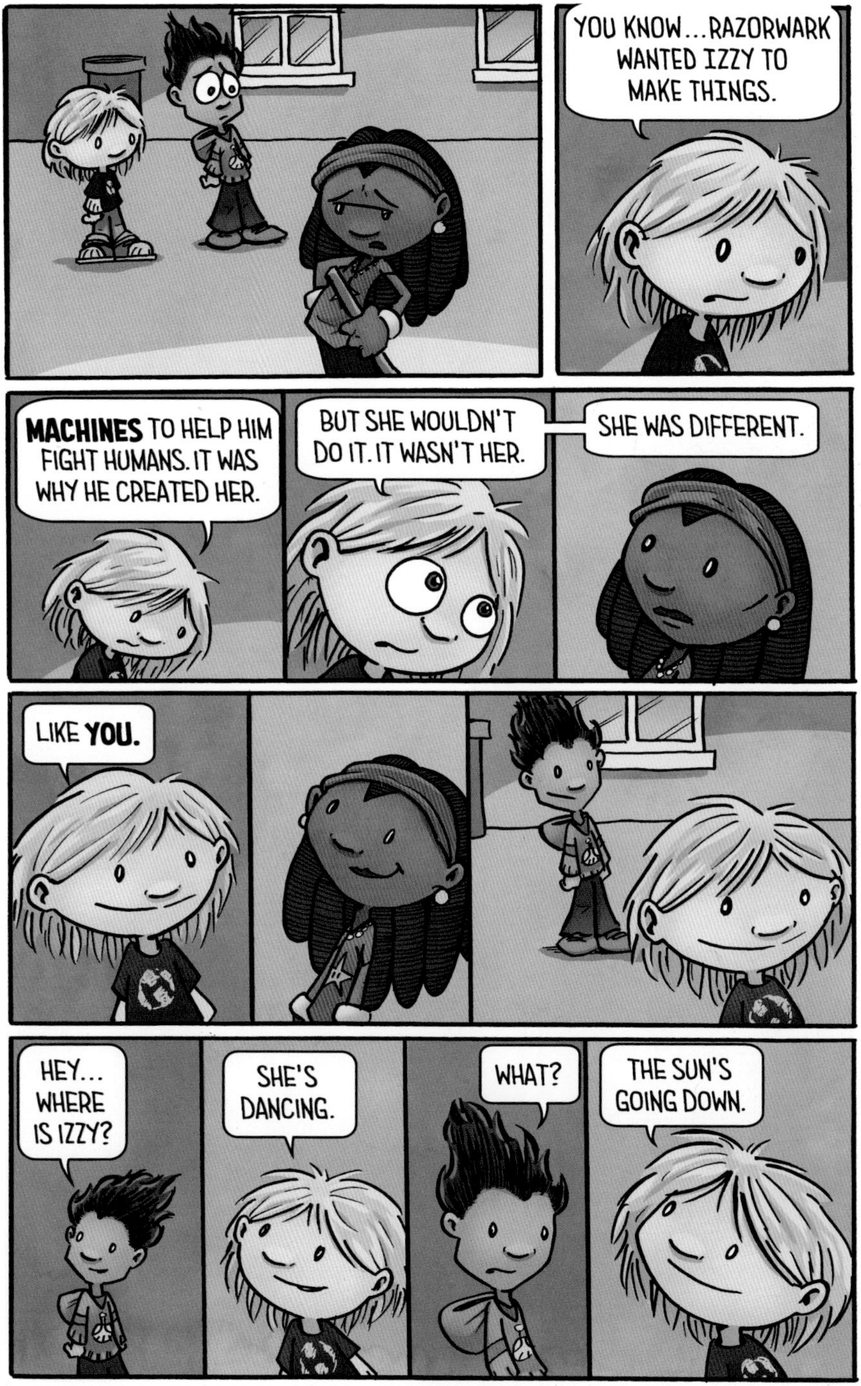
YOU KNOW...RAZORWARK WANTED IZZY TO MAKE THINGS.
MACHINES TO HELP HIM FIGHT HUMANS. IT WAS WHY HE CREATED HER.
BUT SHE WOULDN'T DO IT. IT WASN'T HER.
SHE WAS DIFFERENT.
LIKE **YOU.**
HEY... WHERE IS IZZY?
SHE'S DANCING.
WHAT?
THE SUN'S GOING DOWN.

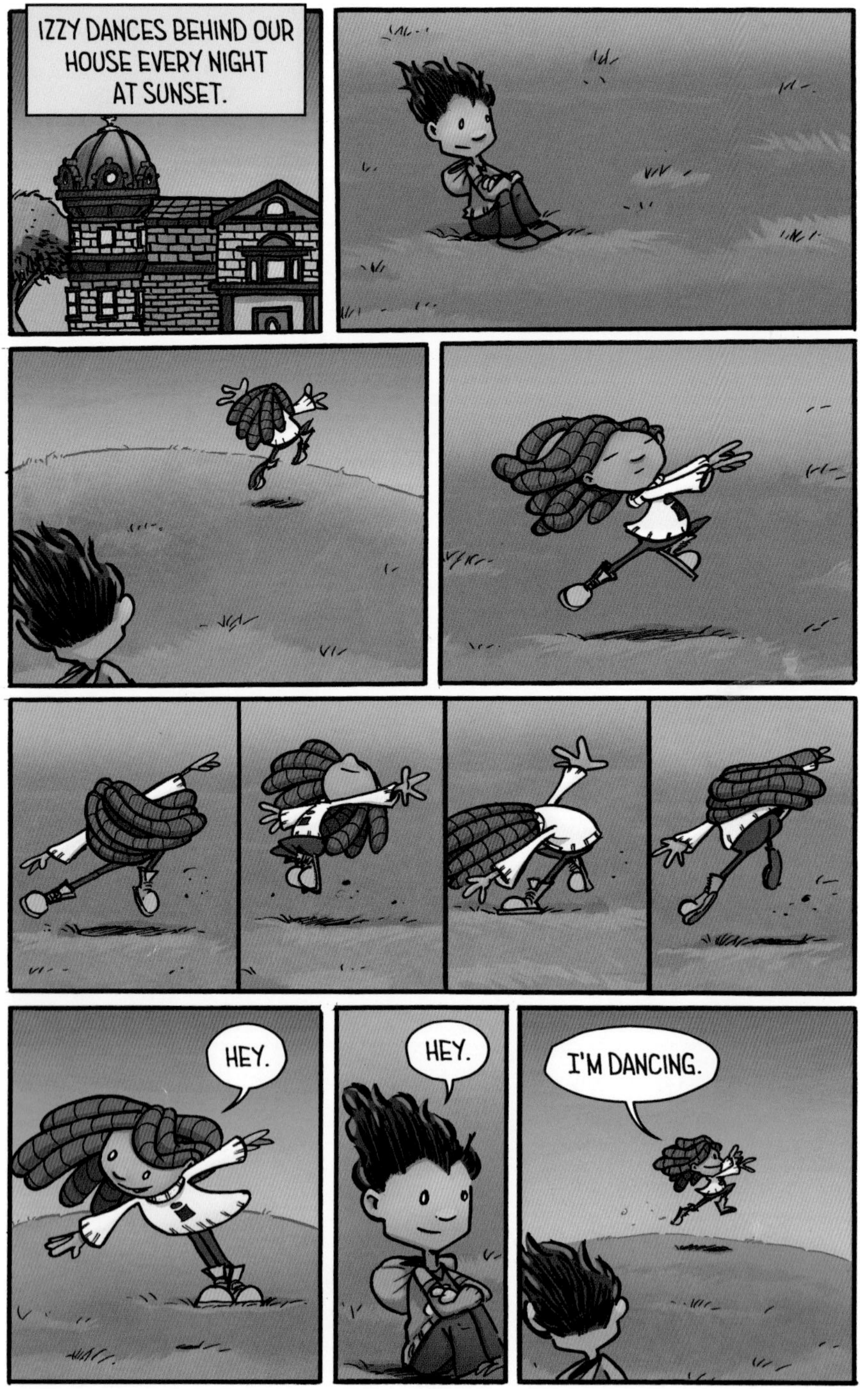
IZZY DANCES BEHIND OUR HOUSE EVERY NIGHT AT SUNSET.
HEY.
HEY.
I'M DANCING.

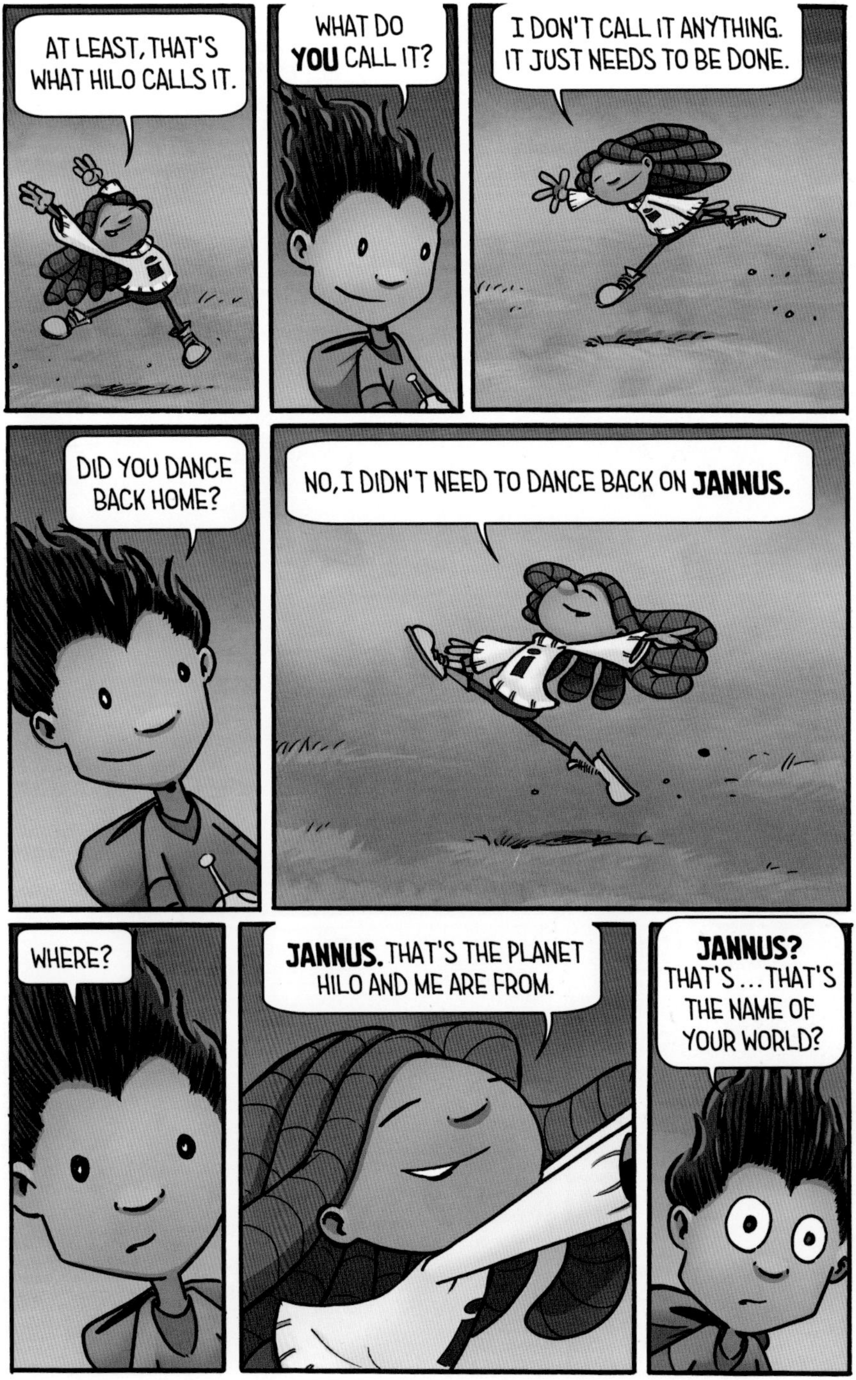
AT LEAST, THAT'S WHAT HILO CALLS IT.
WHAT DO YOU CALL IT?
I DON'T CALL IT ANYTHING. IT JUST NEEDS TO BE DONE.
DID YOU DANCE BACK HOME?
NO, I DIDN'T NEED TO DANCE BACK ON JANNUS.
WHERE?
JANNUS. THAT'S THE PLANET HILO AND ME ARE FROM.
JANNUS? THAT'S . . . THAT'S THE NAME OF YOUR WORLD?

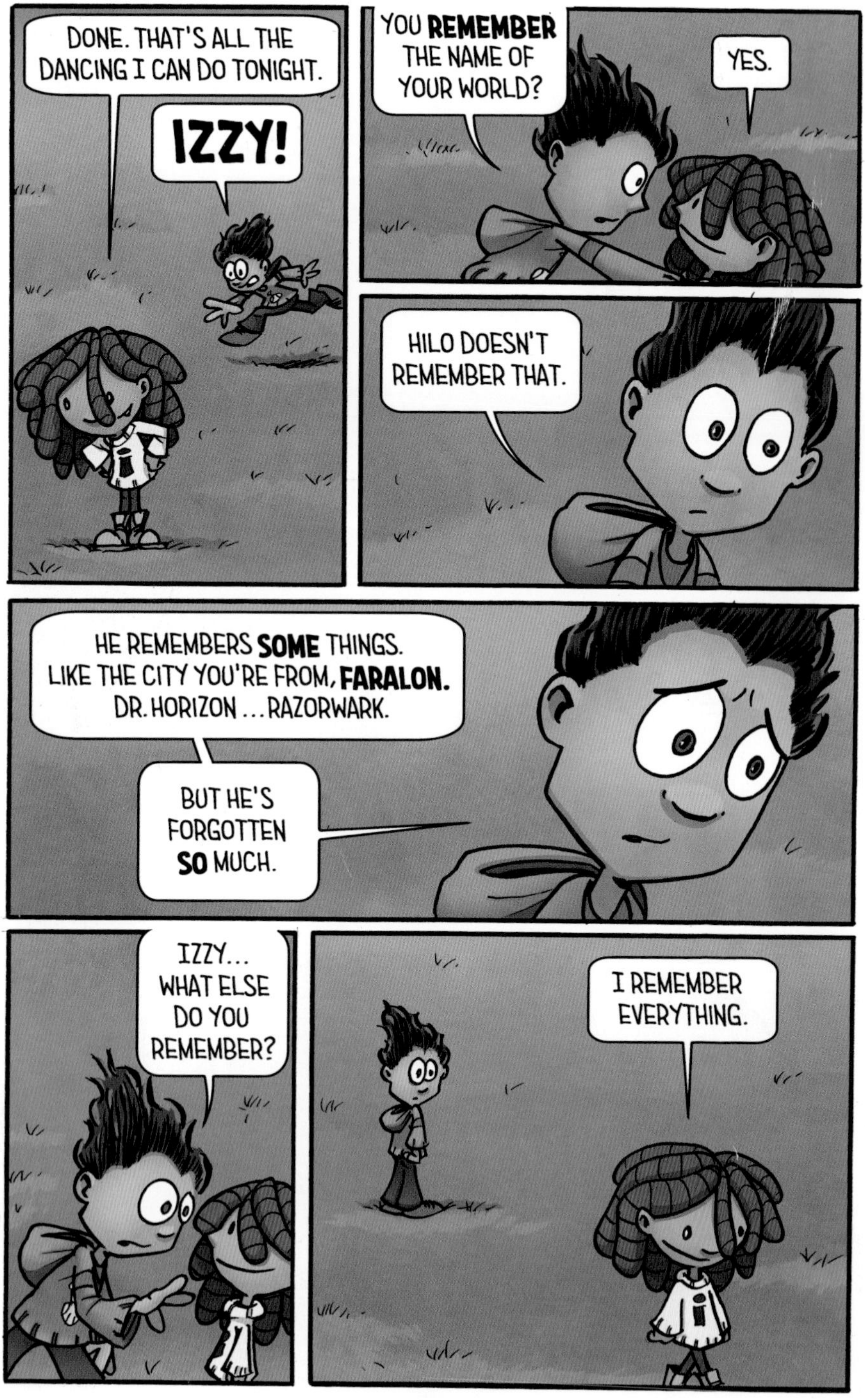
DONE. THAT'S ALL THE DANCING I CAN DO TONIGHT.
IZZY!
YOU **REMEMBER** THE NAME OF YOUR WORLD?
YES.
HILO DOESN'T REMEMBER THAT.
HE REMEMBERS **SOME** THINGS. LIKE THE CITY YOU'RE FROM, **FARALON.** DR. HORIZON ... RAZORWARK.
BUT HE'S FORGOTTEN **SO** MUCH.
IZZY... WHAT ELSE DO YOU REMEMBER?
I REMEMBER EVERYTHING.

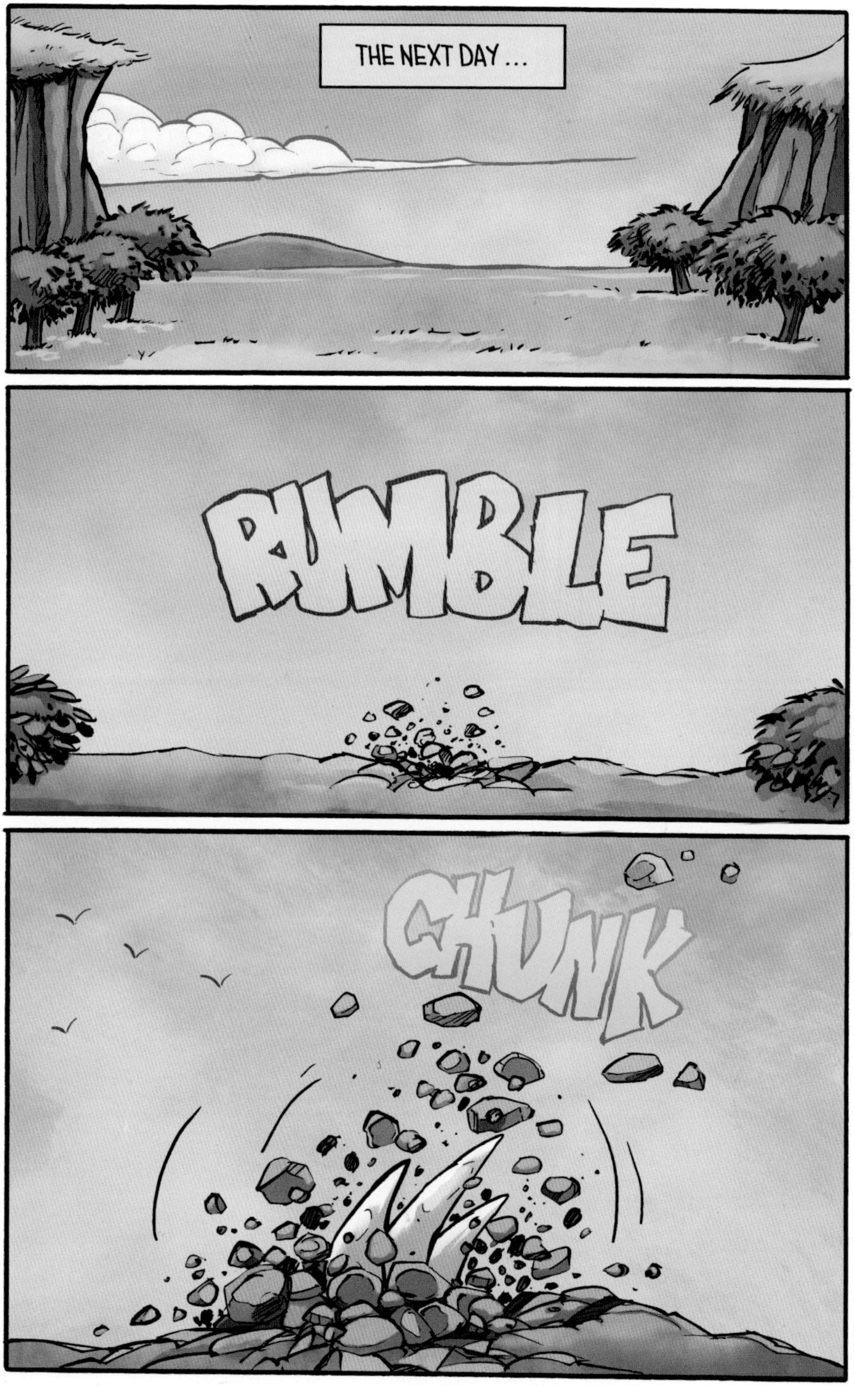
THE NEXT DAY . . .
RUMBLE
CHUNK

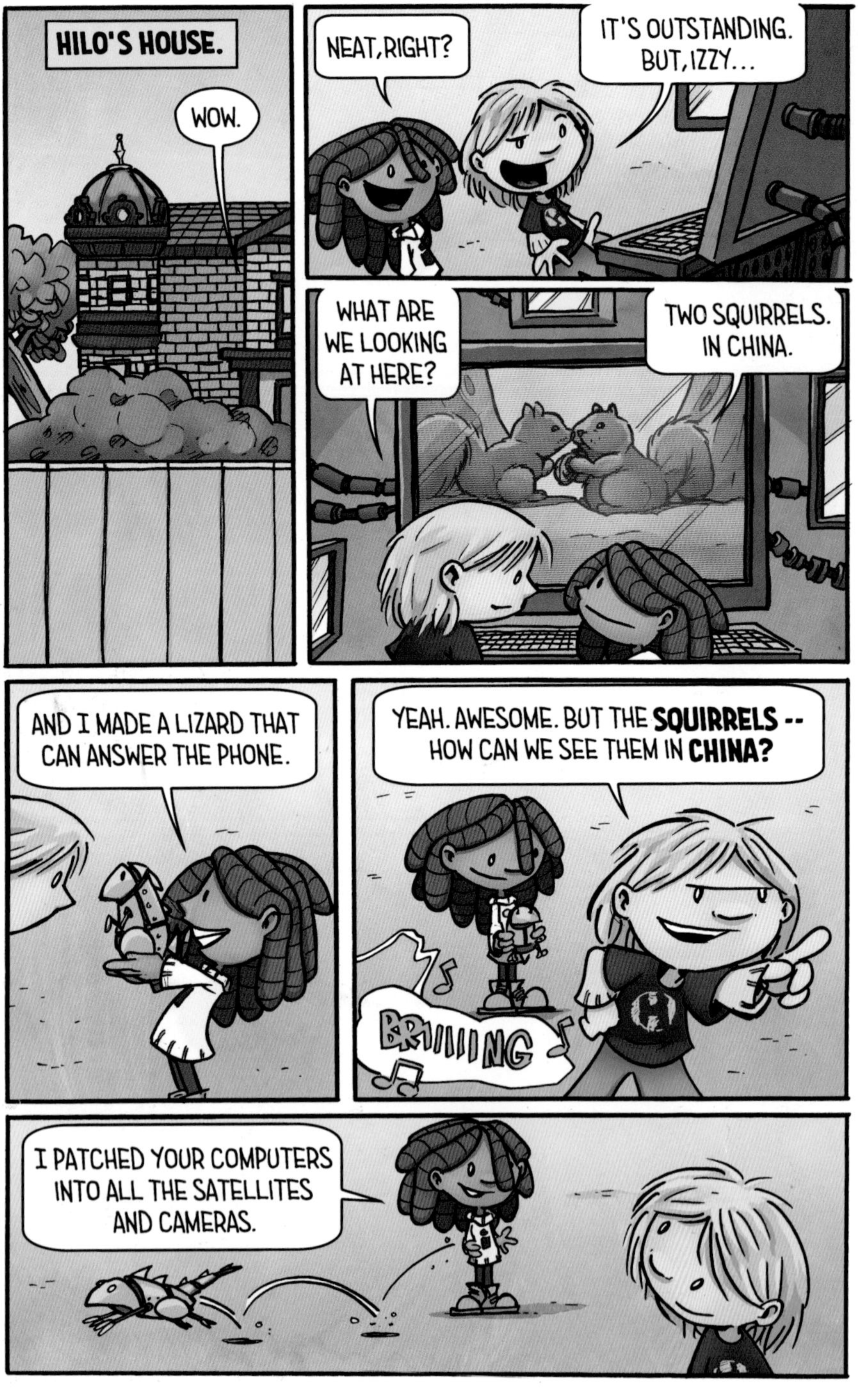
HILO'S HOUSE.
WOW.
NEAT, RIGHT?
IT'S OUTSTANDING. BUT, IZZY...
WHAT ARE WE LOOKING AT HERE?
TWO SQUIRRELS. IN CHINA.
AND I MADE A LIZARD THAT CAN ANSWER THE PHONE.
YEAH. AWESOME. BUT THE **SQUIRRELS** -- HOW CAN WE SEE THEM IN **CHINA?**
BRIIIIING
I PATCHED YOUR COMPUTERS INTO ALL THE SATELLITES AND CAMERAS.

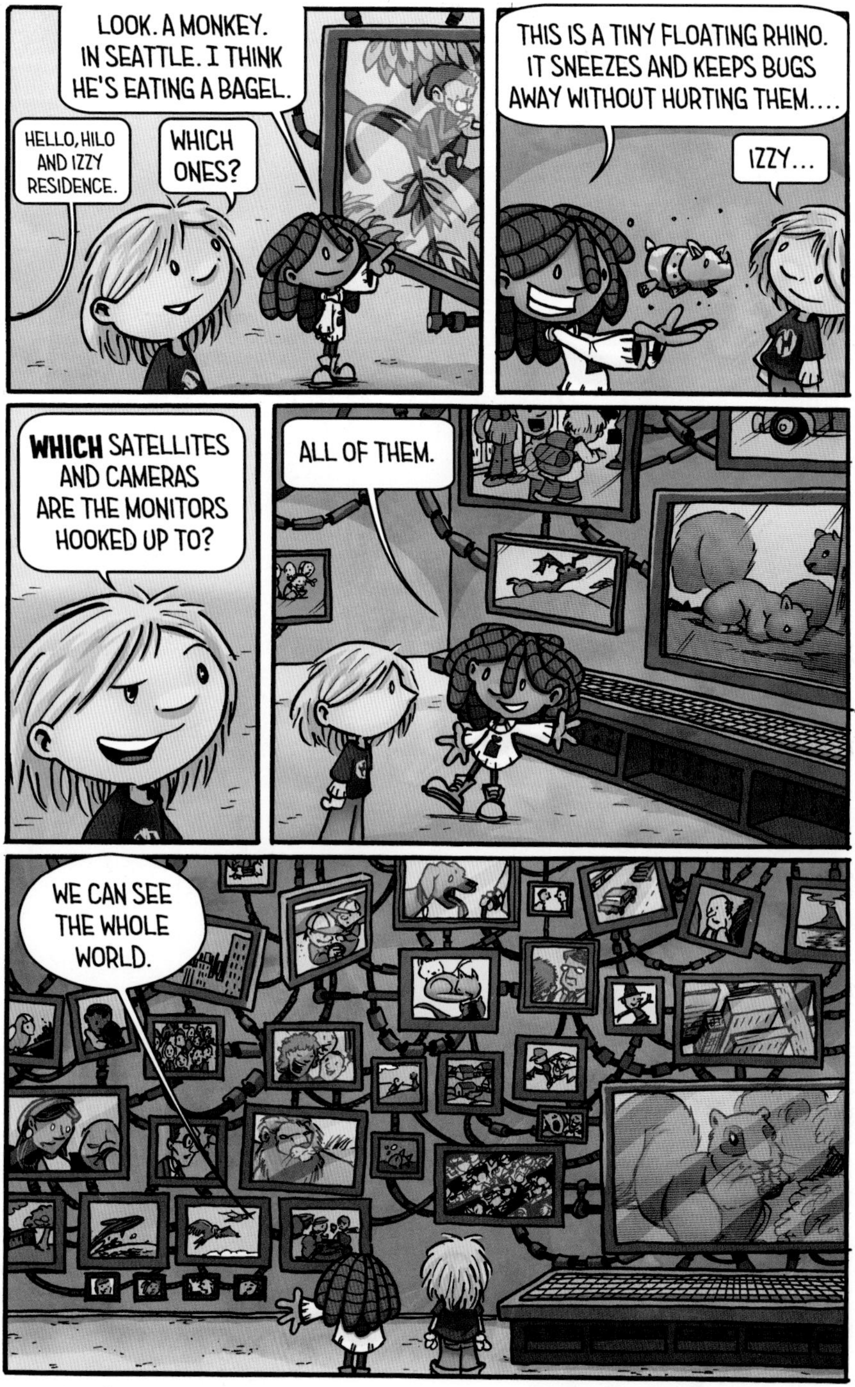
LOOK. A MONKEY. IN SEATTLE. I THINK HE'S EATING A BAGEL.
HELLO, HILO AND IZZY RESIDENCE.
WHICH ONES?
THIS IS A TINY FLOATING RHINO. IT SNEEZES AND KEEPS BUGS AWAY WITHOUT HURTING THEM....
IZZY...
WHICH SATELLITES AND CAMERAS ARE THE MONITORS HOOKED UP TO?
ALL OF THEM.
WE CAN SEE THE WHOLE WORLD.

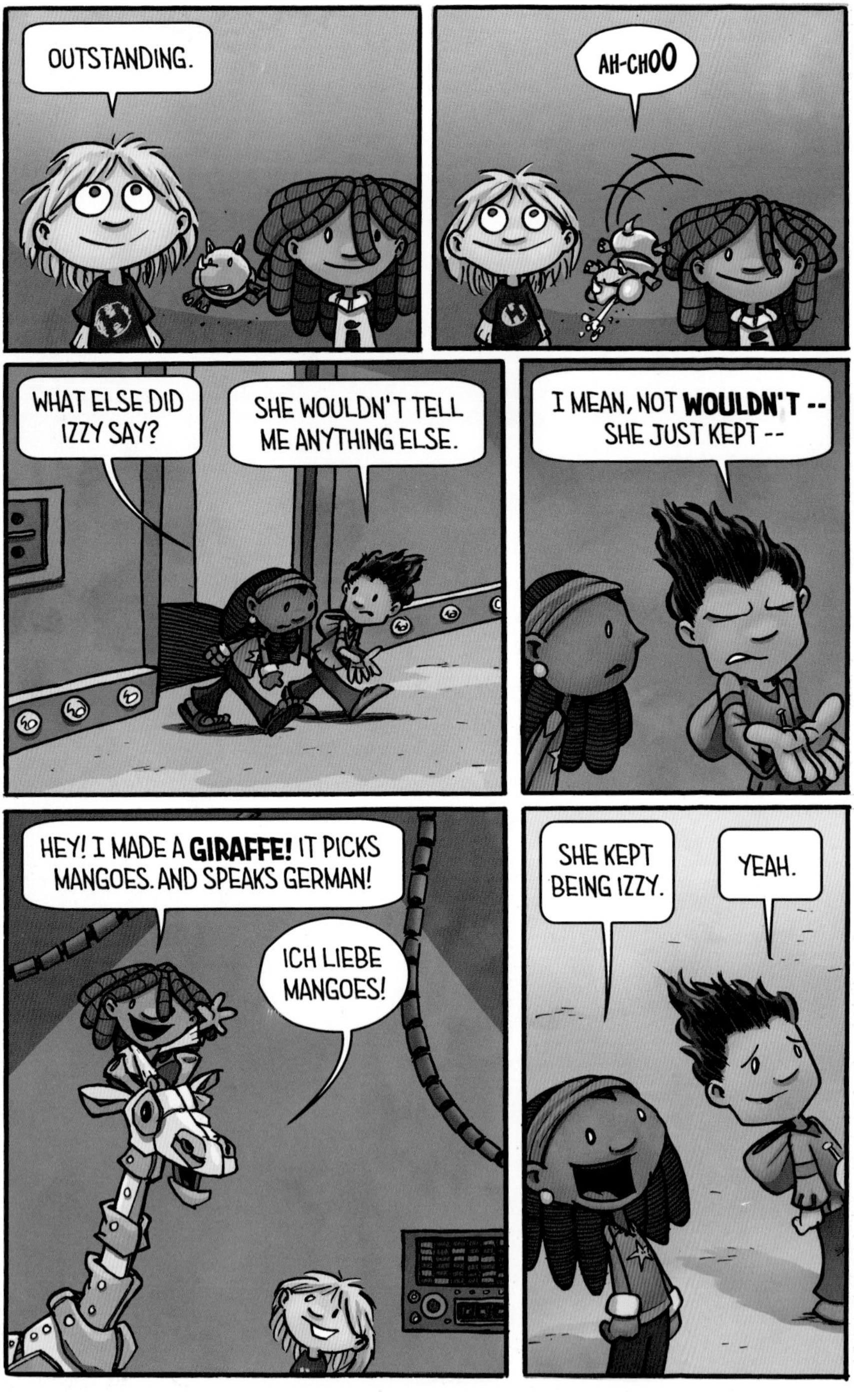
OUTSTANDING.
AH-CHOO
WHAT ELSE DID IZZY SAY?
SHE WOULDN'T TELL ME ANYTHING ELSE.
I MEAN, NOT **WOULDN'T** -- SHE JUST KEPT --
HEY! I MADE A **GIRAFFE!** IT PICKS MANGOES. AND SPEAKS GERMAN!
ICH LIEBE MANGOES!
SHE KEPT BEING IZZY.
YEAH.

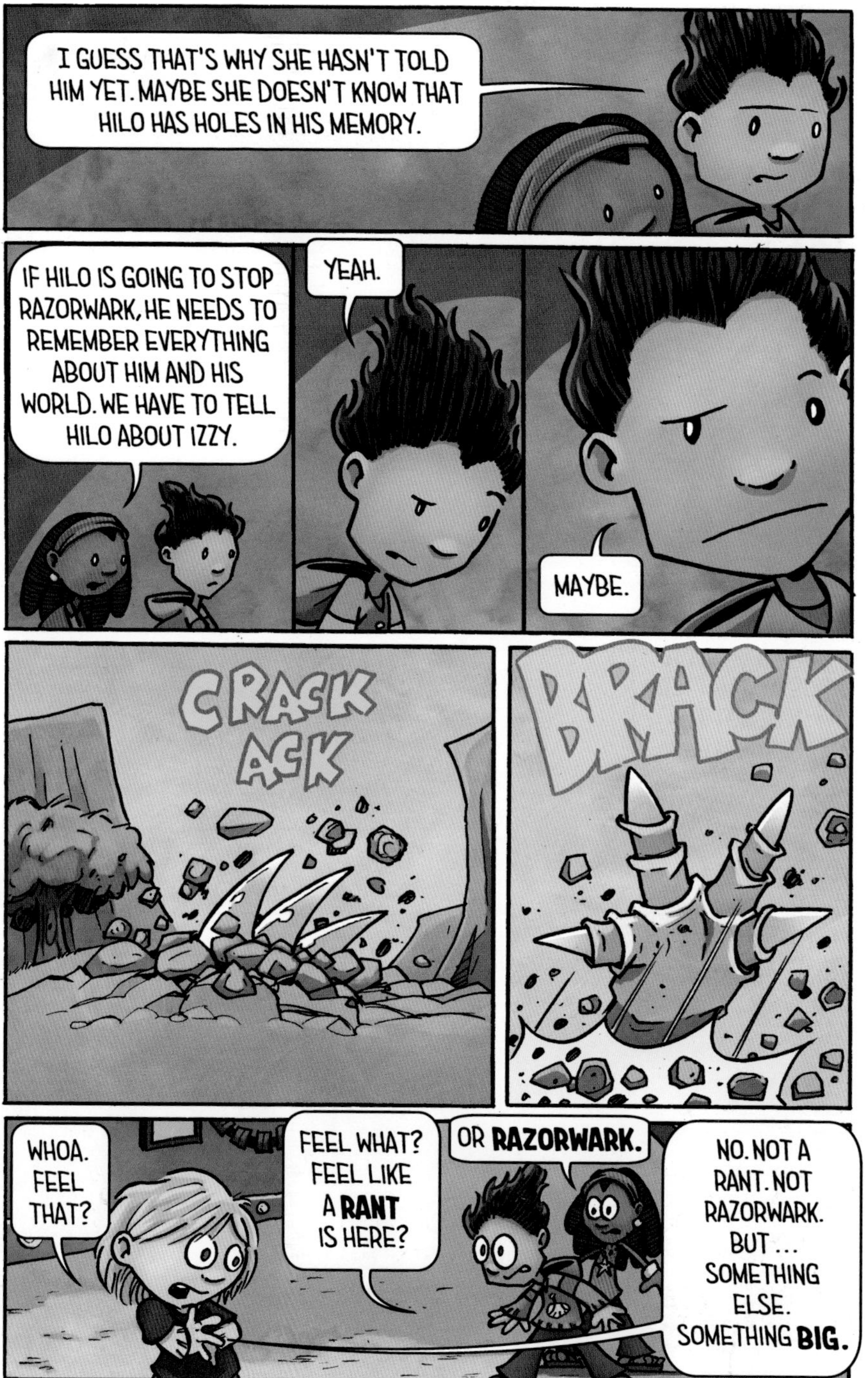
I GUESS THAT'S WHY SHE HASN'T TOLD HIM YET. MAYBE SHE DOESN'T KNOW THAT HILO HAS HOLES IN HIS MEMORY.
IF HILO IS GOING TO STOP RAZORWARK, HE NEEDS TO REMEMBER EVERYTHING ABOUT HIM AND HIS WORLD. WE HAVE TO TELL HILO ABOUT IZZY.
YEAH.
MAYBE.
CRACK ACK
BRACK
WHOA. FEEL THAT?
FEEL WHAT? FEEL LIKE A **RANT** IS HERE?
OR **RAZORWARK.**
NO. NOT A RANT. NOT RAZORWARK. BUT . . . SOMETHING ELSE. SOMETHING **BIG.**

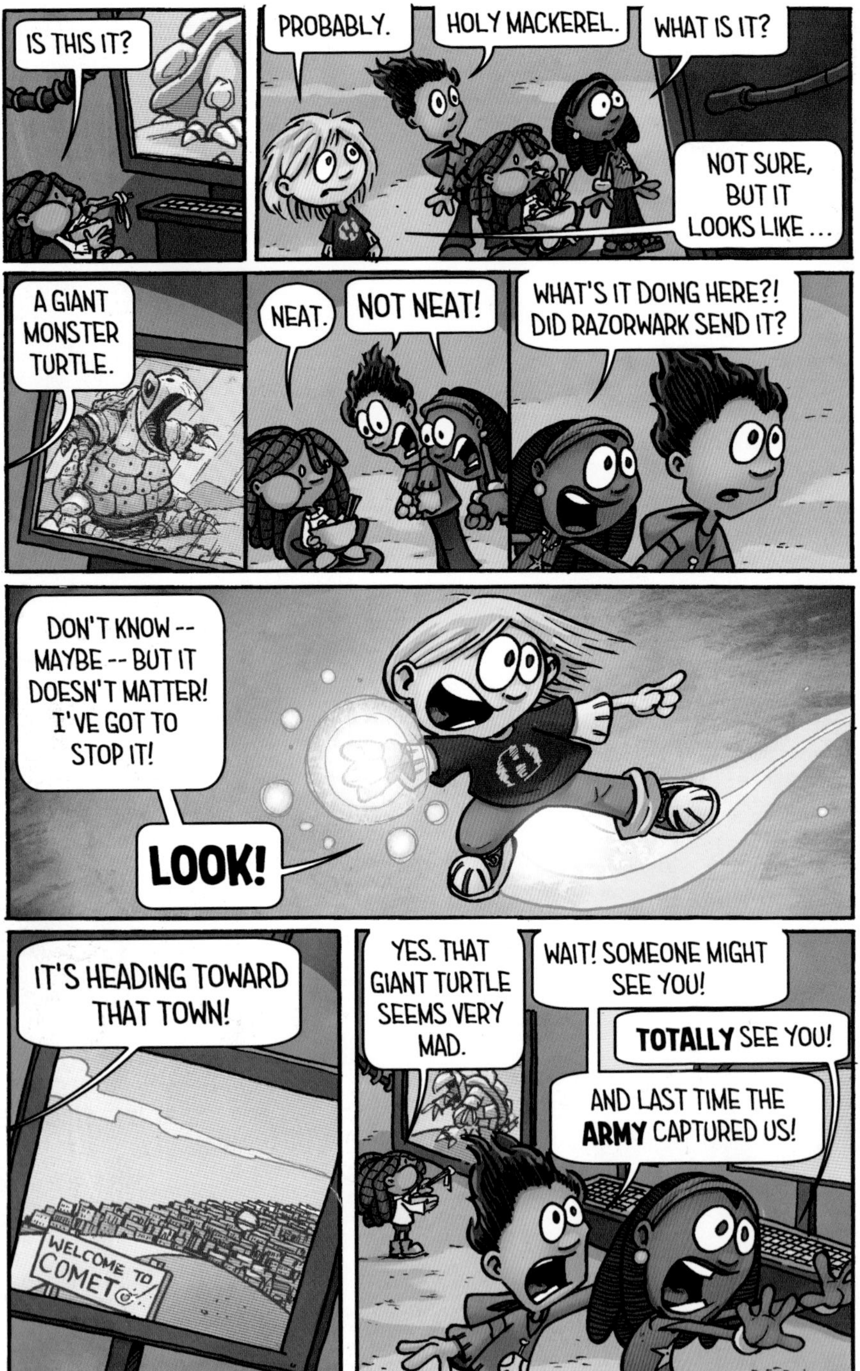
IS THIS IT?
PROBABLY.
HOLY MACKEREL.
WHAT IS IT?
NOT SURE, BUT IT LOOKS LIKE . . .
A GIANT MONSTER TURTLE.
NEAT.
NOT NEAT!
WHAT'S IT DOING HERE?! DID RAZORWARK SEND IT?
DON'T KNOW -- MAYBE -- BUT IT DOESN'T MATTER! I'VE GOT TO STOP IT!
LOOK!
IT'S HEADING TOWARD THAT TOWN!
WELCOME TO COMET
YES. THAT GIANT TURTLE SEEMS VERY MAD.
WAIT! SOMEONE MIGHT SEE YOU!
TOTALLY SEE YOU!
AND LAST TIME THE ARMY CAPTURED US!

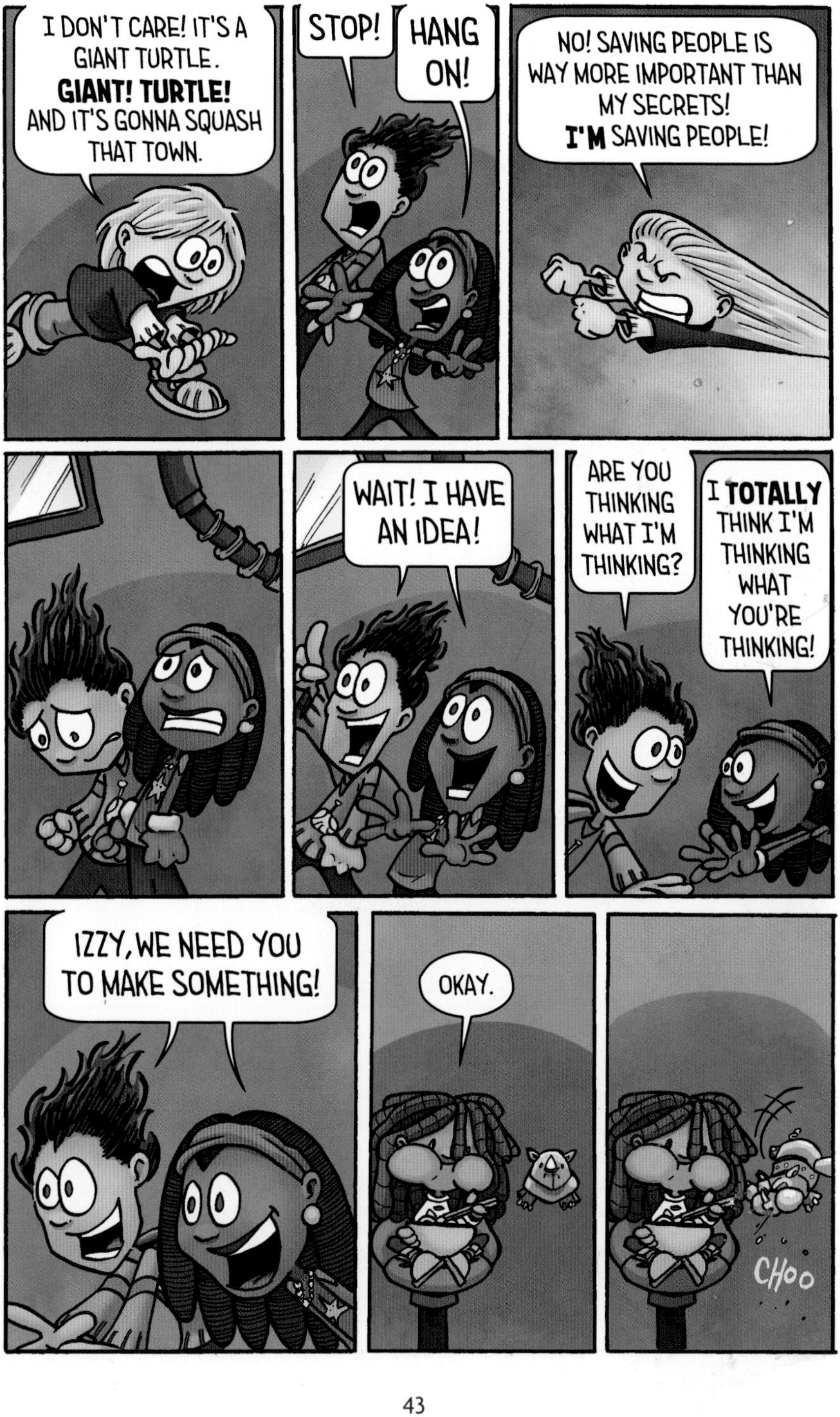

I DON'T CARE! IT'S A GIANT TURTLE. **GIANT! TURTLE!** AND IT'S GONNA SQUASH THAT TOWN.
STOP!
HANG ON!
NO! SAVING PEOPLE IS WAY MORE IMPORTANT THAN MY SECRETS! **I'M** SAVING PEOPLE!
WAIT! I HAVE AN IDEA!
ARE YOU THINKING WHAT I'M THINKING?
I **TOTALLY** THINK I'M THINKING WHAT YOU'RE THINKING!
IZZY, WE NEED YOU TO MAKE SOMETHING!
OKAY.
CHOO

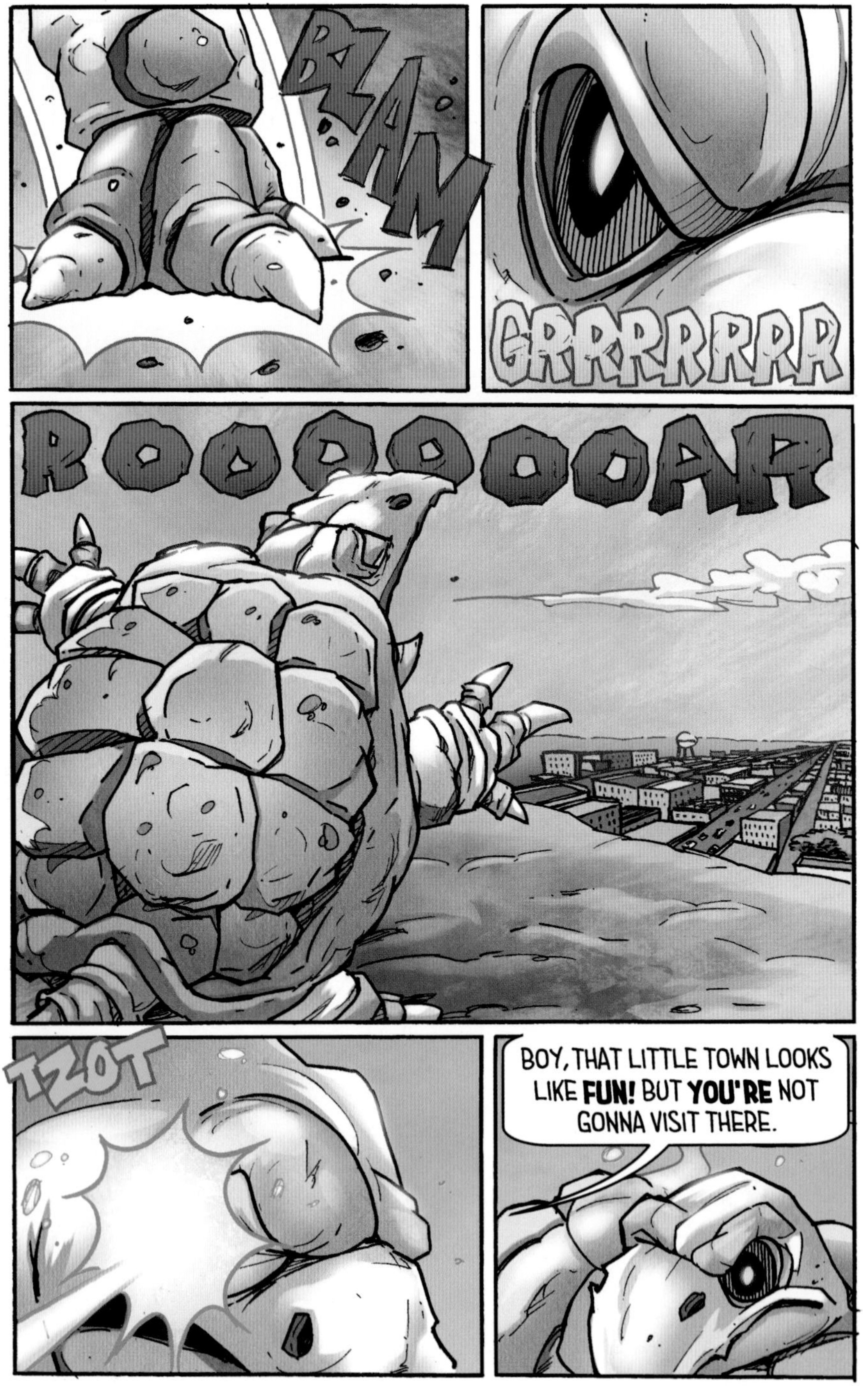
BLAM
GRRRRRRR
ROOOOOOAR
TZOT
BOY, THAT LITTLE TOWN LOOKS LIKE **FUN!** BUT **YOU'RE** NOT GONNA VISIT THERE.

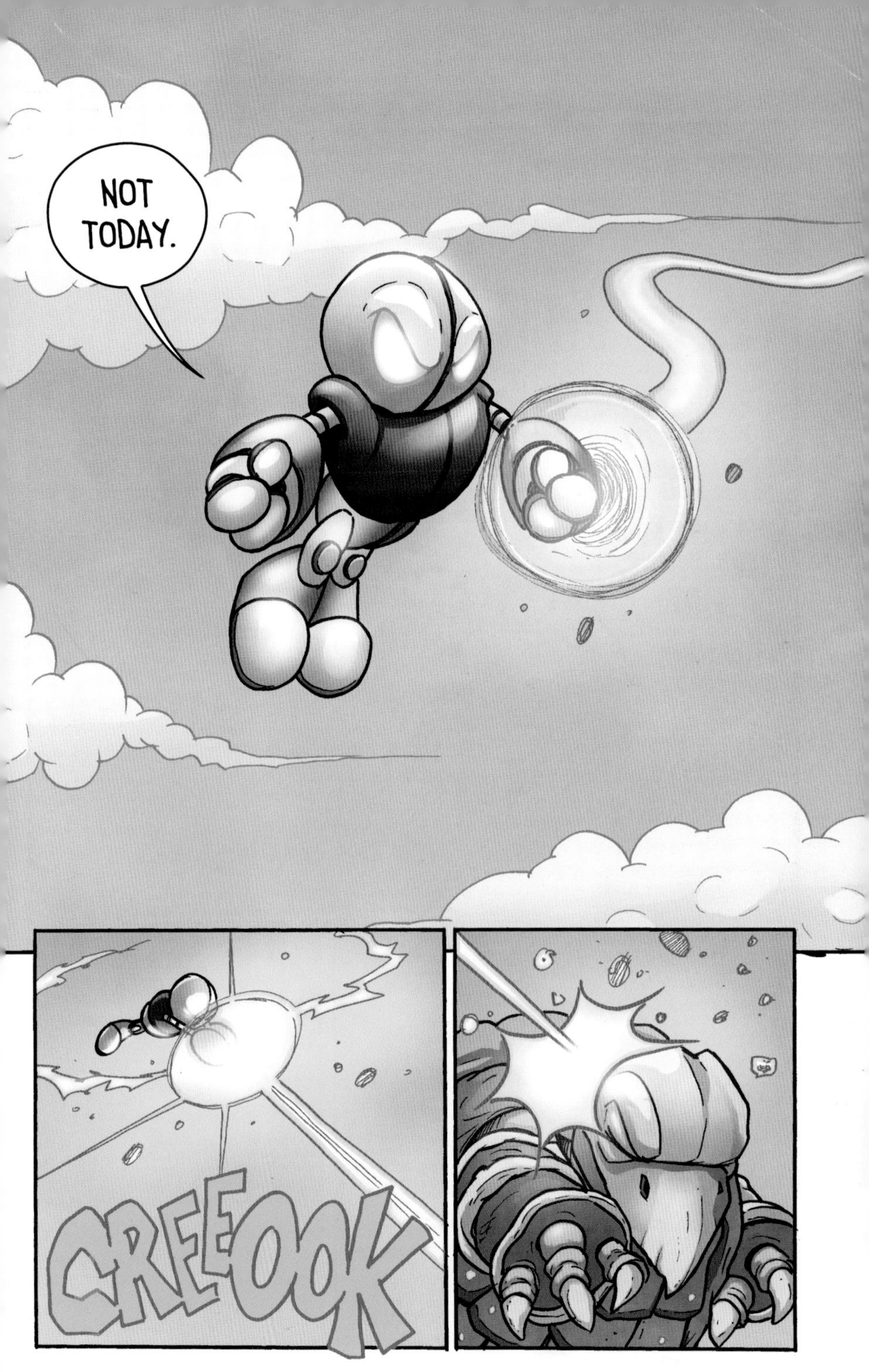
NOT TODAY.
CREEOOK

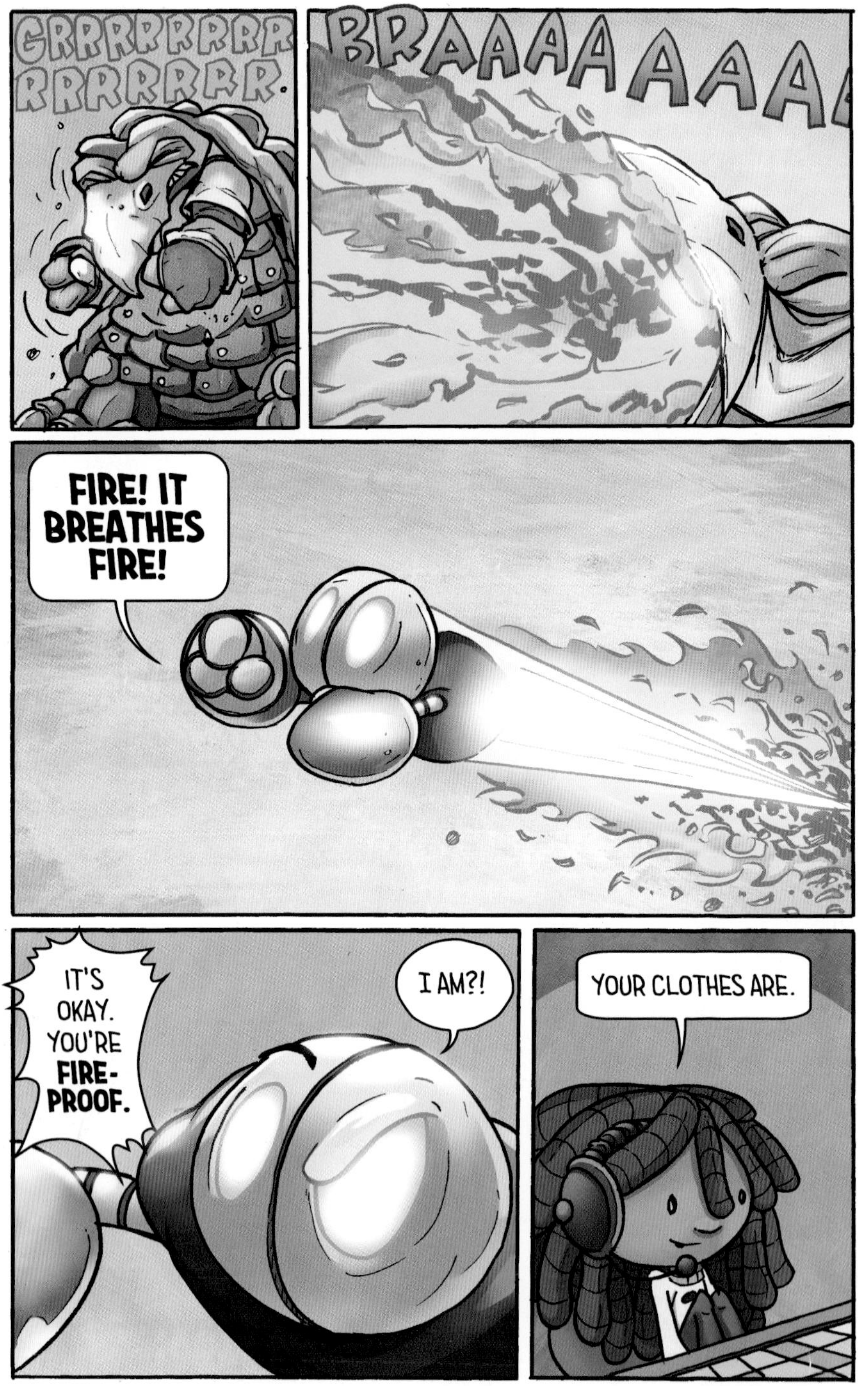
GRRRRRRRR RRRRRRR
BRAAAAAAAA
FIRE! IT BREATHES FIRE!
IT'S OKAY. YOU'RE **FIRE-PROOF.**
I AM?!
YOUR CLOTHES ARE.

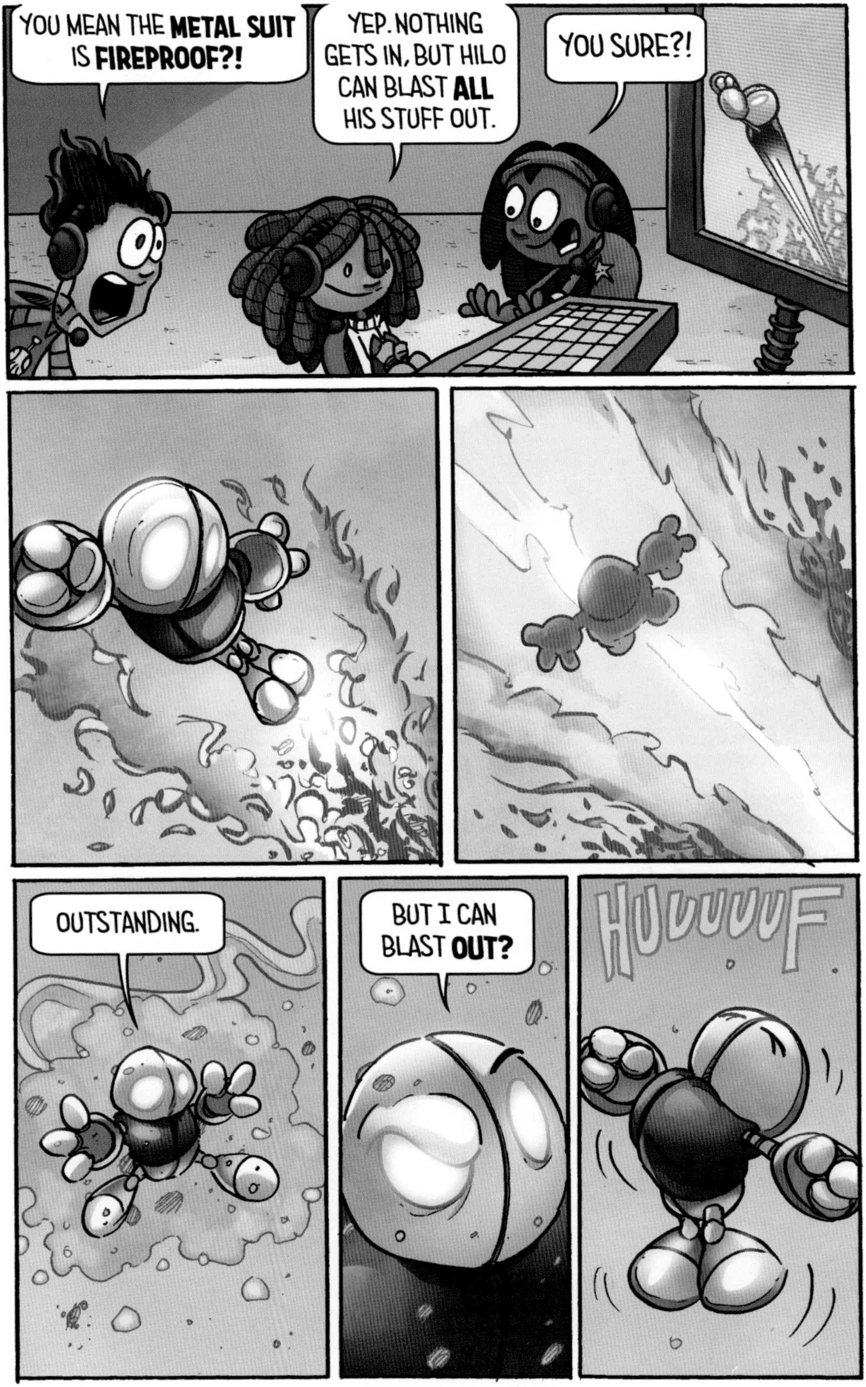

YOU MEAN THE **METAL SUIT** IS **FIREPROOF?!**
YEP. NOTHING GETS IN, BUT HILO CAN BLAST **ALL** HIS STUFF OUT.
YOU SURE?!
OUTSTANDING.
BUT I CAN BLAST **OUT?**
HUUUUUF

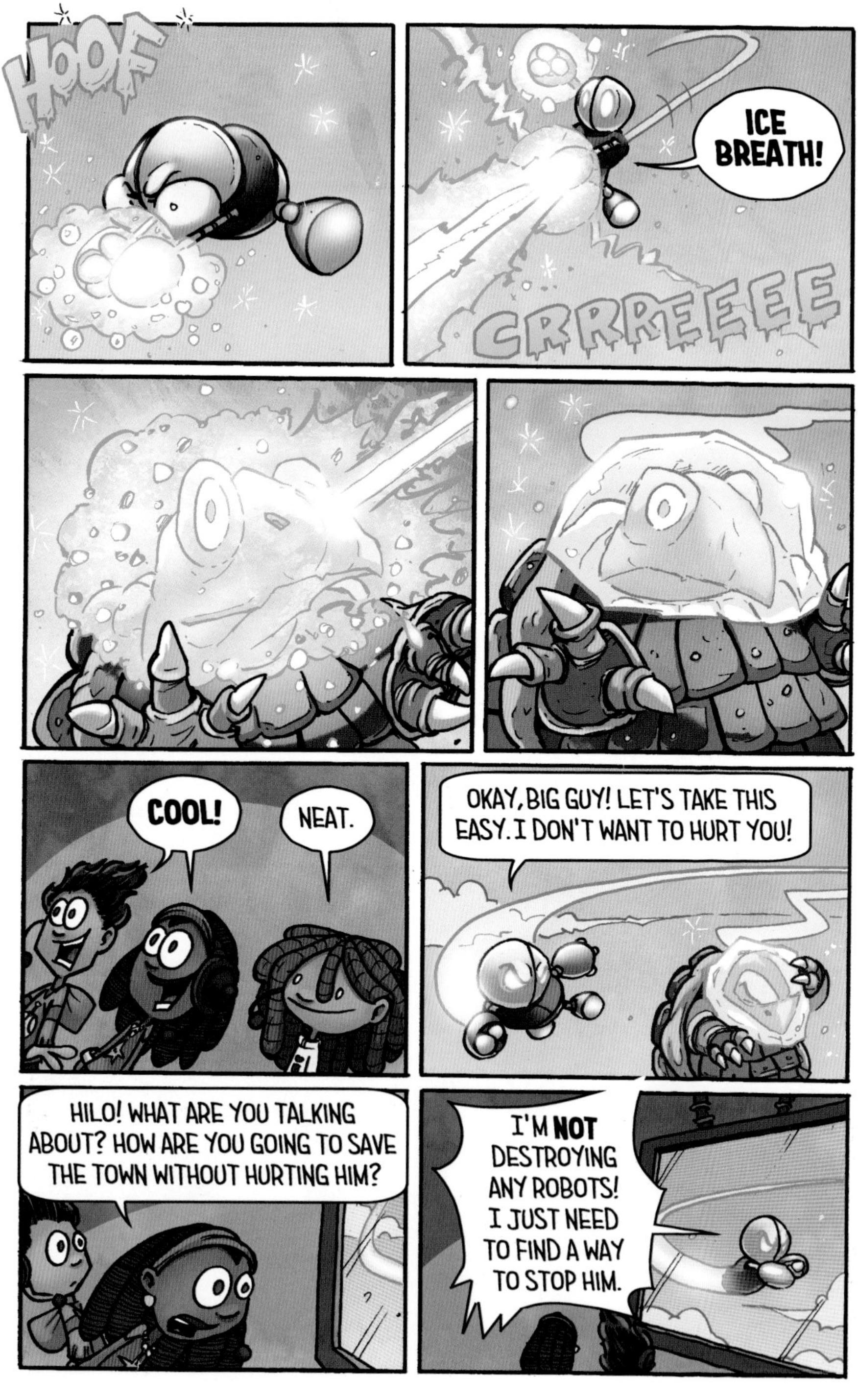
HOOF
ICE BREATH!
CRRREEEE
COOL!
NEAT.
OKAY, BIG GUY! LET'S TAKE THIS EASY. I DON'T WANT TO HURT YOU!
HILO! WHAT ARE YOU TALKING ABOUT? HOW ARE YOU GOING TO SAVE THE TOWN WITHOUT HURTING HIM?
I'M **NOT** DESTROYING ANY ROBOTS! I JUST NEED TO FIND A WAY TO STOP HIM.

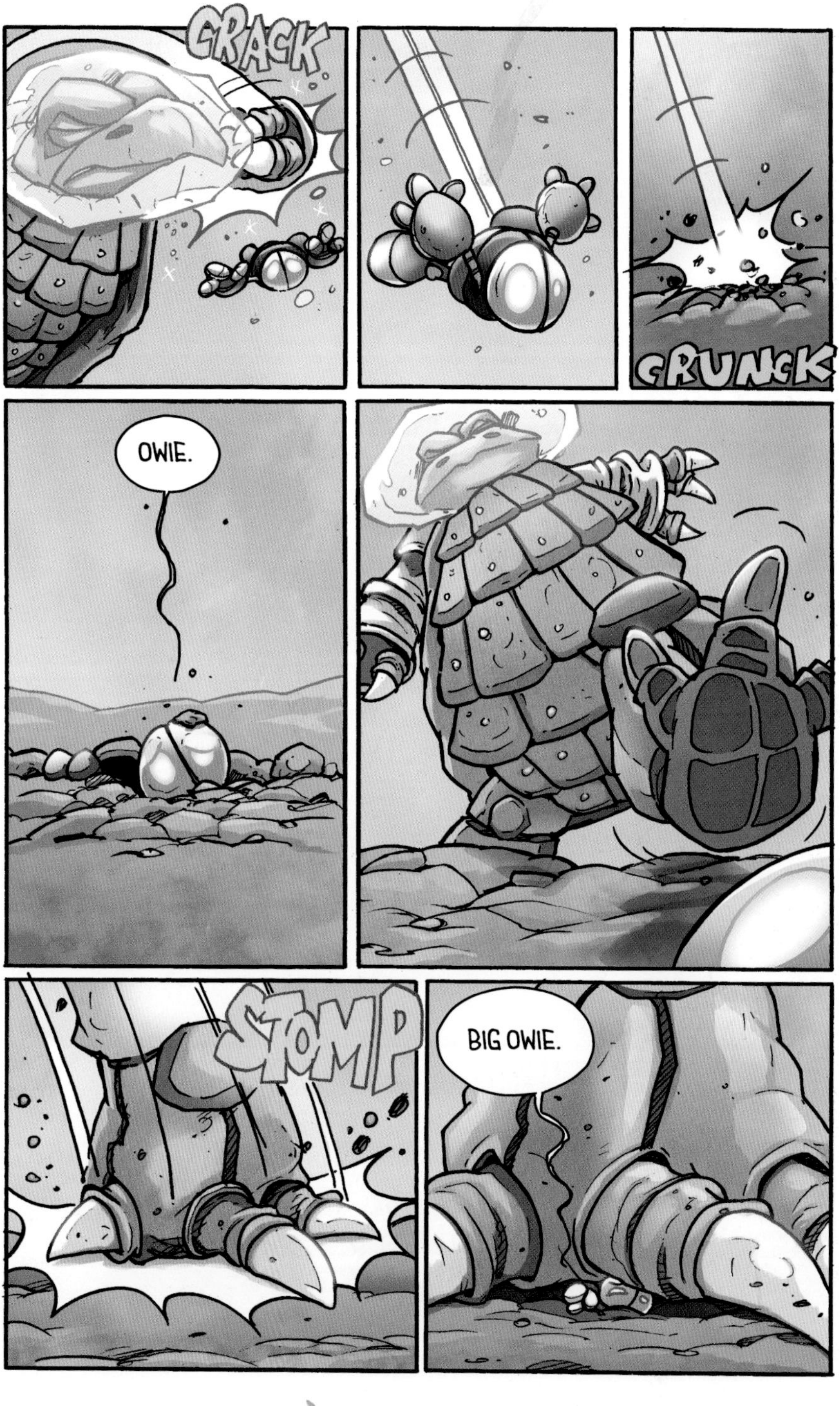
CRACK
CRUNCK
OWIE.
STOMP
BIG OWIE.

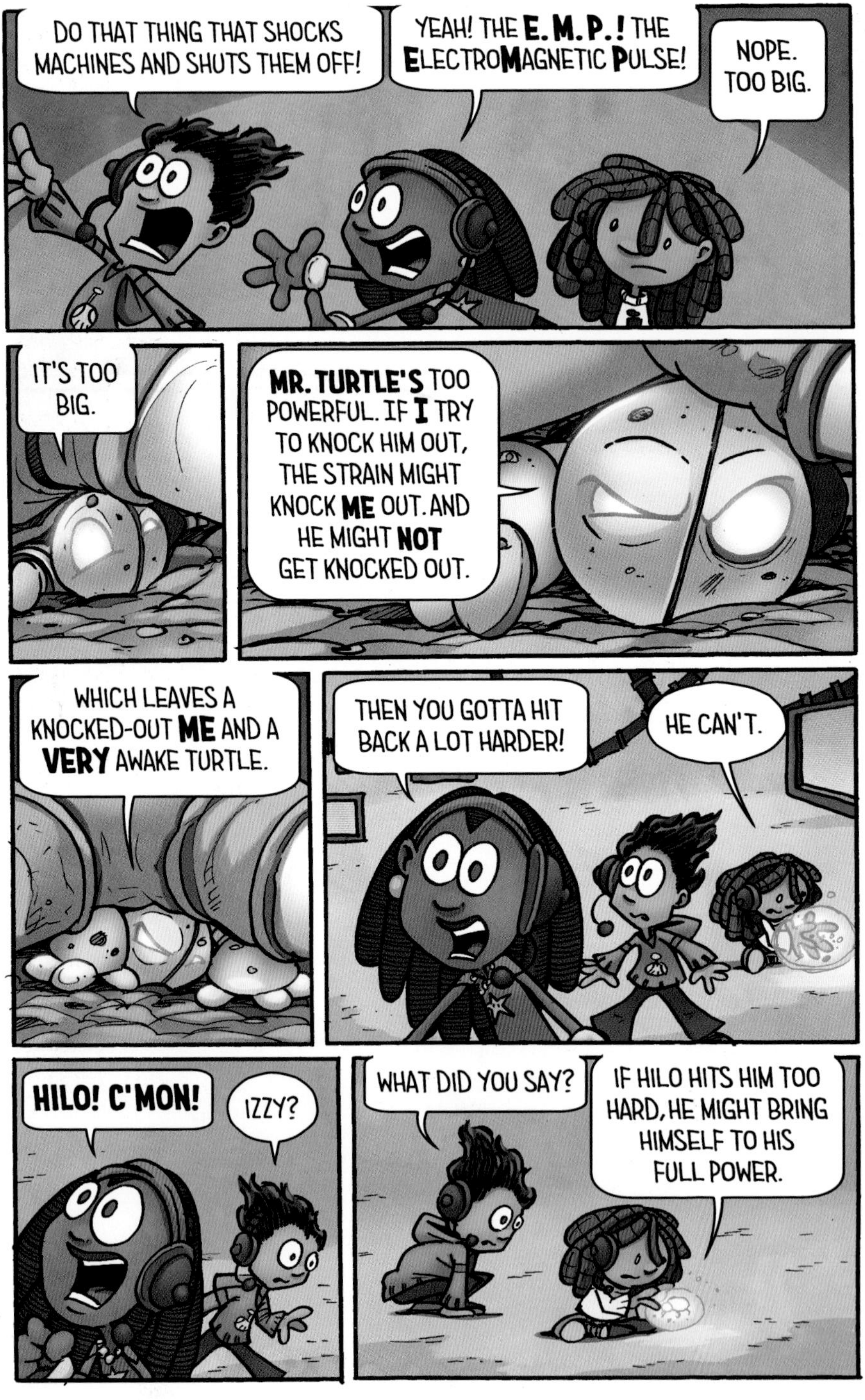
DO THAT THING THAT SHOCKS MACHINES AND SHUTS THEM OFF!
YEAH! THE E.M.P.! THE ELECTROMAGNETIC PULSE!
NOPE. TOO BIG.
IT'S TOO BIG.
MR. TURTLE'S TOO POWERFUL. IF I TRY TO KNOCK HIM OUT, THE STRAIN MIGHT KNOCK ME OUT. AND HE MIGHT NOT GET KNOCKED OUT.
WHICH LEAVES A KNOCKED-OUT ME AND A VERY AWAKE TURTLE.
THEN YOU GOTTA HIT BACK A LOT HARDER!
HE CAN'T.
HILO! C'MON!
IZZY?
WHAT DID YOU SAY?
IF HILO HITS HIM TOO HARD, HE MIGHT BRING HIMSELF TO HIS FULL POWER.

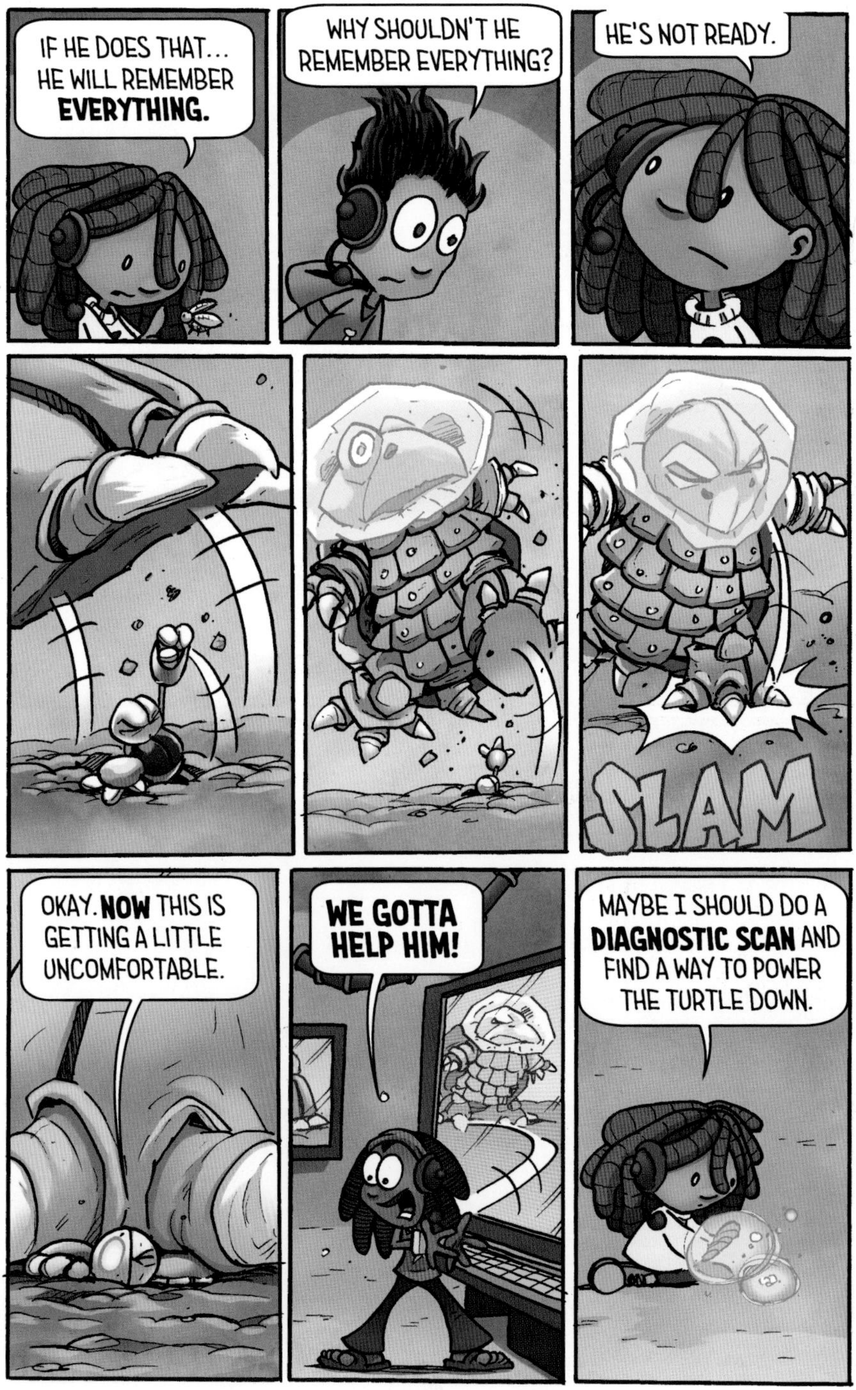

IF HE DOES THAT... HE WILL REMEMBER **EVERYTHING.**
WHY SHOULDN'T HE REMEMBER EVERYTHING?
HE'S NOT READY.
SLAM
OKAY. **NOW** THIS IS GETTING A LITTLE UNCOMFORTABLE.
WE GOTTA HELP HIM!
MAYBE I SHOULD DO A **DIAGNOSTIC SCAN** AND FIND A WAY TO POWER THE TURTLE DOWN.

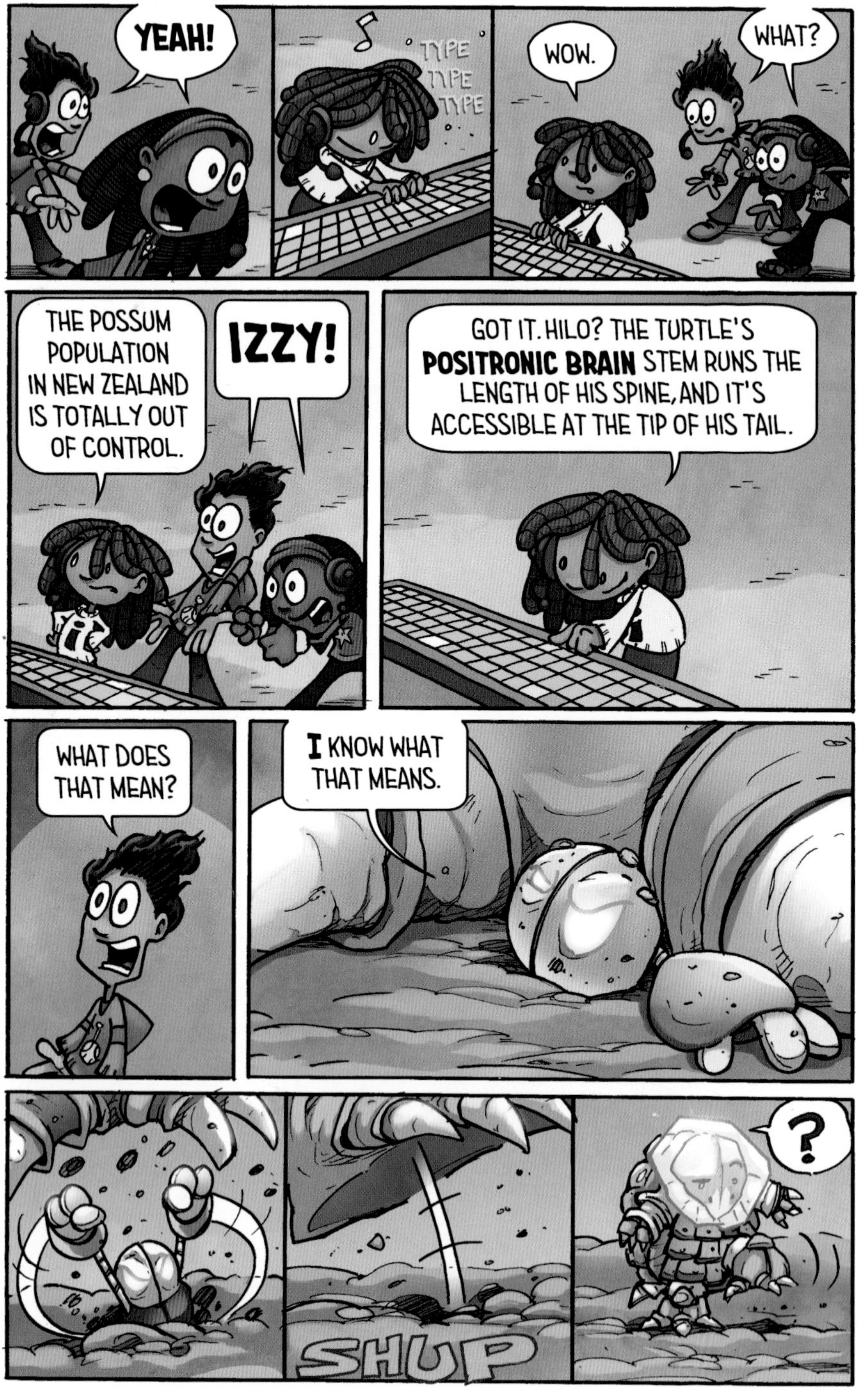
YEAH!
TYPE TYPE TYPE
WOW.
WHAT?
THE POSSUM POPULATION IN NEW ZEALAND IS TOTALLY OUT OF CONTROL.
IZZY!
GOT IT. HILO? THE TURTLE'S **POSITRONIC BRAIN** STEM RUNS THE LENGTH OF HIS SPINE, AND IT'S ACCESSIBLE AT THE TIP OF HIS TAIL.
WHAT DOES THAT MEAN?
I KNOW WHAT THAT MEANS.
SHUP
?

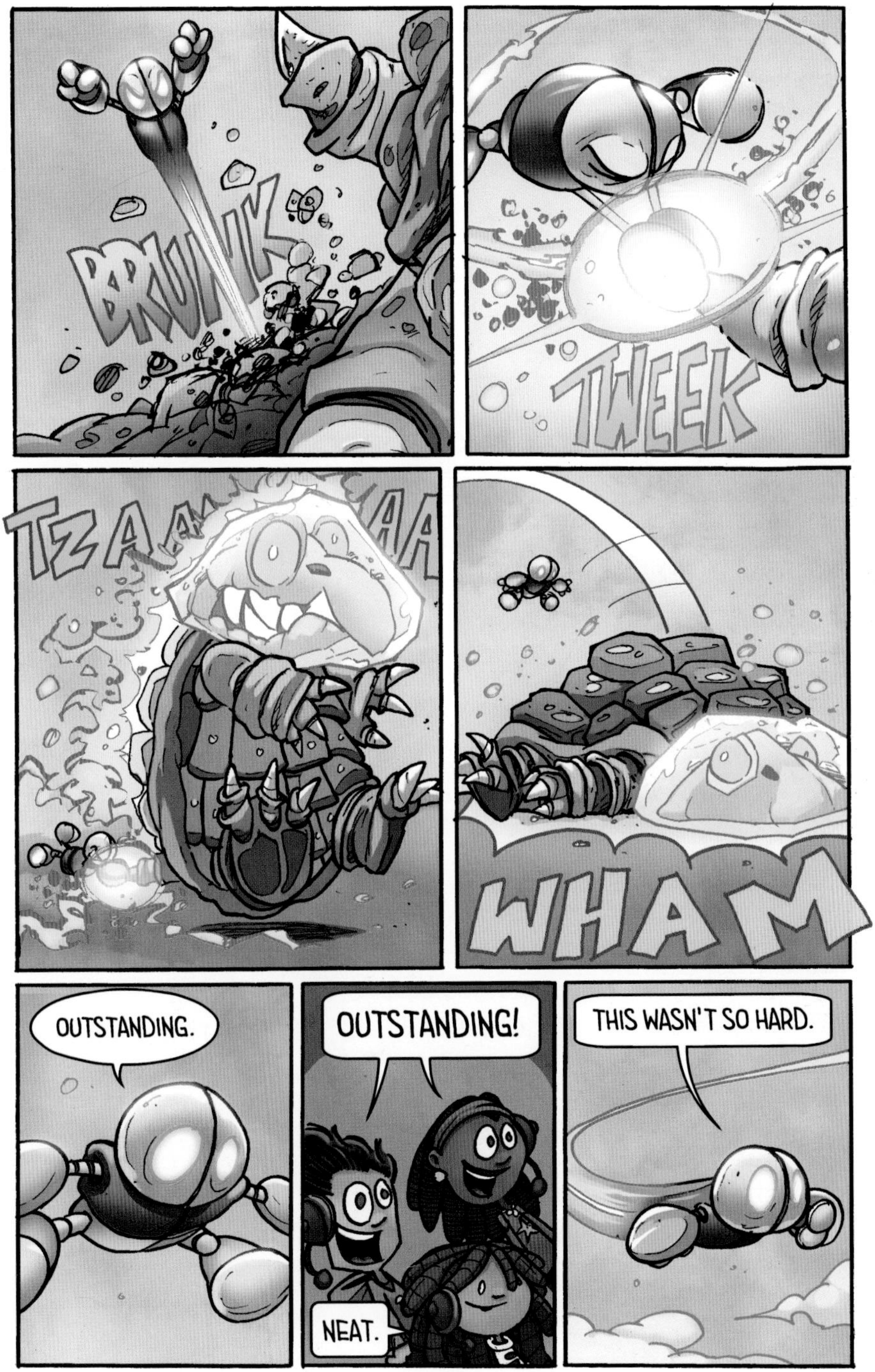
BRUNK
TWEEK
TZAAAAAAAA
WHAM
OUTSTANDING.
OUTSTANDING!
NEAT.
THIS WASN'T SO HARD.

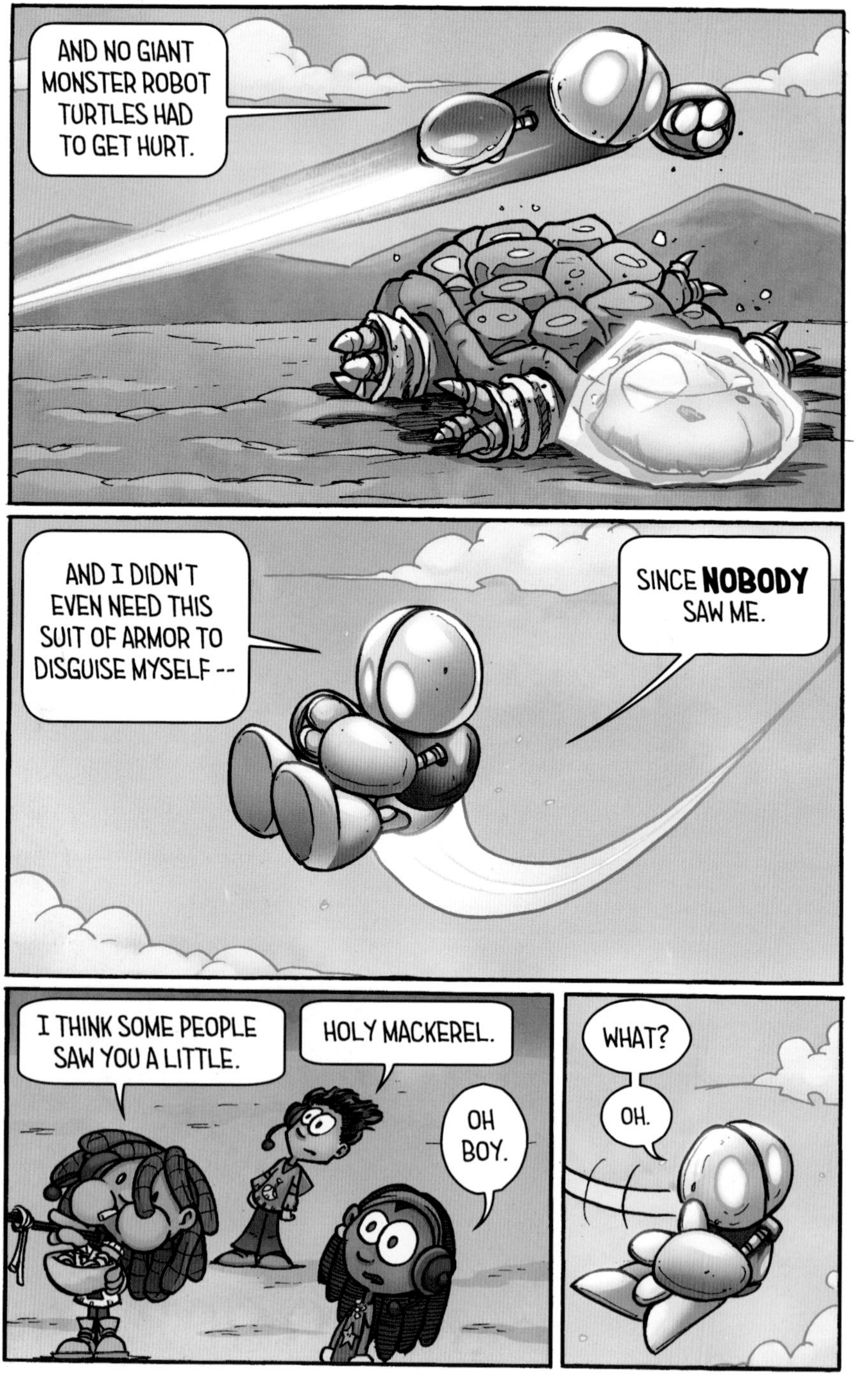
AND NO GIANT MONSTER ROBOT TURTLES HAD TO GET HURT.
AND I DIDN'T EVEN NEED THIS SUIT OF ARMOR TO DISGUISE MYSELF --
SINCE **NOBODY** SAW ME.
I THINK SOME PEOPLE SAW YOU A LITTLE.
HOLY MACKEREL.
OH BOY.
WHAT?
OH.

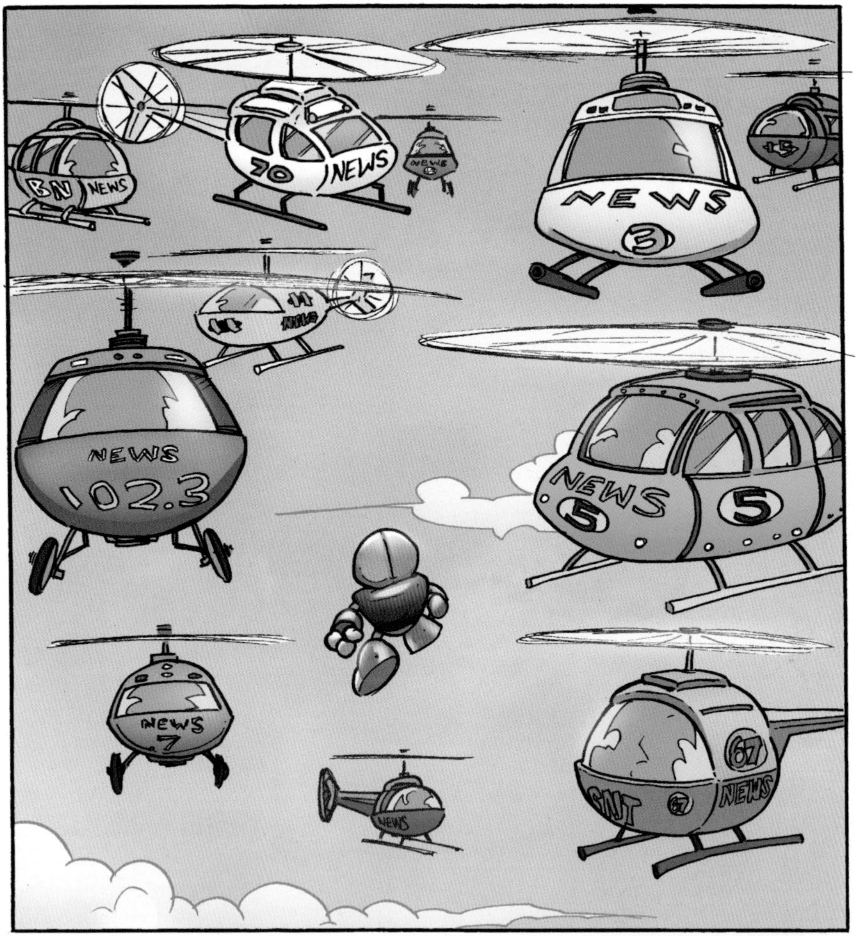
BN NEWS
70 NEWS
NEWS 3
NEWS 102.3
NEWS 5 5
NEWS 7
GNT 67 NEWS

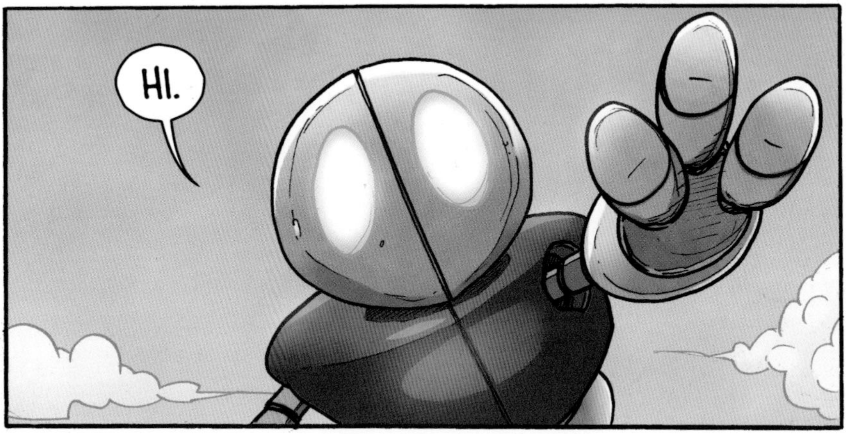
HI.

CHAPTER 4

NEWS

INCREDIBLE!
ASTONISHING!
UNBELIEVABLE!

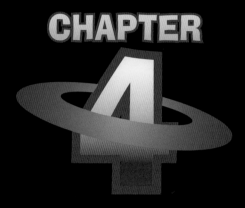

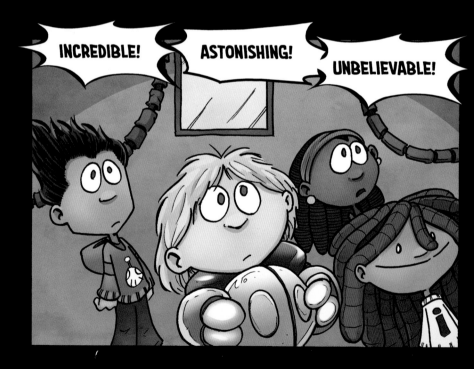

AN ENORMOUS METAL TURTLE!

50 FEET HIGH --

BLASTING FIRE, MARCHING TOWARD THE SMALL TOWN OF **COMET**.

IT'S UNKNOWN AT THIS TIME **WHERE** IT CAME FROM --

WHEN AN ARMORED INDIVIDUAL FLEW -- YES, **FLEW** -- AND FOUGHT OFF THE METAL MONSTER --

SHOOTING **LASERS** FROM HIS HANDS --

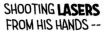

AND A **FREEZE RAY!**

-- ICE BLAST --

A BLIZZARD!

HE SAVED US!

HE SAVED THE WHOLE TOWN OF **COMET!**

THE HERO OF COMET!

HE SAVED US ALL!

HERO!

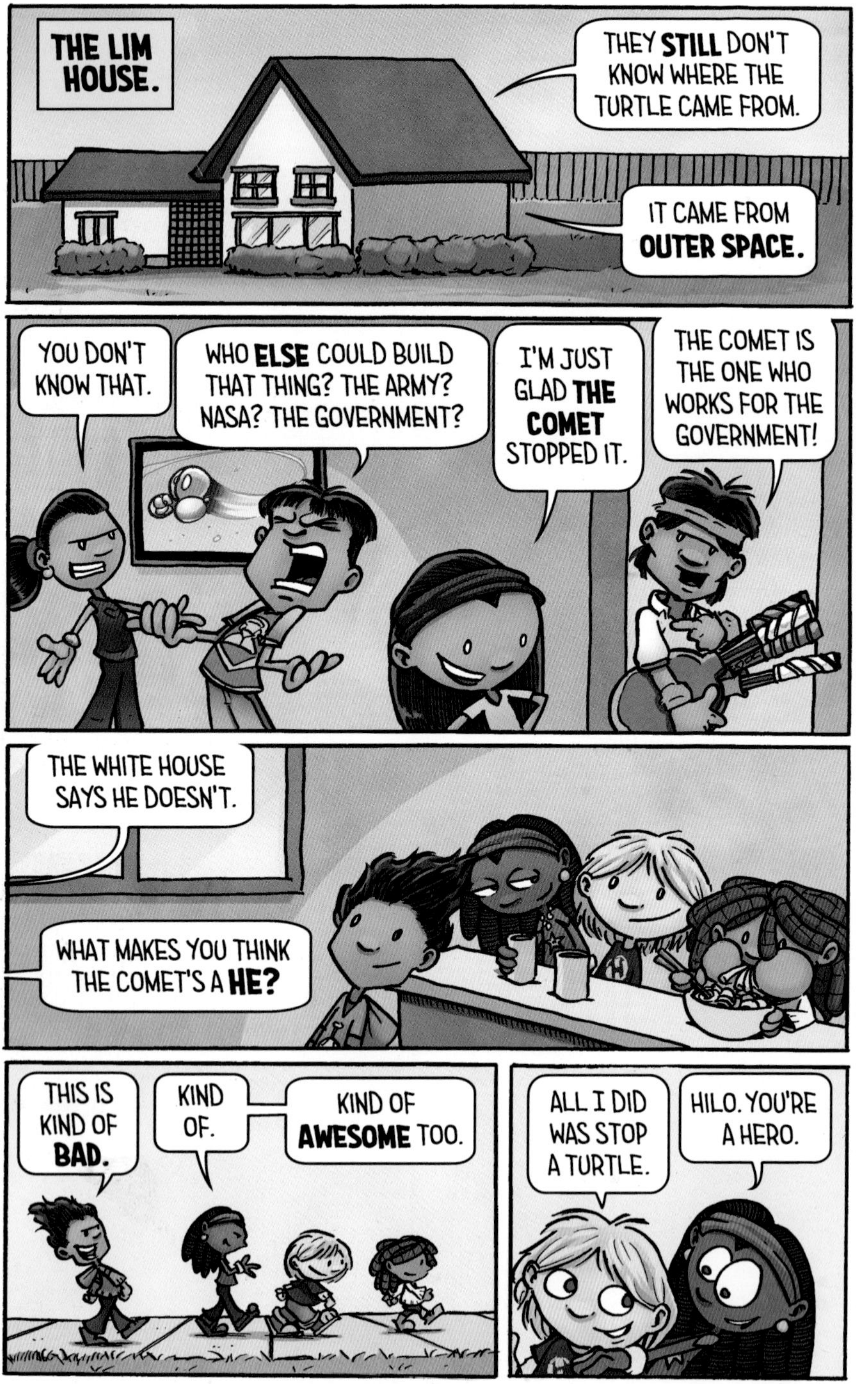
THE LIM HOUSE.
THEY STILL DON'T KNOW WHERE THE TURTLE CAME FROM.
IT CAME FROM OUTER SPACE.
YOU DON'T KNOW THAT.
WHO ELSE COULD BUILD THAT THING? THE ARMY? NASA? THE GOVERNMENT?
I'M JUST GLAD THE COMET STOPPED IT.
THE COMET IS THE ONE WHO WORKS FOR THE GOVERNMENT!
THE WHITE HOUSE SAYS HE DOESN'T.
WHAT MAKES YOU THINK THE COMET'S A HE?
THIS IS KIND OF BAD.
KIND OF.
KIND OF AWESOME TOO.
ALL I DID WAS STOP A TURTLE.
HILO. YOU'RE A HERO.

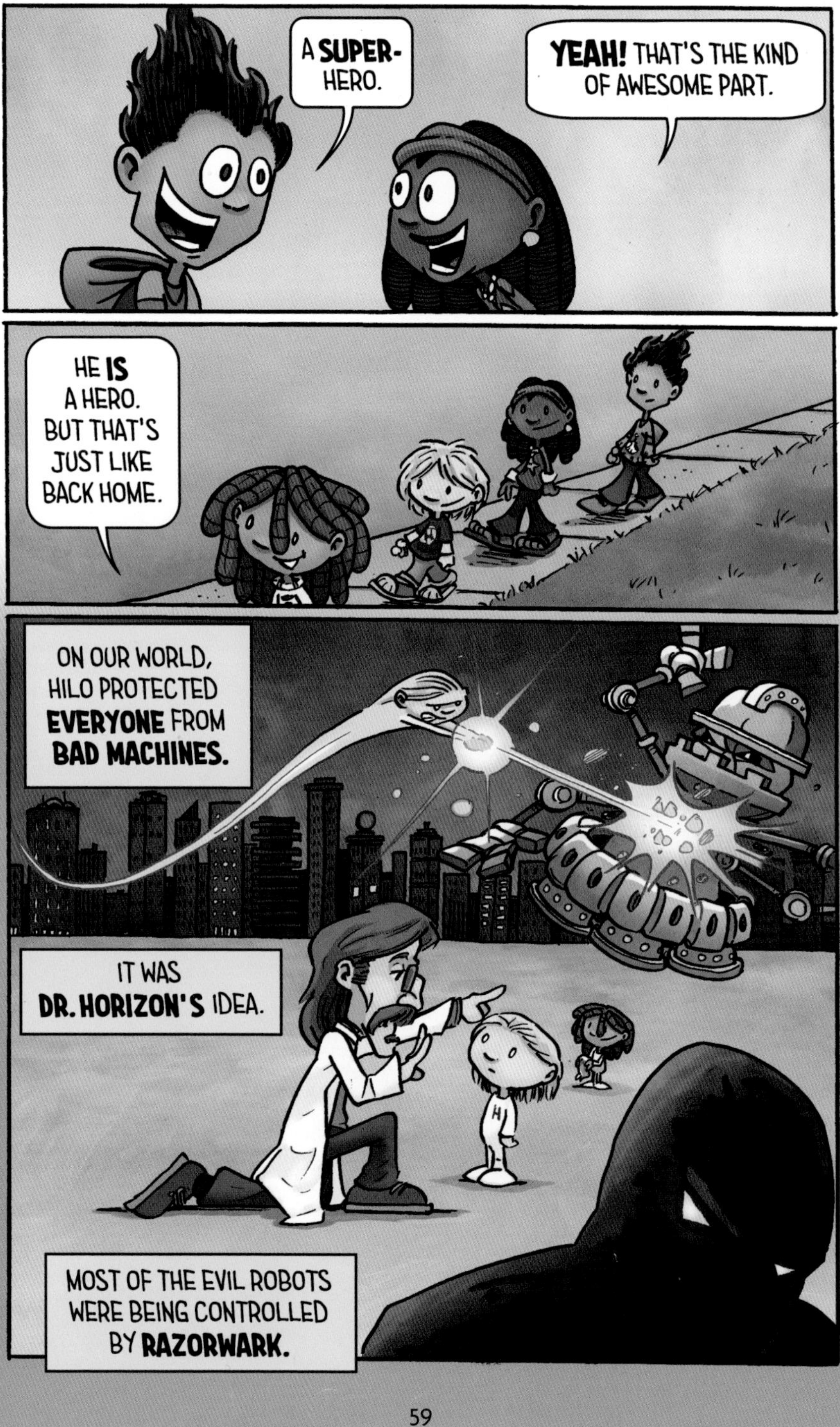
A SUPER-HERO.
YEAH! THAT'S THE KIND OF AWESOME PART.
HE IS A HERO. BUT THAT'S JUST LIKE BACK HOME.
ON OUR WORLD, HILO PROTECTED EVERYONE FROM BAD MACHINES.
IT WAS DR. HORIZON'S IDEA.
MOST OF THE EVIL ROBOTS WERE BEING CONTROLLED BY RAZORWARK.

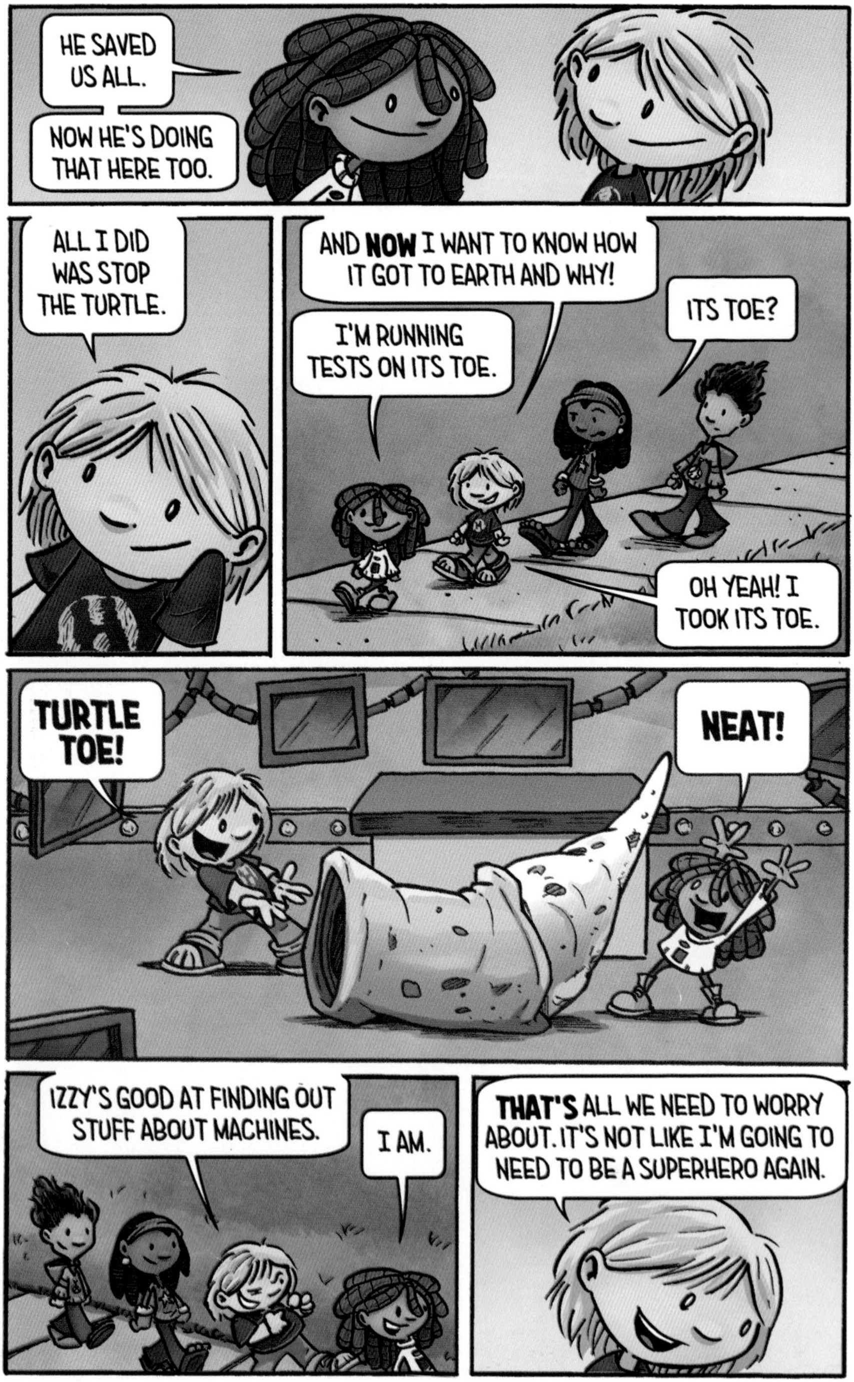
HE SAVED US ALL.
NOW HE'S DOING THAT HERE TOO.
ALL I DID WAS STOP THE TURTLE.
AND **NOW** I WANT TO KNOW HOW IT GOT TO EARTH AND WHY!
I'M RUNNING TESTS ON ITS TOE.
ITS TOE?
OH YEAH! I TOOK ITS TOE.
TURTLE TOE!
NEAT!
IZZY'S GOOD AT FINDING OUT STUFF ABOUT MACHINES.
I AM.
THAT'S ALL WE NEED TO WORRY ABOUT. IT'S NOT LIKE I'M GOING TO NEED TO BE A SUPERHERO AGAIN.

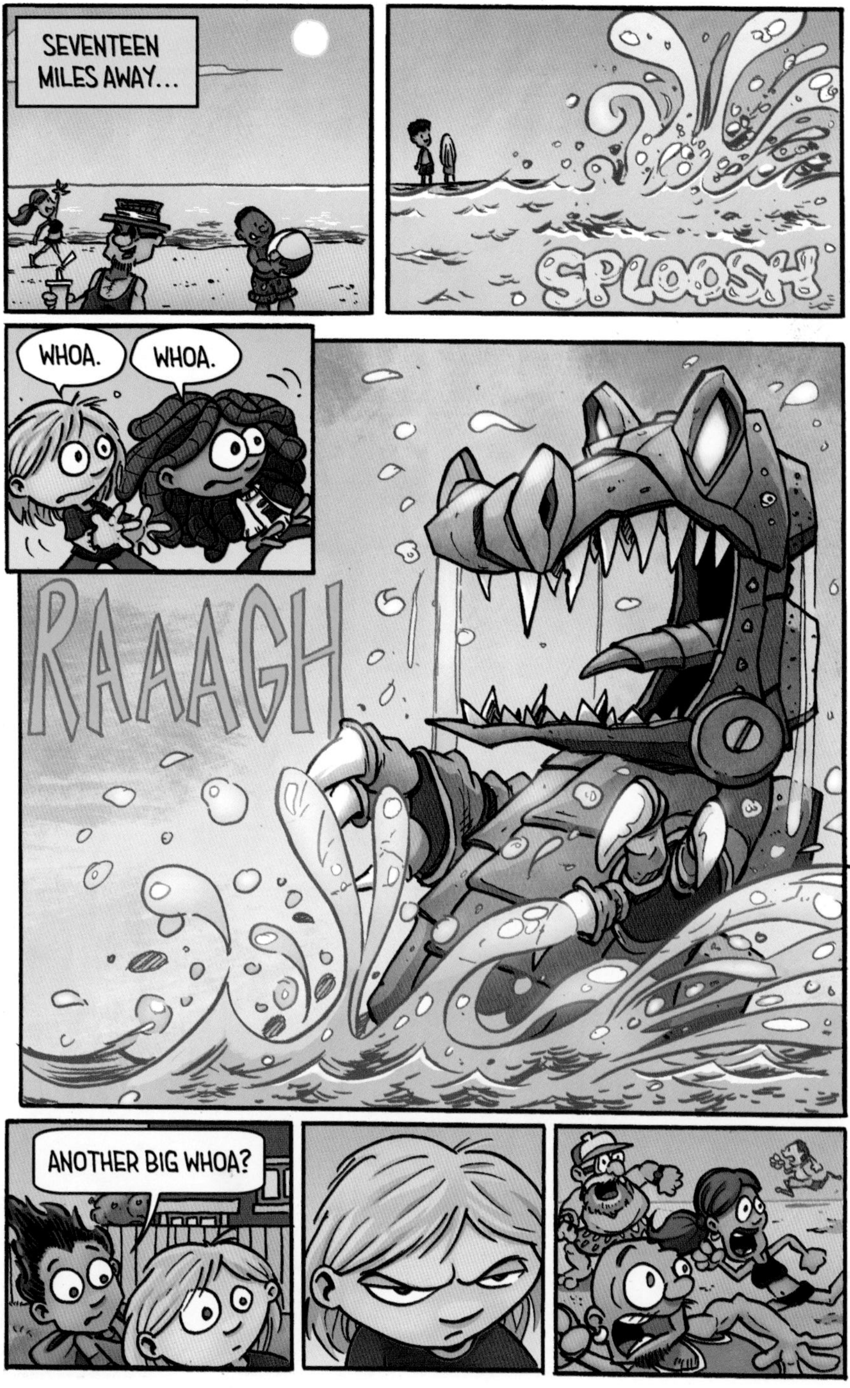
SEVENTEEN MILES AWAY...
SPLOOSH
WHOA.
WHOA.
RAAAGH
ANOTHER BIG WHOA?

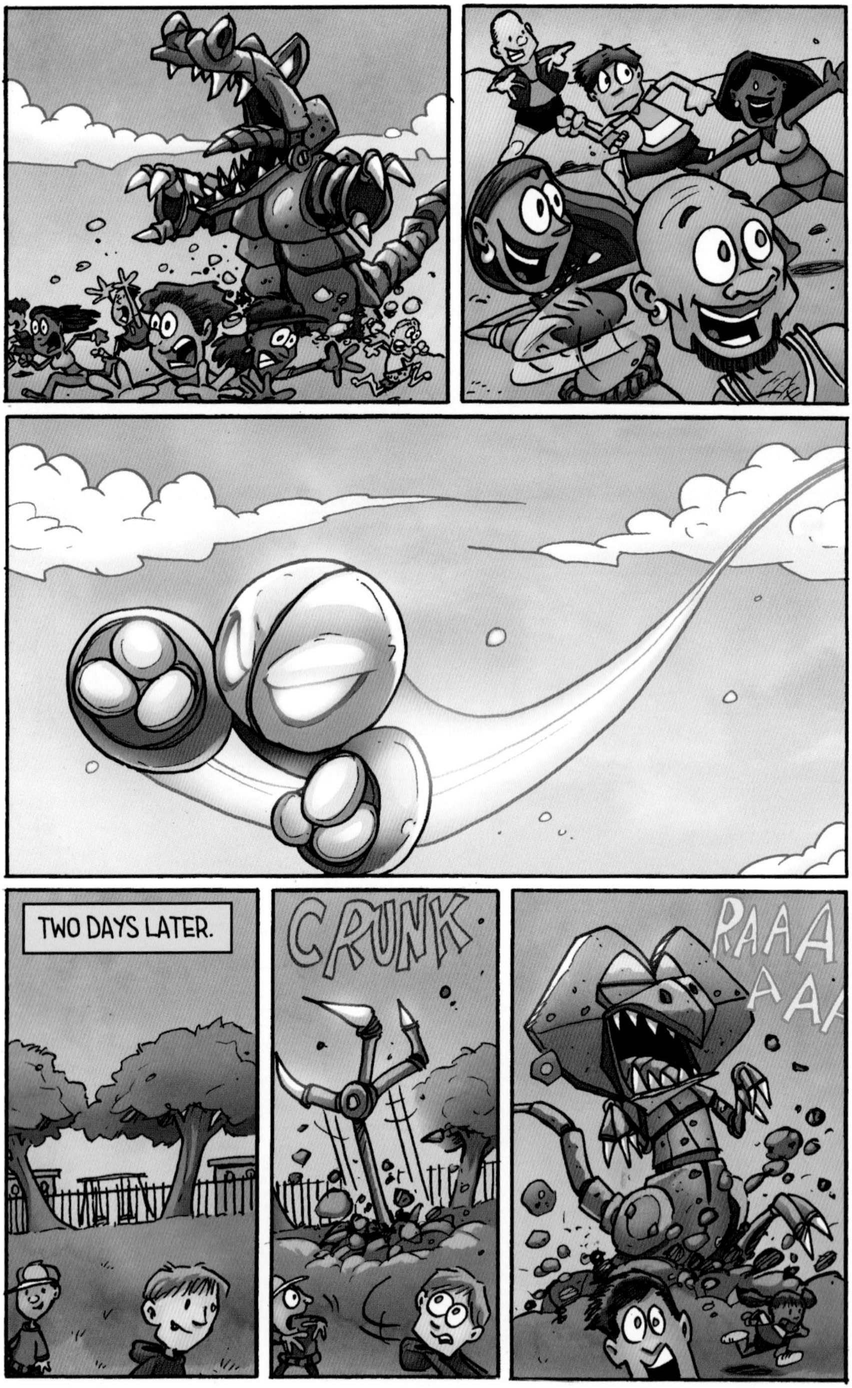
TWO DAYS LATER.
CRUNK
RAAAAAA

FOUR DAYS LATER.

LATER . . .

LATER . . .

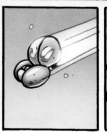

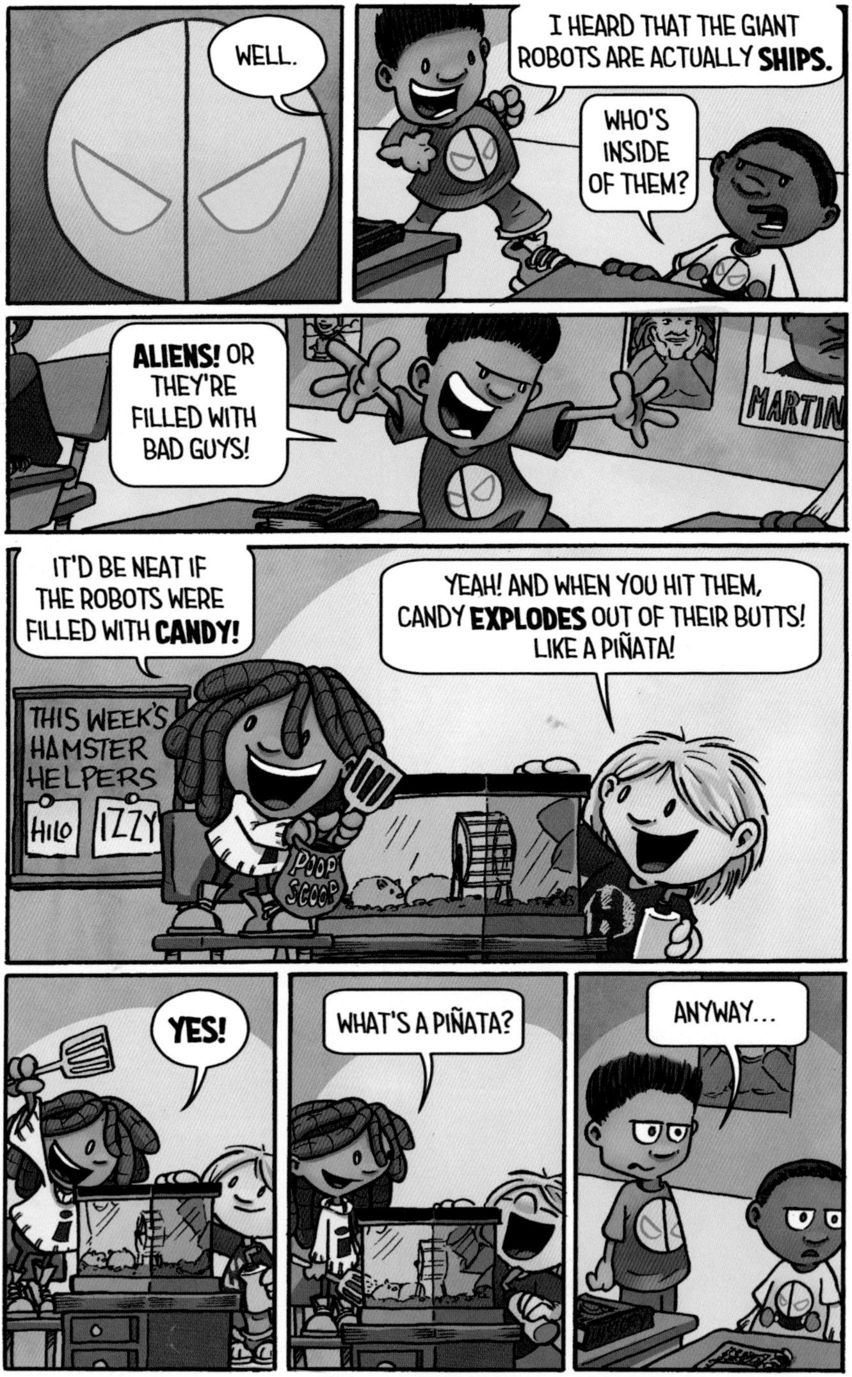

WELL.
I HEARD THAT THE GIANT ROBOTS ARE ACTUALLY **SHIPS.**
WHO'S INSIDE OF THEM?
ALIENS! OR THEY'RE FILLED WITH BAD GUYS!
MARTIN
IT'D BE NEAT IF THE ROBOTS WERE FILLED WITH **CANDY!**
YEAH! AND WHEN YOU HIT THEM, CANDY **EXPLODES** OUT OF THEIR BUTTS! LIKE A PIÑATA!
THIS WEEK'S HAMSTER HELPERS
HILO
IZZY
POOP SCOOP
YES!
WHAT'S A PIÑATA?
ANYWAY...

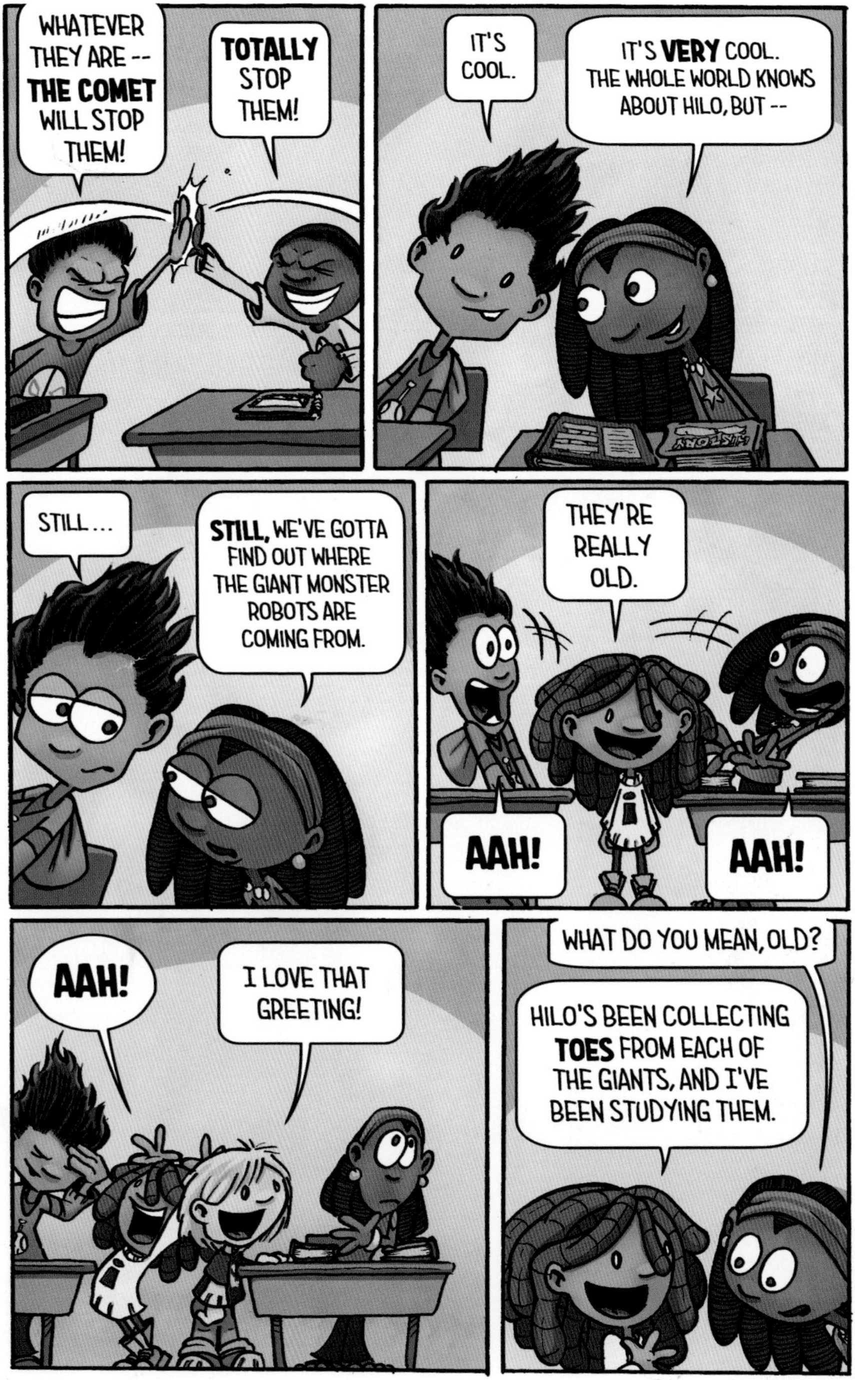
WHATEVER THEY ARE -- **THE COMET** WILL STOP THEM!
TOTALLY STOP THEM!
IT'S COOL.
IT'S **VERY** COOL. THE WHOLE WORLD KNOWS ABOUT HILO, BUT --
STILL . . .
STILL, WE'VE GOTTA FIND OUT WHERE THE GIANT MONSTER ROBOTS ARE COMING FROM.
THEY'RE REALLY OLD.
AAH!
AAH!
AAH!
I LOVE THAT GREETING!
WHAT DO YOU MEAN, OLD?
HILO'S BEEN COLLECTING **TOES** FROM EACH OF THE GIANTS, AND I'VE BEEN STUDYING THEM.

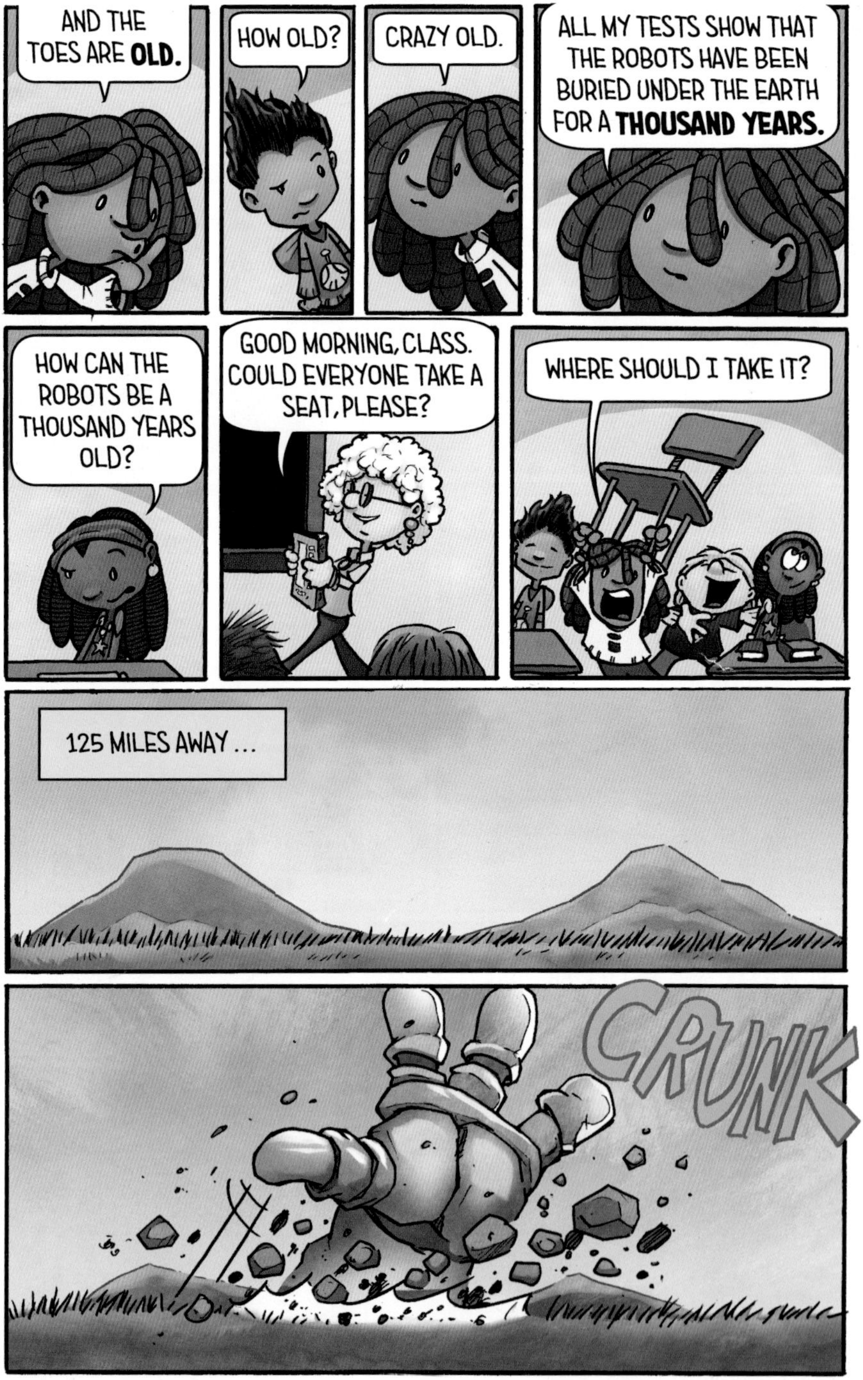
AND THE TOES ARE **OLD.**
HOW OLD?
CRAZY OLD.
ALL MY TESTS SHOW THAT THE ROBOTS HAVE BEEN BURIED UNDER THE EARTH FOR A **THOUSAND YEARS.**
HOW CAN THE ROBOTS BE A THOUSAND YEARS OLD?
GOOD MORNING, CLASS. COULD EVERYONE TAKE A SEAT, PLEASE?
WHERE SHOULD I TAKE IT?
125 MILES AWAY . . .
CRUNK

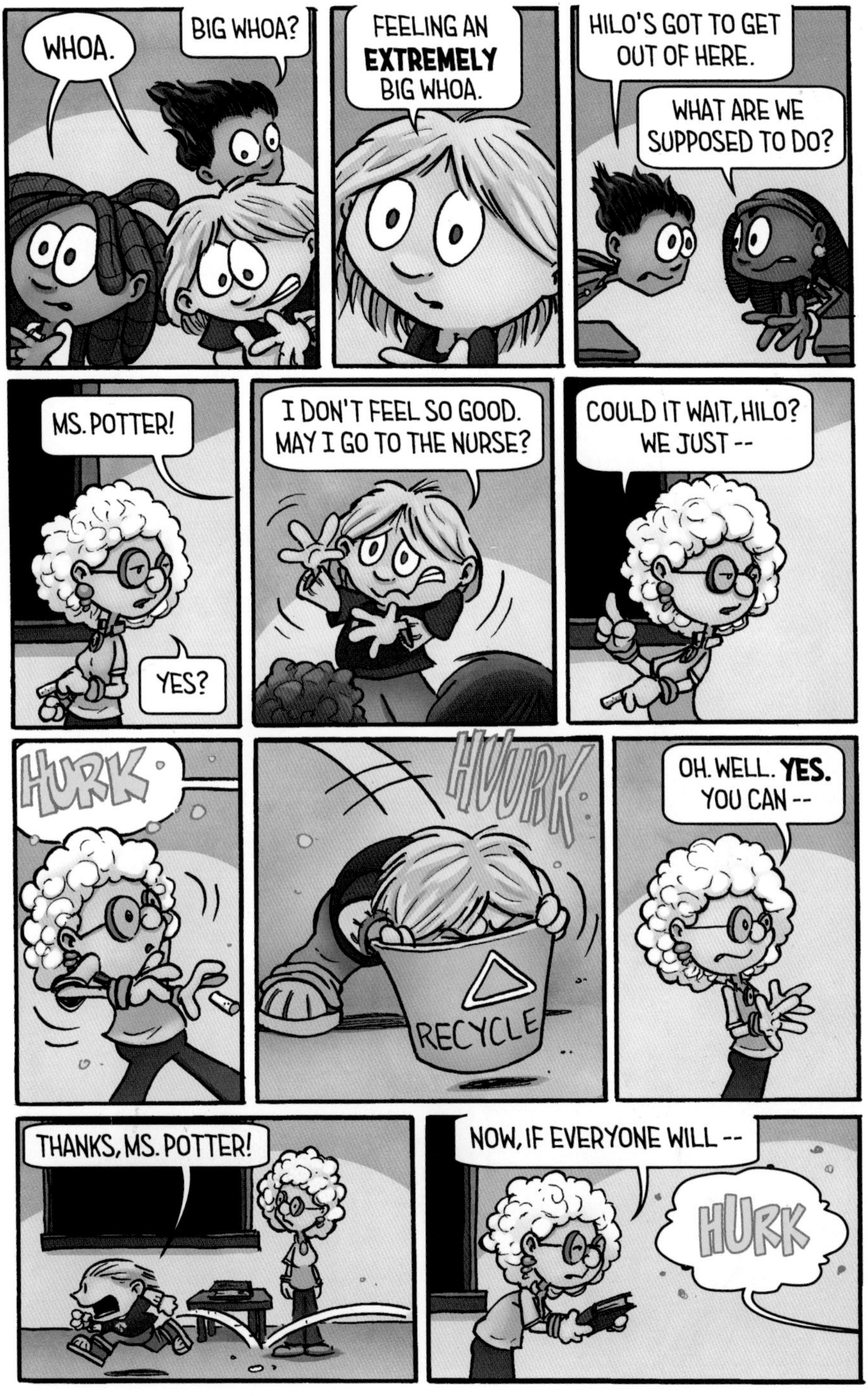

WHOA.
BIG WHOA?
FEELING AN **EXTREMELY** BIG WHOA.
HILO'S GOT TO GET OUT OF HERE.
WHAT ARE WE SUPPOSED TO DO?
MS. POTTER!
YES?
I DON'T FEEL SO GOOD. MAY I GO TO THE NURSE?
COULD IT WAIT, HILO? WE JUST --
HURK
HUURK
RECYCLE
OH. WELL. **YES.** YOU CAN --
THANKS, MS. POTTER!
NOW, IF EVERYONE WILL --
HURK

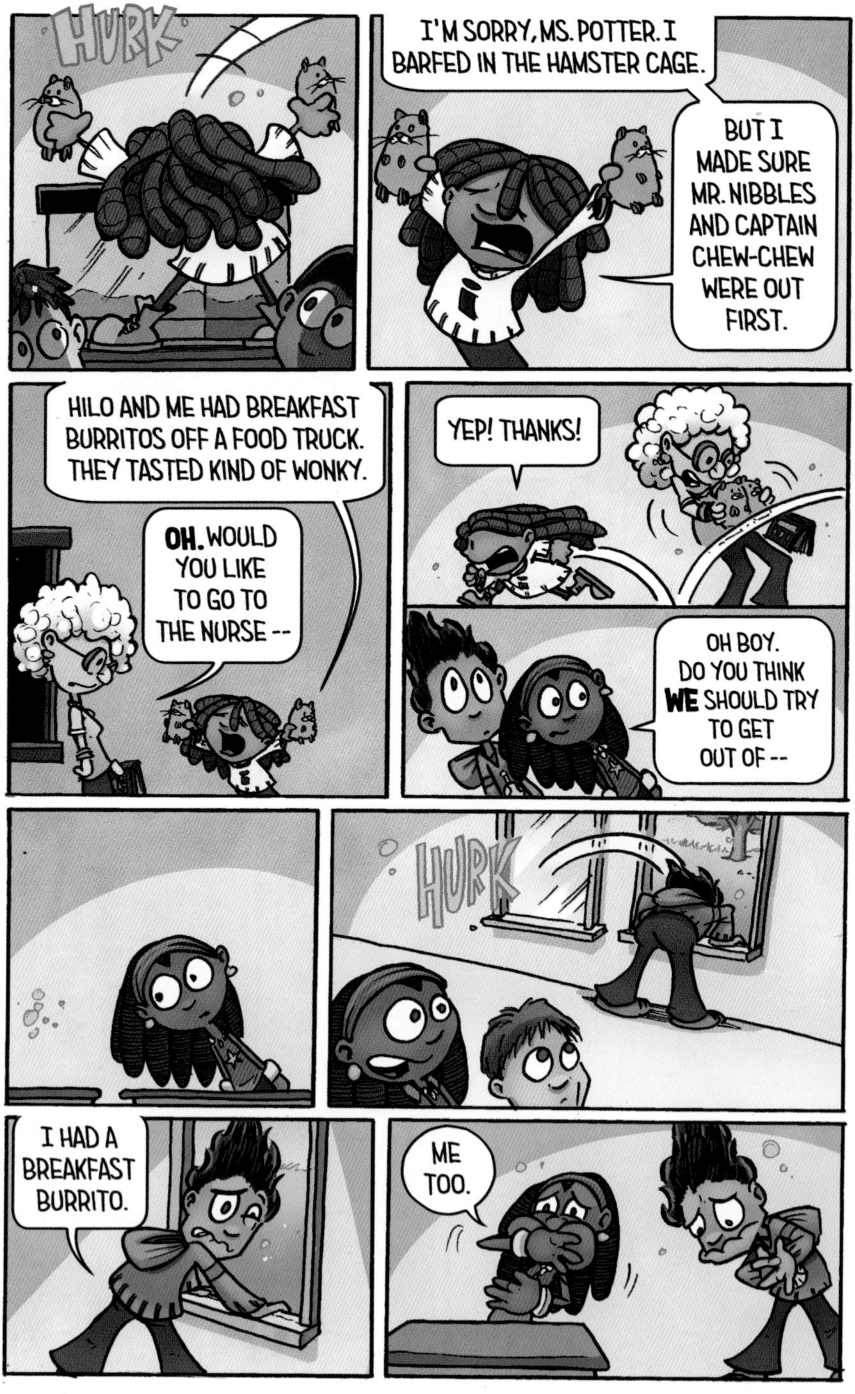
HURK
I'M SORRY, MS. POTTER. I BARFED IN THE HAMSTER CAGE.
BUT I MADE SURE MR. NIBBLES AND CAPTAIN CHEW-CHEW WERE OUT FIRST.
HILO AND ME HAD BREAKFAST BURRITOS OFF A FOOD TRUCK. THEY TASTED KIND OF WONKY.
OH. WOULD YOU LIKE TO GO TO THE NURSE --
YEP! THANKS!
OH BOY. DO YOU THINK WE SHOULD TRY TO GET OUT OF --
HURK
I HAD A BREAKFAST BURRITO.
ME TOO.

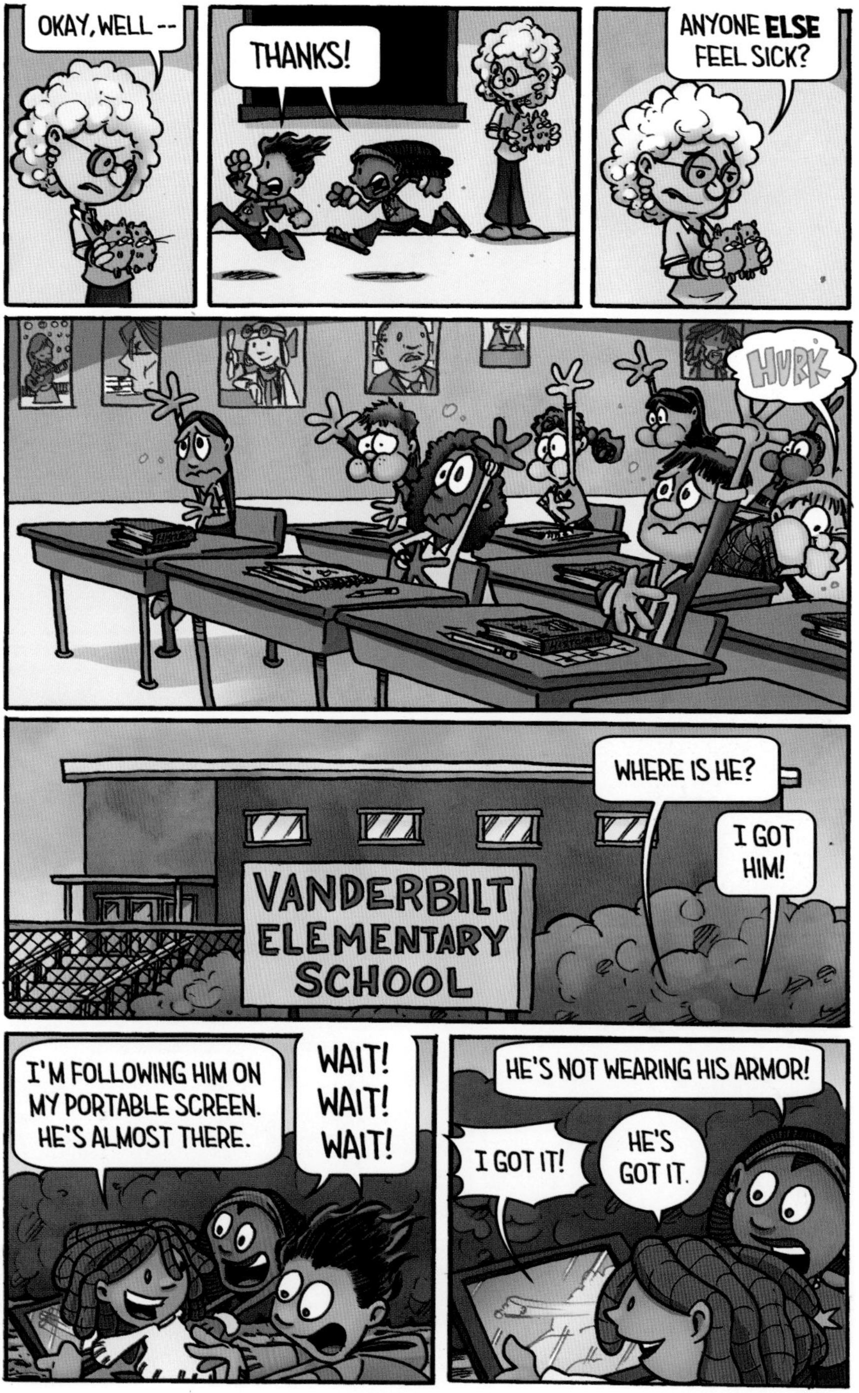
OKAY, WELL --
THANKS!
ANYONE ELSE FEEL SICK?
HURK
VANDERBILT ELEMENTARY SCHOOL
WHERE IS HE?
I GOT HIM!
I'M FOLLOWING HIM ON MY PORTABLE SCREEN. HE'S ALMOST THERE.
WAIT! WAIT! WAIT!
HE'S NOT WEARING HIS ARMOR!
I GOT IT!
HE'S GOT IT.

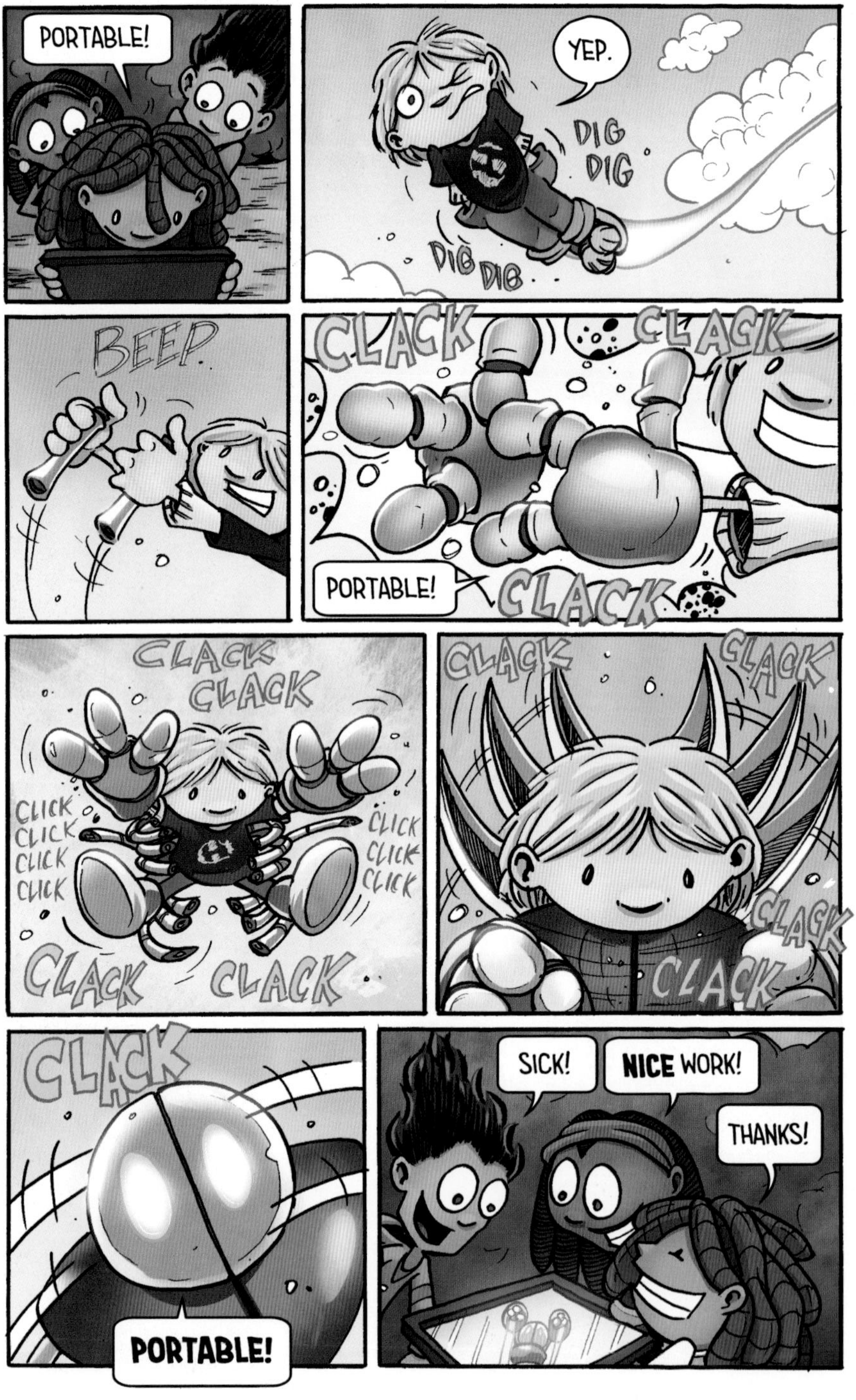
PORTABLE!
YEP.
DIG DIG
DIG DIG
BEEP
CLACK
CLACK
PORTABLE!
CLACK
CLACK CLACK
CLICK CLICK CLICK CLICK
CLICK CLICK CLICK
CLACK CLACK
CLACK
CLACK
CLACK
CLACK
CLACK
PORTABLE!
SICK!
NICE WORK!
THANKS!

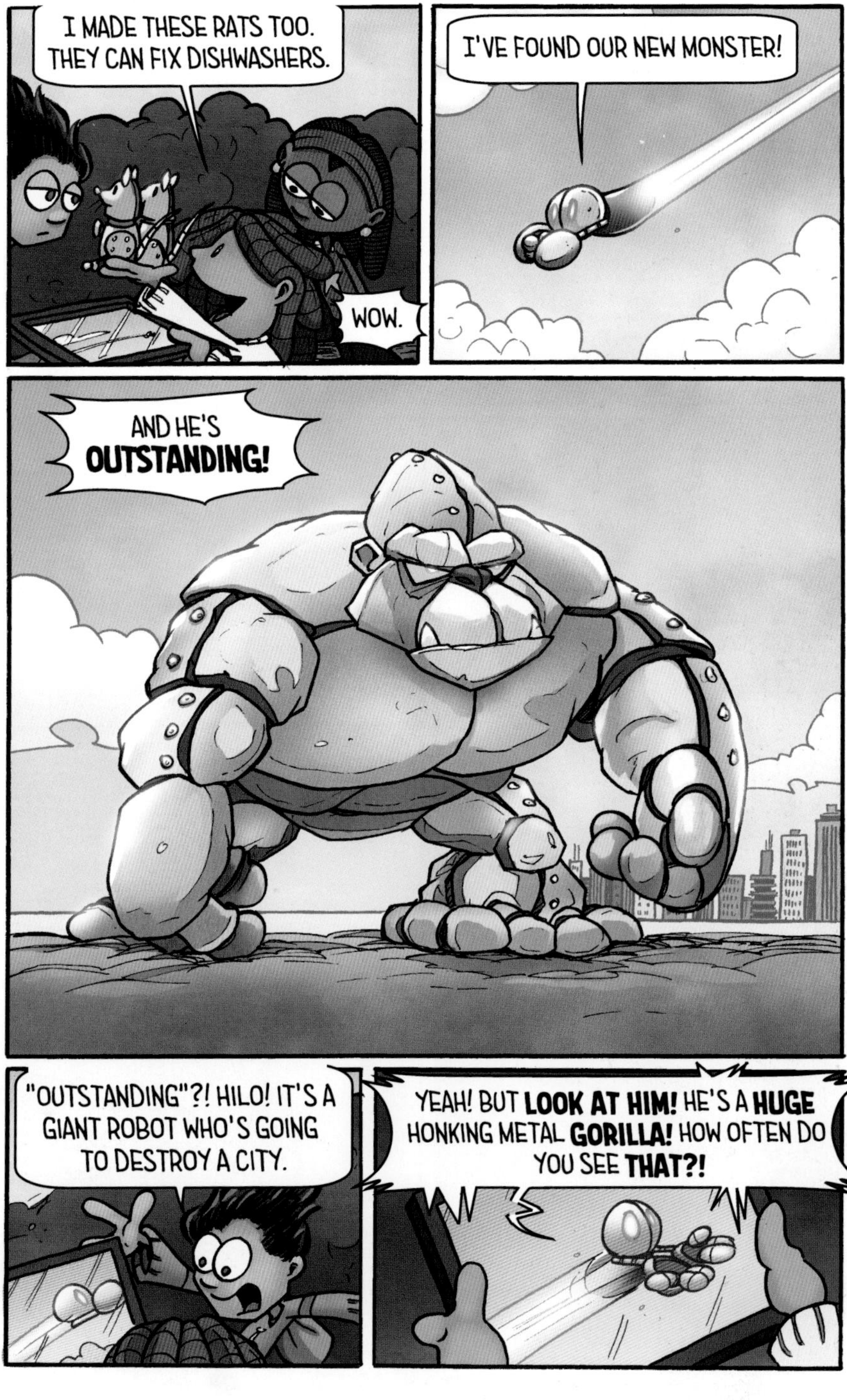
I MADE THESE RATS TOO. THEY CAN FIX DISHWASHERS.
WOW.
I'VE FOUND OUR NEW MONSTER!
AND HE'S **OUTSTANDING!**
"OUTSTANDING"?! HILO! IT'S A GIANT ROBOT WHO'S GOING TO DESTROY A CITY.
YEAH! BUT **LOOK AT HIM!** HE'S A **HUGE** HONKING METAL **GORILLA!** HOW OFTEN DO YOU SEE **THAT?!**

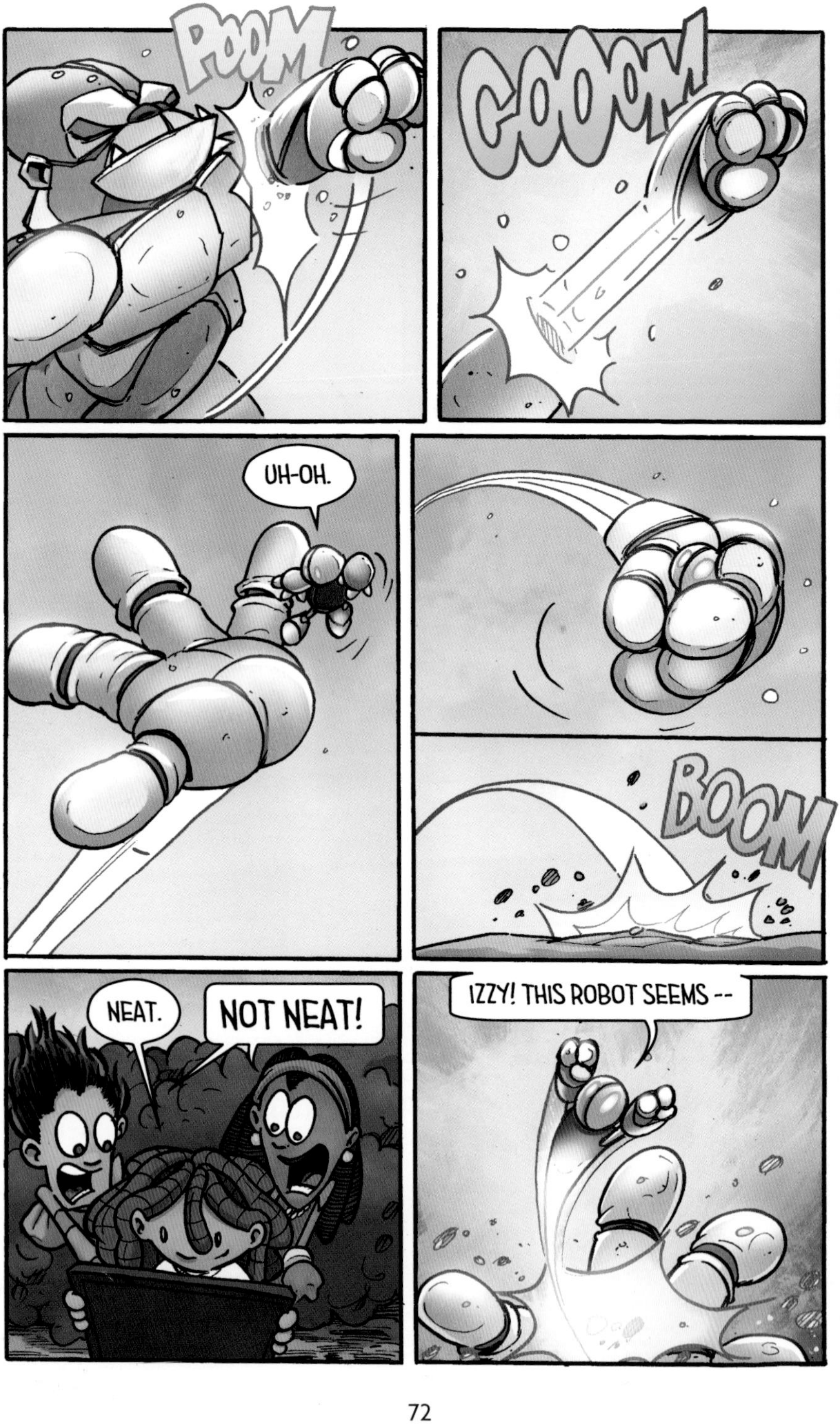
POOM
GOOOM
UH-OH.
BOOM
NEAT.
NOT NEAT!
IZZY! THIS ROBOT SEEMS --

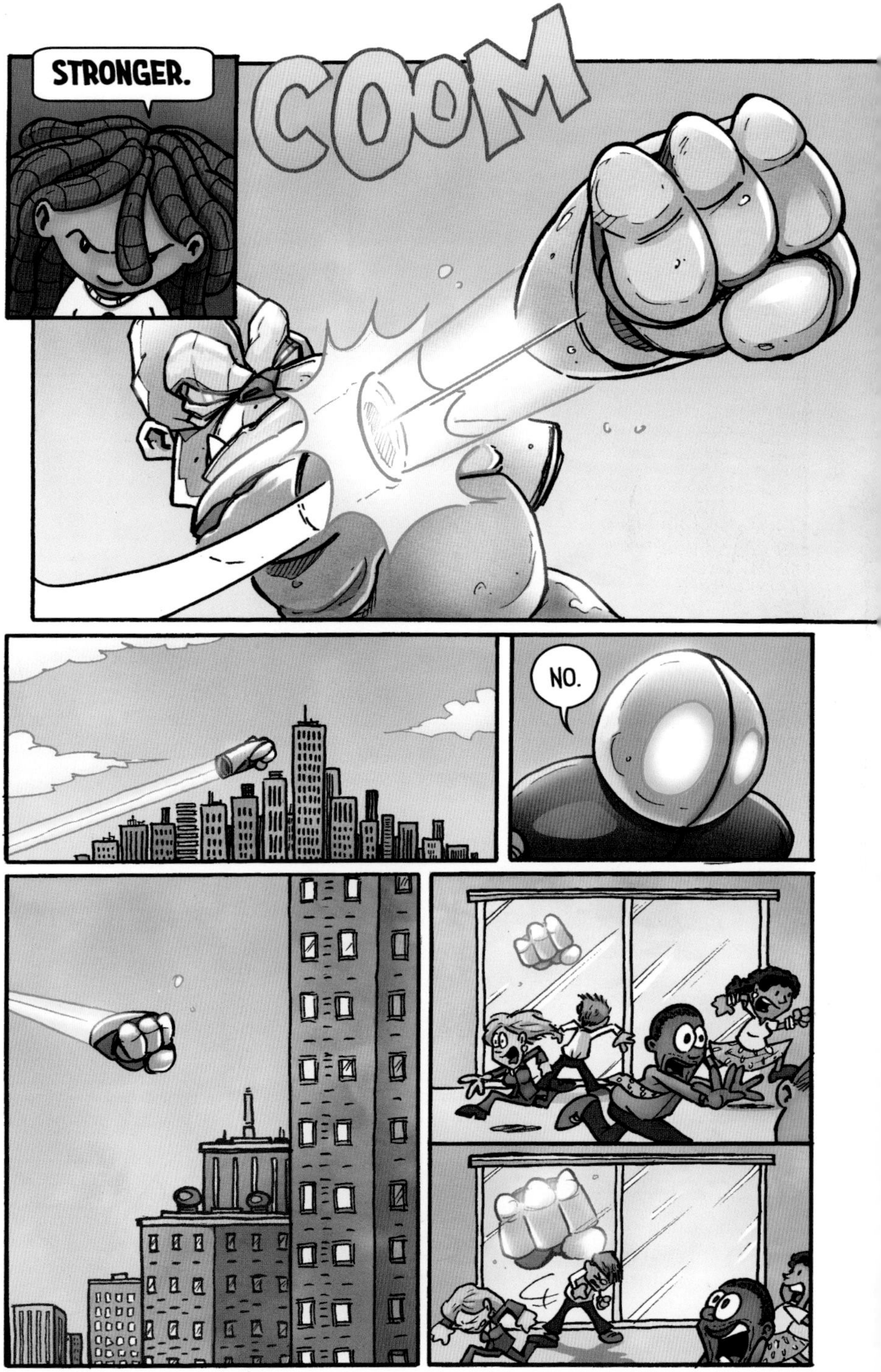
STRONGER.
COOM
NO.

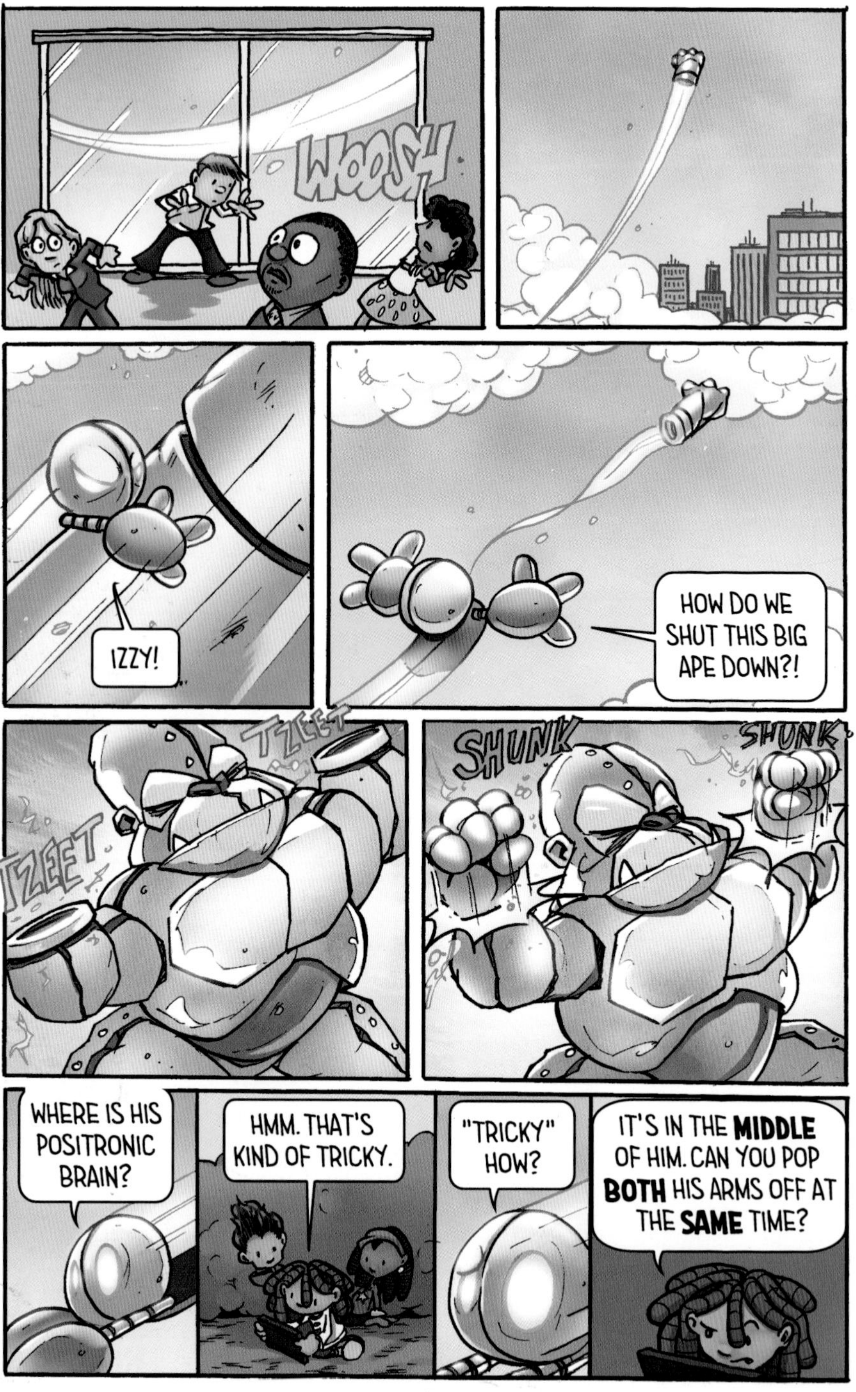
WOOSH
IZZY!
HOW DO WE SHUT THIS BIG APE DOWN?!
TZEET
TZEET
SHUNK
SHUNK
WHERE IS HIS POSITRONIC BRAIN?
HMM. THAT'S KIND OF TRICKY.
"TRICKY" HOW?
IT'S IN THE **MIDDLE** OF HIM. CAN YOU POP **BOTH** HIS ARMS OFF AT THE **SAME** TIME?

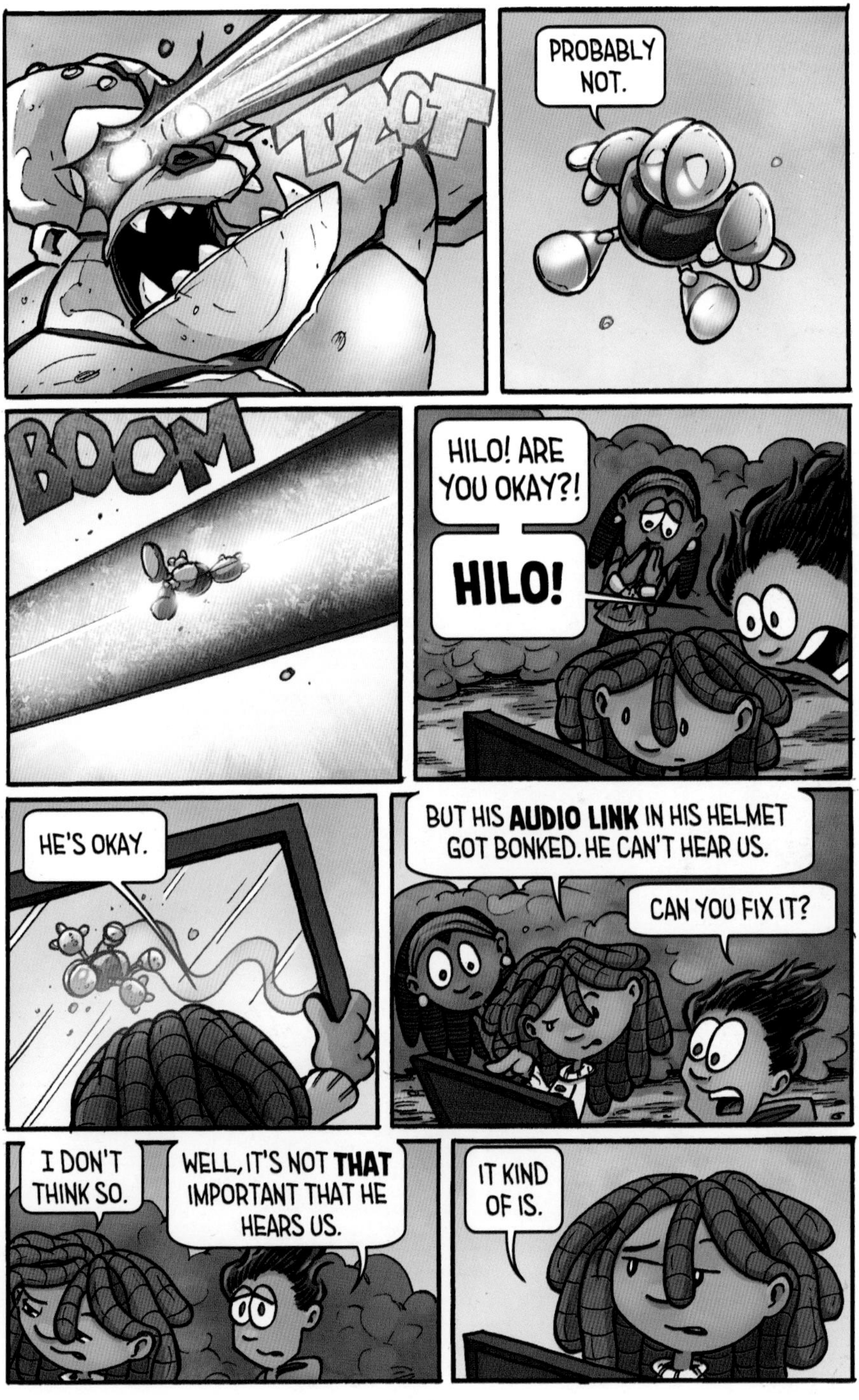
TZOT
PROBABLY NOT.
BOOM
HILO! ARE YOU OKAY?!
HILO!
HE'S OKAY.
BUT HIS **AUDIO LINK** IN HIS HELMET GOT BONKED. HE CAN'T HEAR US.
CAN YOU FIX IT?
I DON'T THINK SO.
WELL, IT'S NOT **THAT** IMPORTANT THAT HE HEARS US.
IT KIND OF IS.

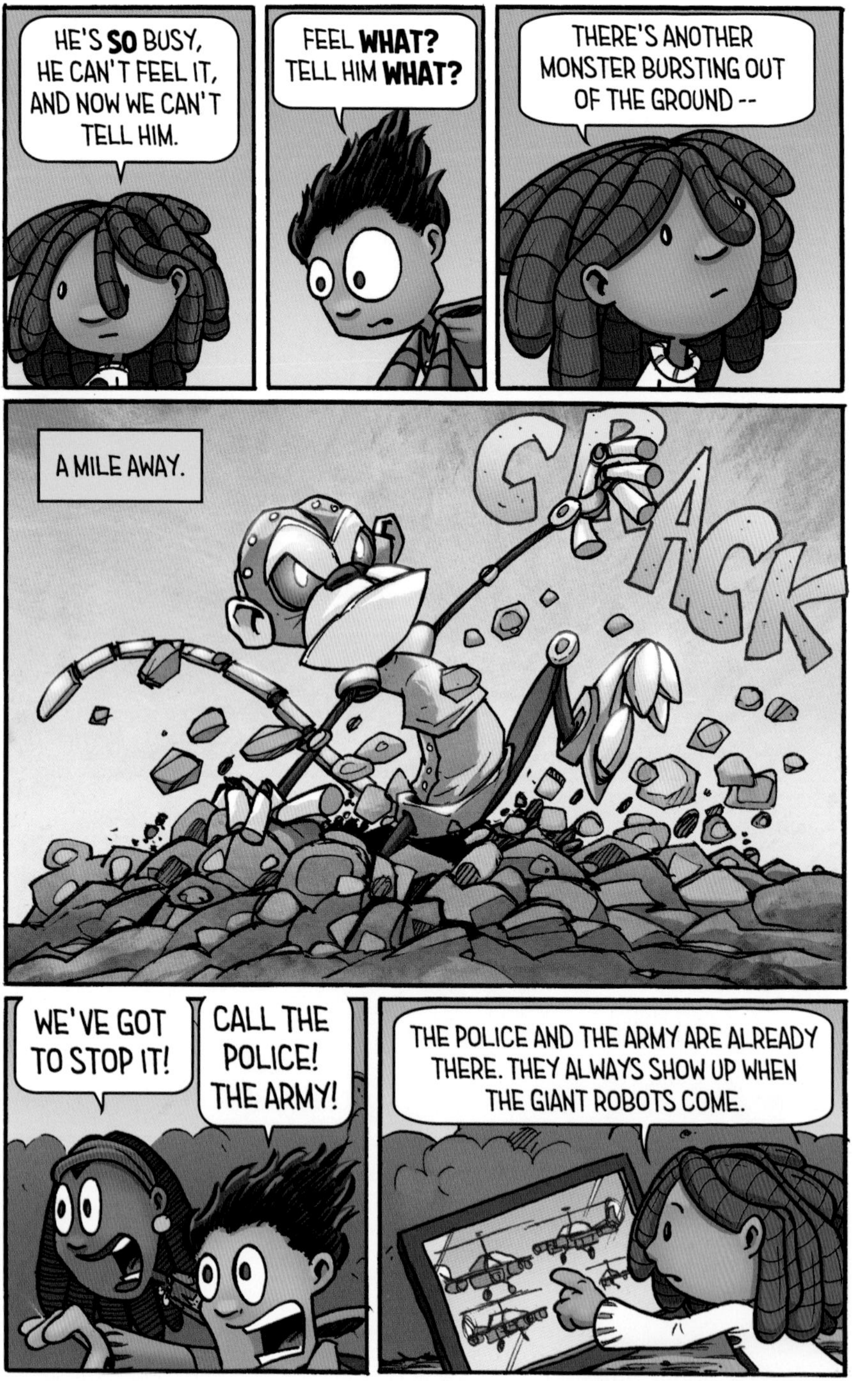
HE'S **SO** BUSY, HE CAN'T FEEL IT, AND NOW WE CAN'T TELL HIM.
FEEL **WHAT?** TELL HIM **WHAT?**
THERE'S ANOTHER MONSTER BURSTING OUT OF THE GROUND --
A MILE AWAY.
CRACK
WE'VE GOT TO STOP IT!
CALL THE POLICE! THE ARMY!
THE POLICE AND THE ARMY ARE ALREADY THERE. THEY ALWAYS SHOW UP WHEN THE GIANT ROBOTS COME.

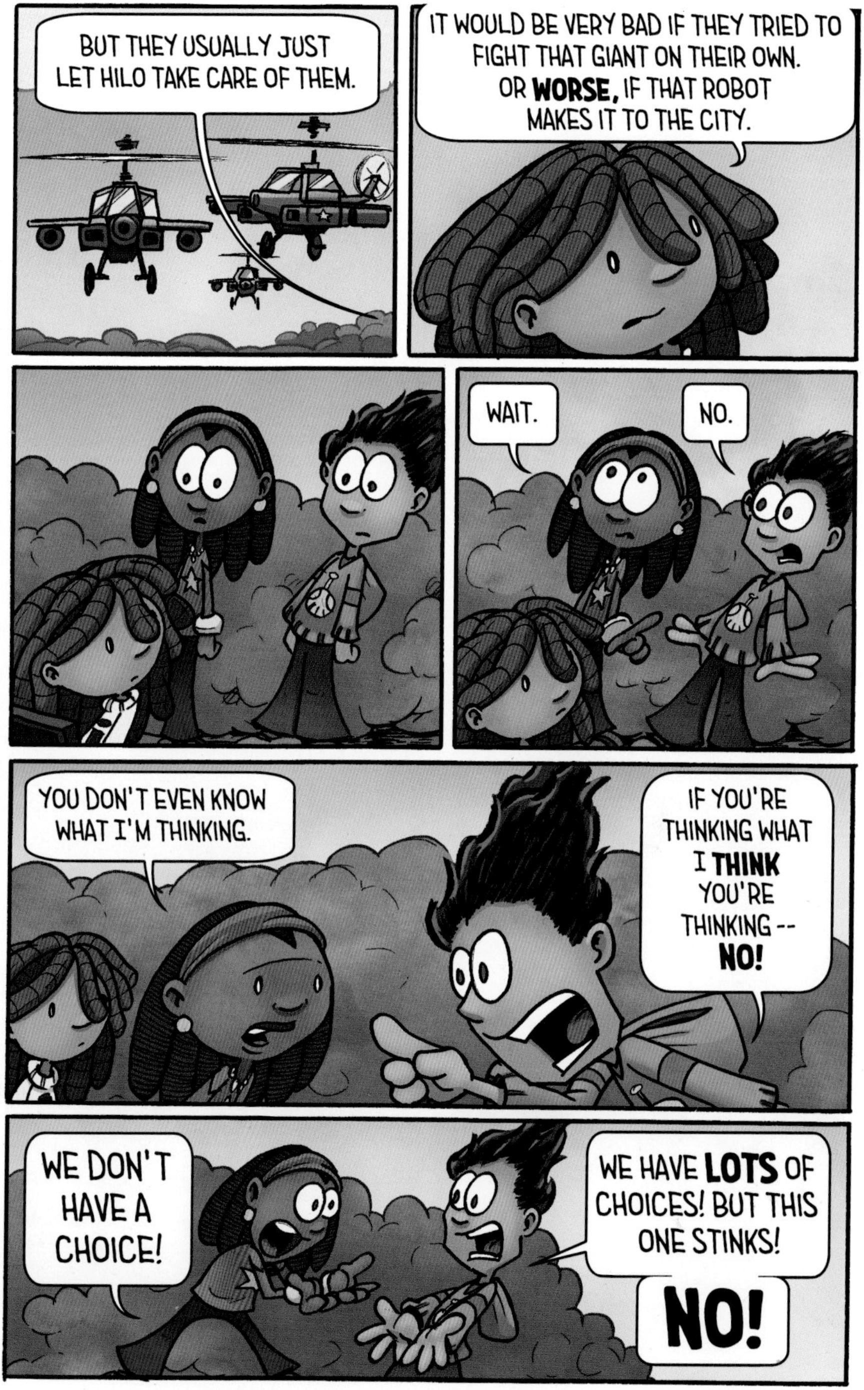
BUT THEY USUALLY JUST LET HILO TAKE CARE OF THEM.
IT WOULD BE VERY BAD IF THEY TRIED TO FIGHT THAT GIANT ON THEIR OWN. OR **WORSE,** IF THAT ROBOT MAKES IT TO THE CITY.
WAIT.
NO.
YOU DON'T EVEN KNOW WHAT I'M THINKING.
IF YOU'RE THINKING WHAT I **THINK** YOU'RE THINKING -- **NO!**
WE DON'T HAVE A CHOICE!
WE HAVE **LOTS** OF CHOICES! BUT THIS ONE STINKS!
NO!

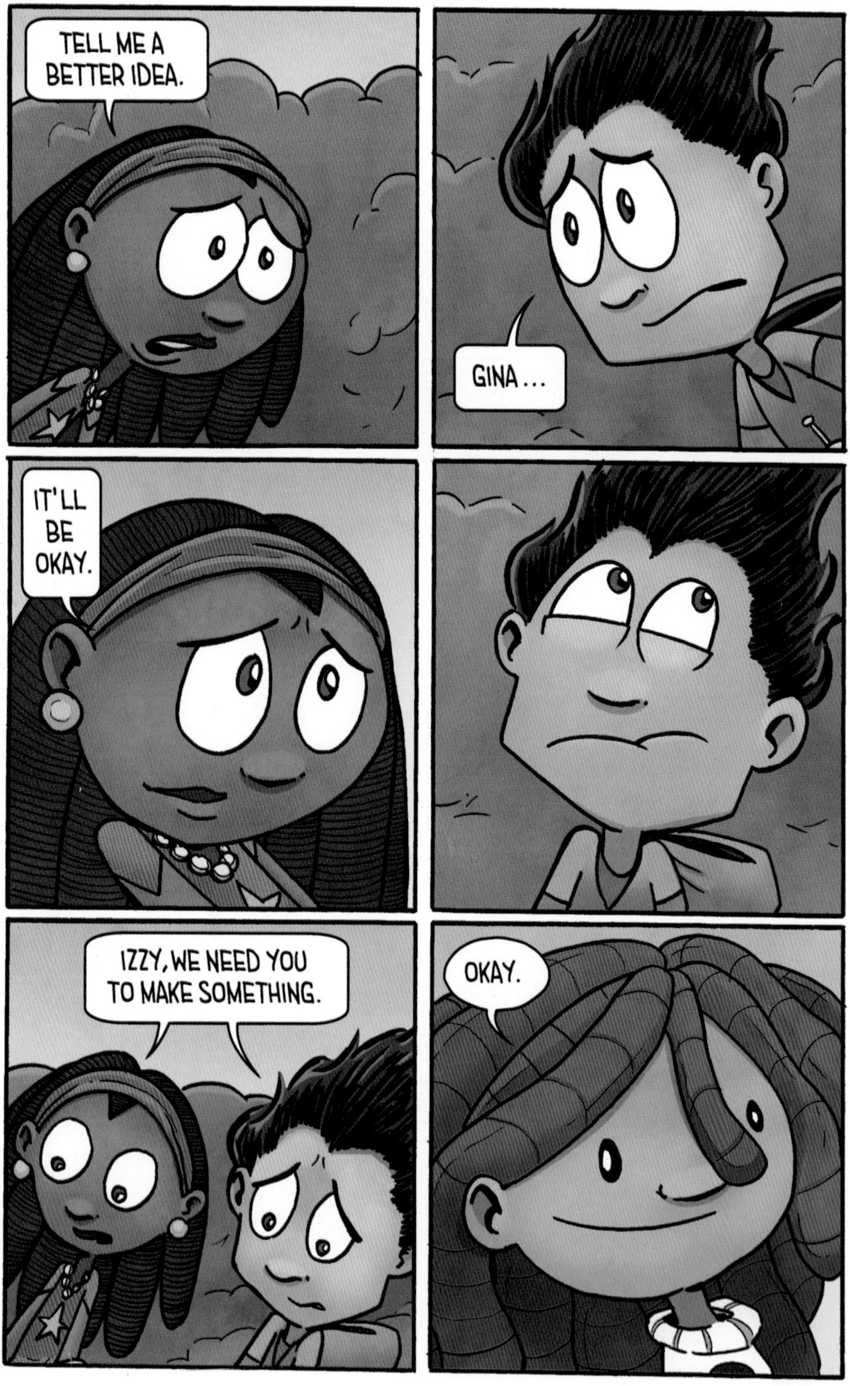
TELL ME A BETTER IDEA.
GINA...
IT'LL BE OKAY.
IZZY, WE NEED YOU TO MAKE SOMETHING.
OKAY.

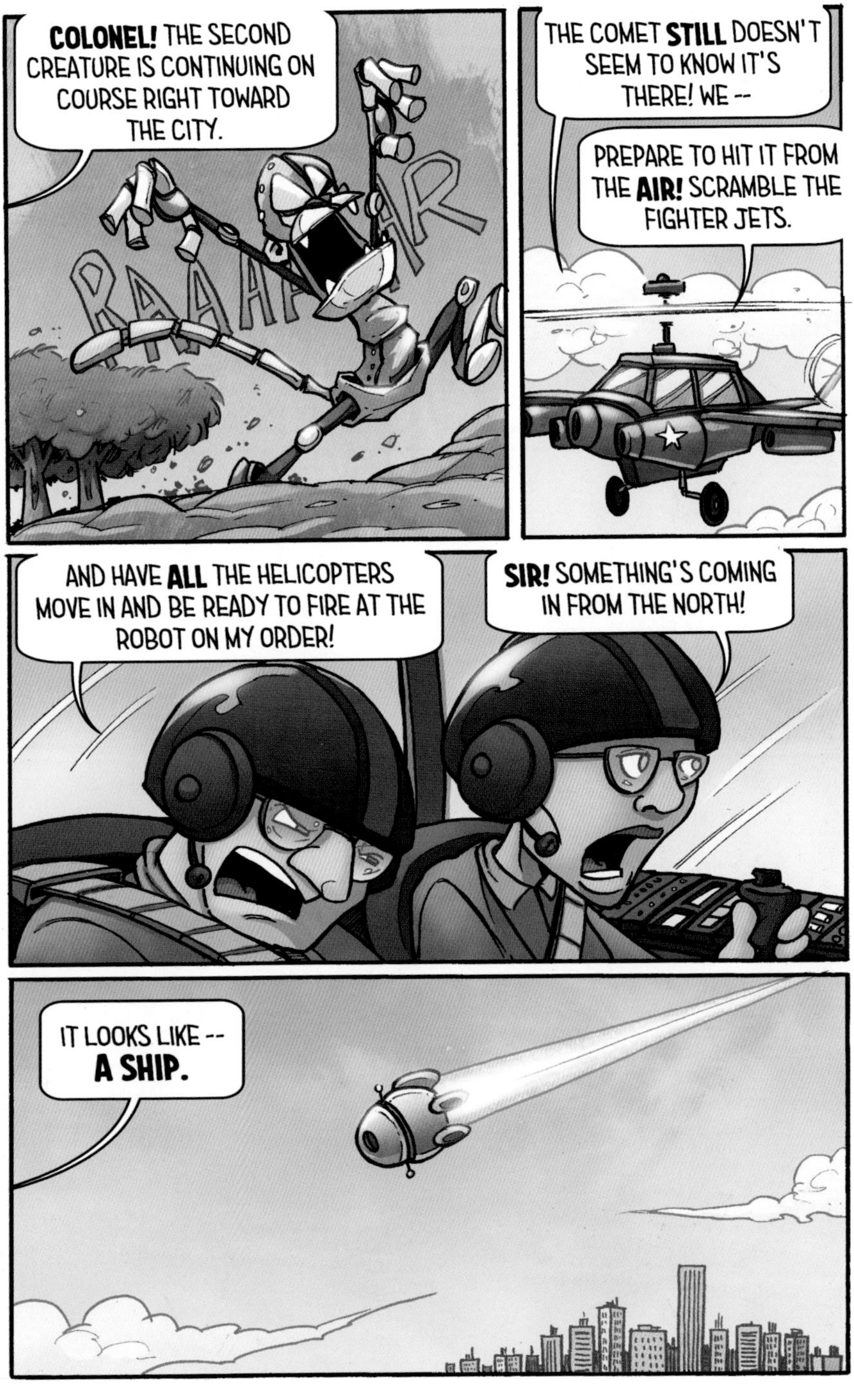
COLONEL! THE SECOND CREATURE IS CONTINUING ON COURSE RIGHT TOWARD THE CITY.
RAAAAR
THE COMET **STILL** DOESN'T SEEM TO KNOW IT'S THERE! WE --
PREPARE TO HIT IT FROM THE **AIR!** SCRAMBLE THE FIGHTER JETS.
AND HAVE **ALL** THE HELICOPTERS MOVE IN AND BE READY TO FIRE AT THE ROBOT ON MY ORDER!
SIR! SOMETHING'S COMING IN FROM THE NORTH!
IT LOOKS LIKE --
A SHIP.

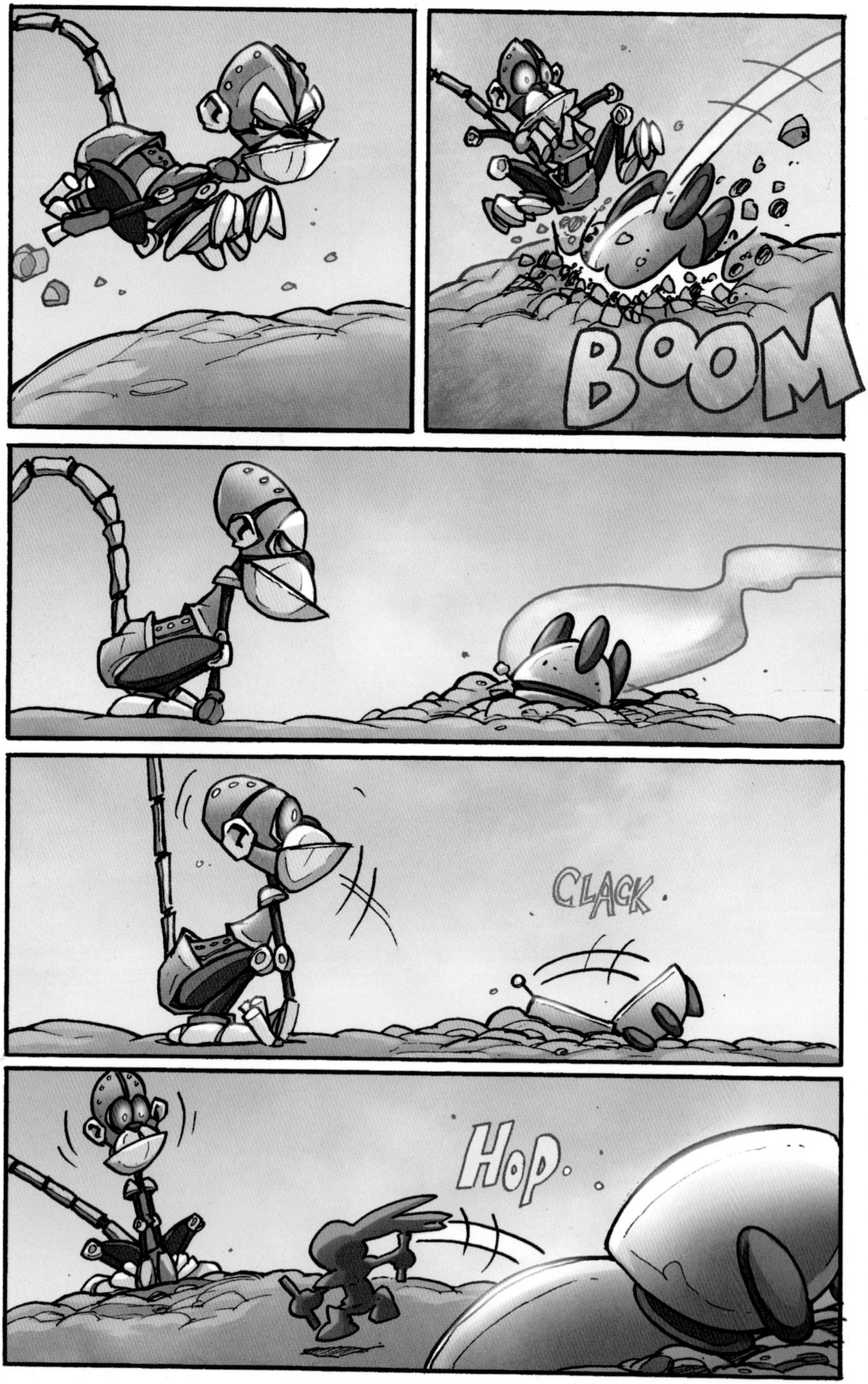
BOOM
CLACK.
HOP.

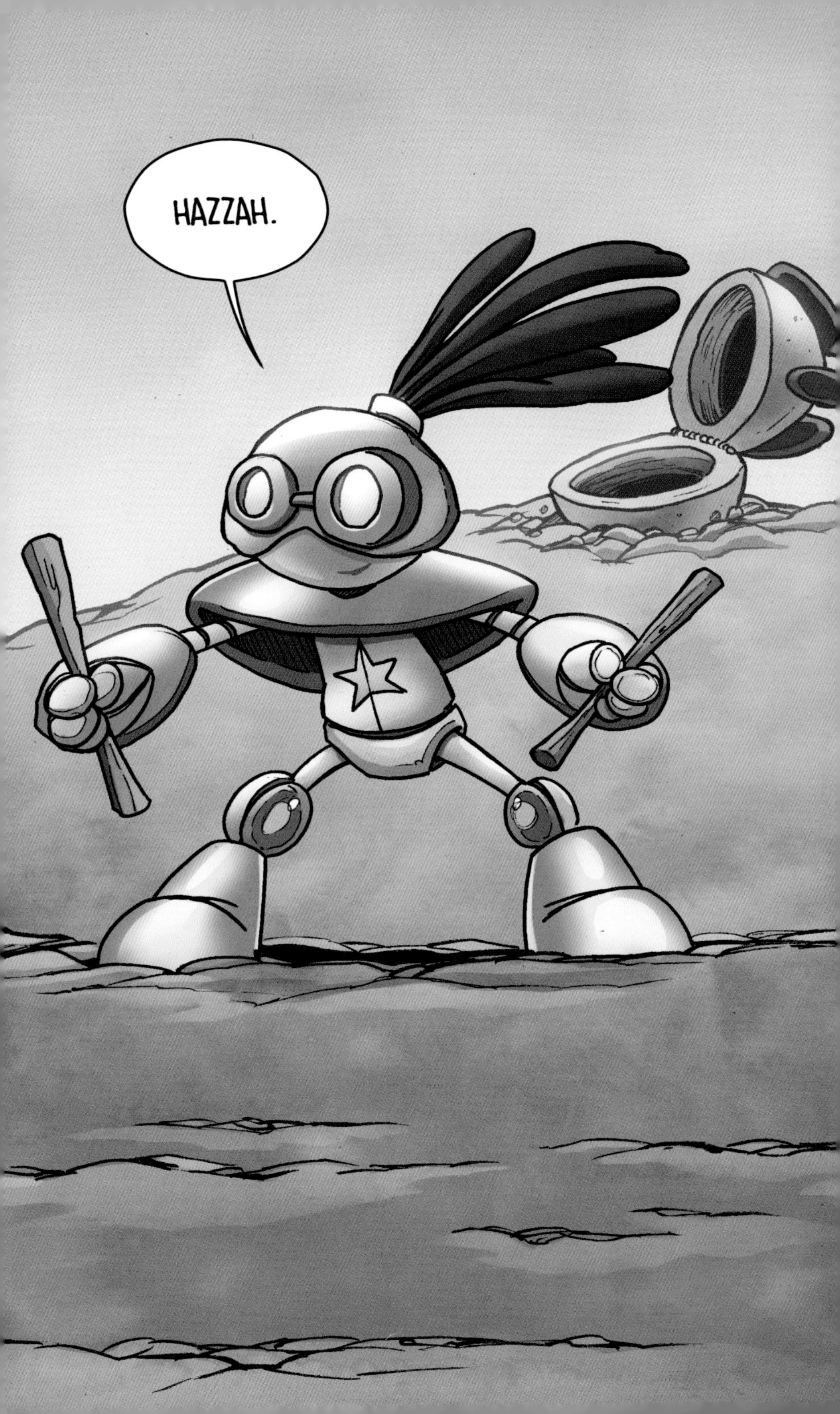
HAZZAH.

CHAPTER 5

HAZZAH

MAYBE I LOOK **SO** TOUGH THAT HE DOESN'T WANT TO FIGHT.

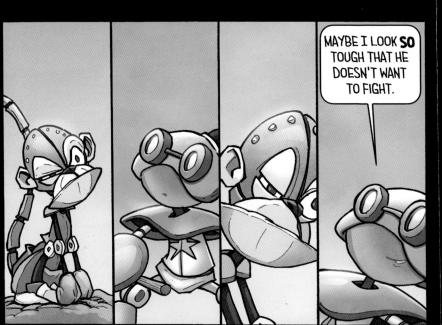

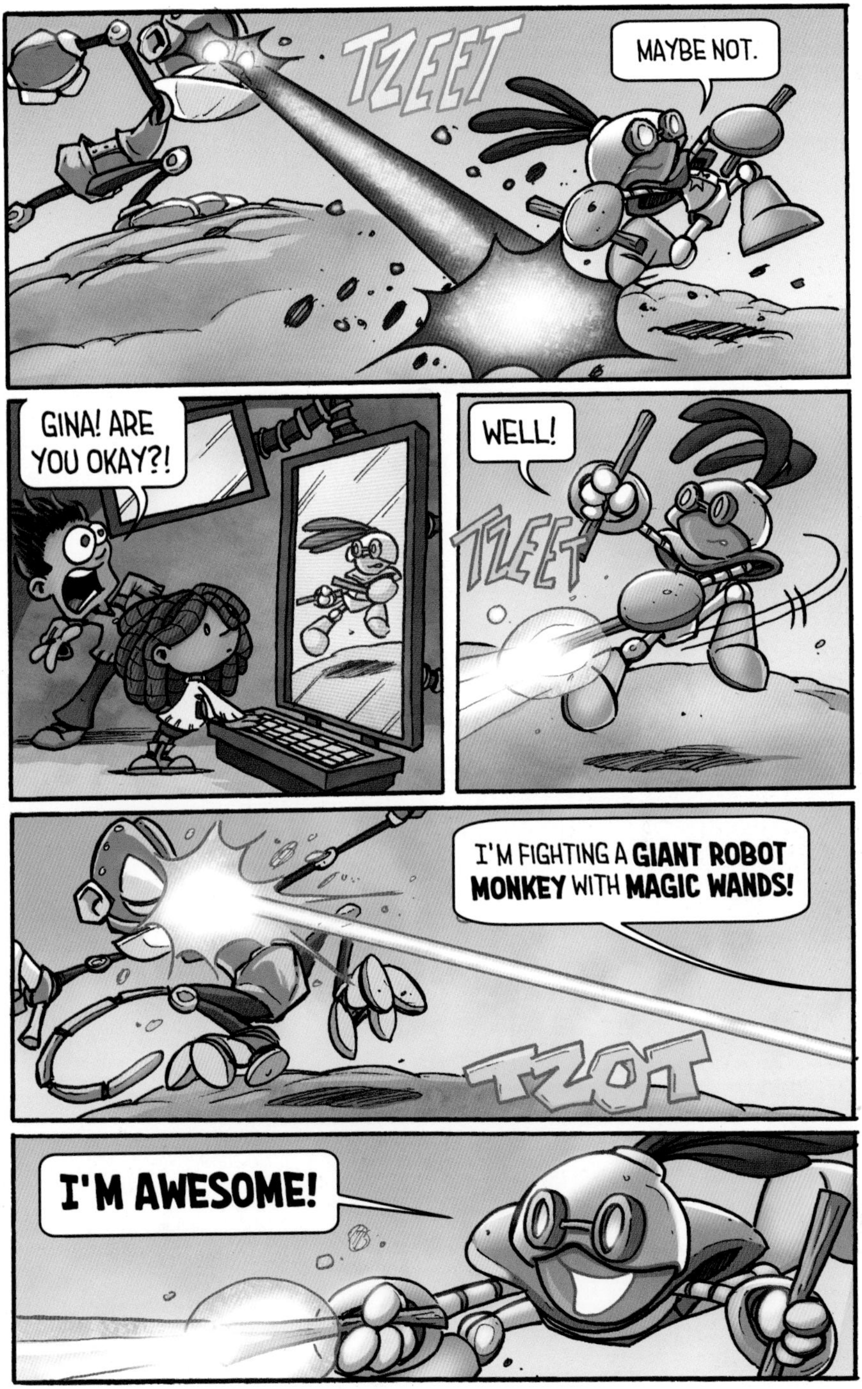
TZEET
MAYBE NOT.
GINA! ARE YOU OKAY?!
WELL!
TZEET
I'M FIGHTING A **GIANT ROBOT MONKEY** WITH **MAGIC WANDS!**
TZOT
I'M AWESOME!

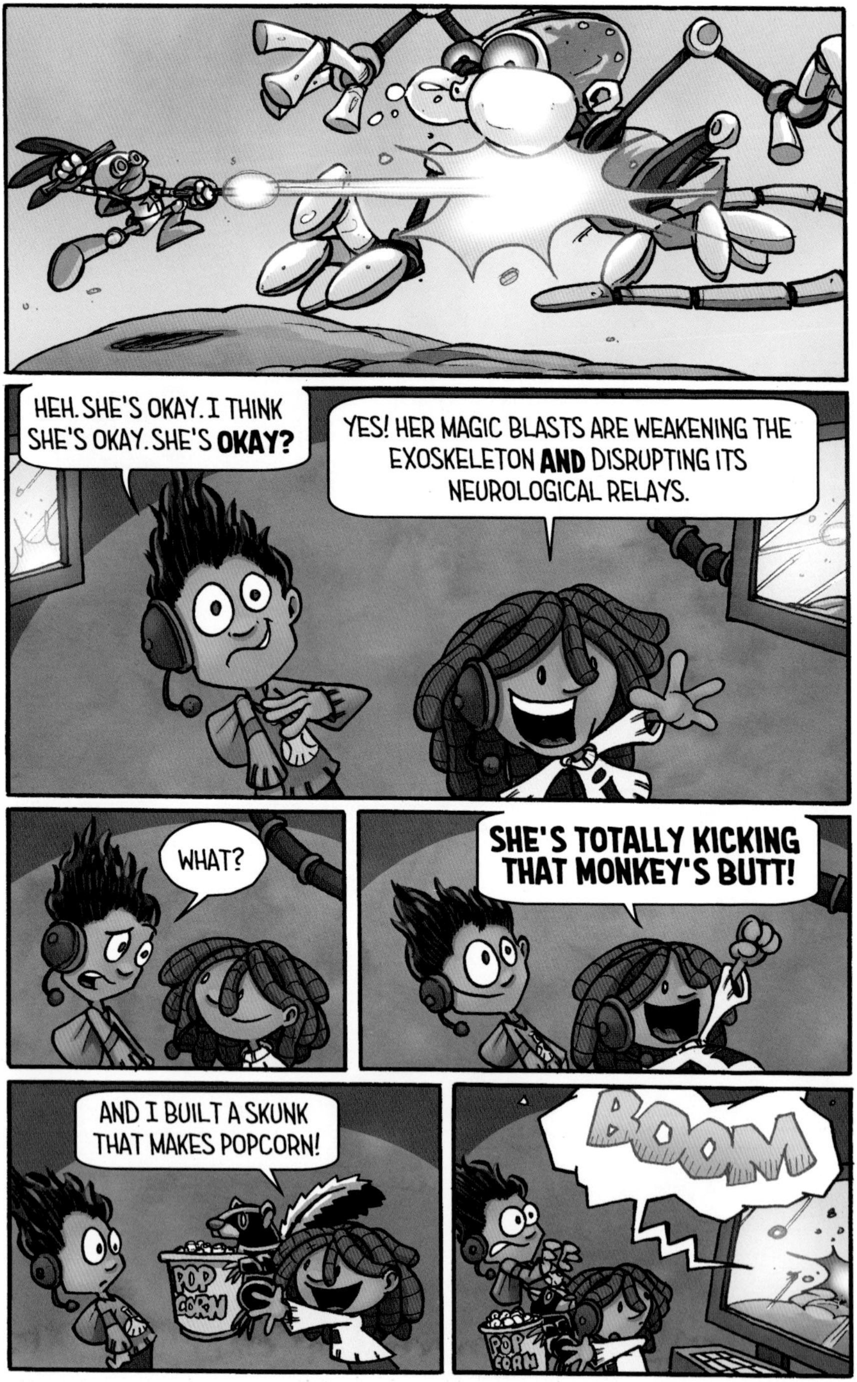
HEH. SHE'S OKAY. I THINK SHE'S OKAY. SHE'S **OKAY?**
YES! HER MAGIC BLASTS ARE WEAKENING THE EXOSKELETON **AND** DISRUPTING ITS NEUROLOGICAL RELAYS.
WHAT?
SHE'S TOTALLY KICKING THAT MONKEY'S BUTT!
AND I BUILT A SKUNK THAT MAKES POPCORN!
POP CORN
BOOM
POP CORN

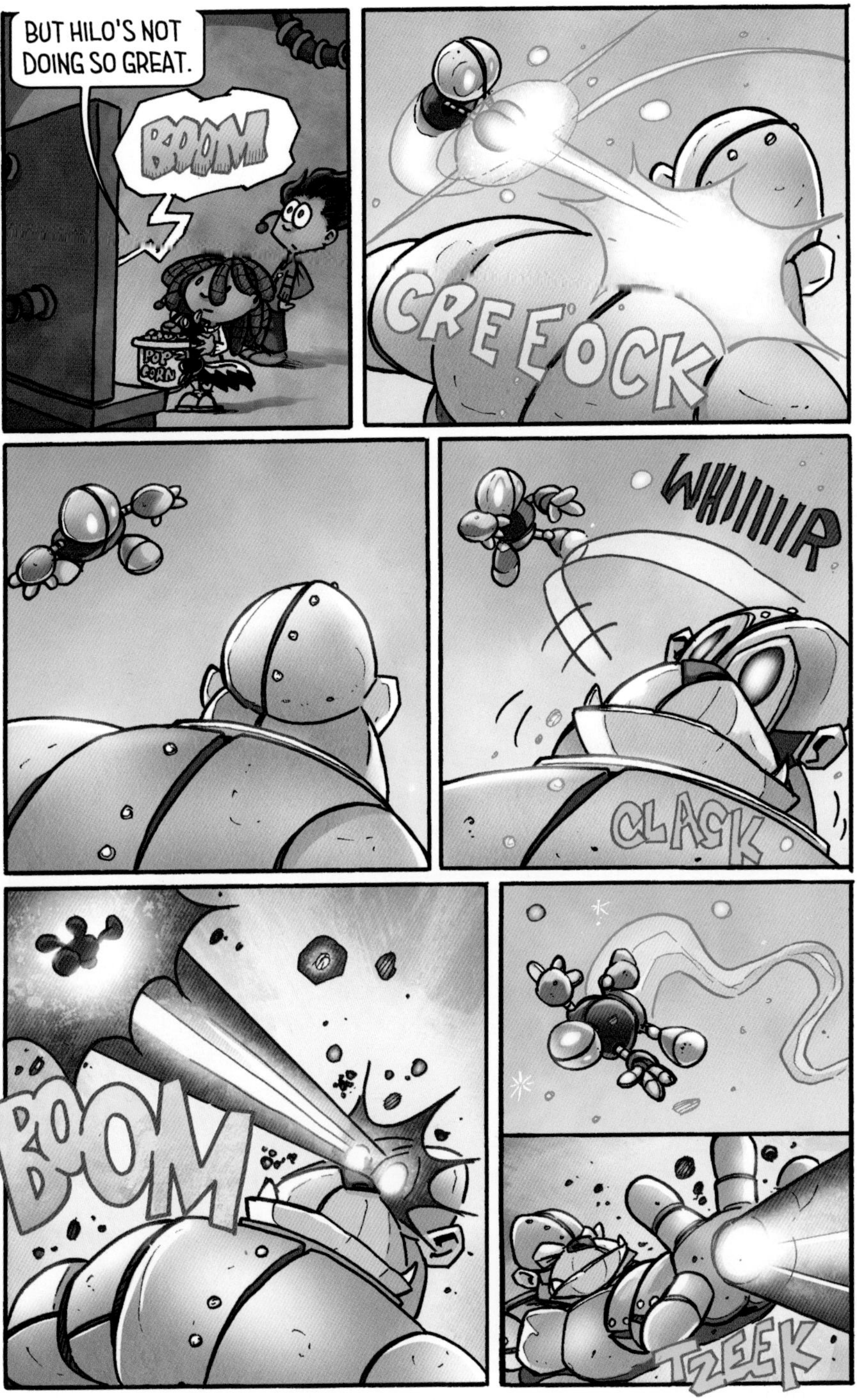
BUT HILO'S NOT DOING SO GREAT.
BOOM
POP CORN
CREEOCK
WHIIIIR
CLACK
BOOM
TZEEK

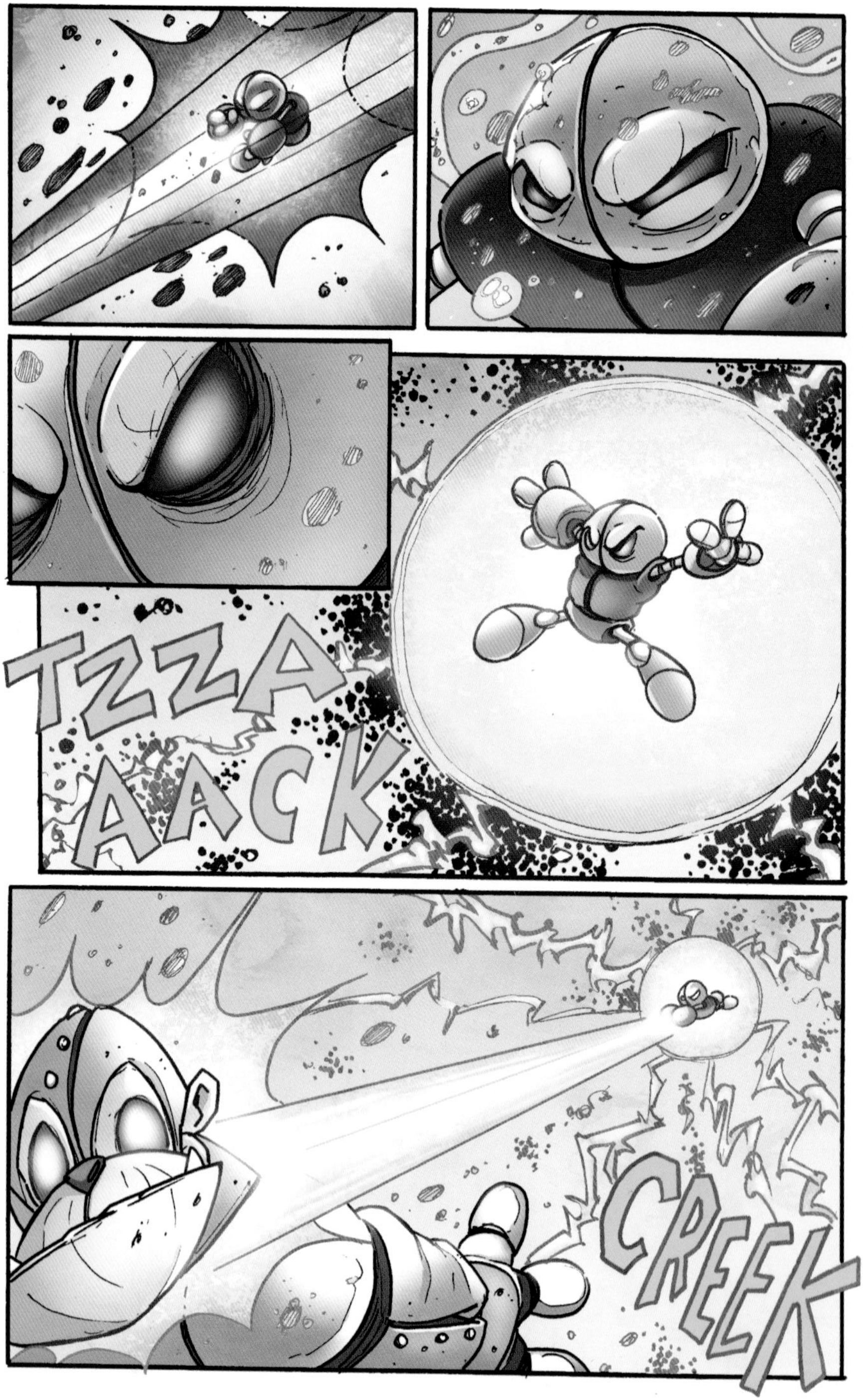
TZZA
AACK
CREEK

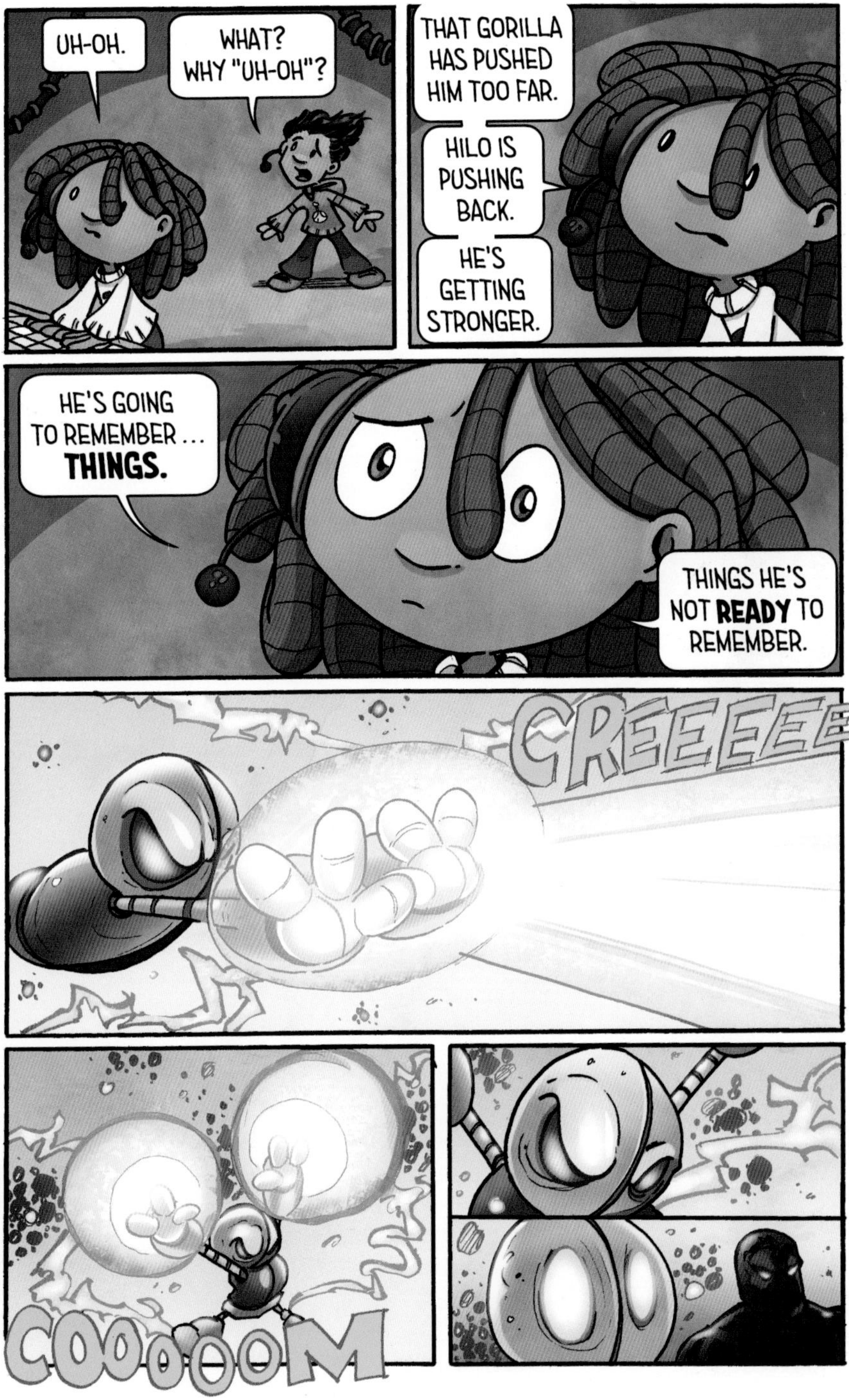
UH-OH.
WHAT? WHY "UH-OH"?
THAT GORILLA HAS PUSHED HIM TOO FAR.
HILO IS PUSHING BACK.
HE'S GETTING STRONGER.
HE'S GOING TO REMEMBER ... **THINGS.**
THINGS HE'S NOT **READY** TO REMEMBER.
CREEEEE
COOOOOOM

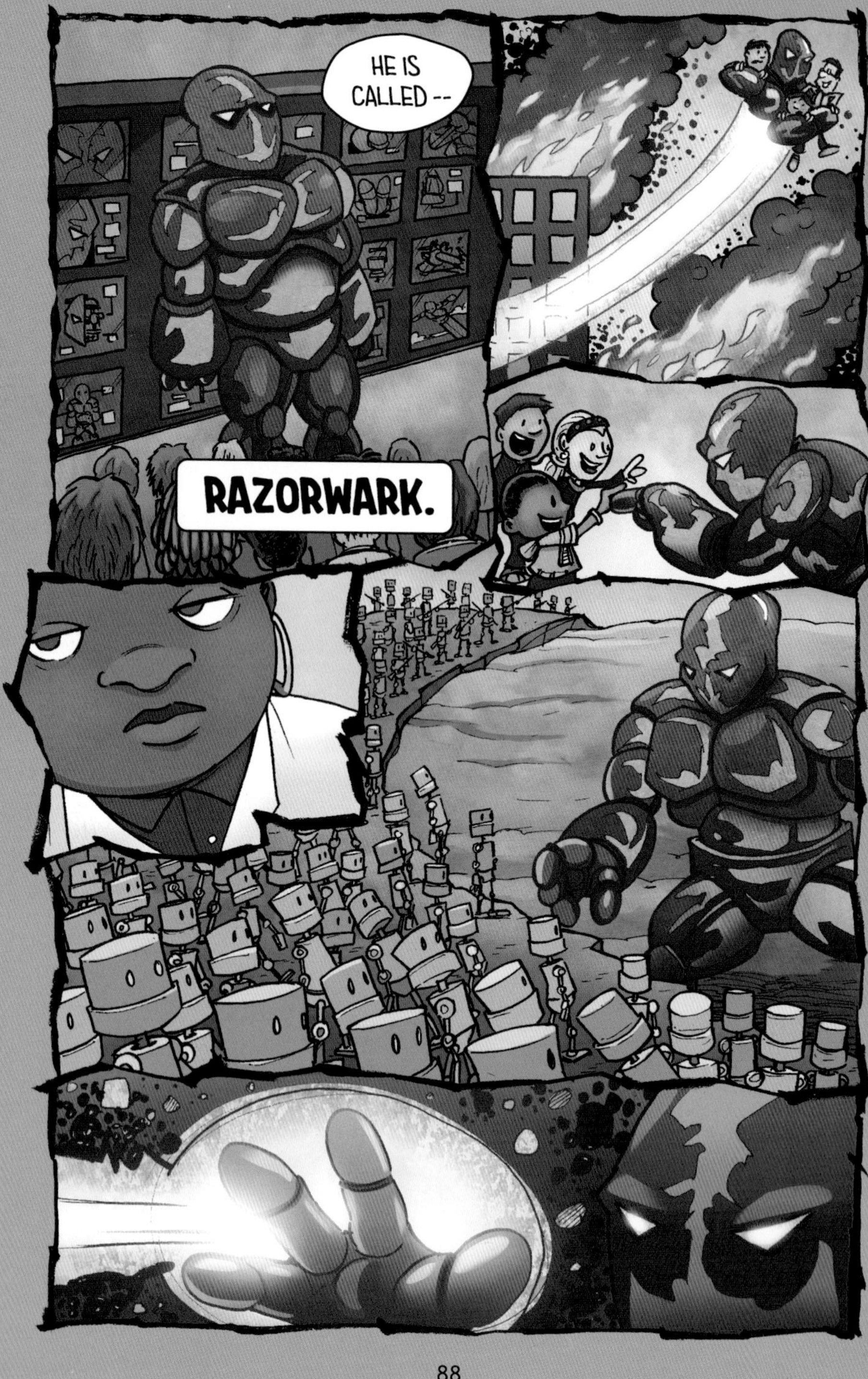
HE IS CALLED --
RAZORWARK.

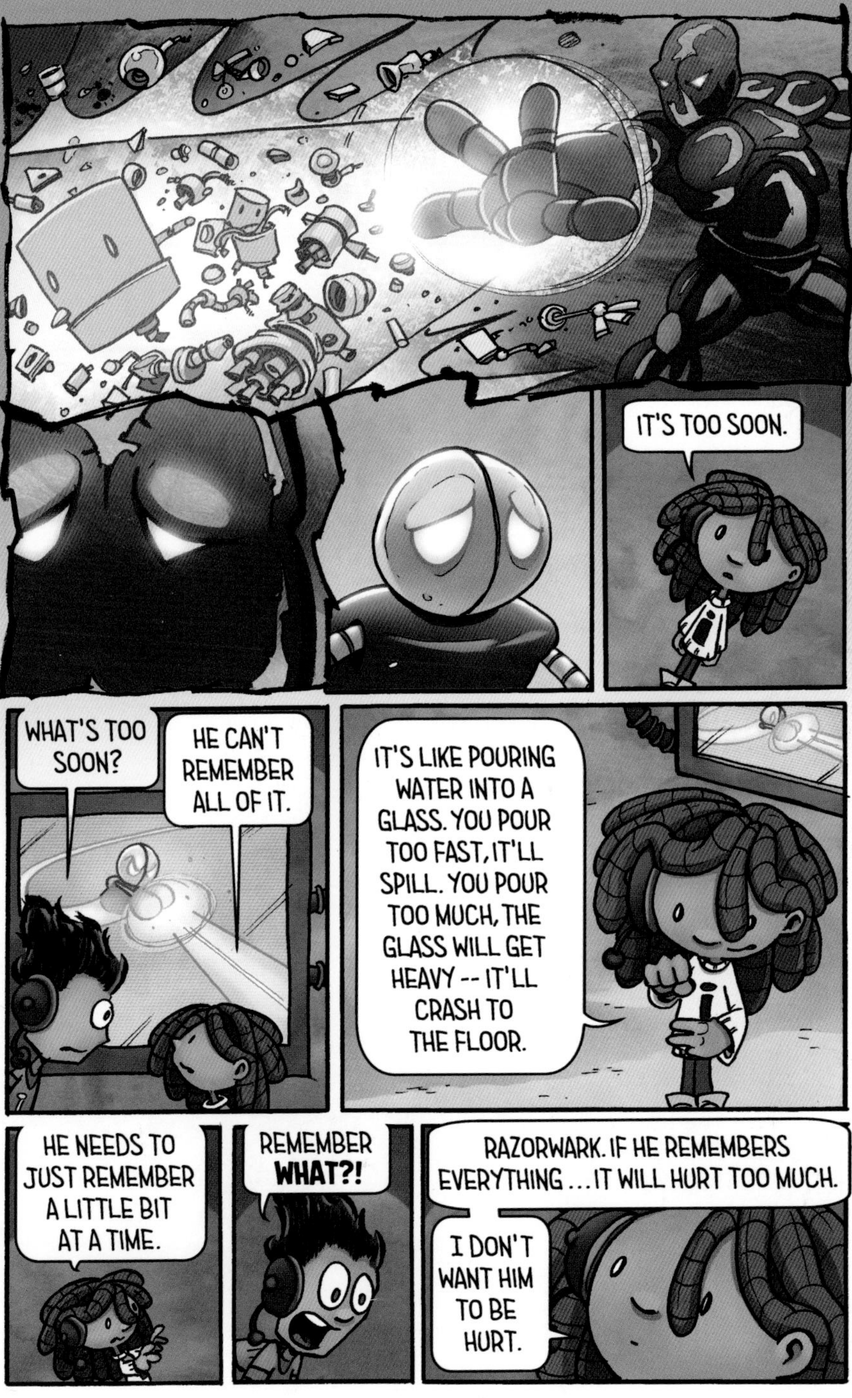
IT'S TOO SOON.
WHAT'S TOO SOON?
HE CAN'T REMEMBER ALL OF IT.
IT'S LIKE POURING WATER INTO A GLASS. YOU POUR TOO FAST, IT'LL SPILL. YOU POUR TOO MUCH, THE GLASS WILL GET HEAVY -- IT'LL CRASH TO THE FLOOR.
HE NEEDS TO JUST REMEMBER A LITTLE BIT AT A TIME.
REMEMBER **WHAT?!**
RAZORWARK. IF HE REMEMBERS EVERYTHING . . . IT WILL HURT TOO MUCH.
I DON'T WANT HIM TO BE HURT.

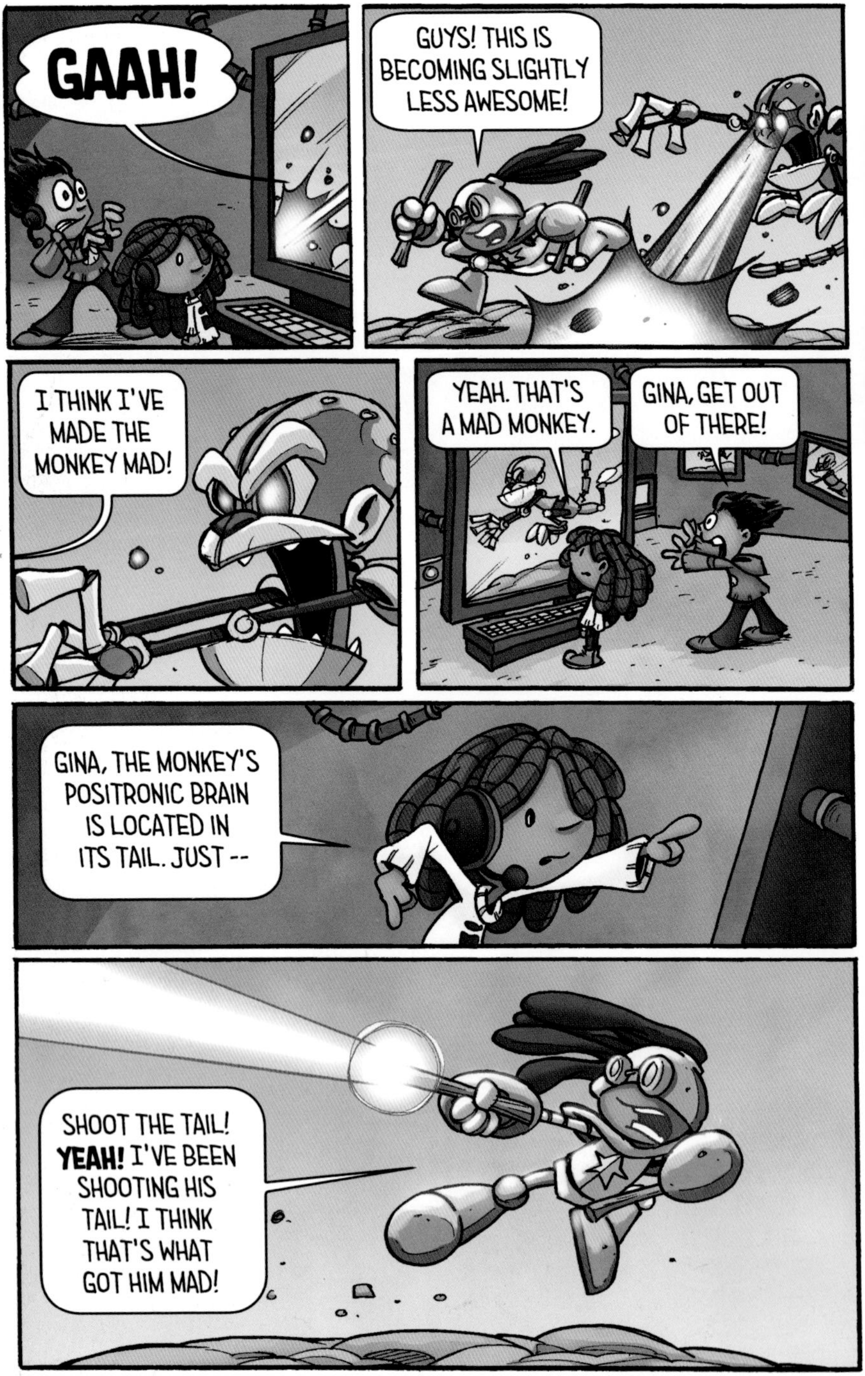
GAAH!
GUYS! THIS IS BECOMING SLIGHTLY LESS AWESOME!
I THINK I'VE MADE THE MONKEY MAD!
YEAH. THAT'S A MAD MONKEY.
GINA, GET OUT OF THERE!
GINA, THE MONKEY'S POSITRONIC BRAIN IS LOCATED IN ITS TAIL. JUST --
SHOOT THE TAIL! **YEAH!** I'VE BEEN SHOOTING HIS TAIL! I THINK THAT'S WHAT GOT HIM MAD!

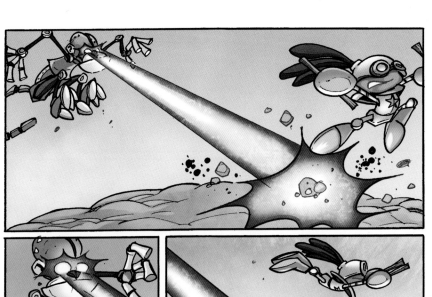

MY BLASTS DON'T HURT HIM ANYMORE!

HE MAY HAVE CALIBRATED YOUR BLASTS AND BUILT UP A RESISTANCE.

WHAT?

YOUR BLASTS DON'T HURT HIM ANYMORE.

OUTSTANDING.

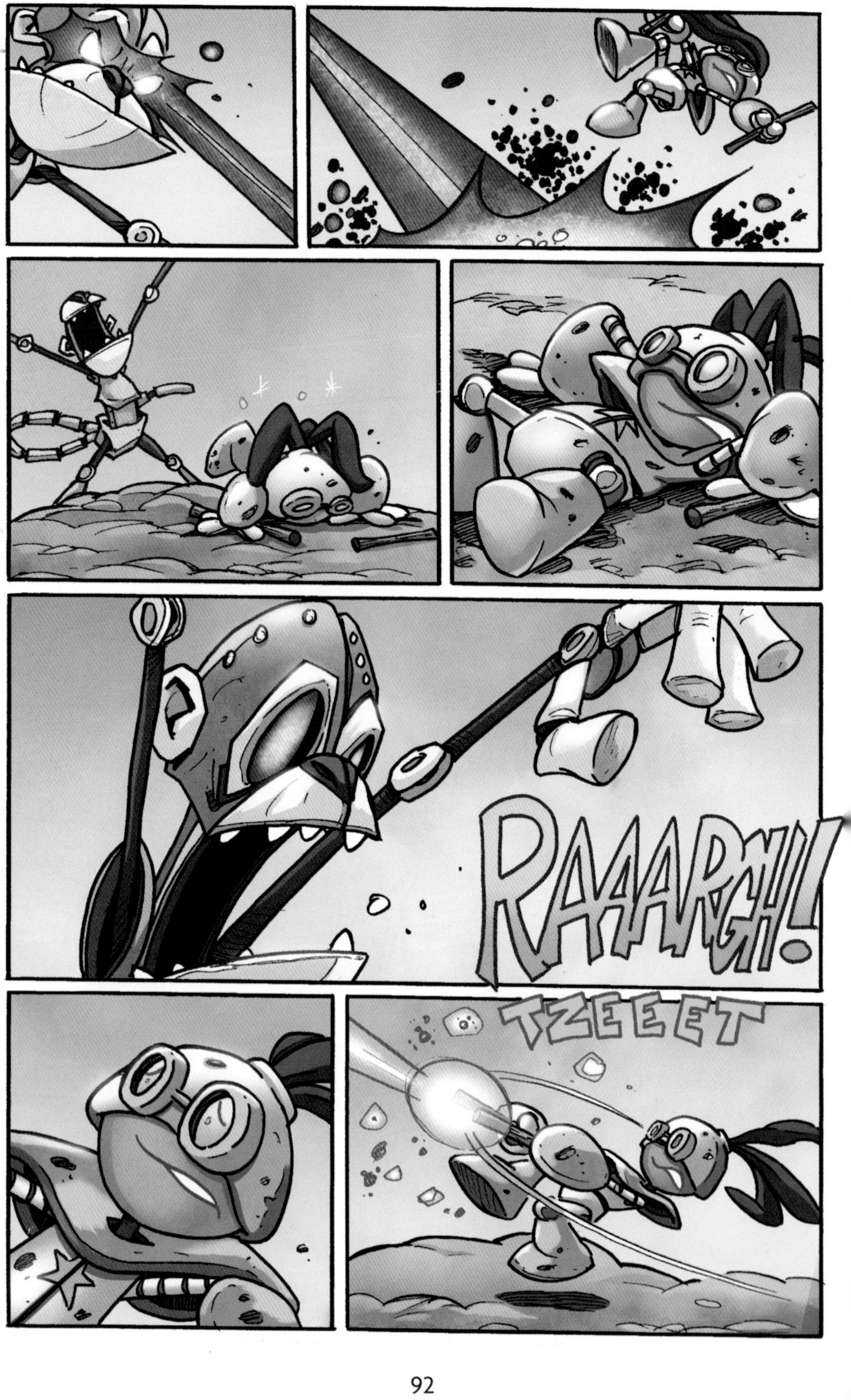
RAAARGH!!
TZEEET

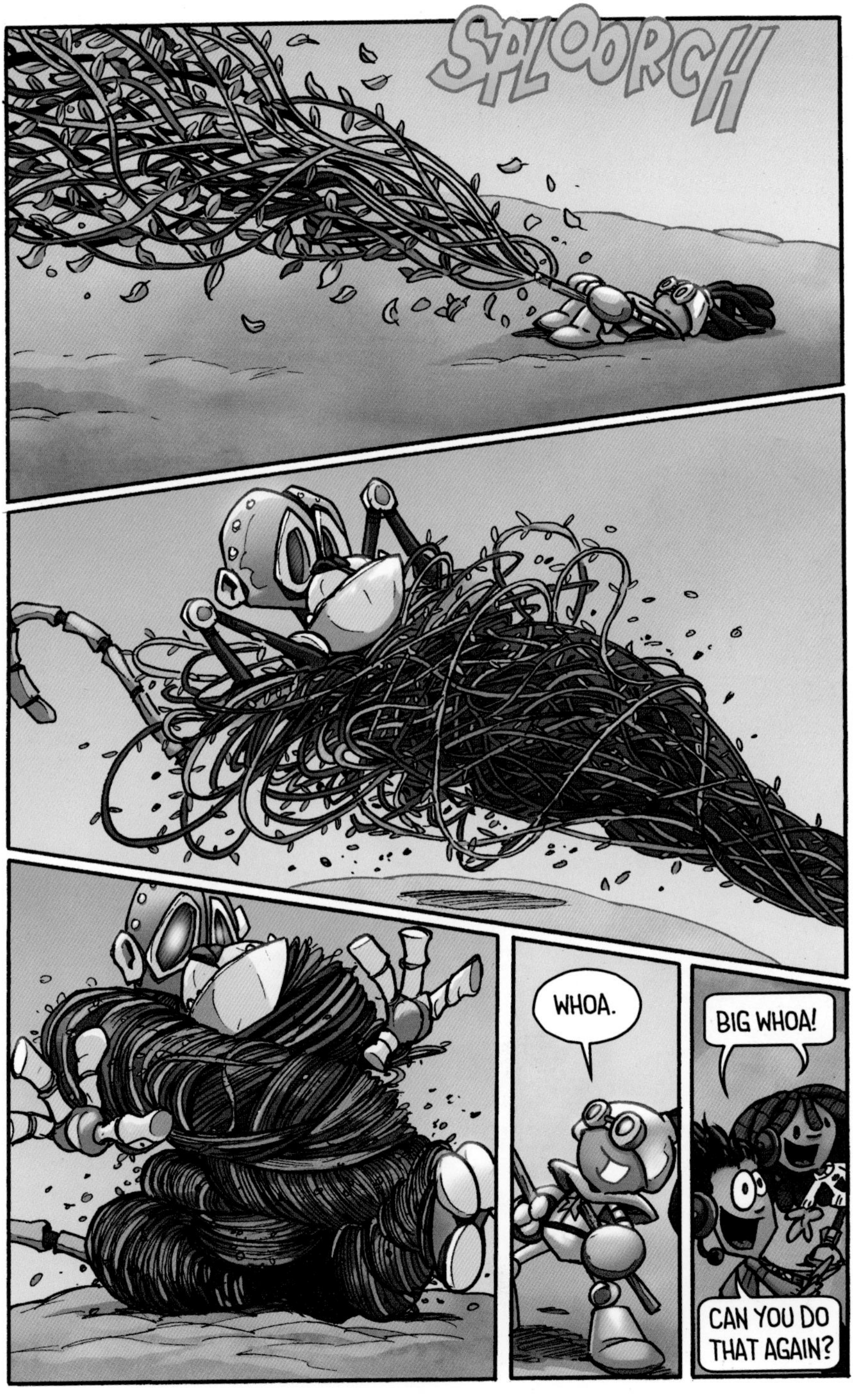
SPLOORCH
WHOA.
BIG WHOA!
CAN YOU DO THAT AGAIN?

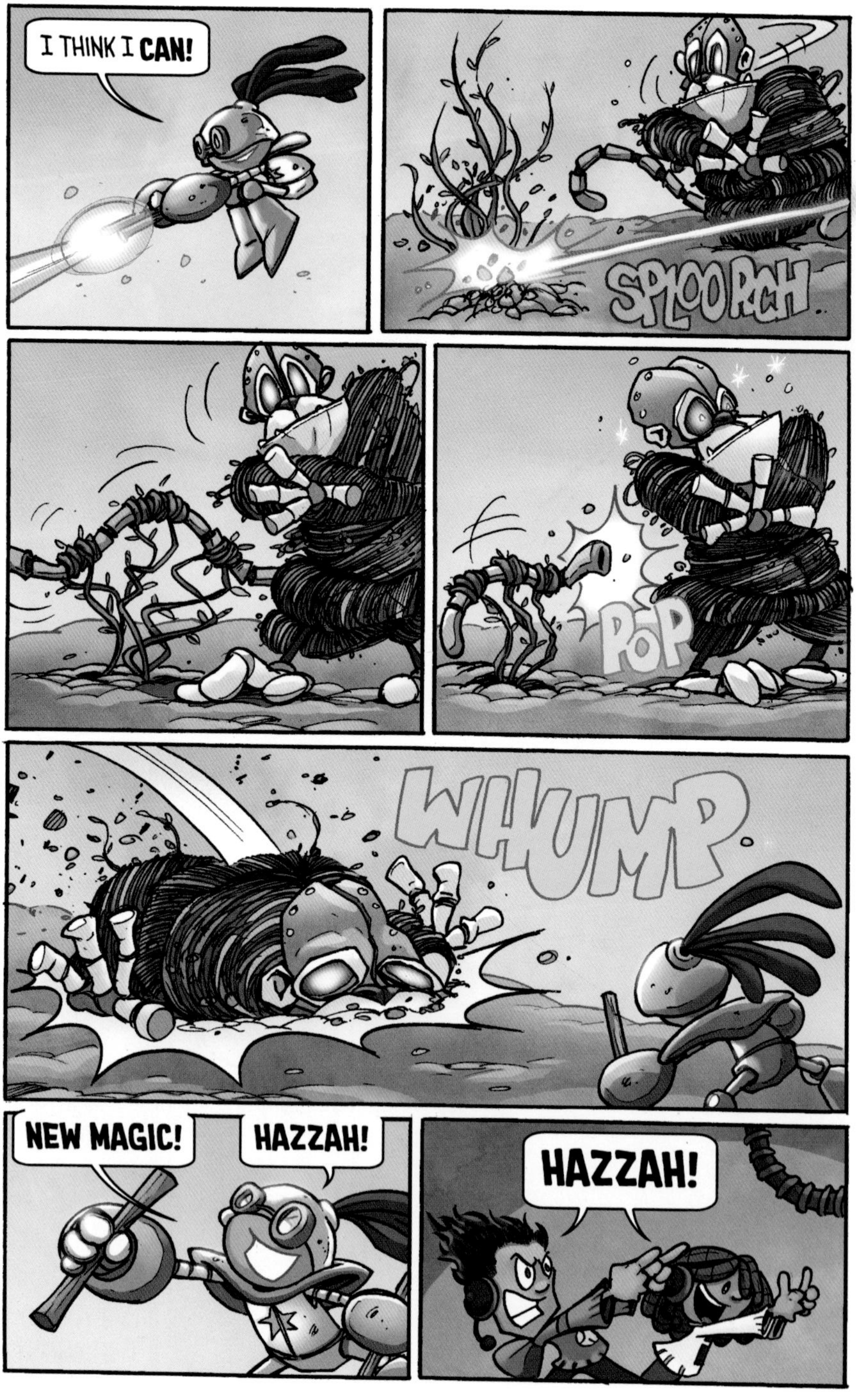
I THINK I CAN!
SPLOORCH
POP
WHUMP
NEW MAGIC!
HAZZAH!
HAZZAH!

BOOM

UH-OH.

GINA. THAT MEMORY'S GOT HILO CONFUSED.

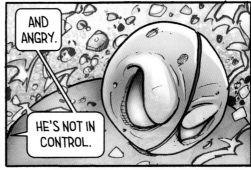

AND ANGRY.

HE'S NOT IN CONTROL.

HE MIGHT DESTROY THAT OTHER ROBOT.

HE DOESN'T WANT TO DO THAT ANYMORE.

HE JUST WANTS TO SHUT THEM OFF.

HELP HIM.

WHAT DO YOU MEAN, HE'S --

ANGRY?

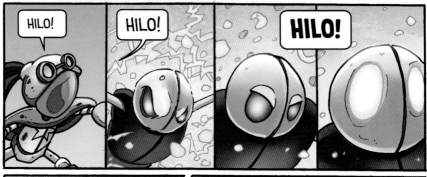

HILO!

HILO!

HILO!

HILO!

GINA?

YEAH.

YOU LOOK **OUTSTANDING!** DID IZZY MAKE THAT FOR YOU? YOUR **HELMET** IS WICKED NUTS!

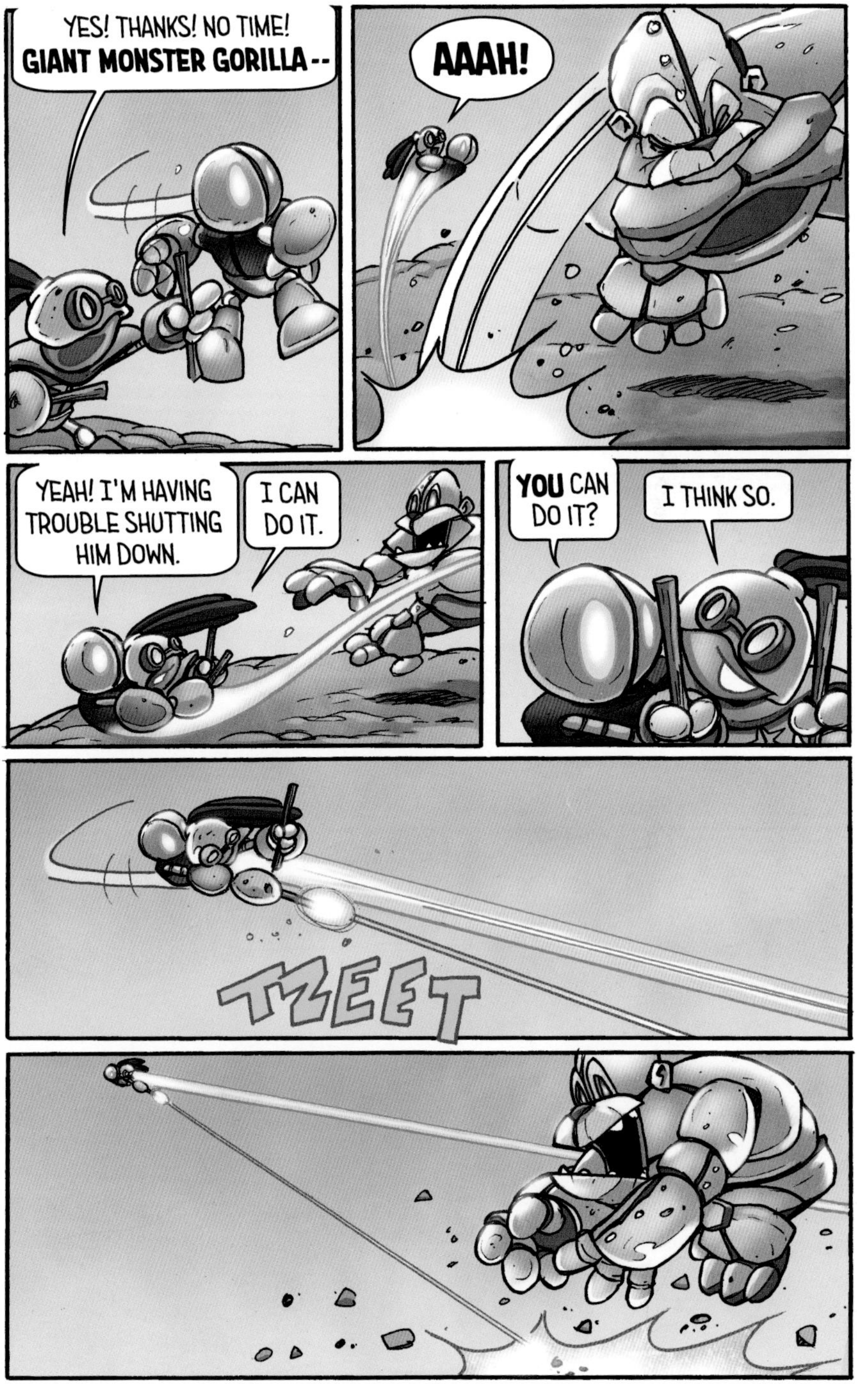
YES! THANKS! NO TIME! **GIANT MONSTER GORILLA --**
AAAH!
YEAH! I'M HAVING TROUBLE SHUTTING HIM DOWN.
I CAN DO IT.
YOU CAN DO IT?
I THINK SO.
TZEET

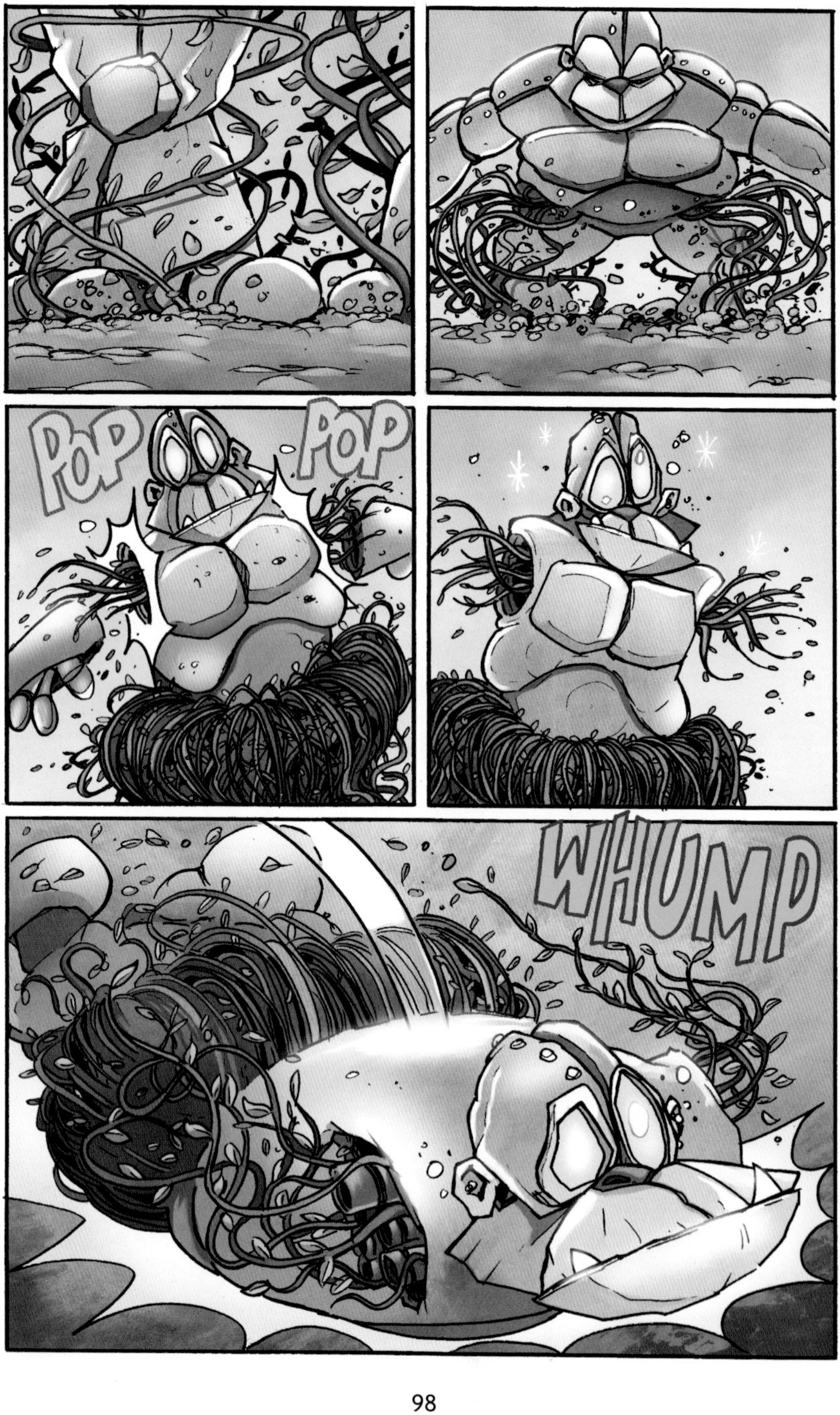
POP
POP
WHUMP

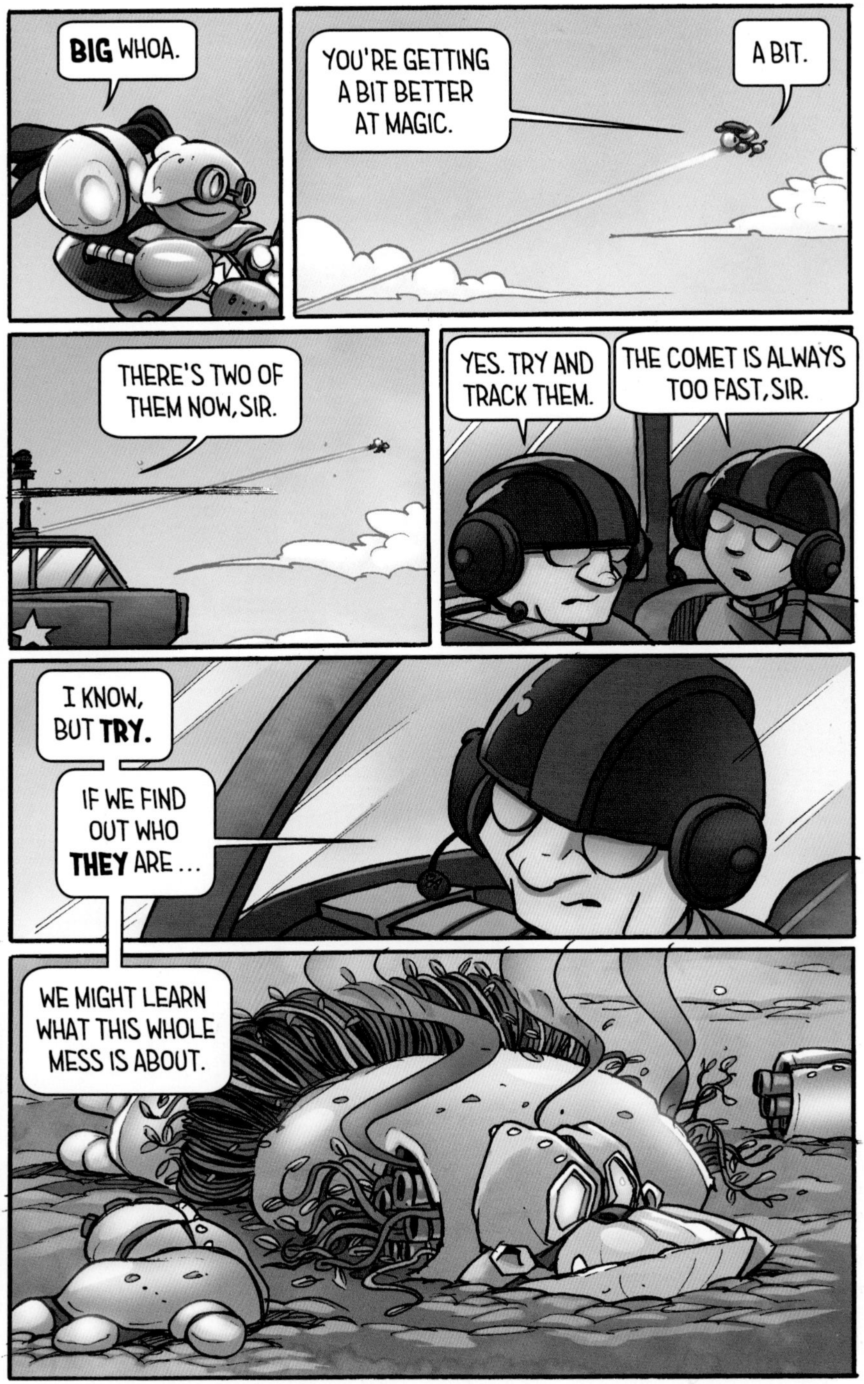
BIG WHOA.
YOU'RE GETTING A BIT BETTER AT MAGIC.
A BIT.
THERE'S TWO OF THEM NOW, SIR.
YES. TRY AND TRACK THEM.
THE COMET IS ALWAYS TOO FAST, SIR.
I KNOW, BUT TRY.
IF WE FIND OUT WHO THEY ARE ...
WE MIGHT LEARN WHAT THIS WHOLE MESS IS ABOUT.

CHAPTER 6

WE CAN BE HEROES

A GIANT METAL GORILLA AND A **HUGE** ROBOT MONKEY --

MARCHED ON THE CITY -- DISASTER SURELY JUST MOMENTS AWAY.

THIS TIME **THE COMET** CAME TO THE RESCUE WITH A **NEW** SUPERHERO BY HIS SIDE.

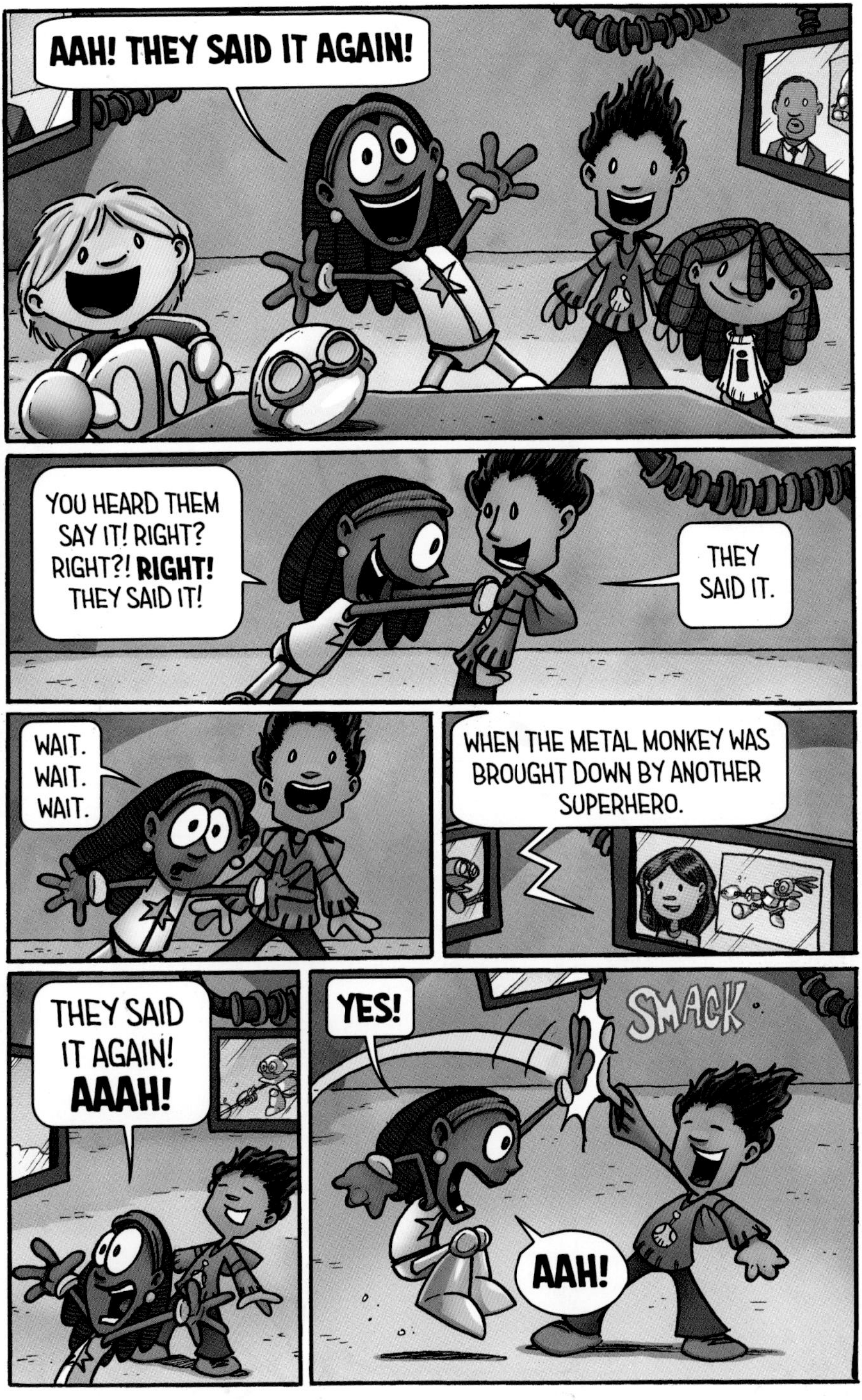

AAH! THEY SAID IT AGAIN!
YOU HEARD THEM SAY IT! RIGHT? RIGHT?! **RIGHT!** THEY SAID IT!
THEY SAID IT.
WAIT. WAIT. WAIT.
WHEN THE METAL MONKEY WAS BROUGHT DOWN BY ANOTHER SUPERHERO.
THEY SAID IT AGAIN! **AAAH!**
YES!
SMACK
AAH!

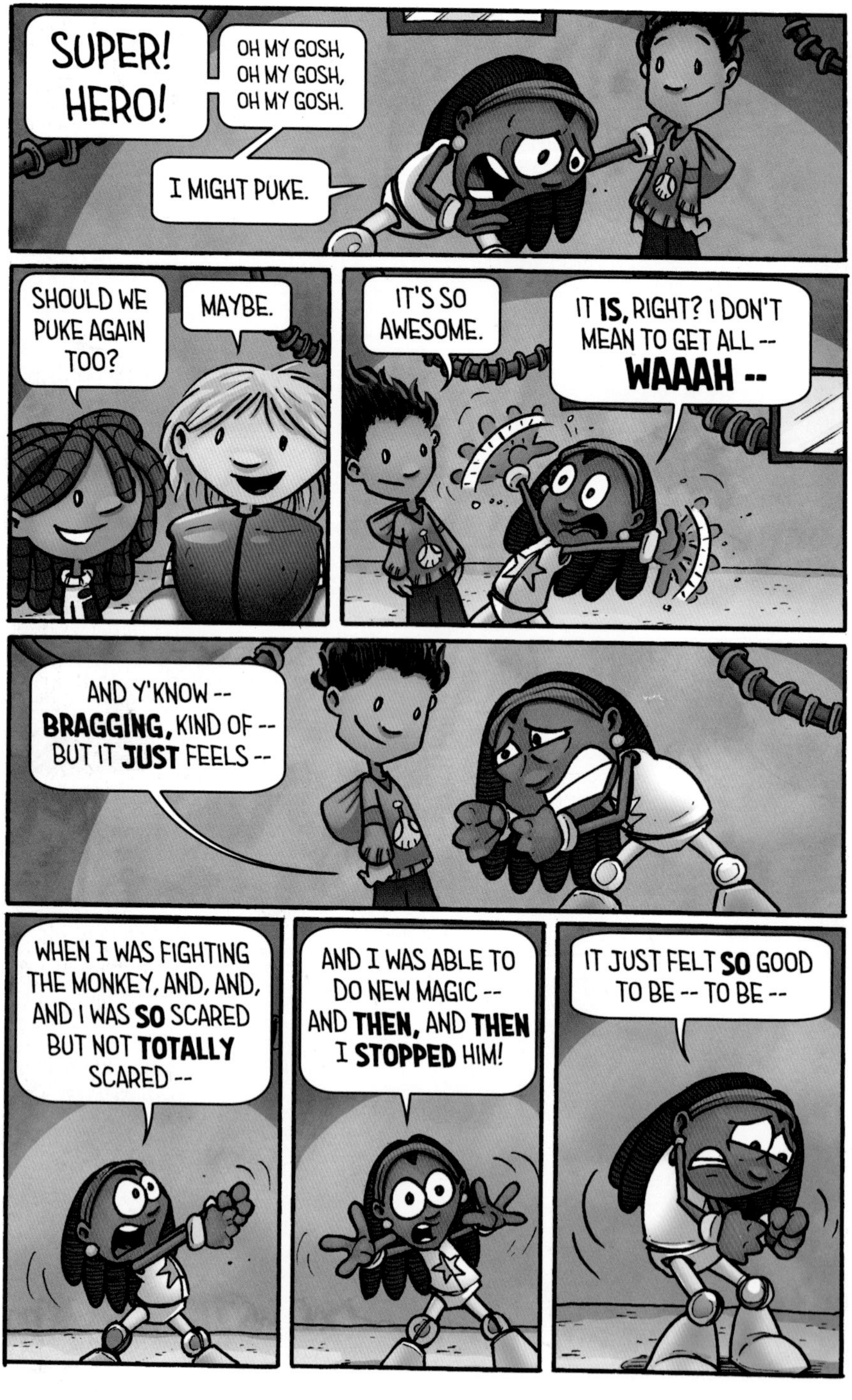
SUPER! HERO!
OH MY GOSH, OH MY GOSH, OH MY GOSH.
I MIGHT PUKE.
SHOULD WE PUKE AGAIN TOO?
MAYBE.
IT'S SO AWESOME.
IT **IS,** RIGHT? I DON'T MEAN TO GET ALL -- **WAAAH --**
AND Y'KNOW -- **BRAGGING,** KIND OF -- BUT IT **JUST** FEELS --
WHEN I WAS FIGHTING THE MONKEY, AND, AND, AND I WAS **SO** SCARED BUT NOT **TOTALLY** SCARED --
AND I WAS ABLE TO DO NEW MAGIC -- AND **THEN,** AND **THEN** I **STOPPED** HIM!
IT JUST FELT **SO** GOOD TO BE -- TO BE --

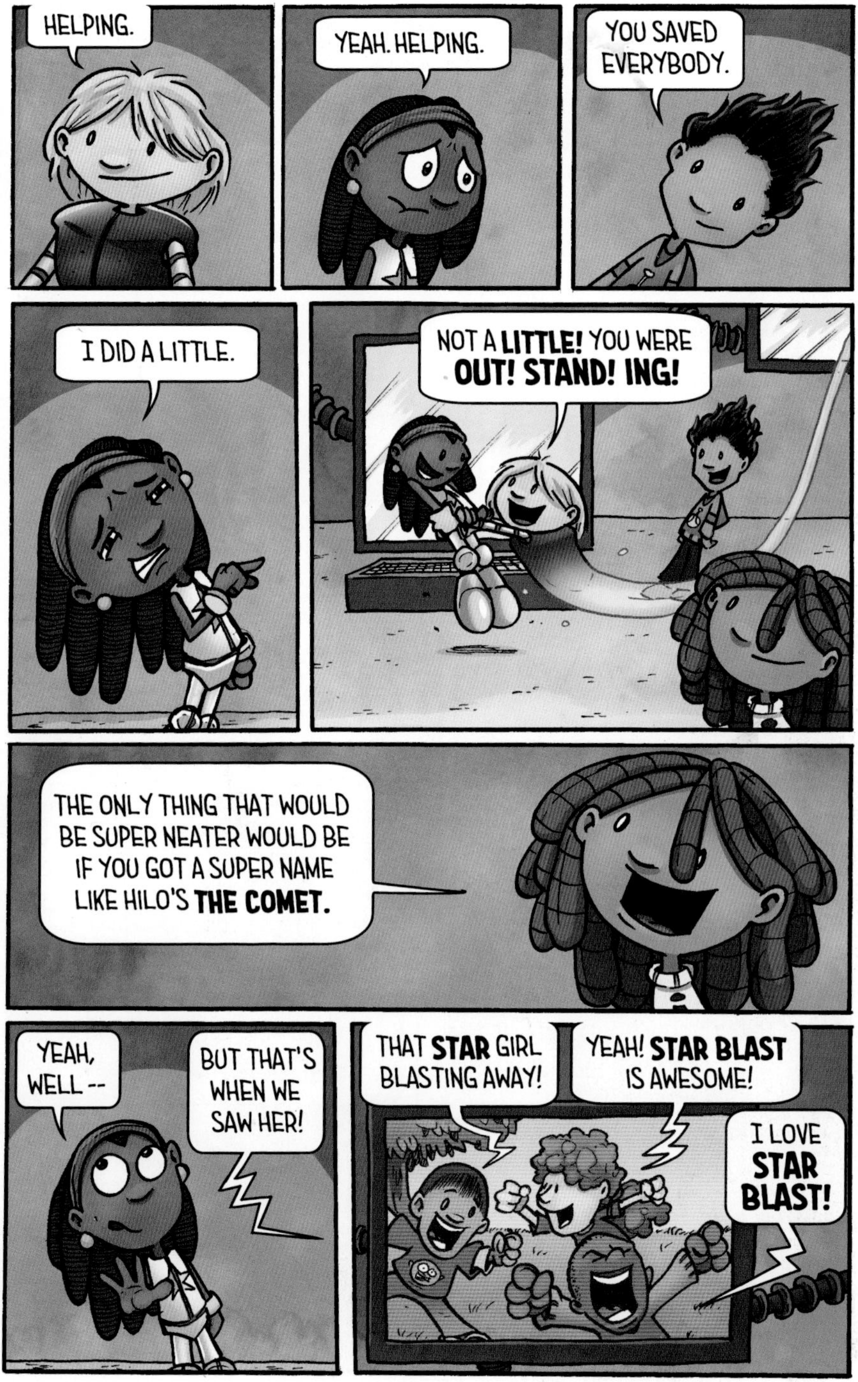
HELPING.
YEAH. HELPING.
YOU SAVED EVERYBODY.
I DID A LITTLE.
NOT A **LITTLE!** YOU WERE **OUT! STAND! ING!**
THE ONLY THING THAT WOULD BE SUPER NEATER WOULD BE IF YOU GOT A SUPER NAME LIKE HILO'S **THE COMET.**
YEAH, WELL --
BUT THAT'S WHEN WE SAW HER!
THAT **STAR** GIRL BLASTING AWAY!
YEAH! **STAR BLAST** IS AWESOME!
I LOVE **STAR BLAST!**

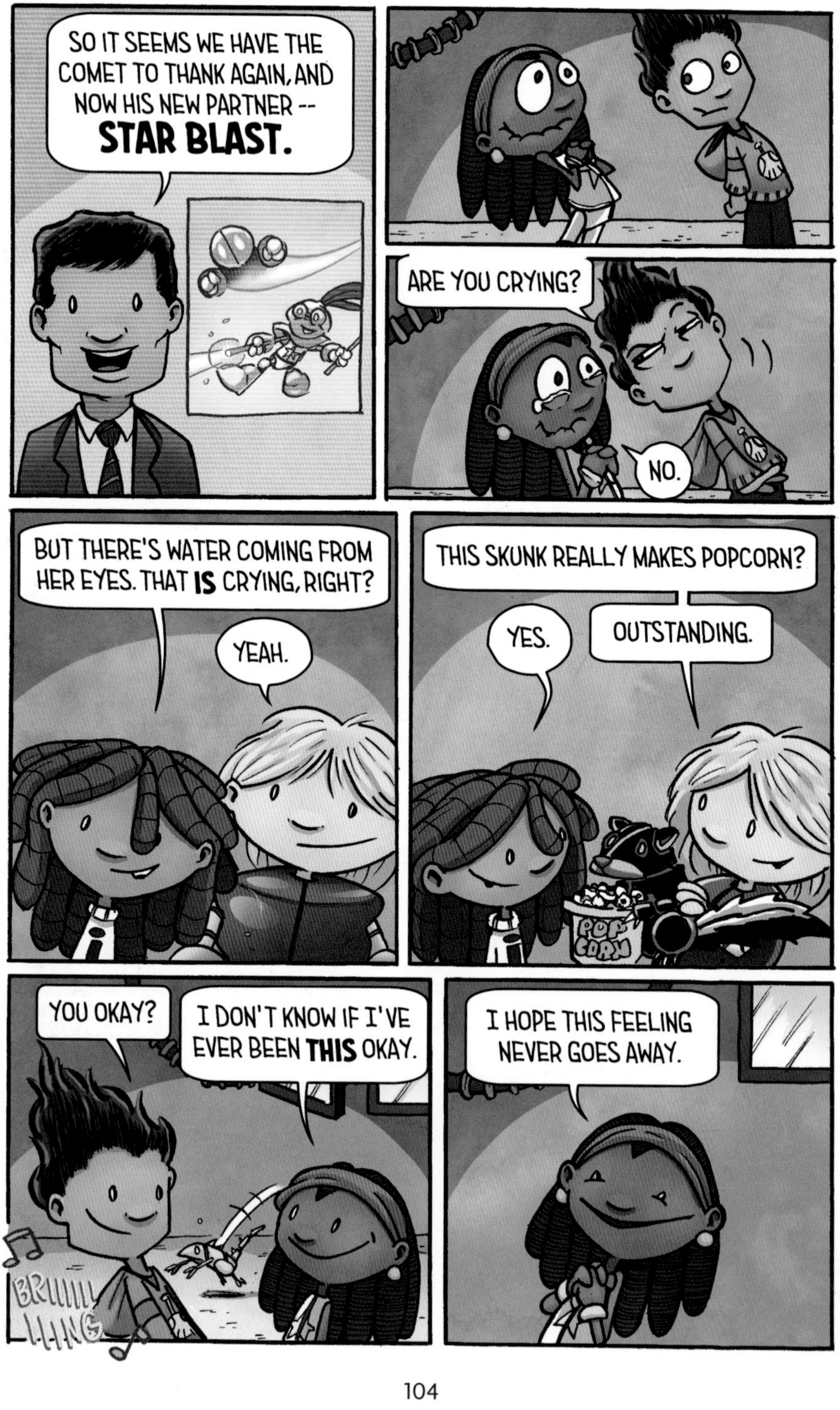
SO IT SEEMS WE HAVE THE COMET TO THANK AGAIN, AND NOW HIS NEW PARTNER -- **STAR BLAST.**
ARE YOU CRYING?
NO.
BUT THERE'S WATER COMING FROM HER EYES. THAT **IS** CRYING, RIGHT?
YEAH.
THIS SKUNK REALLY MAKES POPCORN?
YES.
OUTSTANDING.
POP CORN
YOU OKAY?
I DON'T KNOW IF I'VE EVER BEEN **THIS** OKAY.
BRIIIII IIING
I HOPE THIS FEELING NEVER GOES AWAY.

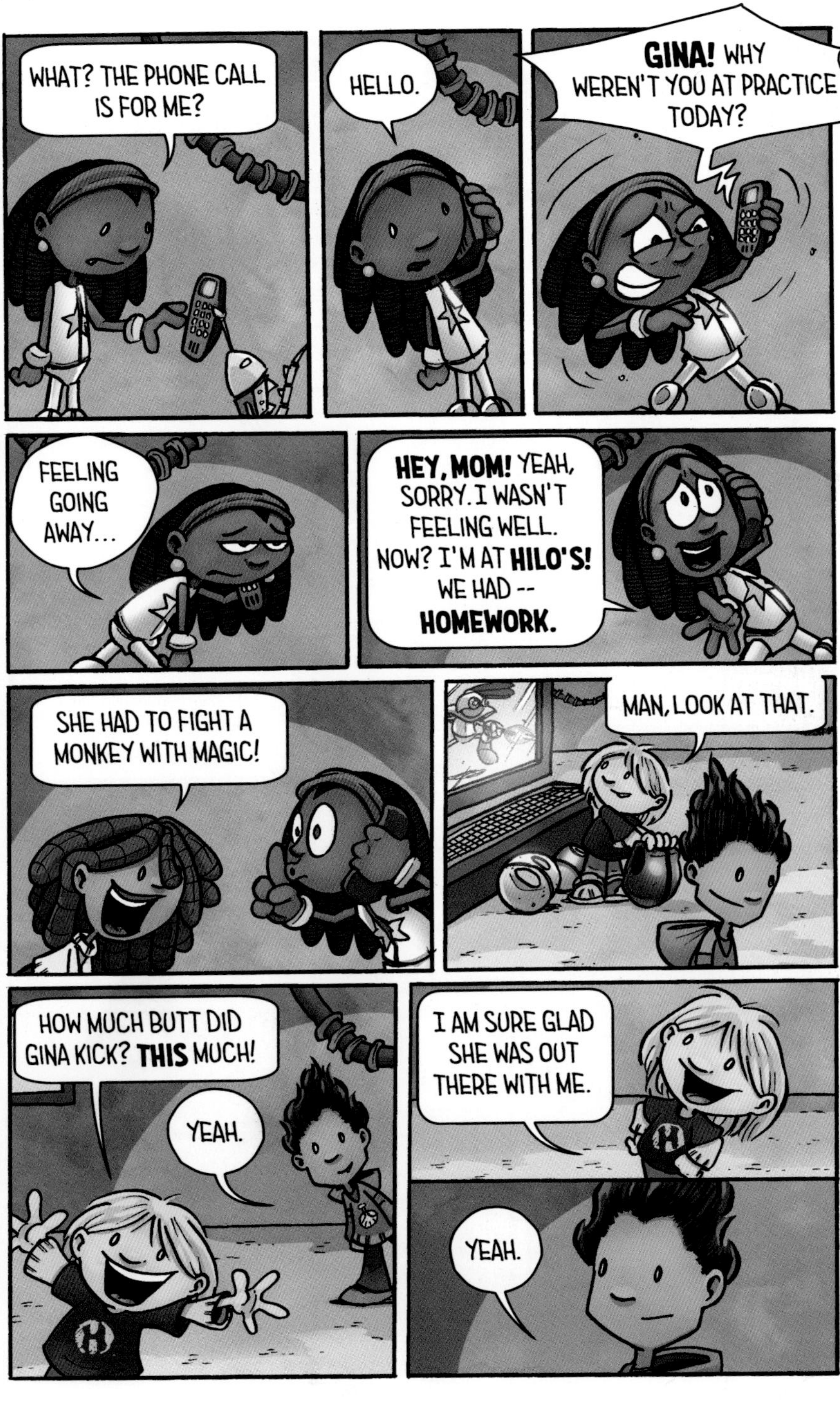
WHAT? THE PHONE CALL IS FOR ME?
HELLO.
GINA! WHY WEREN'T YOU AT PRACTICE TODAY?
FEELING GOING AWAY...
HEY, MOM! YEAH, SORRY. I WASN'T FEELING WELL. NOW? I'M AT HILO'S! WE HAD -- HOMEWORK.
SHE HAD TO FIGHT A MONKEY WITH MAGIC!
MAN, LOOK AT THAT.
HOW MUCH BUTT DID GINA KICK? THIS MUCH!
YEAH.
I AM SURE GLAD SHE WAS OUT THERE WITH ME.
YEAH.

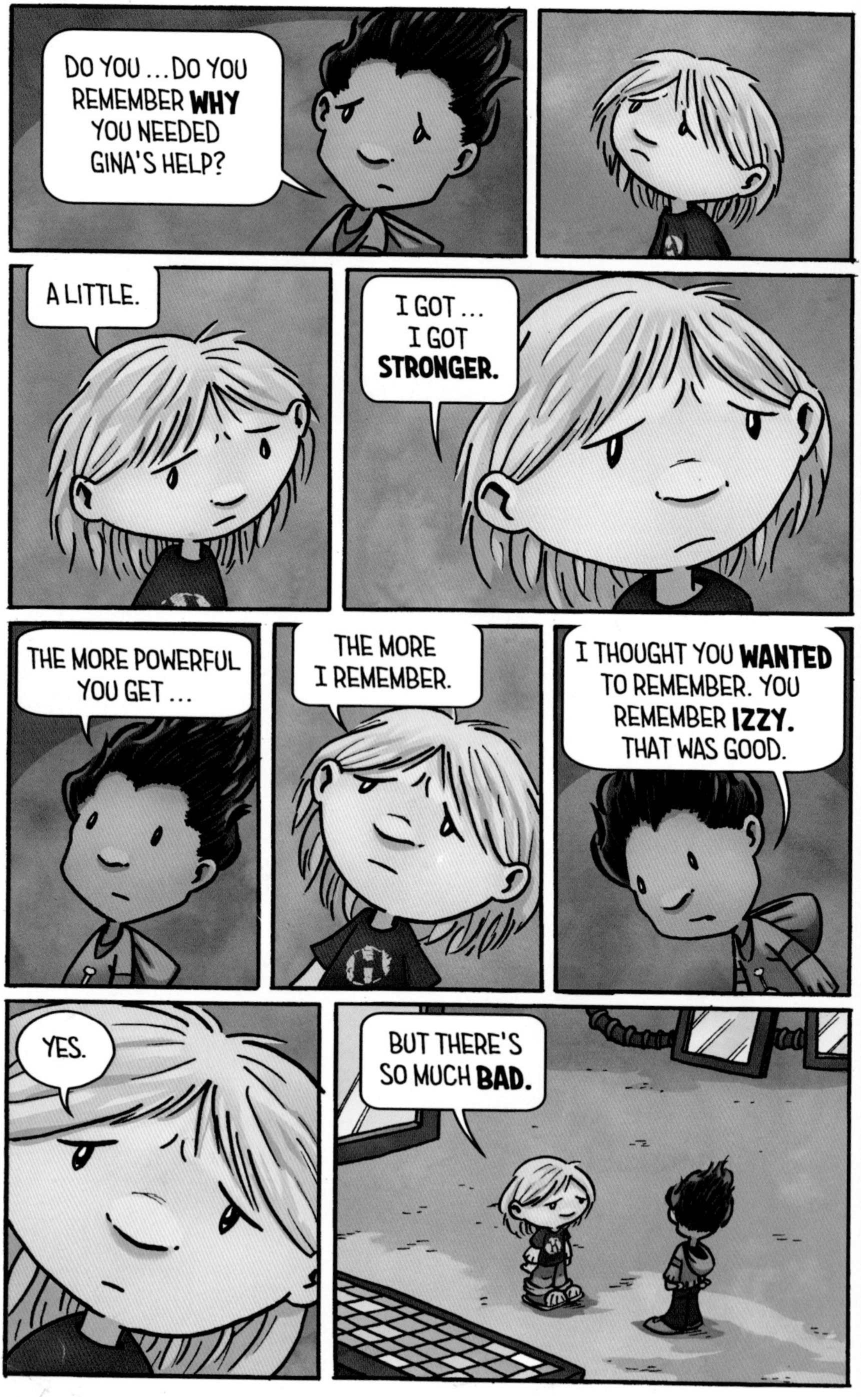
DO YOU ... DO YOU REMEMBER **WHY** YOU NEEDED GINA'S HELP?
A LITTLE.
I GOT ... I GOT **STRONGER.**
THE MORE POWERFUL YOU GET ...
THE MORE I REMEMBER.
I THOUGHT YOU **WANTED** TO REMEMBER. YOU REMEMBER **IZZY.** THAT WAS GOOD.
YES.
BUT THERE'S SO MUCH **BAD.**

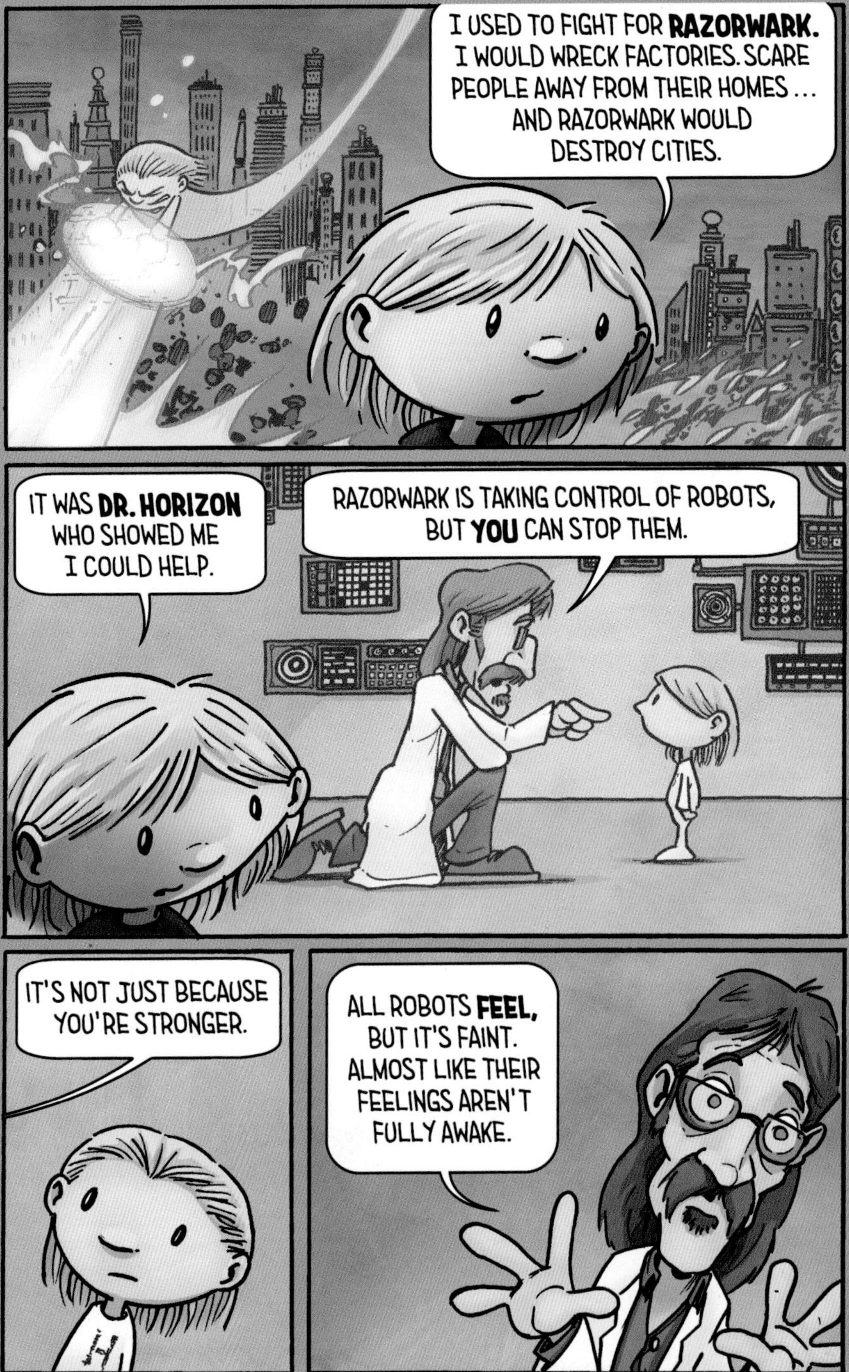
I USED TO FIGHT FOR **RAZORWARK.** I WOULD WRECK FACTORIES. SCARE PEOPLE AWAY FROM THEIR HOMES . . . AND RAZORWARK WOULD DESTROY CITIES.
IT WAS **DR. HORIZON** WHO SHOWED ME I COULD HELP.
RAZORWARK IS TAKING CONTROL OF ROBOTS, BUT **YOU** CAN STOP THEM.
IT'S NOT JUST BECAUSE YOU'RE STRONGER.
ALL ROBOTS **FEEL,** BUT IT'S FAINT. ALMOST LIKE THEIR FEELINGS AREN'T FULLY AWAKE.

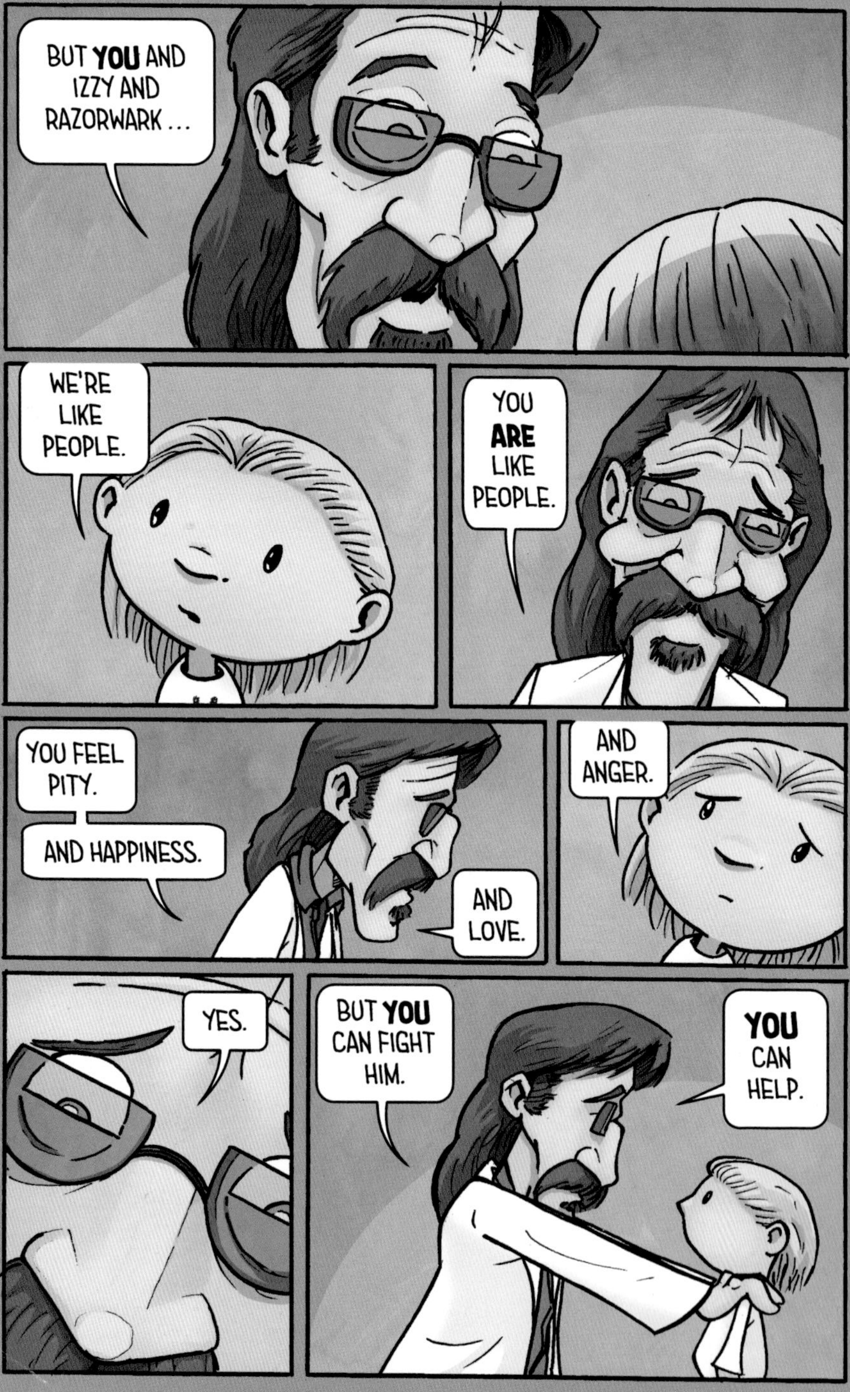
BUT **YOU** AND IZZY AND RAZORWARK . . .
WE'RE LIKE PEOPLE.
YOU **ARE** LIKE PEOPLE.
YOU FEEL PITY.
AND HAPPINESS.
AND LOVE.
AND ANGER.
YES.
BUT **YOU** CAN FIGHT HIM.
YOU CAN HELP.

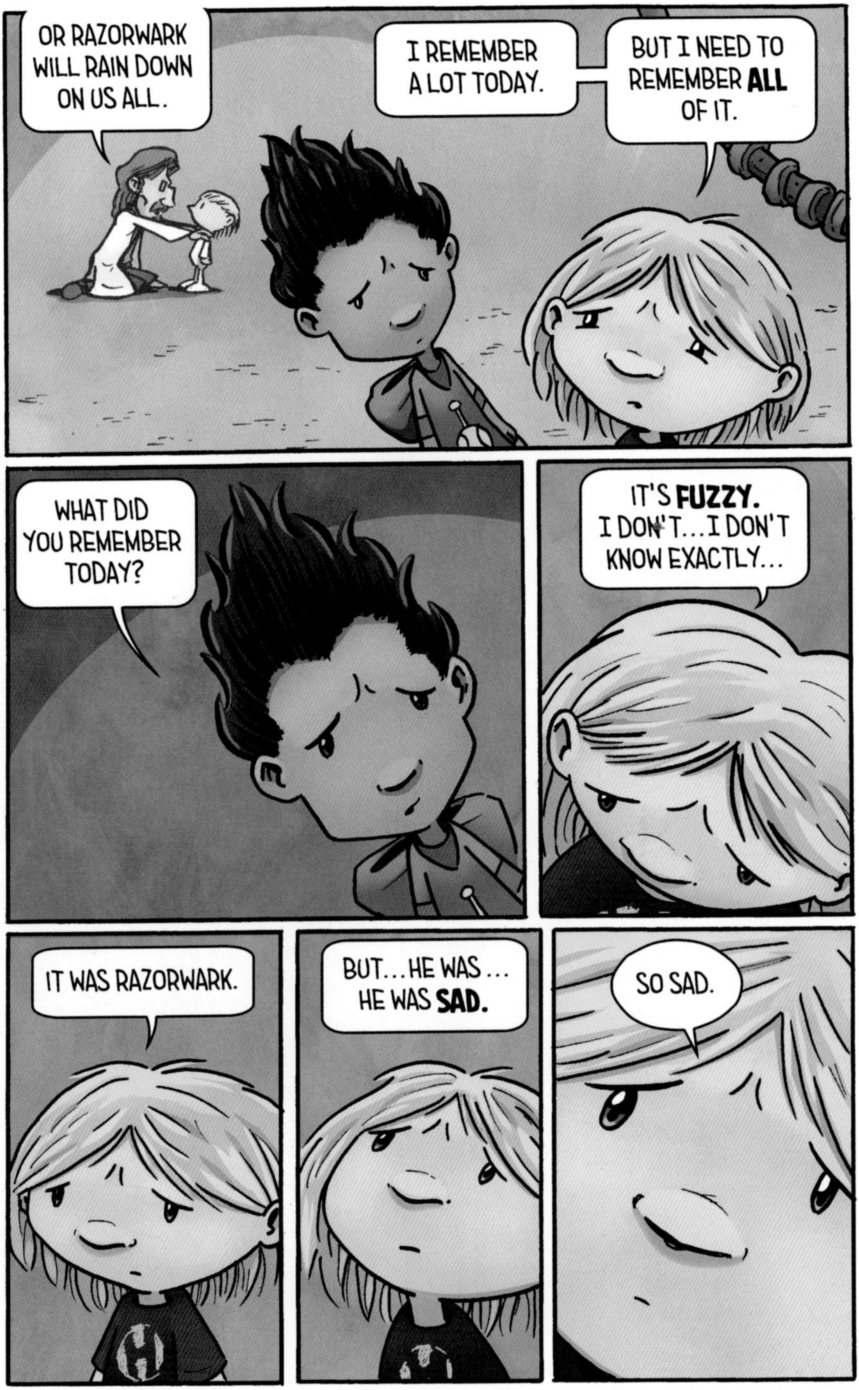
OR RAZORWARK WILL RAIN DOWN ON US ALL.
I REMEMBER A LOT TODAY.
BUT I NEED TO REMEMBER **ALL** OF IT.
WHAT DID YOU REMEMBER TODAY?
IT'S **FUZZY.** I DON'T... I DON'T KNOW EXACTLY...
IT WAS RAZORWARK.
BUT... HE WAS ... HE WAS **SAD.**
SO SAD.

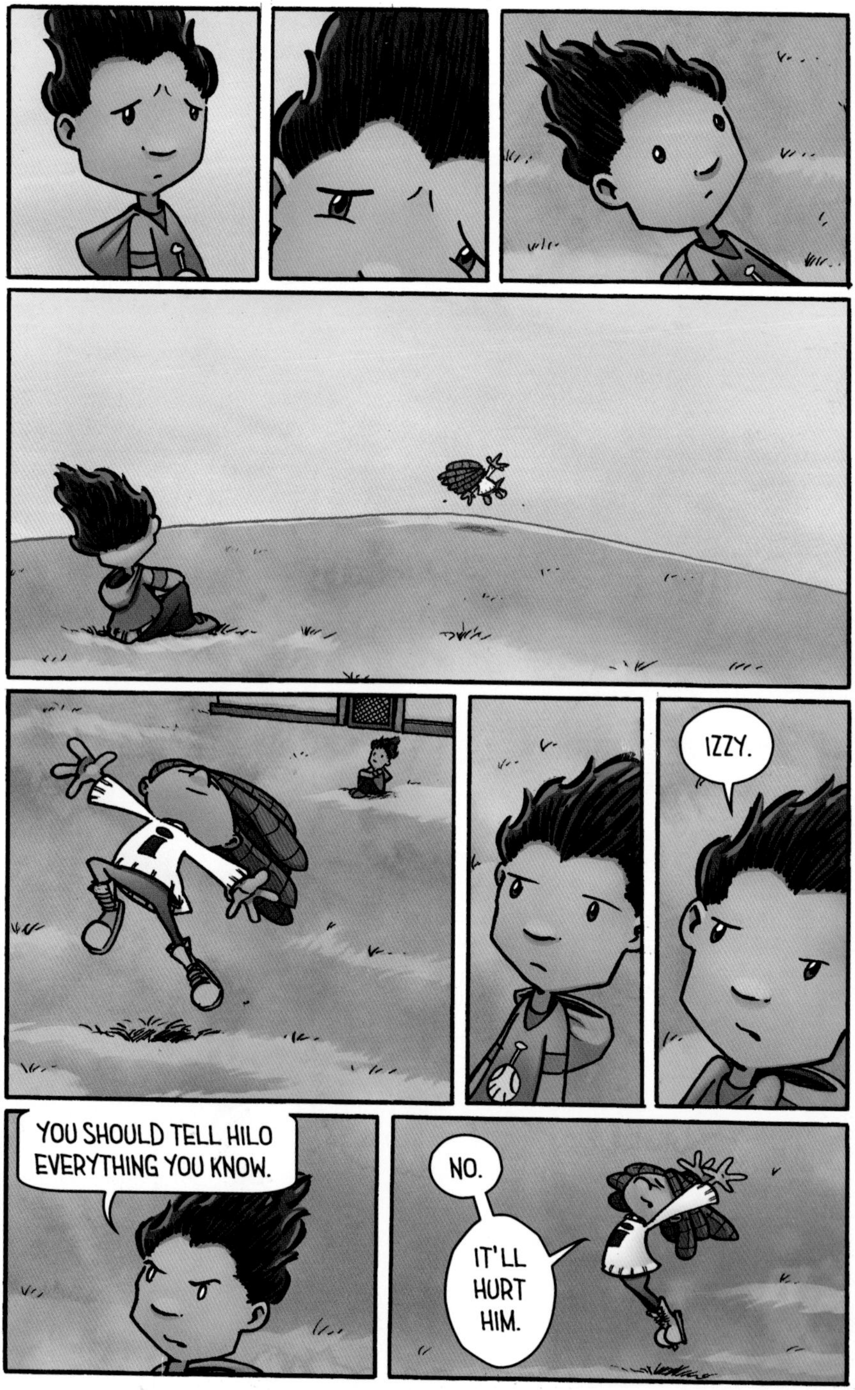
IZZY.
YOU SHOULD TELL HILO EVERYTHING YOU KNOW.
NO.
IT'LL HURT HIM.

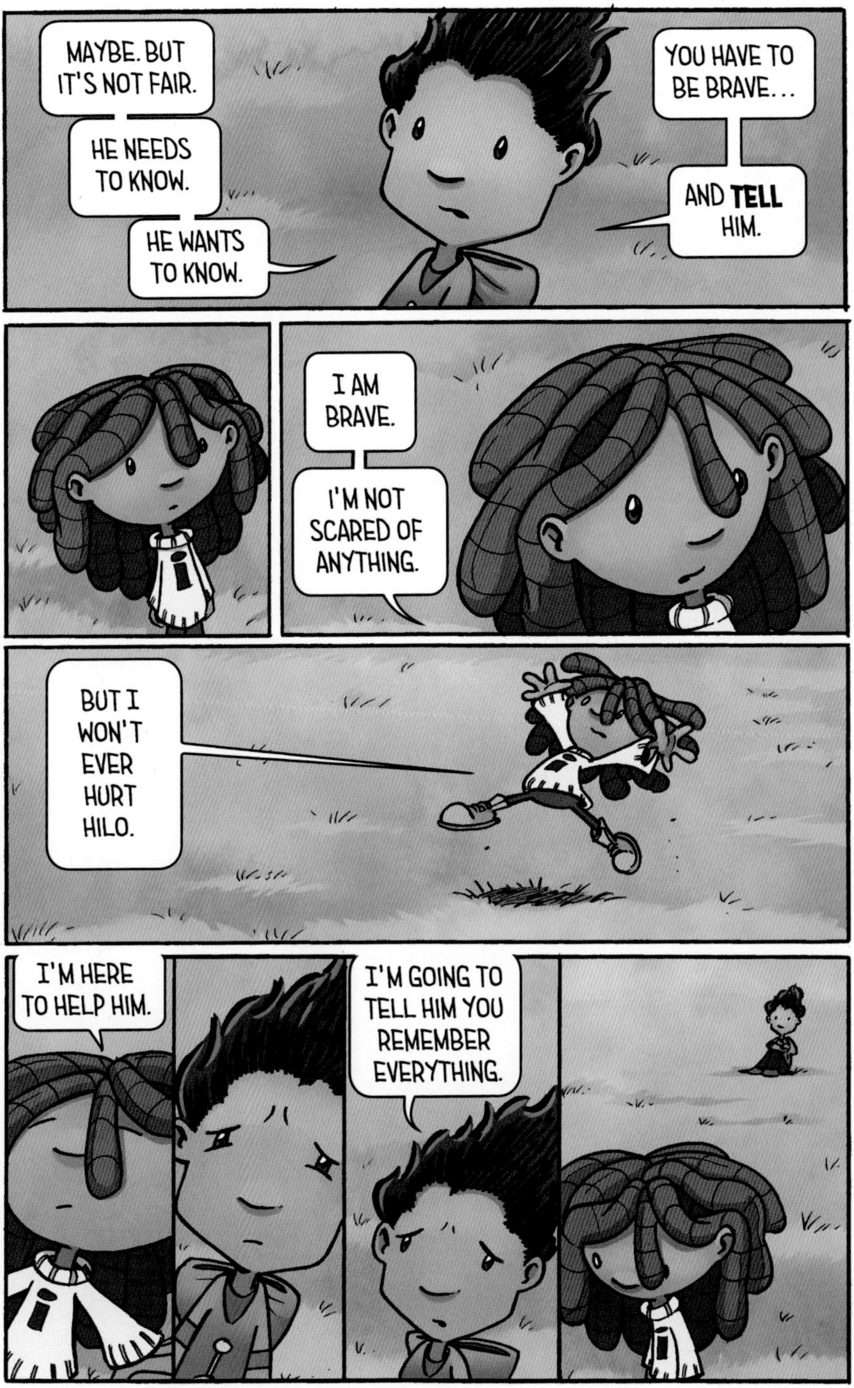
MAYBE. BUT IT'S NOT FAIR.
HE NEEDS TO KNOW.
HE WANTS TO KNOW.
YOU HAVE TO BE BRAVE...
AND **TELL** HIM.
I AM BRAVE.
I'M NOT SCARED OF ANYTHING.
BUT I WON'T EVER HURT HILO.
I'M HERE TO HELP HIM.
I'M GOING TO TELL HIM YOU REMEMBER EVERYTHING.

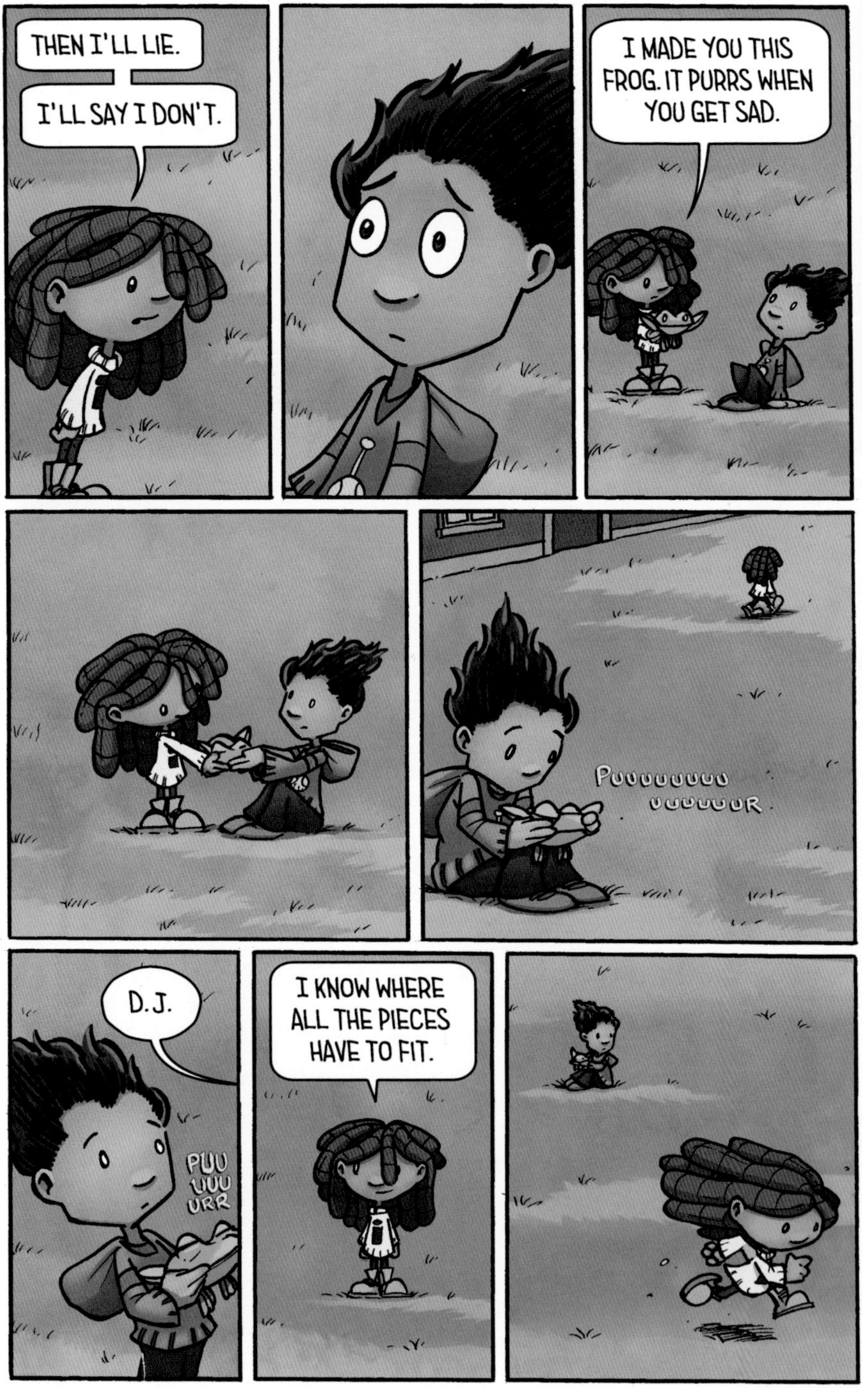
THEN I'LL LIE.
I'LL SAY I DON'T.
I MADE YOU THIS FROG. IT PURRS WHEN YOU GET SAD.
PUUUUUUUU UUUUUUR.
D.J.
PUU UUU URR
I KNOW WHERE ALL THE PIECES HAVE TO FIT.

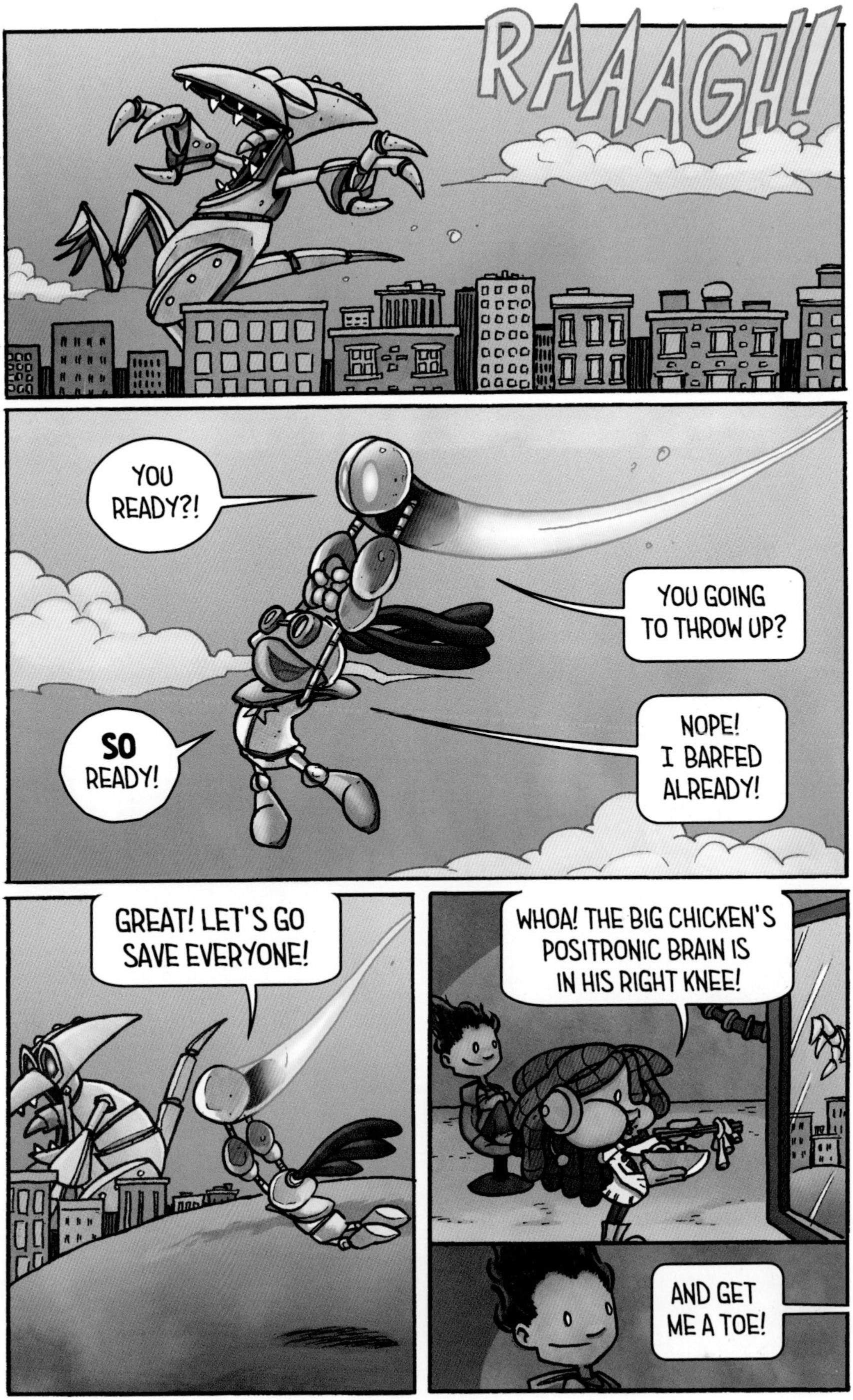
RAAAGH!!
YOU READY?!
YOU GOING TO THROW UP?
SO READY!
NOPE! I BARFED ALREADY!
GREAT! LET'S GO SAVE EVERYONE!
WHOA! THE BIG CHICKEN'S POSITRONIC BRAIN IS IN HIS RIGHT KNEE!
AND GET ME A TOE!

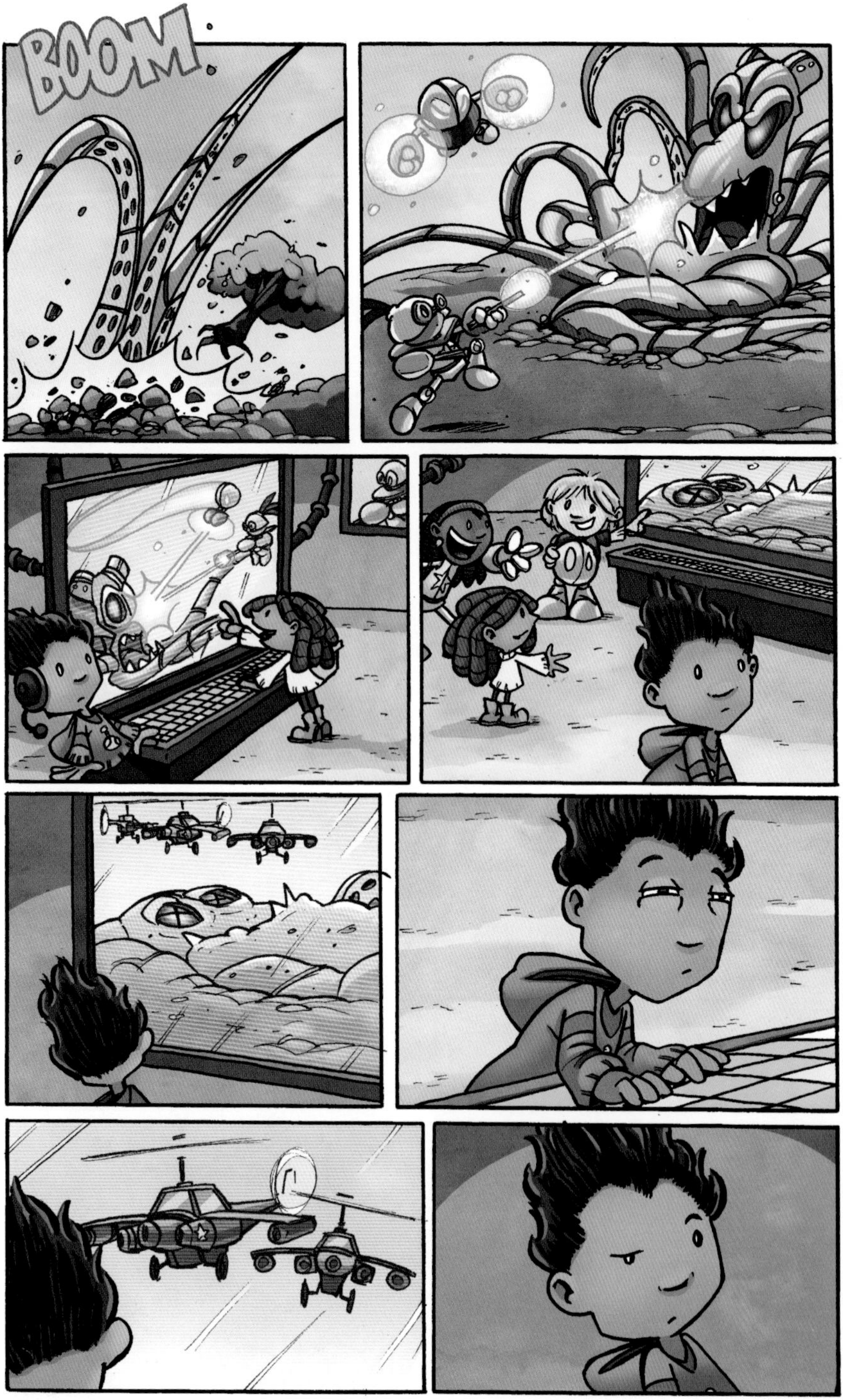
BOOM

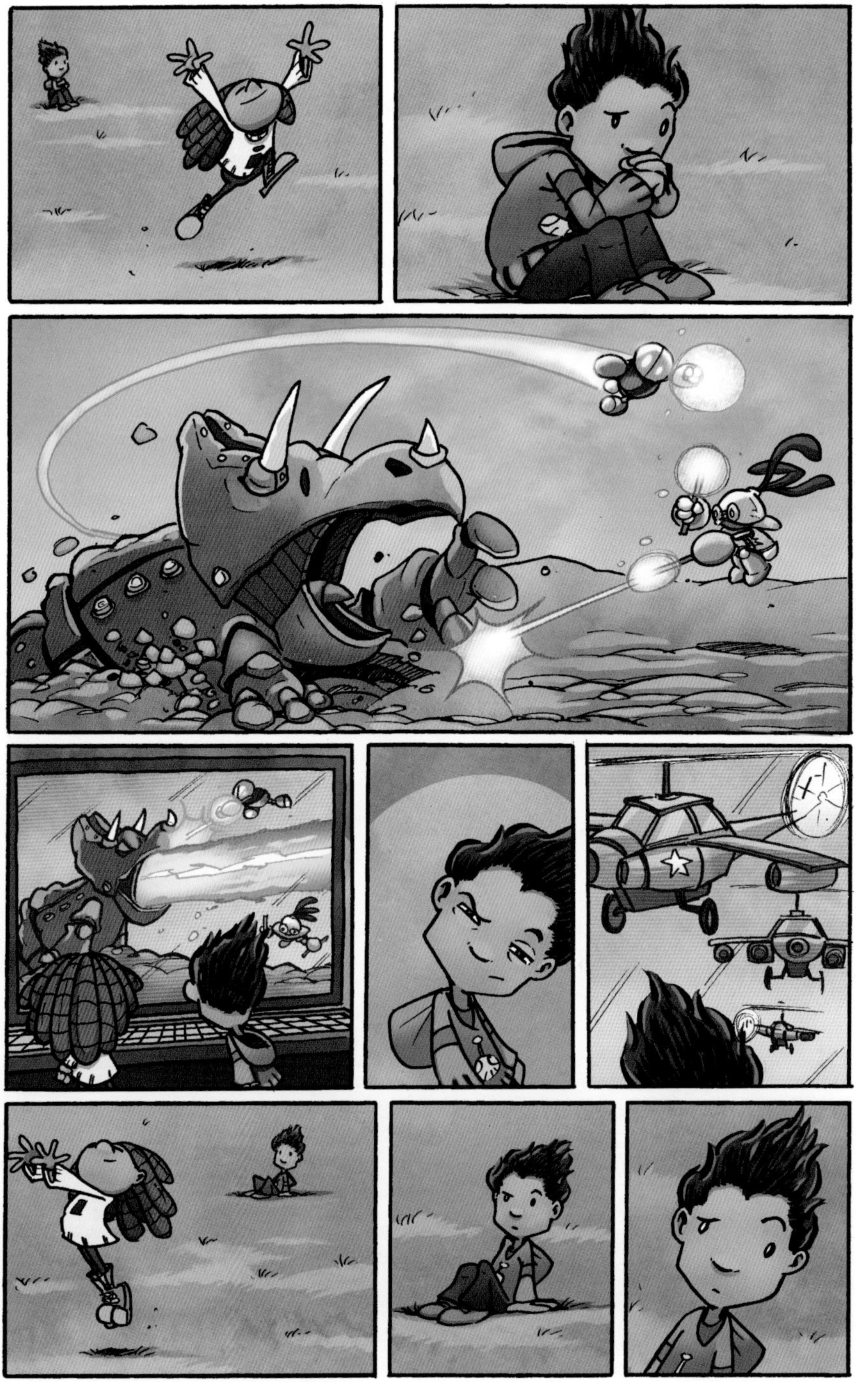

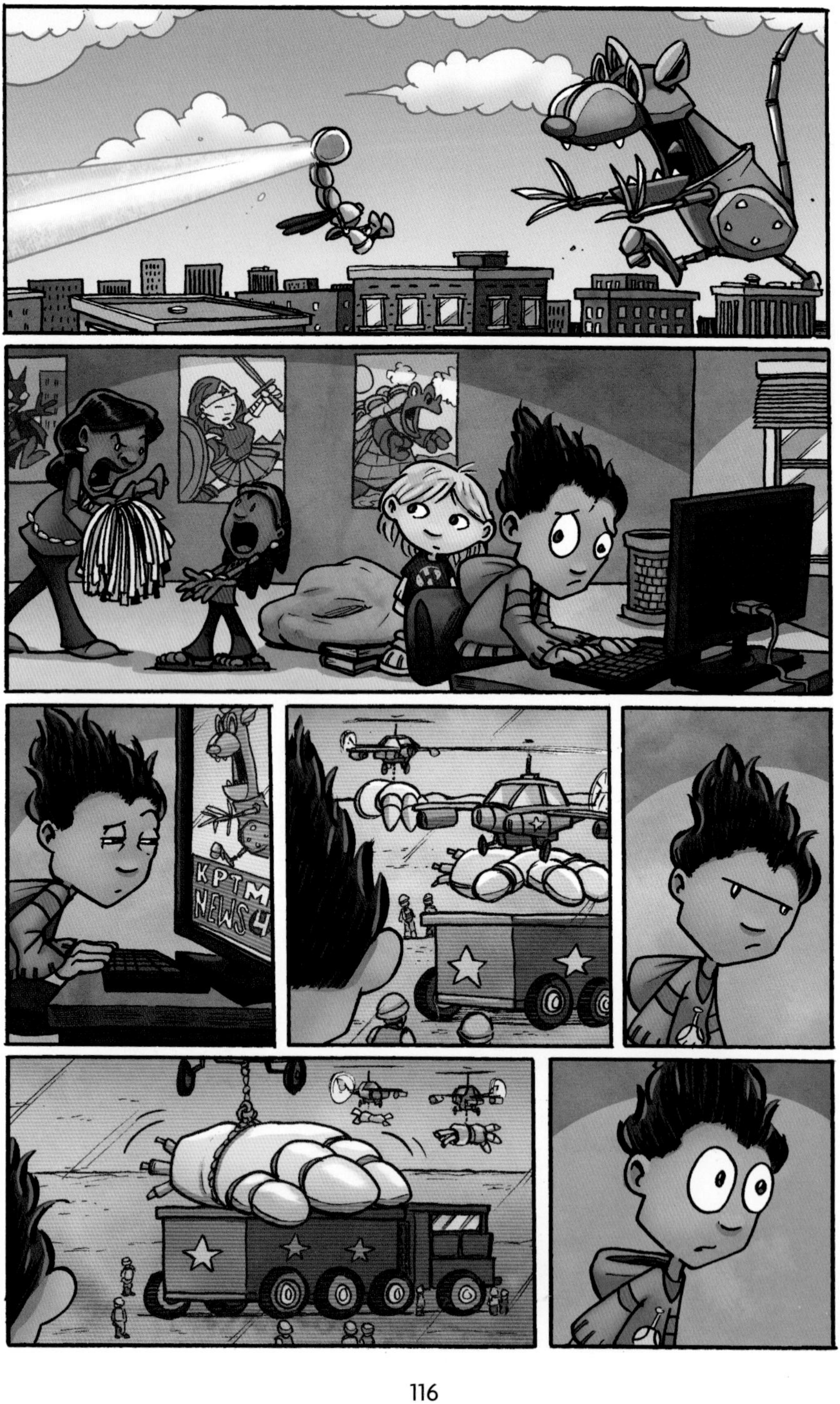
KPTM
NEWS

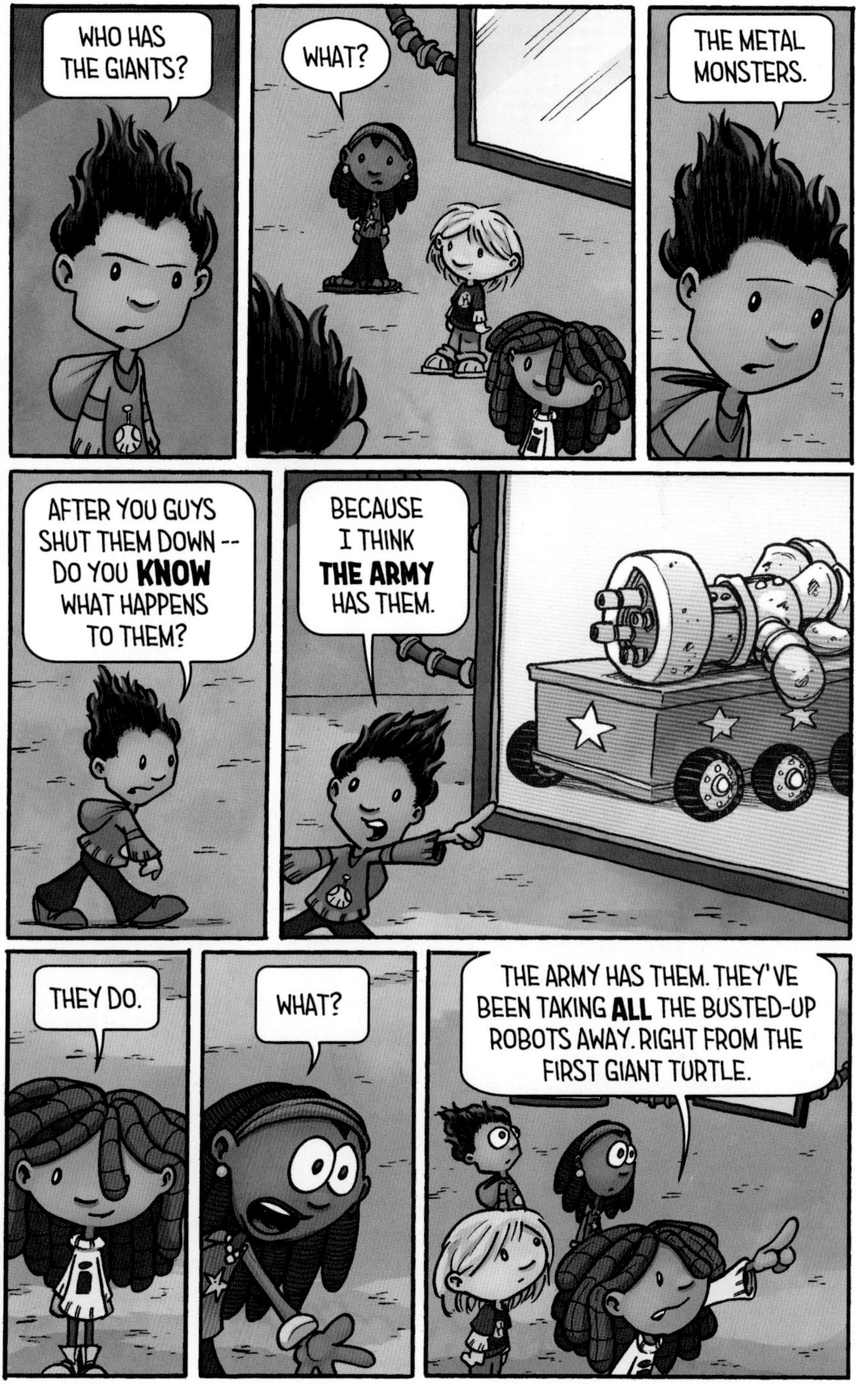
WHO HAS THE GIANTS?
WHAT?
THE METAL MONSTERS.
AFTER YOU GUYS SHUT THEM DOWN -- DO YOU **KNOW** WHAT HAPPENS TO THEM?
BECAUSE I THINK **THE ARMY** HAS THEM.
THEY DO.
WHAT?
THE ARMY HAS THEM. THEY'VE BEEN TAKING **ALL** THE BUSTED-UP ROBOTS AWAY. RIGHT FROM THE FIRST GIANT TURTLE.

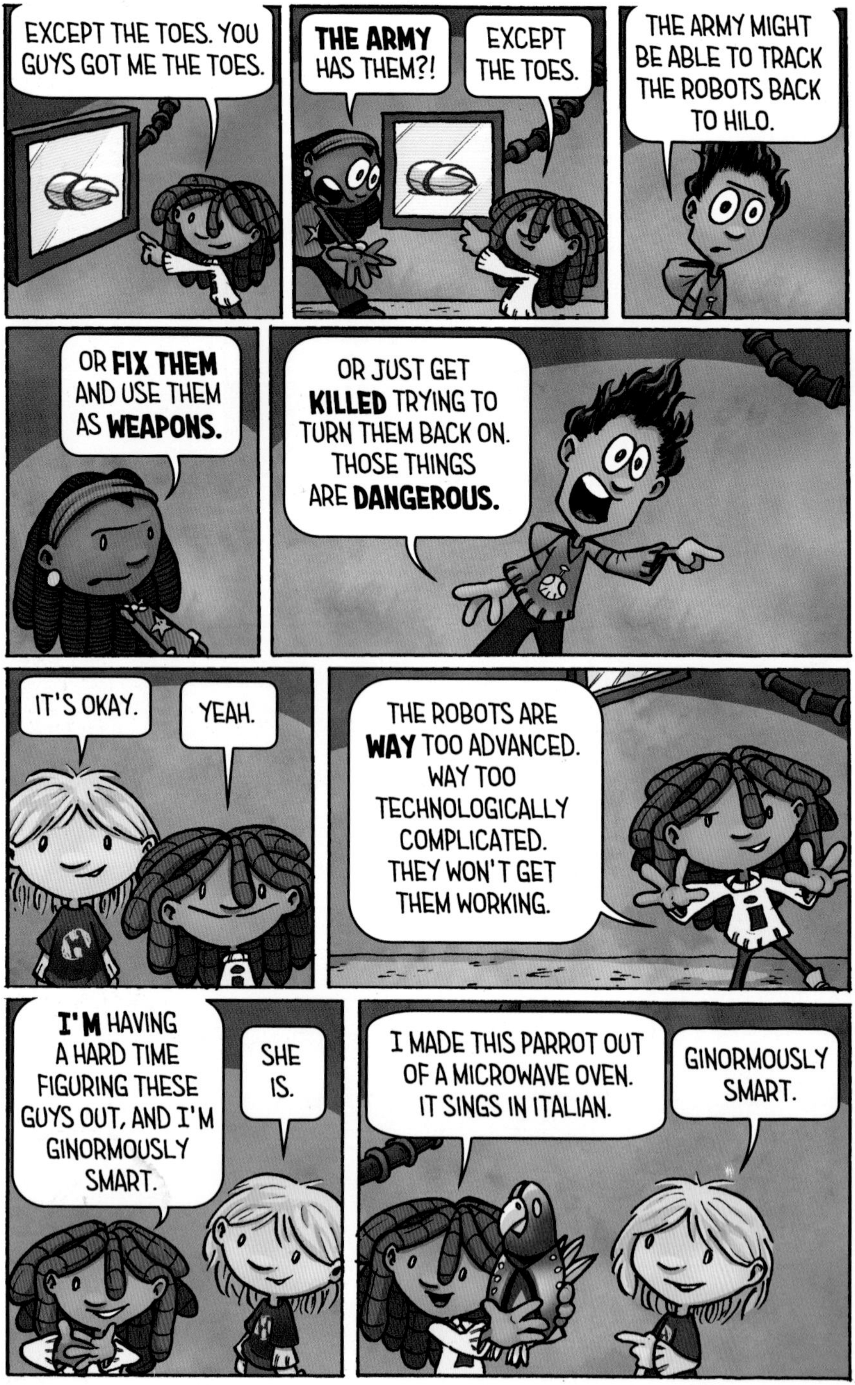
EXCEPT THE TOES. YOU GUYS GOT ME THE TOES.
THE ARMY HAS THEM?!
EXCEPT THE TOES.
THE ARMY MIGHT BE ABLE TO TRACK THE ROBOTS BACK TO HILO.
OR FIX THEM AND USE THEM AS WEAPONS.
OR JUST GET KILLED TRYING TO TURN THEM BACK ON. THOSE THINGS ARE DANGEROUS.
IT'S OKAY.
YEAH.
THE ROBOTS ARE WAY TOO ADVANCED. WAY TOO TECHNOLOGICALLY COMPLICATED. THEY WON'T GET THEM WORKING.
I'M HAVING A HARD TIME FIGURING THESE GUYS OUT, AND I'M GINORMOUSLY SMART.
SHE IS.
I MADE THIS PARROT OUT OF A MICROWAVE OVEN. IT SINGS IN ITALIAN.
GINORMOUSLY SMART.

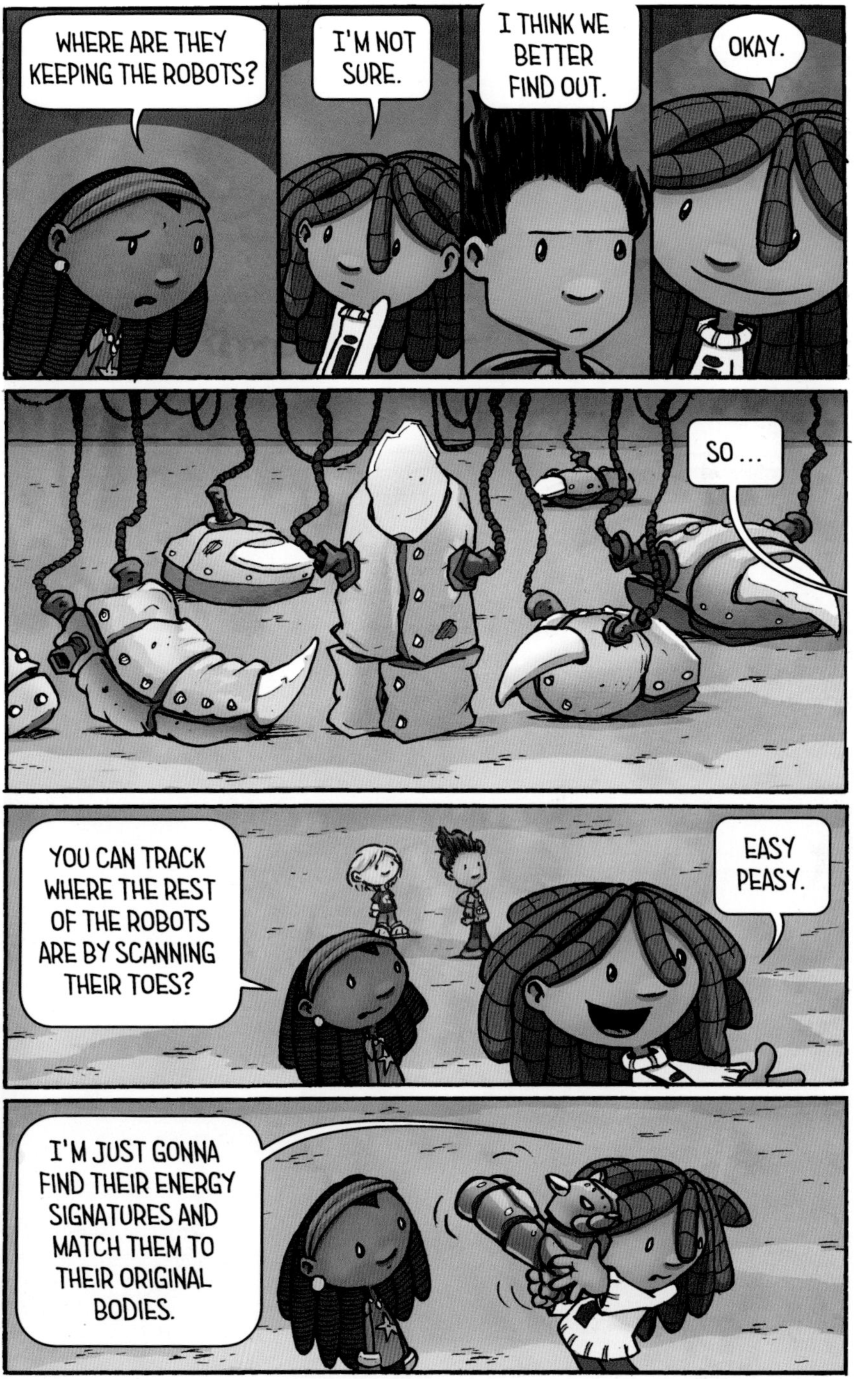
WHERE ARE THEY KEEPING THE ROBOTS?
I'M NOT SURE.
I THINK WE BETTER FIND OUT.
OKAY.
SO...
YOU CAN TRACK WHERE THE REST OF THE ROBOTS ARE BY SCANNING THEIR TOES?
EASY PEASY.
I'M JUST GONNA FIND THEIR ENERGY SIGNATURES AND MATCH THEM TO THEIR ORIGINAL BODIES.

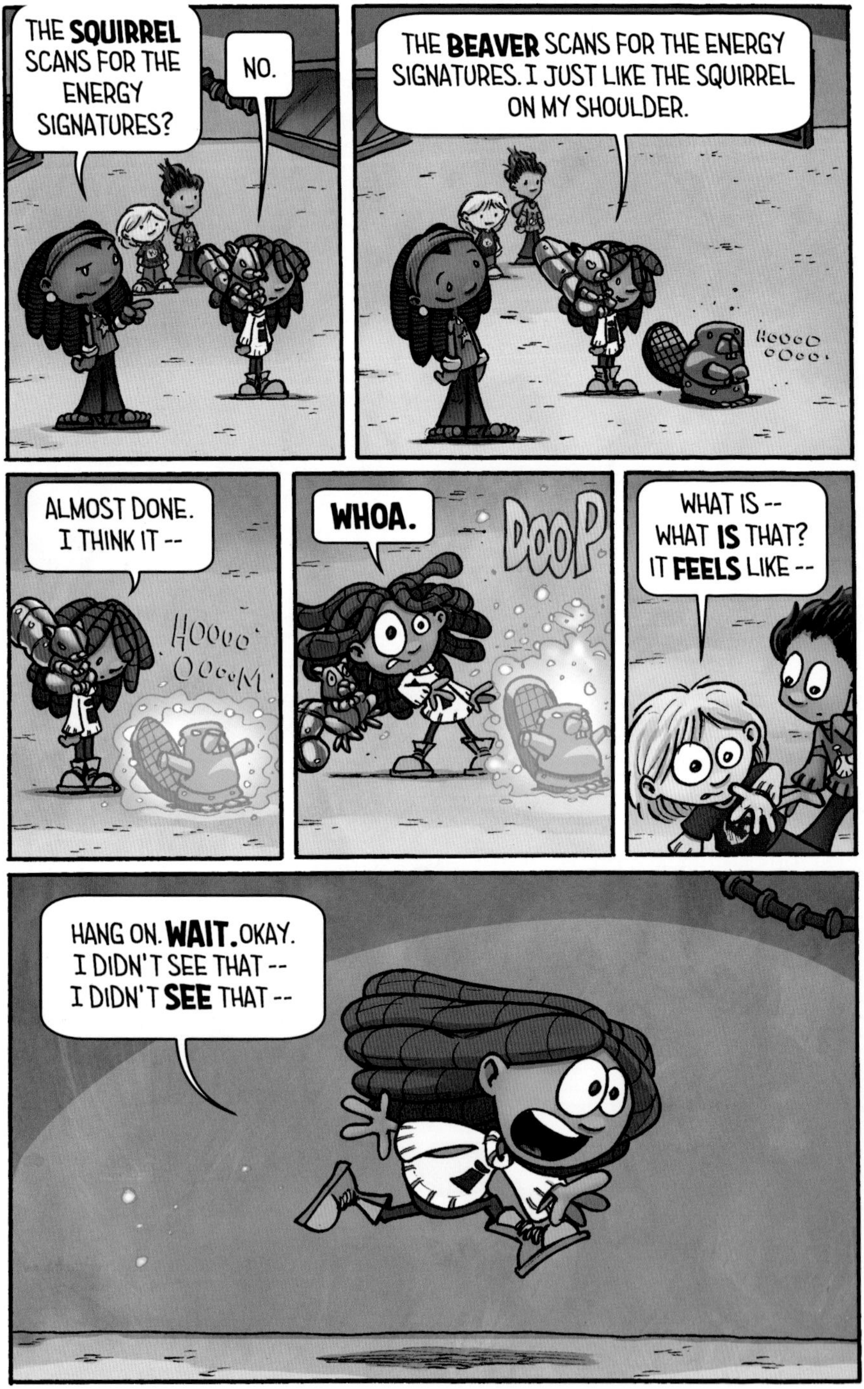
THE **SQUIRREL** SCANS FOR THE ENERGY SIGNATURES?
NO.
THE **BEAVER** SCANS FOR THE ENERGY SIGNATURES. I JUST LIKE THE SQUIRREL ON MY SHOULDER.
HOOOO OOOO.
ALMOST DONE. I THINK IT --
HOOOO OOOOM
WHOA.
DOOP
WHAT IS -- WHAT **IS** THAT? IT **FEELS** LIKE --
HANG ON. **WAIT.** OKAY. I DIDN'T SEE THAT -- I DIDN'T **SEE** THAT --

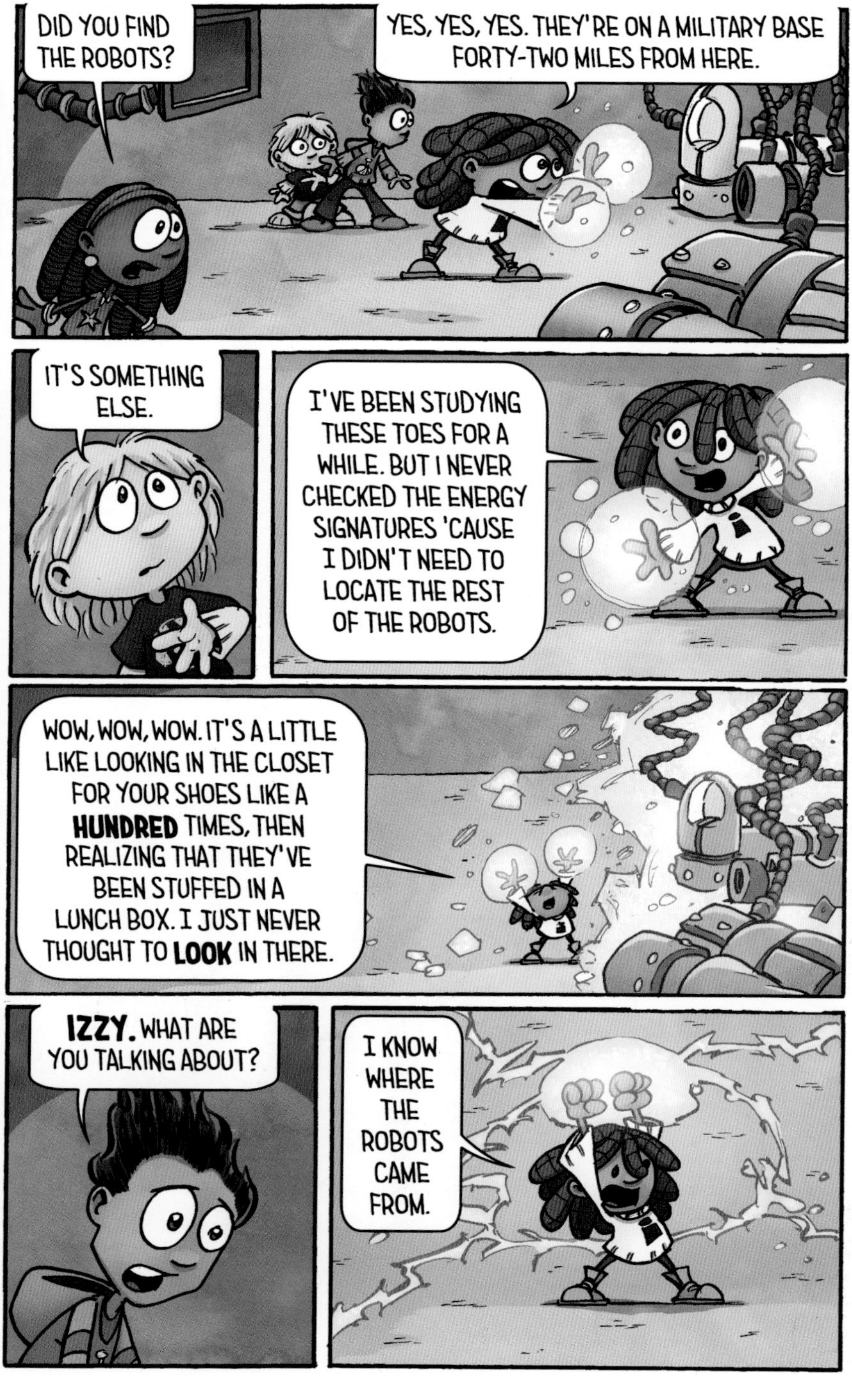

DID YOU FIND THE ROBOTS?
YES, YES, YES. THEY'RE ON A MILITARY BASE FORTY-TWO MILES FROM HERE.
IT'S SOMETHING ELSE.
I'VE BEEN STUDYING THESE TOES FOR A WHILE. BUT I NEVER CHECKED THE ENERGY SIGNATURES 'CAUSE I DIDN'T NEED TO LOCATE THE REST OF THE ROBOTS.
WOW, WOW, WOW. IT'S A LITTLE LIKE LOOKING IN THE CLOSET FOR YOUR SHOES LIKE A **HUNDRED** TIMES, THEN REALIZING THAT THEY'VE BEEN STUFFED IN A LUNCH BOX. I JUST NEVER THOUGHT TO **LOOK** IN THERE.
IZZY. WHAT ARE YOU TALKING ABOUT?
I KNOW WHERE THE ROBOTS CAME FROM.

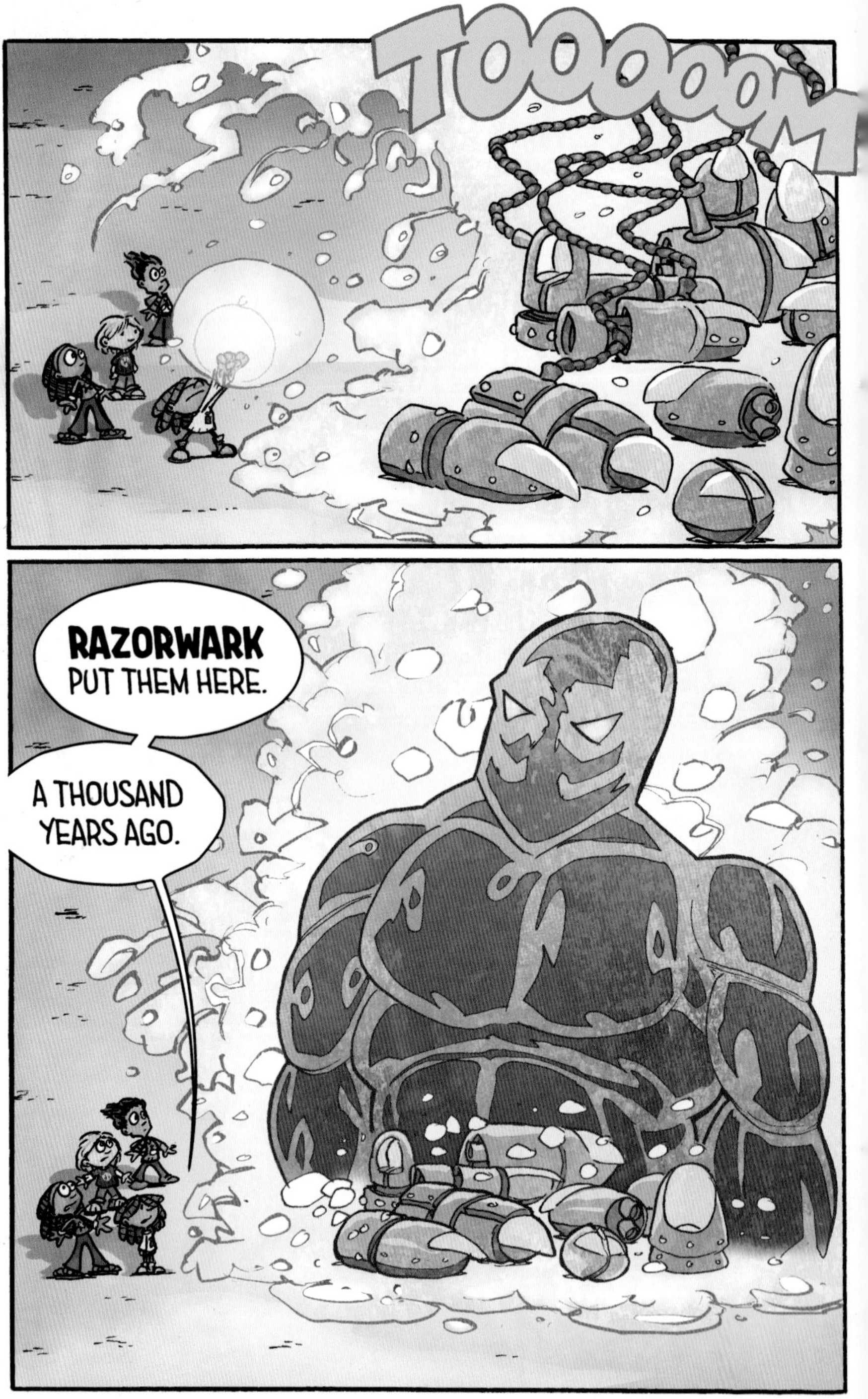
TOOOOOM
RAZORWARK PUT THEM HERE.
A THOUSAND YEARS AGO.

7

SECTOR E

YOU SEE, HE DID IT SO WELL -- HE MASKED THEM -- HE MADE THEM DIFFERENT -- LIKE A CAT DRESSED IN RABBIT FUR --
NEED TO FIND, NEED TO FIND -- **THERE! THE PORTAL --** TOTALLY DIFFERENT PORTAL -- BUT STILL -- **YES --** THAT WAS HOW --

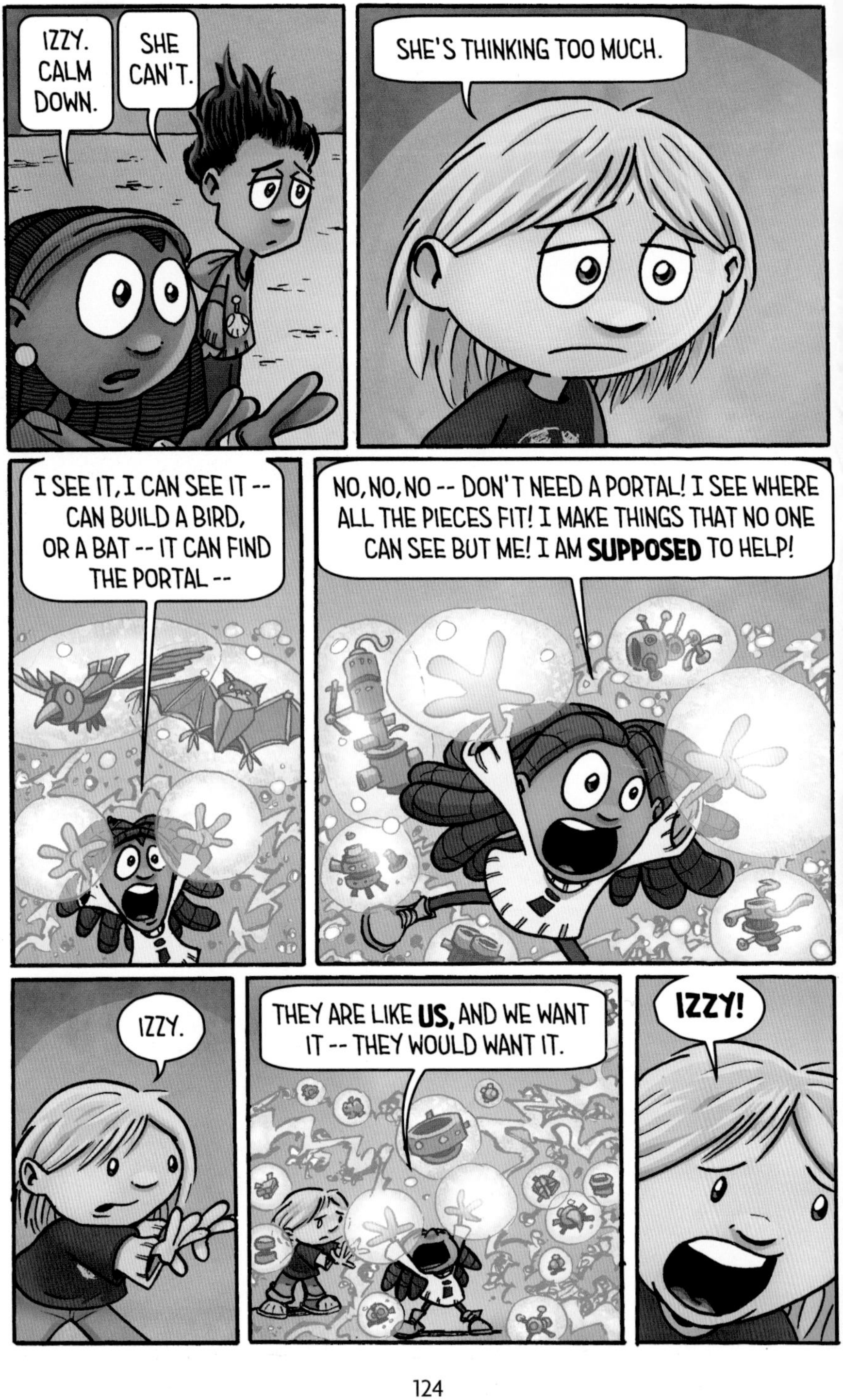
IZZY. CALM DOWN.
SHE CAN'T.
SHE'S THINKING TOO MUCH.
I SEE IT, I CAN SEE IT -- CAN BUILD A BIRD, OR A BAT -- IT CAN FIND THE PORTAL --
NO, NO, NO -- DON'T NEED A PORTAL! I SEE WHERE ALL THE PIECES FIT! I MAKE THINGS THAT NO ONE CAN SEE BUT ME! I AM SUPPOSED TO HELP!
IZZY.
THEY ARE LIKE US, AND WE WANT IT -- THEY WOULD WANT IT.
IZZY!

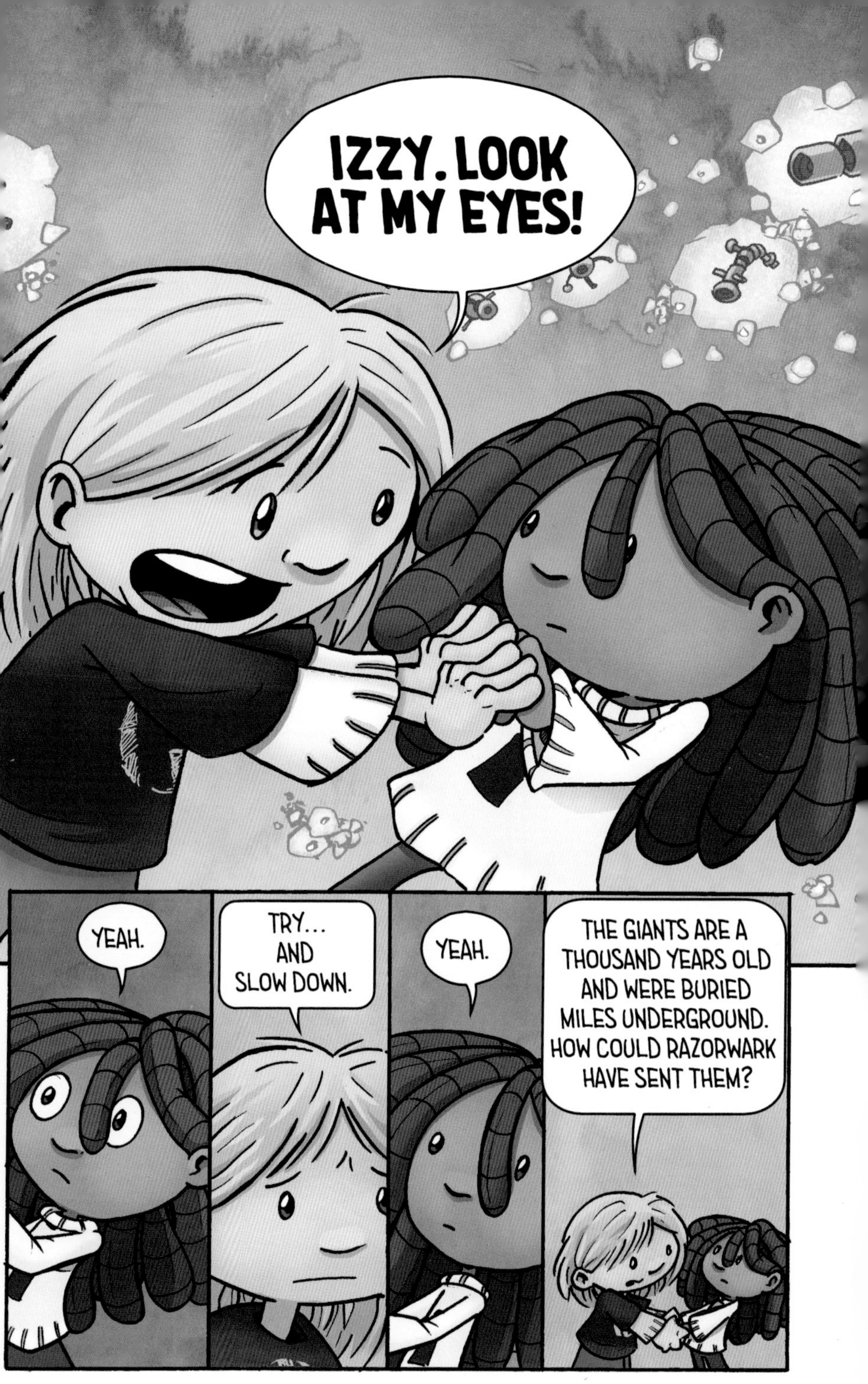
IZZY. LOOK AT MY EYES!
YEAH.
TRY... AND SLOW DOWN.
YEAH.
THE GIANTS ARE A THOUSAND YEARS OLD AND WERE BURIED MILES UNDERGROUND. HOW COULD RAZORWARK HAVE SENT THEM?

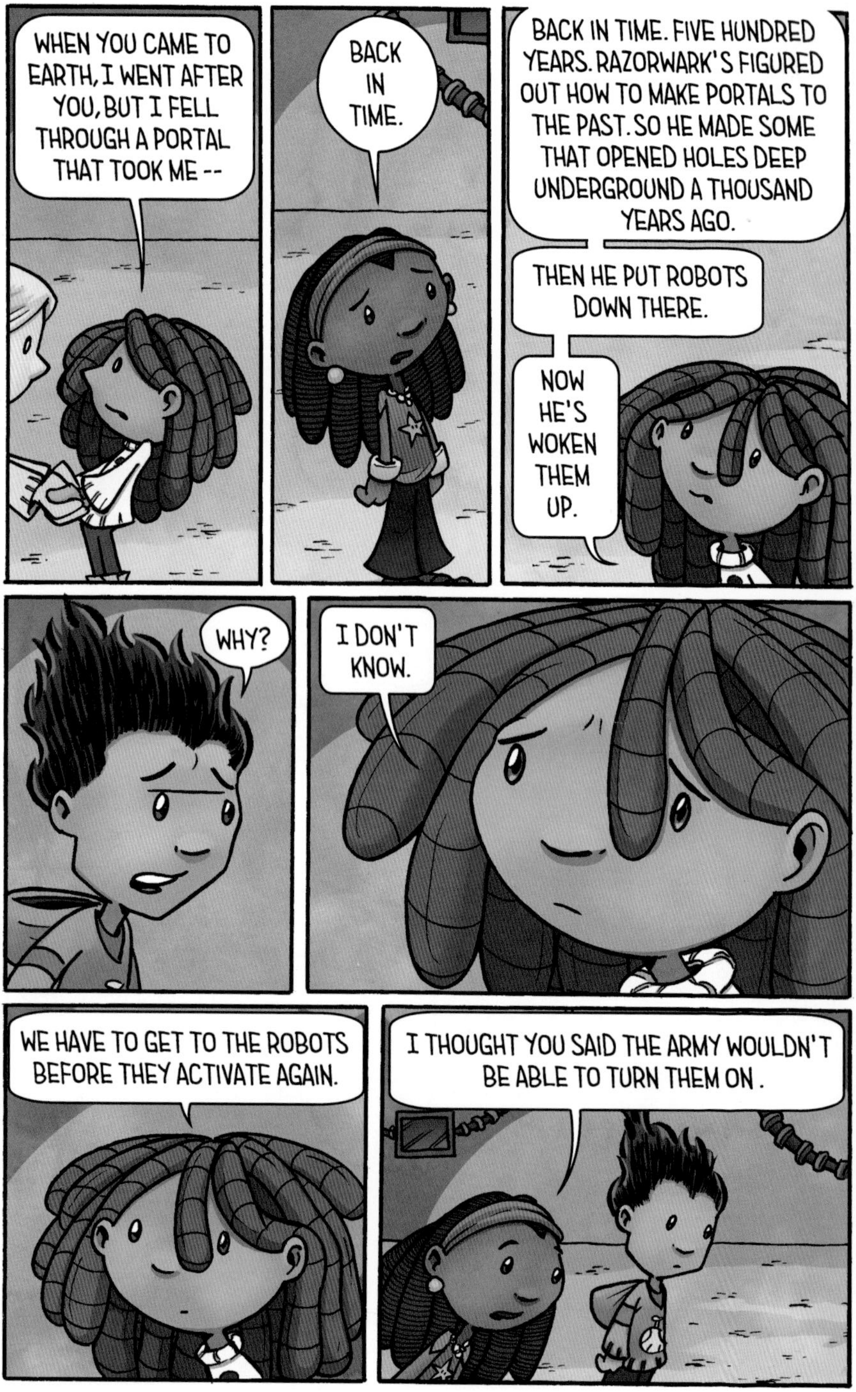
WHEN YOU CAME TO EARTH, I WENT AFTER YOU, BUT I FELL THROUGH A PORTAL THAT TOOK ME --
BACK IN TIME.
BACK IN TIME. FIVE HUNDRED YEARS. RAZORWARK'S FIGURED OUT HOW TO MAKE PORTALS TO THE PAST. SO HE MADE SOME THAT OPENED HOLES DEEP UNDERGROUND A THOUSAND YEARS AGO.
THEN HE PUT ROBOTS DOWN THERE.
NOW HE'S WOKEN THEM UP.
WHY?
I DON'T KNOW.
WE HAVE TO GET TO THE ROBOTS BEFORE THEY ACTIVATE AGAIN.
I THOUGHT YOU SAID THE ARMY WOULDN'T BE ABLE TO TURN THEM ON.

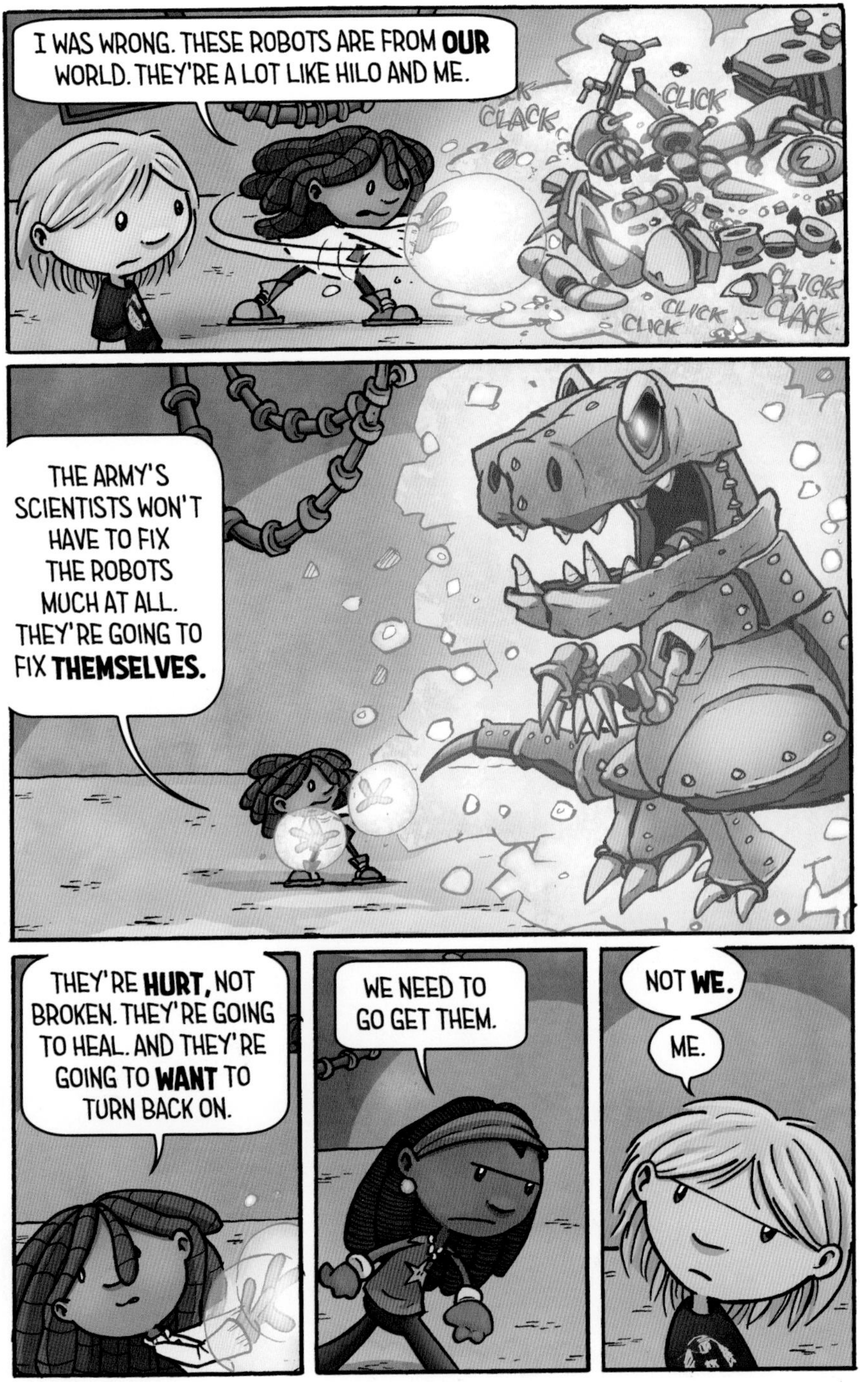
I WAS WRONG. THESE ROBOTS ARE FROM **OUR** WORLD. THEY'RE A LOT LIKE HILO AND ME.
CLACK
CLICK
CLICK
CLICK
CLICK
CLACK
CLICK
CLACK
THE ARMY'S SCIENTISTS WON'T HAVE TO FIX THE ROBOTS MUCH AT ALL. THEY'RE GOING TO FIX **THEMSELVES.**
THEY'RE **HURT,** NOT BROKEN. THEY'RE GOING TO HEAL. AND THEY'RE GOING TO **WANT** TO TURN BACK ON.
WE NEED TO GO GET THEM.
NOT **WE.**
ME.

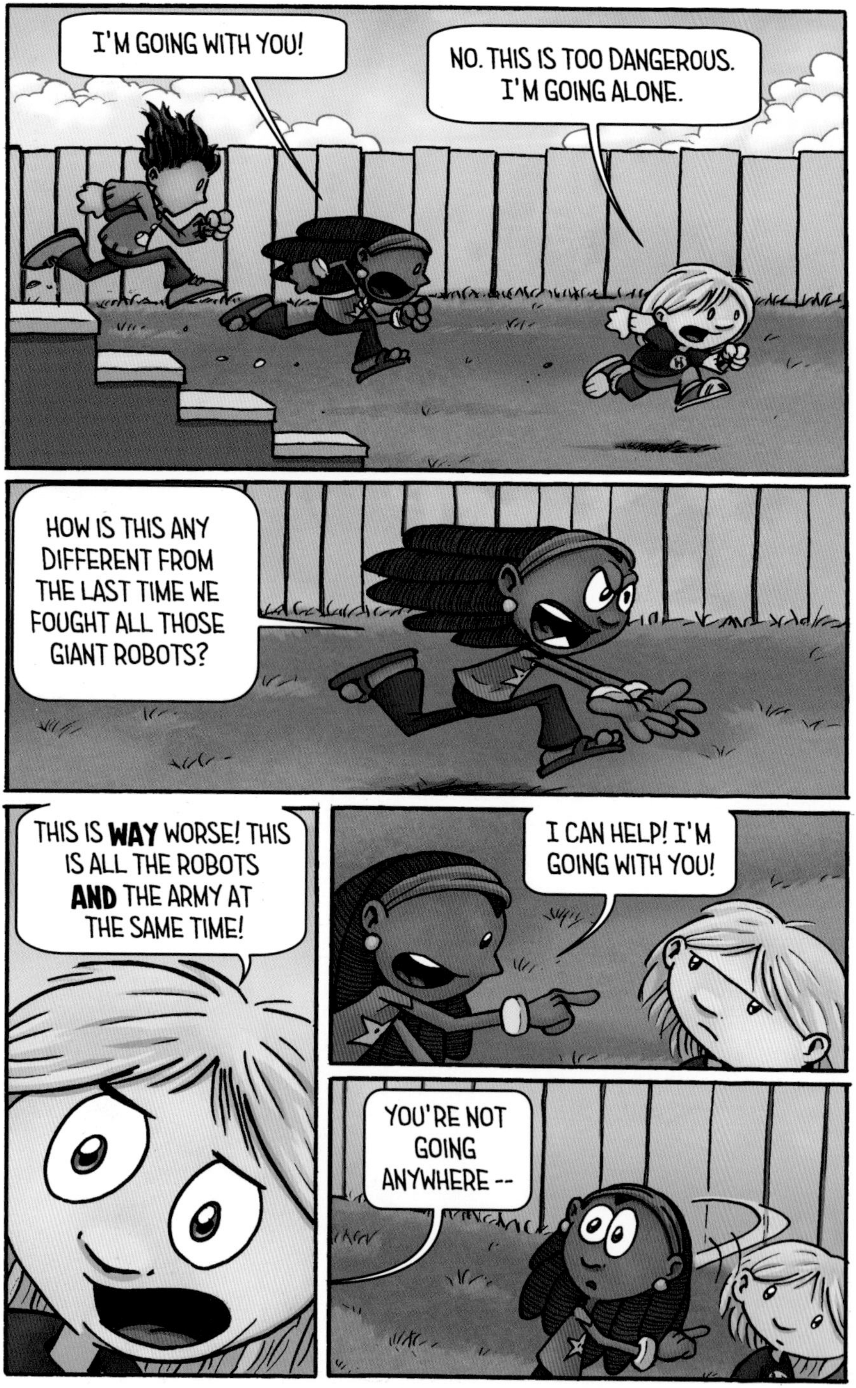
I'M GOING WITH YOU!
NO. THIS IS TOO DANGEROUS. I'M GOING ALONE.
HOW IS THIS ANY DIFFERENT FROM THE LAST TIME WE FOUGHT ALL THOSE GIANT ROBOTS?
THIS IS **WAY** WORSE! THIS IS ALL THE ROBOTS **AND** THE ARMY AT THE SAME TIME!
I CAN HELP! I'M GOING WITH YOU!
YOU'RE NOT GOING ANYWHERE --

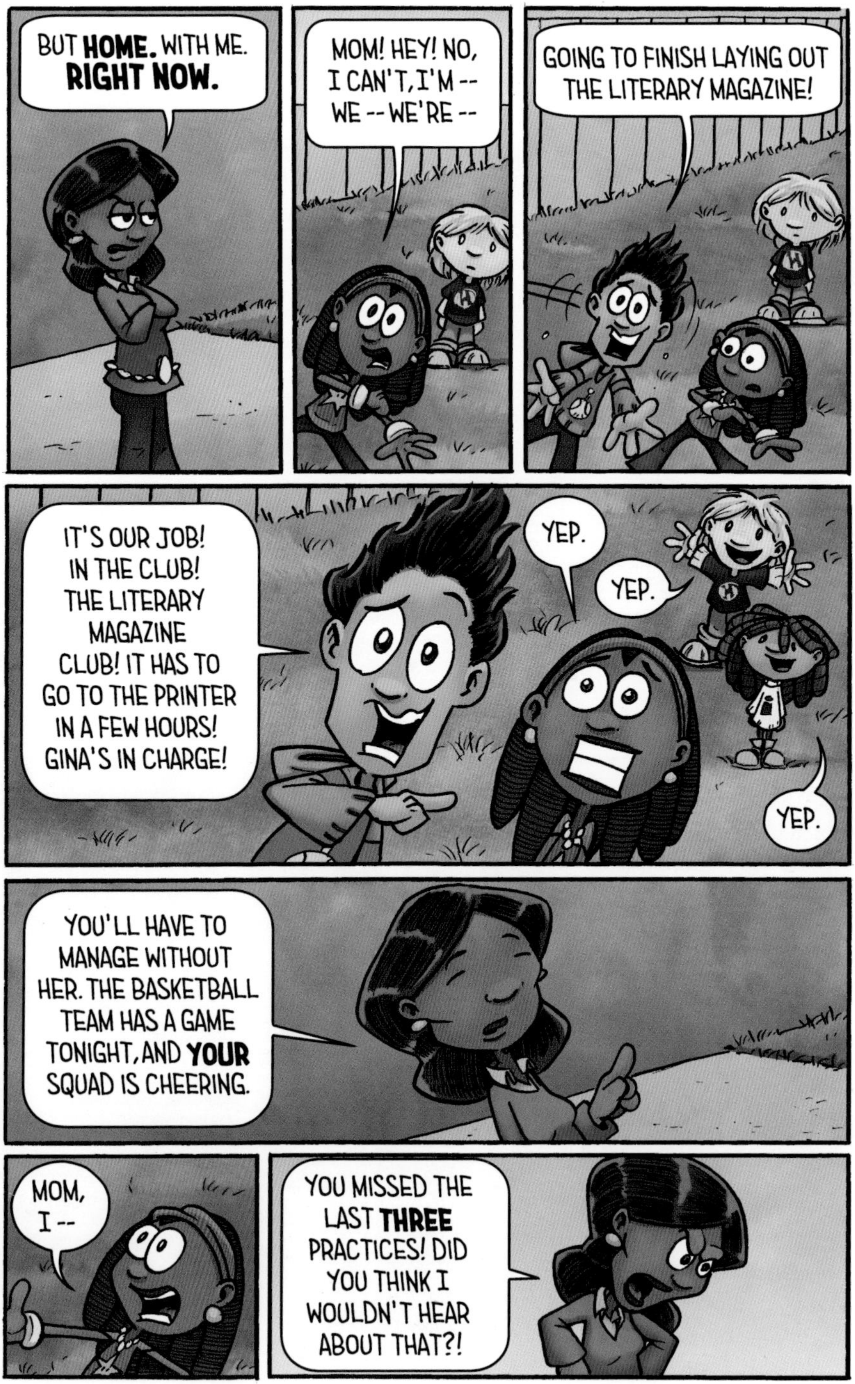
BUT **HOME.** WITH ME. **RIGHT NOW.**
MOM! HEY! NO, I CAN'T, I'M -- WE -- WE'RE --
GOING TO FINISH LAYING OUT THE LITERARY MAGAZINE!
IT'S OUR JOB! IN THE CLUB! THE LITERARY MAGAZINE CLUB! IT HAS TO GO TO THE PRINTER IN A FEW HOURS! GINA'S IN CHARGE!
YEP.
YEP.
YEP.
YOU'LL HAVE TO MANAGE WITHOUT HER. THE BASKETBALL TEAM HAS A GAME TONIGHT, AND **YOUR** SQUAD IS CHEERING.
MOM, I --
YOU MISSED THE LAST **THREE** PRACTICES! DID YOU THINK I WOULDN'T HEAR ABOUT THAT?!

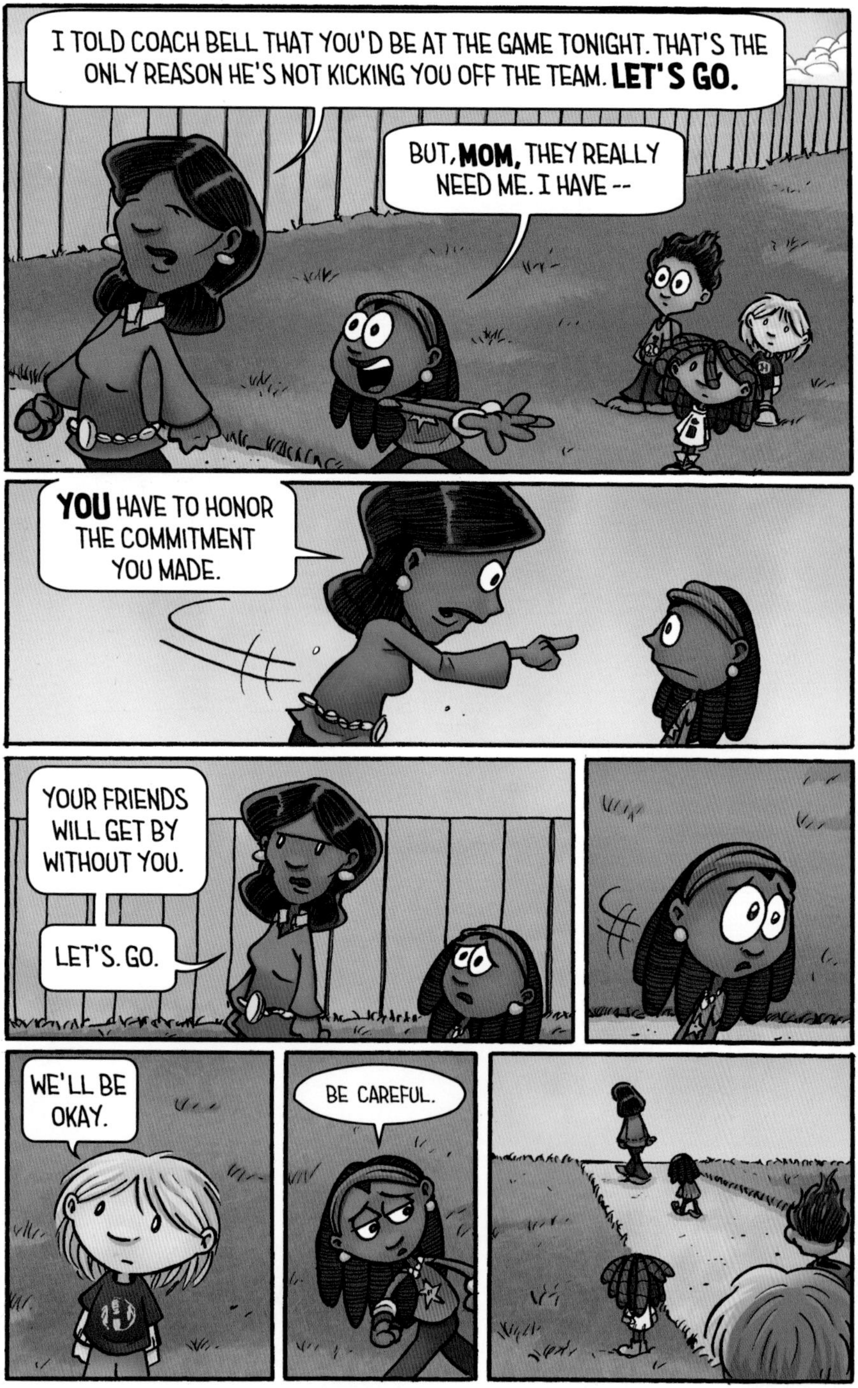

I TOLD COACH BELL THAT YOU'D BE AT THE GAME TONIGHT. THAT'S THE ONLY REASON HE'S NOT KICKING YOU OFF THE TEAM. **LET'S GO.**
BUT, **MOM,** THEY REALLY NEED ME. I HAVE --
YOU HAVE TO HONOR THE COMMITMENT YOU MADE.
YOUR FRIENDS WILL GET BY WITHOUT YOU.
LET'S. GO.
WE'LL BE OKAY.
BE CAREFUL.

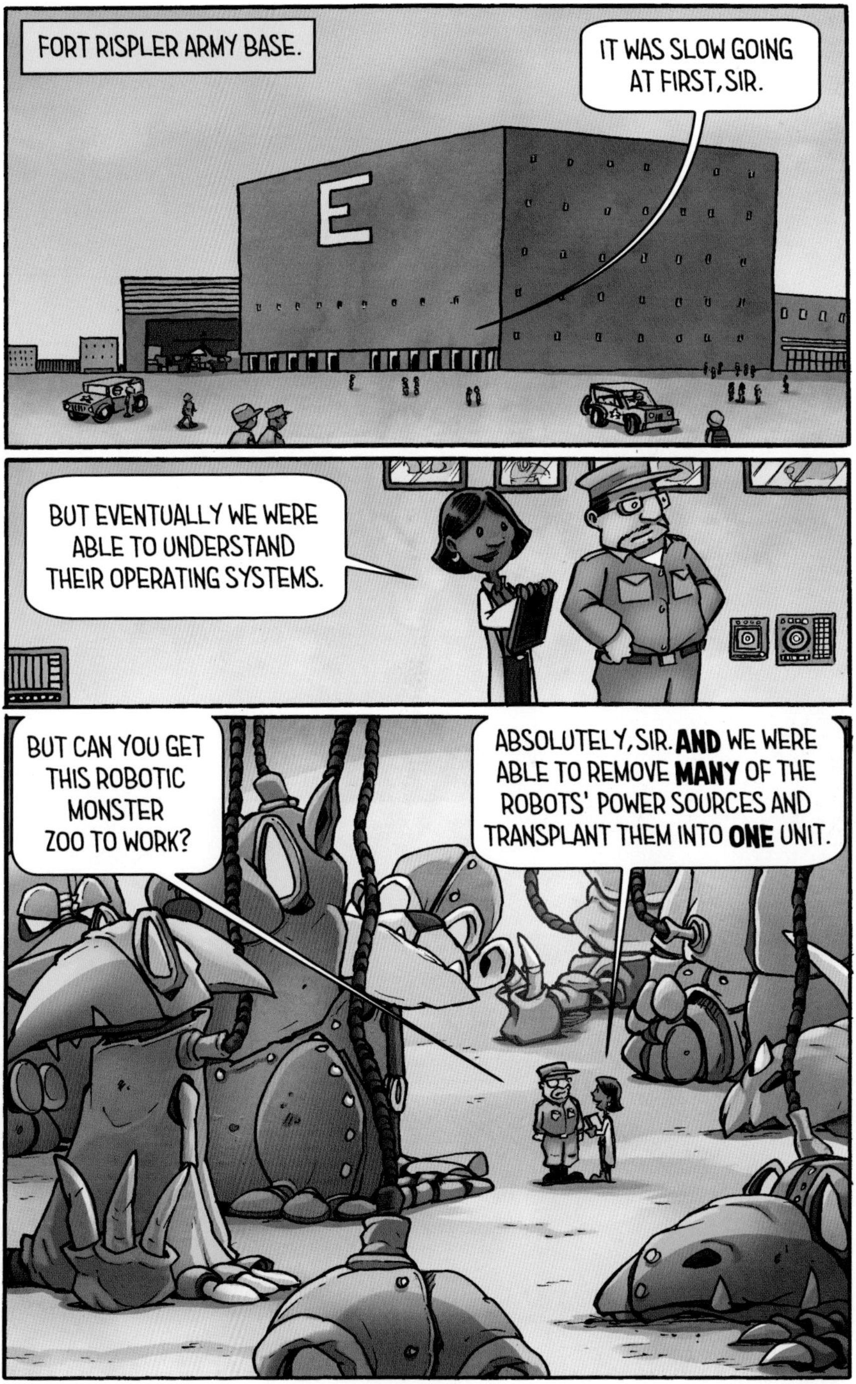
FORT RISPLER ARMY BASE.
IT WAS SLOW GOING AT FIRST, SIR.
E
BUT EVENTUALLY WE WERE ABLE TO UNDERSTAND THEIR OPERATING SYSTEMS.
BUT CAN YOU GET THIS ROBOTIC MONSTER ZOO TO WORK?
ABSOLUTELY, SIR. **AND** WE WERE ABLE TO REMOVE **MANY** OF THE ROBOTS' POWER SOURCES AND TRANSPLANT THEM INTO **ONE** UNIT.

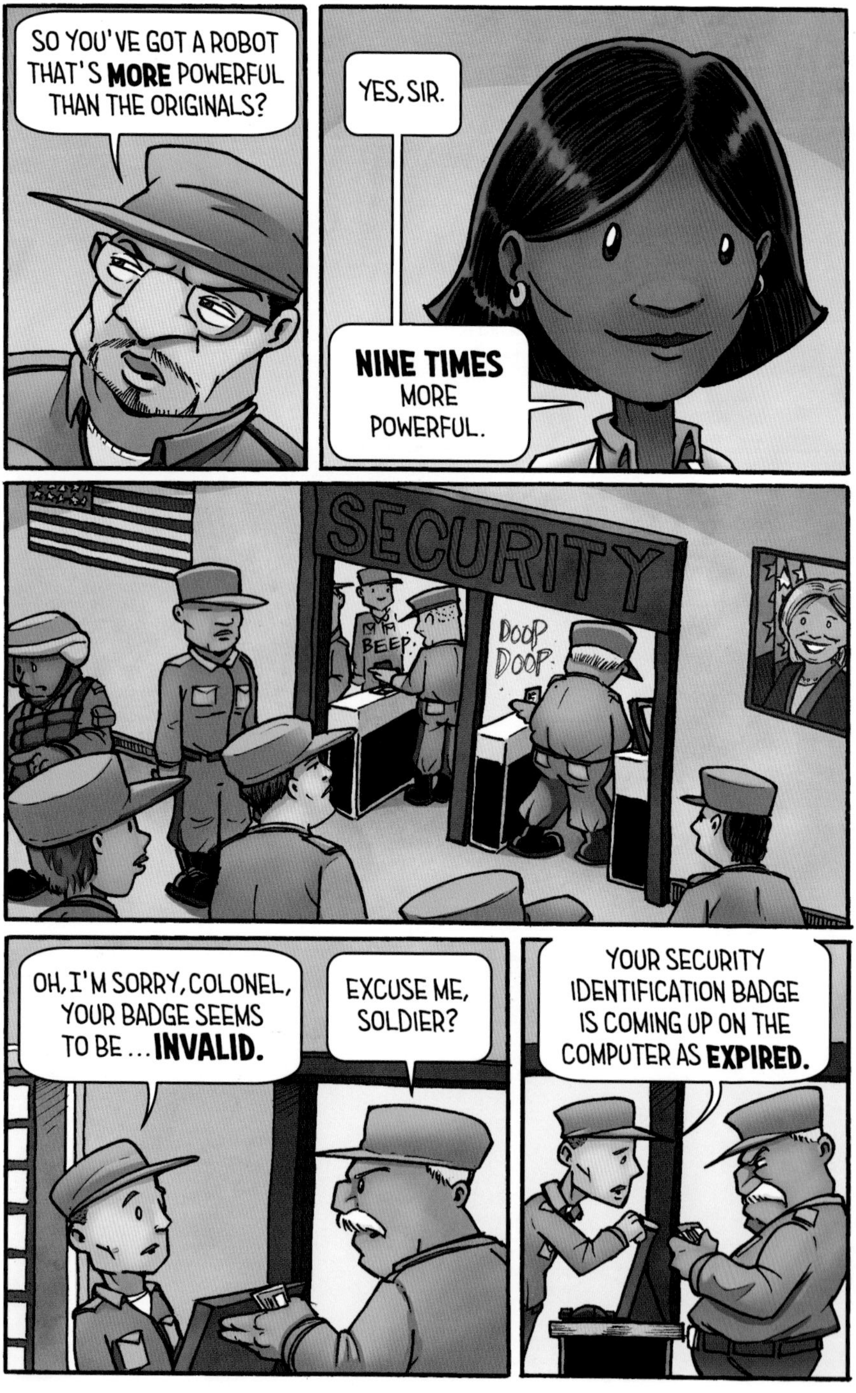
SO YOU'VE GOT A ROBOT THAT'S **MORE** POWERFUL THAN THE ORIGINALS?
YES, SIR.
NINE TIMES MORE POWERFUL.
SECURITY
BEEP
DOOP DOOP
OH, I'M SORRY, COLONEL, YOUR BADGE SEEMS TO BE . . . **INVALID.**
EXCUSE ME, SOLDIER?
YOUR SECURITY IDENTIFICATION BADGE IS COMING UP ON THE COMPUTER AS **EXPIRED.**

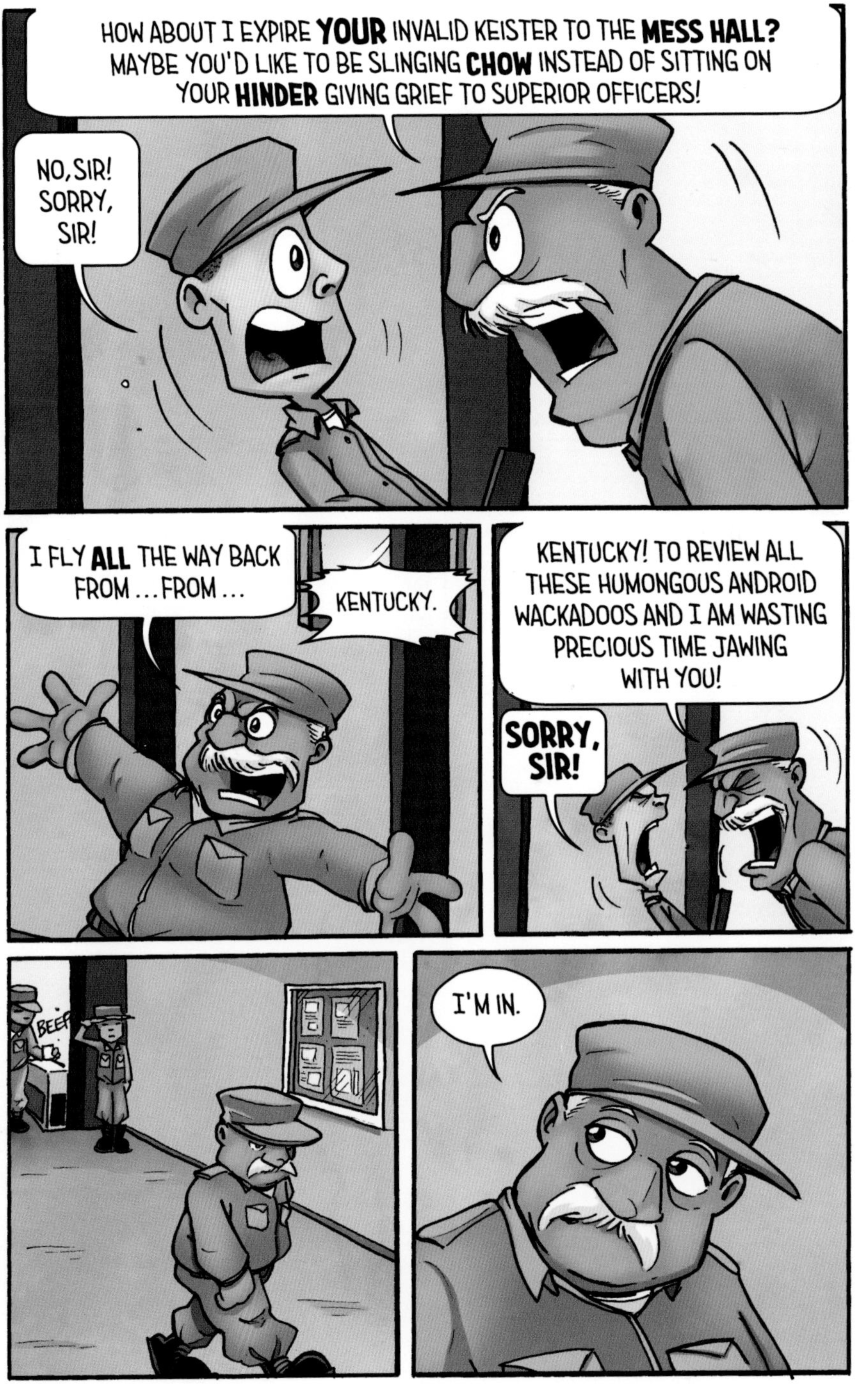
HOW ABOUT I EXPIRE **YOUR** INVALID KEISTER TO THE **MESS HALL?** MAYBE YOU'D LIKE TO BE SLINGING **CHOW** INSTEAD OF SITTING ON YOUR **HINDER** GIVING GRIEF TO SUPERIOR OFFICERS!
NO, SIR! SORRY, SIR!
I FLY **ALL** THE WAY BACK FROM ... FROM ...
KENTUCKY.
KENTUCKY! TO REVIEW ALL THESE HUMONGOUS ANDROID WACKADOOS AND I AM WASTING PRECIOUS TIME JAWING WITH YOU!
SORRY, SIR!
BEEP
I'M IN.

BUT MY **ARMPITS** ITCH.

DON'T SCRATCH!

SCRETCH

BOOP

IT DISRUPTS THE HOLOGRAM.

DEE BOOP

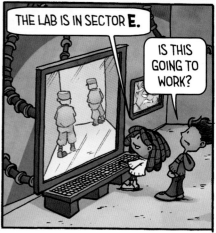

THE LAB IS IN SECTOR **E.**

IS THIS GOING TO WORK?

YEP. ALL HILO HAS TO DO IS GET TO THE LAB, FIND THE ROBOTS, ACTIVATE THE **TELEPORTER** I MADE HIM -- LIKE THIS ONE -- AND **ZAP** THE ROBOTS BACK TO US.

HERE? BUT THEY'RE **ENORMOUS!** WHERE ARE WE GOING TO PUT THEM?

I MADE ROOM.

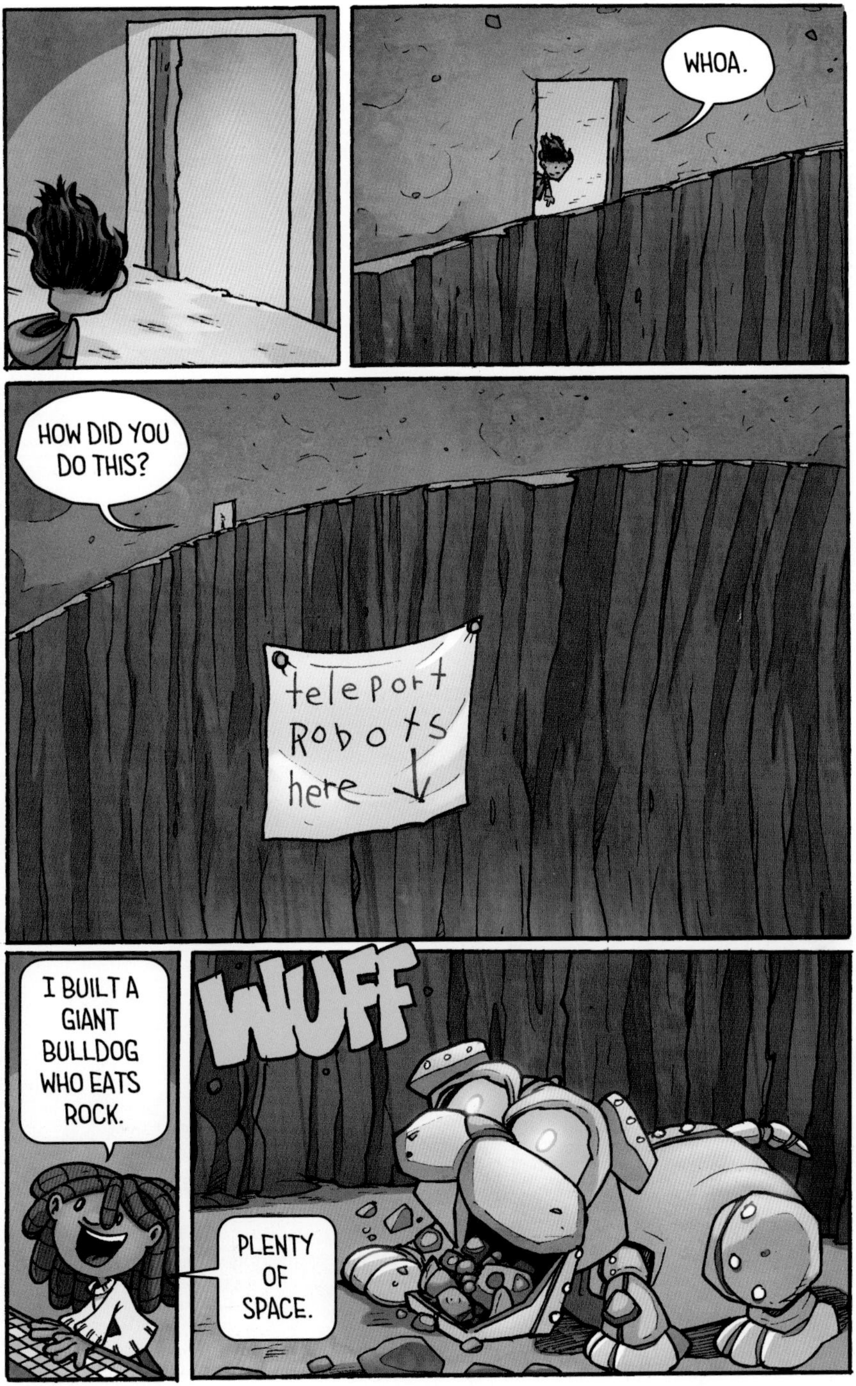
WHOA.
HOW DID YOU DO THIS?
teleport Robots here
I BUILT A GIANT BULLDOG WHO EATS ROCK.
PLENTY OF SPACE.
WUFF

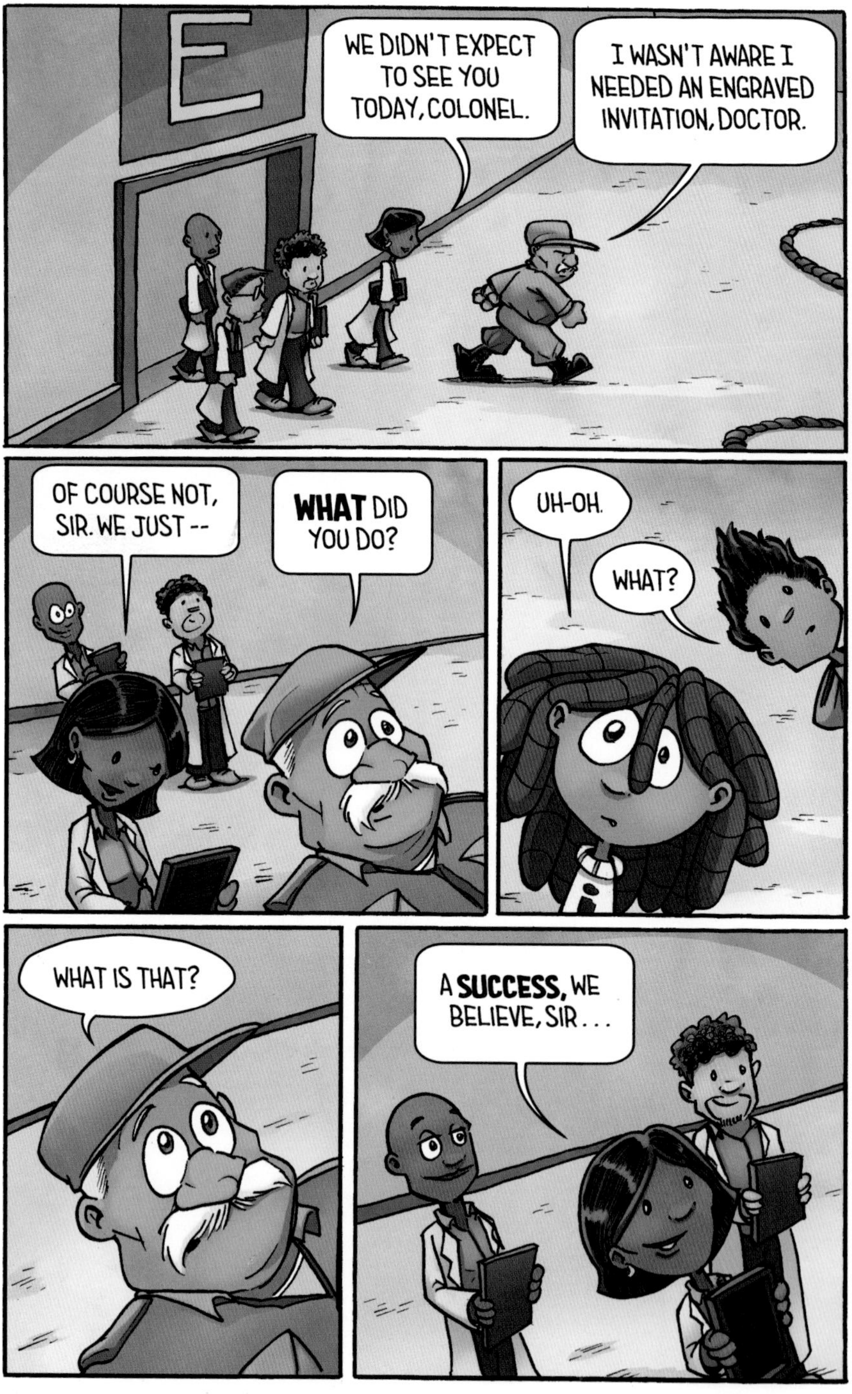
WE DIDN'T EXPECT TO SEE YOU TODAY, COLONEL.
I WASN'T AWARE I NEEDED AN ENGRAVED INVITATION, DOCTOR.
OF COURSE NOT, SIR. WE JUST --
WHAT DID YOU DO?
UH-OH.
WHAT?
WHAT IS THAT?
A SUCCESS, WE BELIEVE, SIR . . .

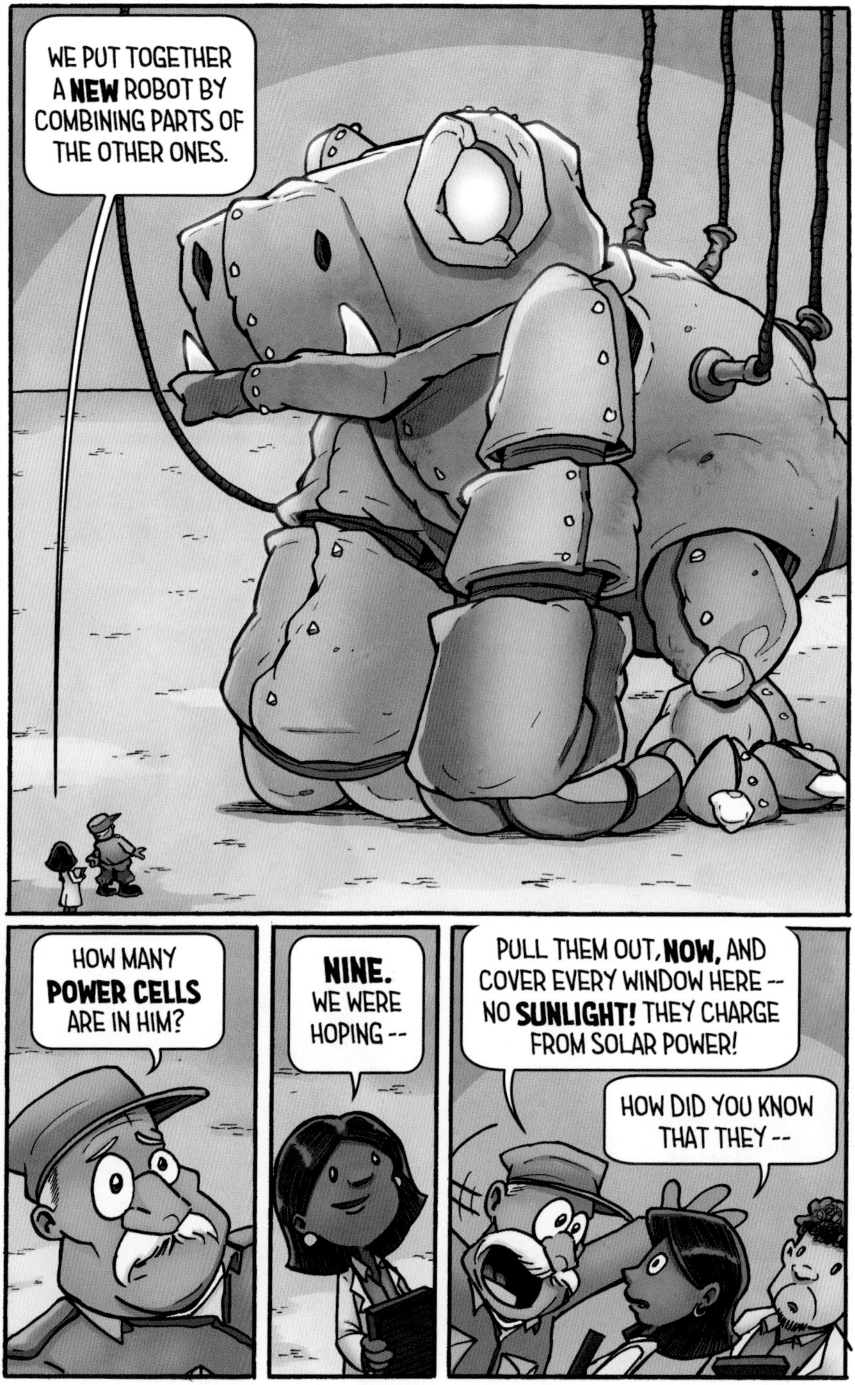
WE PUT TOGETHER A NEW ROBOT BY COMBINING PARTS OF THE OTHER ONES.
HOW MANY POWER CELLS ARE IN HIM?
NINE. WE WERE HOPING --
PULL THEM OUT, NOW, AND COVER EVERY WINDOW HERE -- NO SUNLIGHT! THEY CHARGE FROM SOLAR POWER!
HOW DID YOU KNOW THAT THEY --

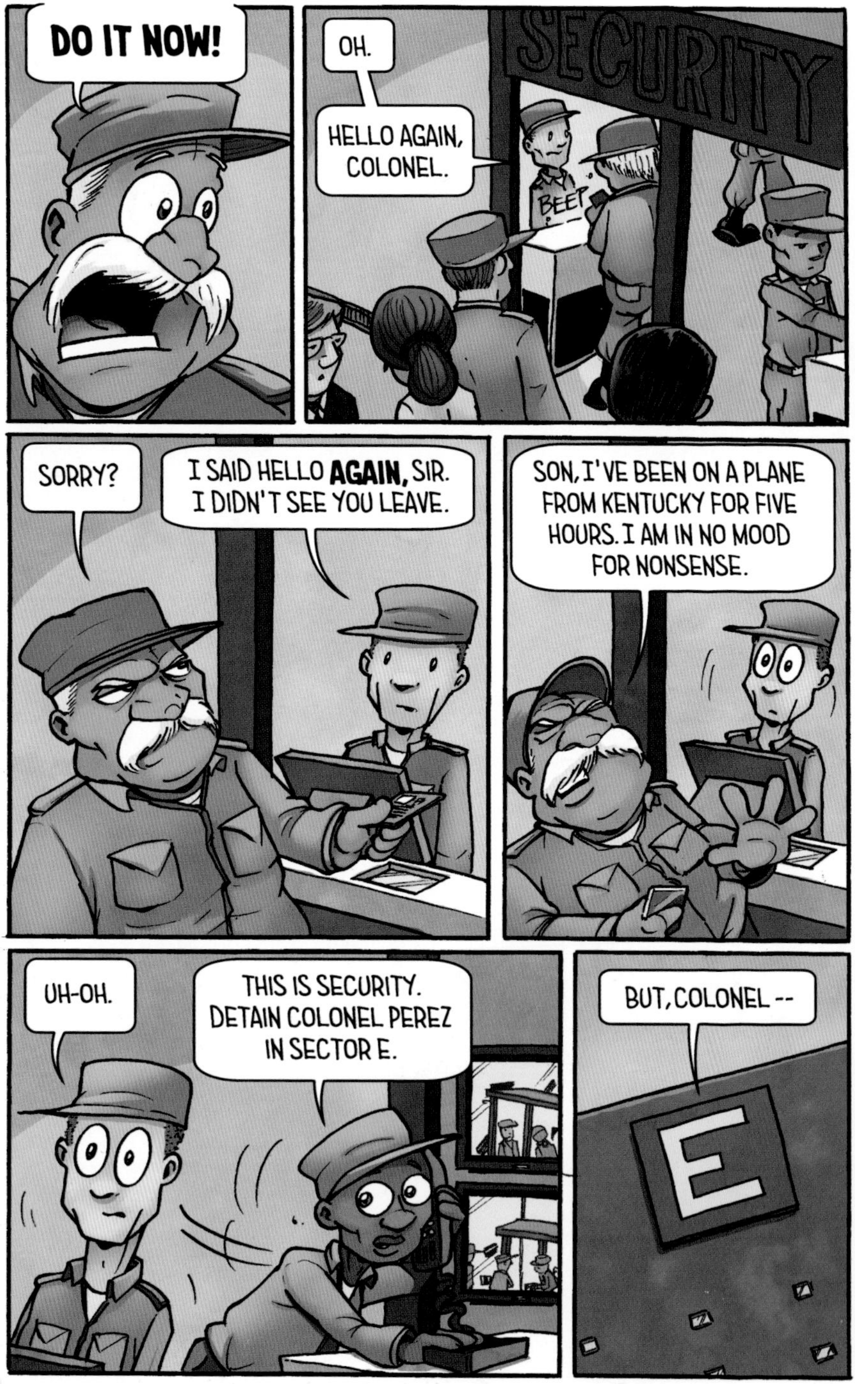
DO IT NOW!
OH.
HELLO AGAIN, COLONEL.
SECURITY
BEEP
SORRY?
I SAID HELLO **AGAIN,** SIR. I DIDN'T SEE YOU LEAVE.
SON, I'VE BEEN ON A PLANE FROM KENTUCKY FOR FIVE HOURS. I AM IN NO MOOD FOR NONSENSE.
UH-OH.
THIS IS SECURITY. DETAIN COLONEL PEREZ IN SECTOR E.
BUT, COLONEL --
E

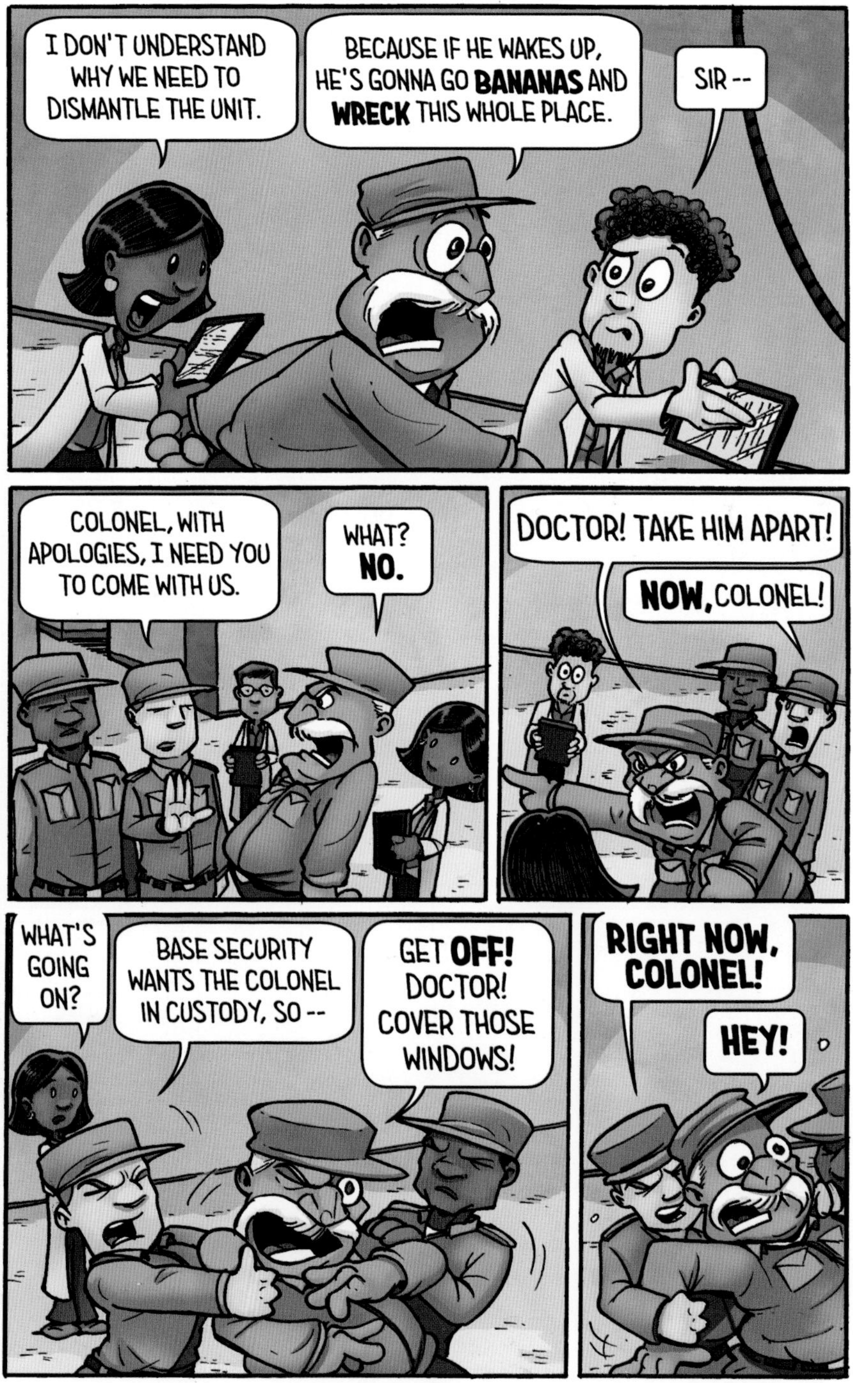
I DON'T UNDERSTAND WHY WE NEED TO DISMANTLE THE UNIT.
BECAUSE IF HE WAKES UP, HE'S GONNA GO **BANANAS** AND **WRECK** THIS WHOLE PLACE.
SIR --
COLONEL, WITH APOLOGIES, I NEED YOU TO COME WITH US.
WHAT? **NO.**
DOCTOR! TAKE HIM APART!
NOW, COLONEL!
WHAT'S GOING ON?
BASE SECURITY WANTS THE COLONEL IN CUSTODY, SO --
GET **OFF!** DOCTOR! COVER THOSE WINDOWS!
RIGHT NOW, COLONEL!
HEY!

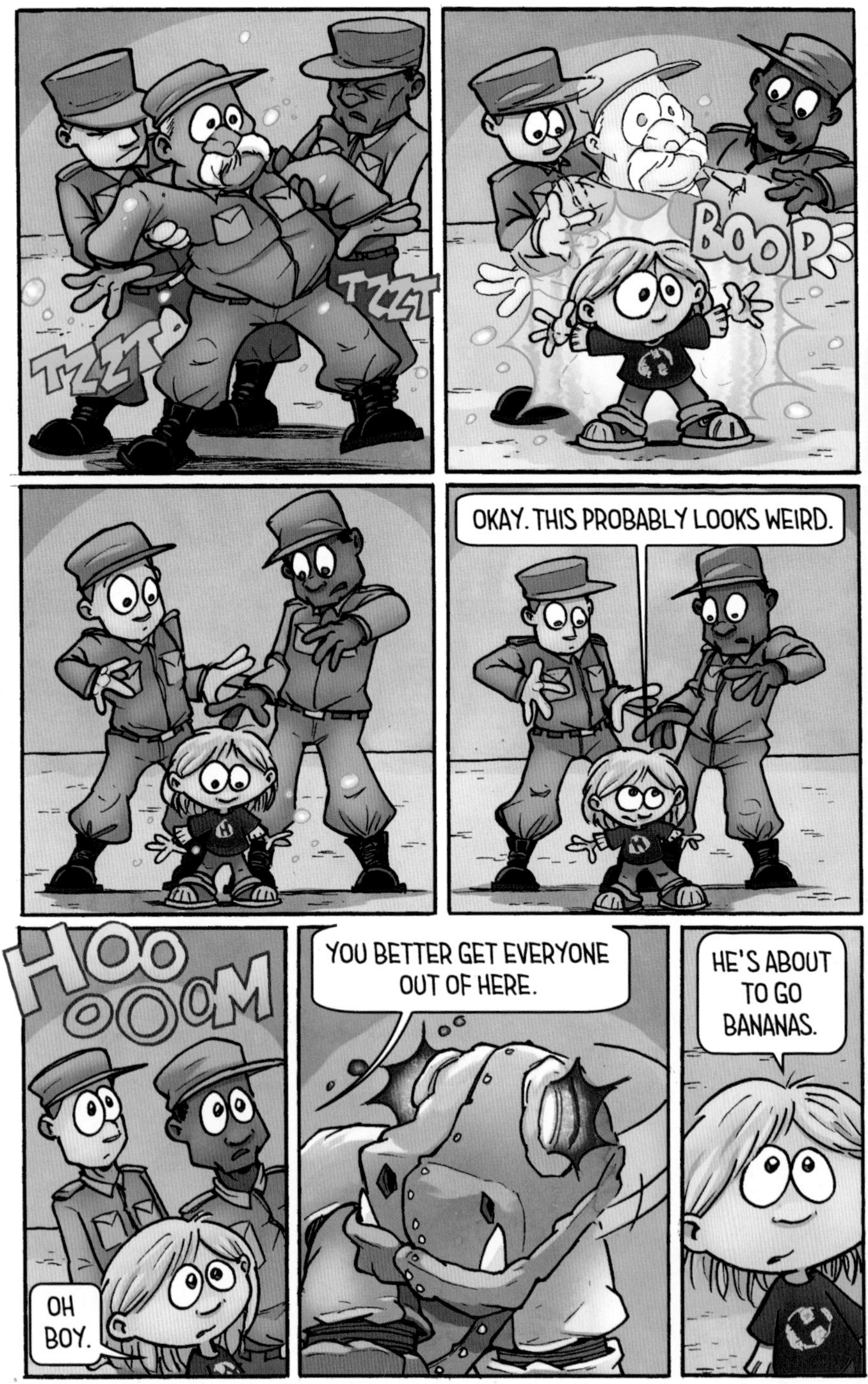
TZZT
TZZT
BOOP
OKAY. THIS PROBABLY LOOKS WEIRD.
HOOOOOM
OH BOY.
YOU BETTER GET EVERYONE OUT OF HERE.
HE'S ABOUT TO GO BANANAS.

CHAPTER 8

BANANAS

BOOM

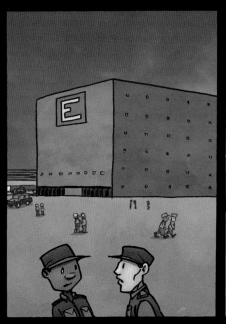

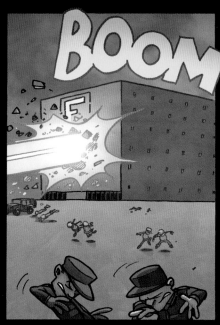

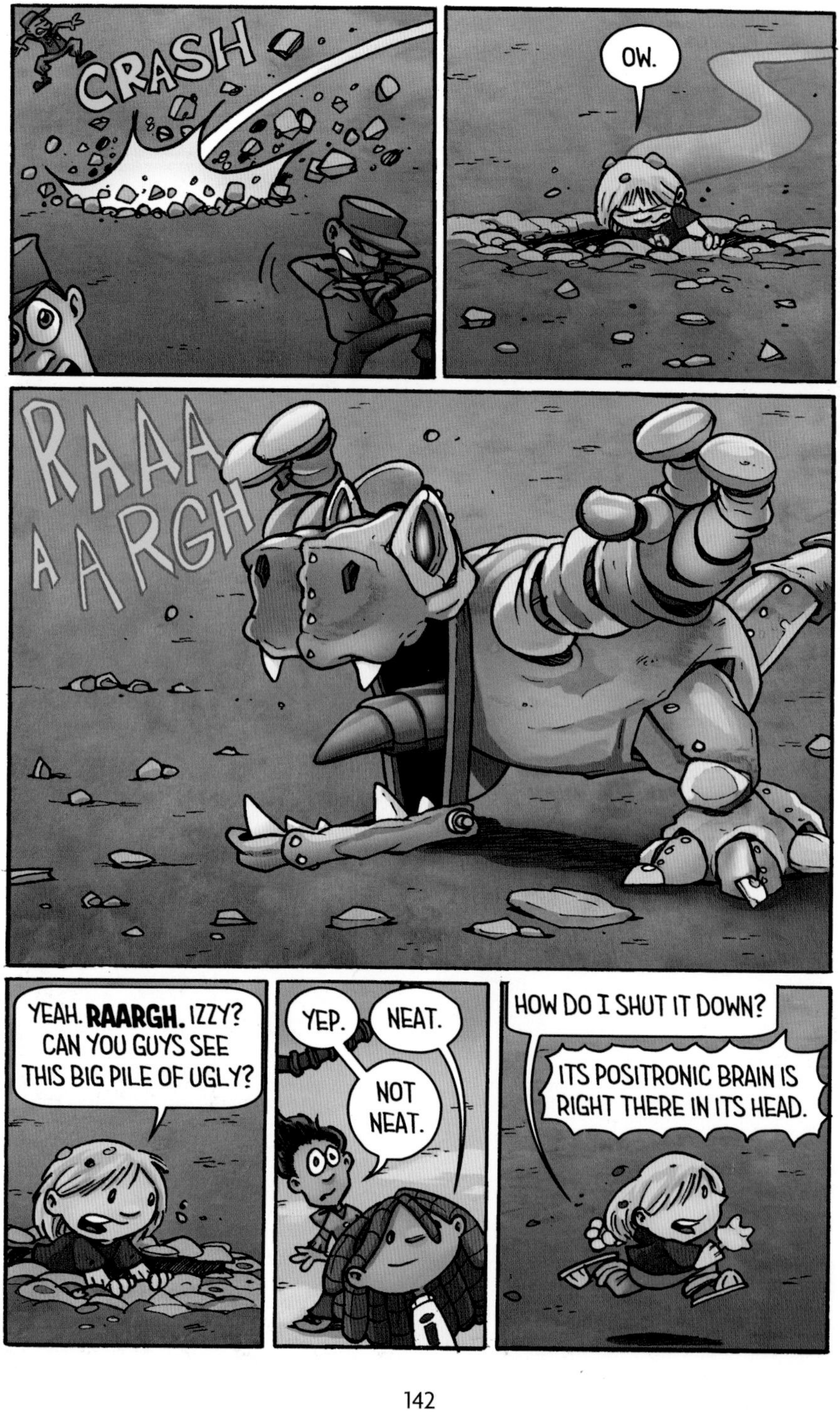
CRASH
OW.
RAAAAARGH
YEAH. **RAARGH.** IZZY? CAN YOU GUYS SEE THIS BIG PILE OF UGLY?
YEP.
NEAT.
NOT NEAT.
HOW DO I SHUT IT DOWN?
ITS POSITRONIC BRAIN IS RIGHT THERE IN ITS HEAD.

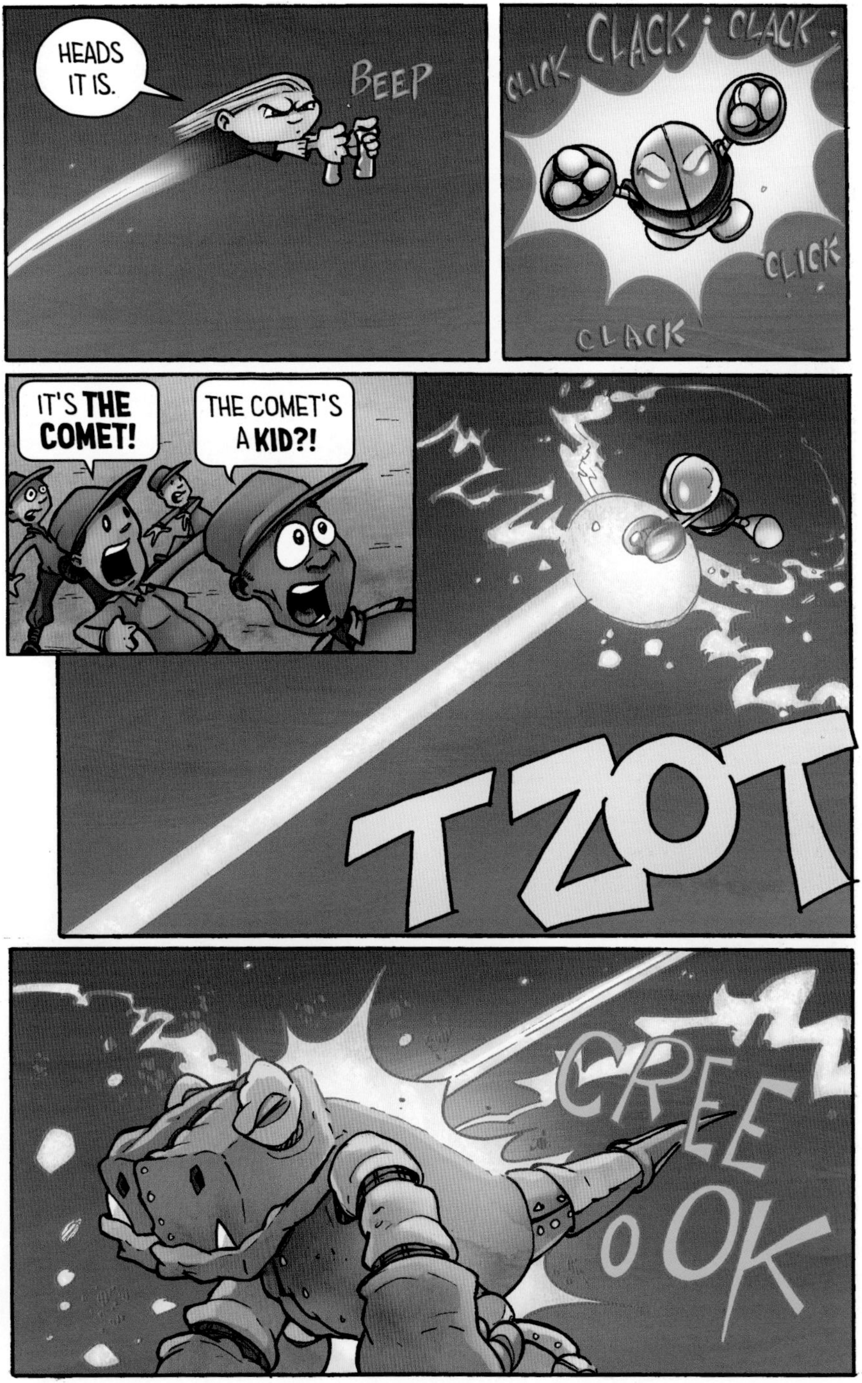
HEADS IT IS.
BEEP
CLICK CLACK CLACK
CLICK
CLACK
IT'S **THE COMET!**
THE COMET'S A **KID?!**
TZOT
CREE OOK

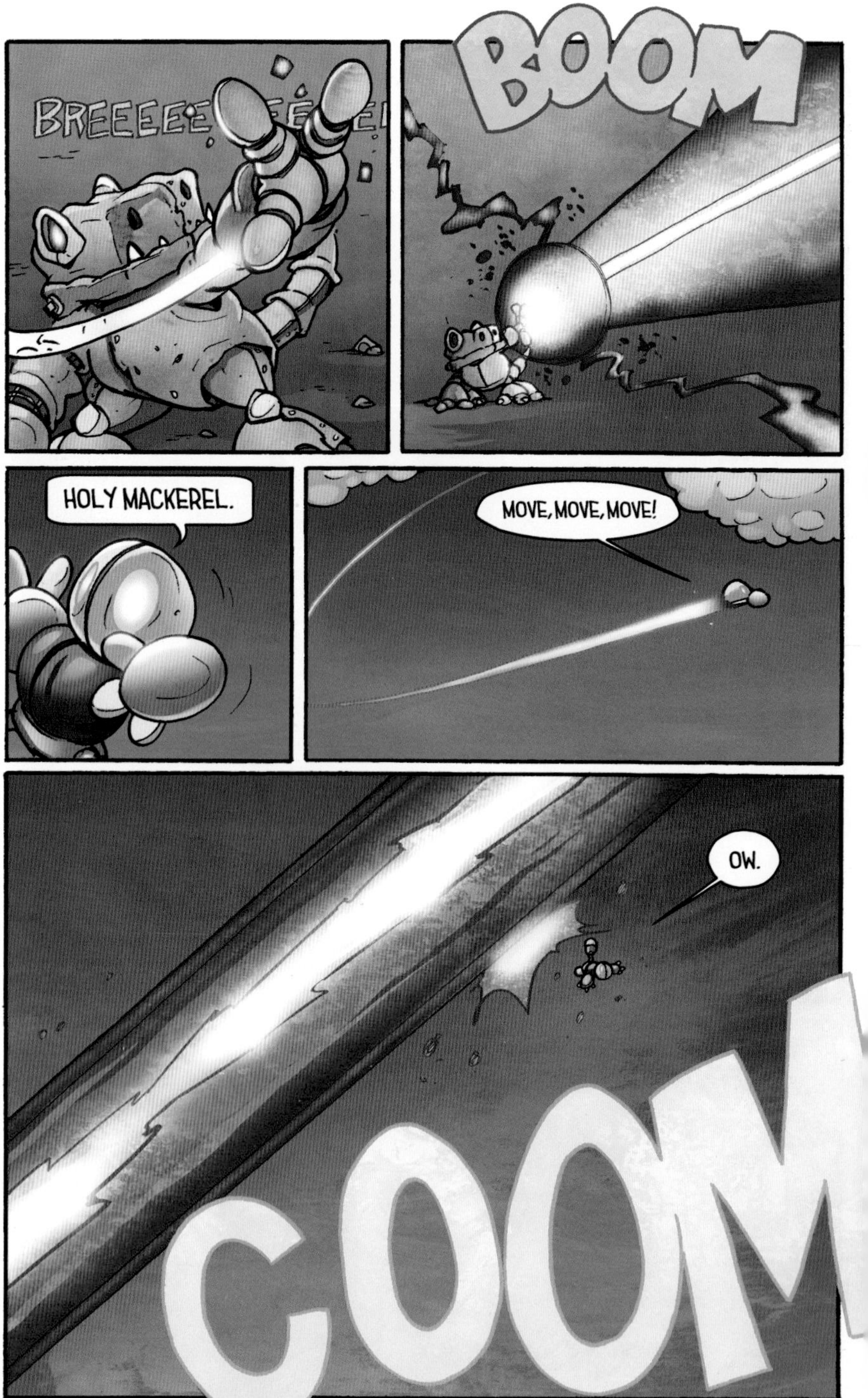
BREEEEEEEEEEEEE
BOOM
HOLY MACKEREL.
MOVE, MOVE, MOVE!
OW.
COOM

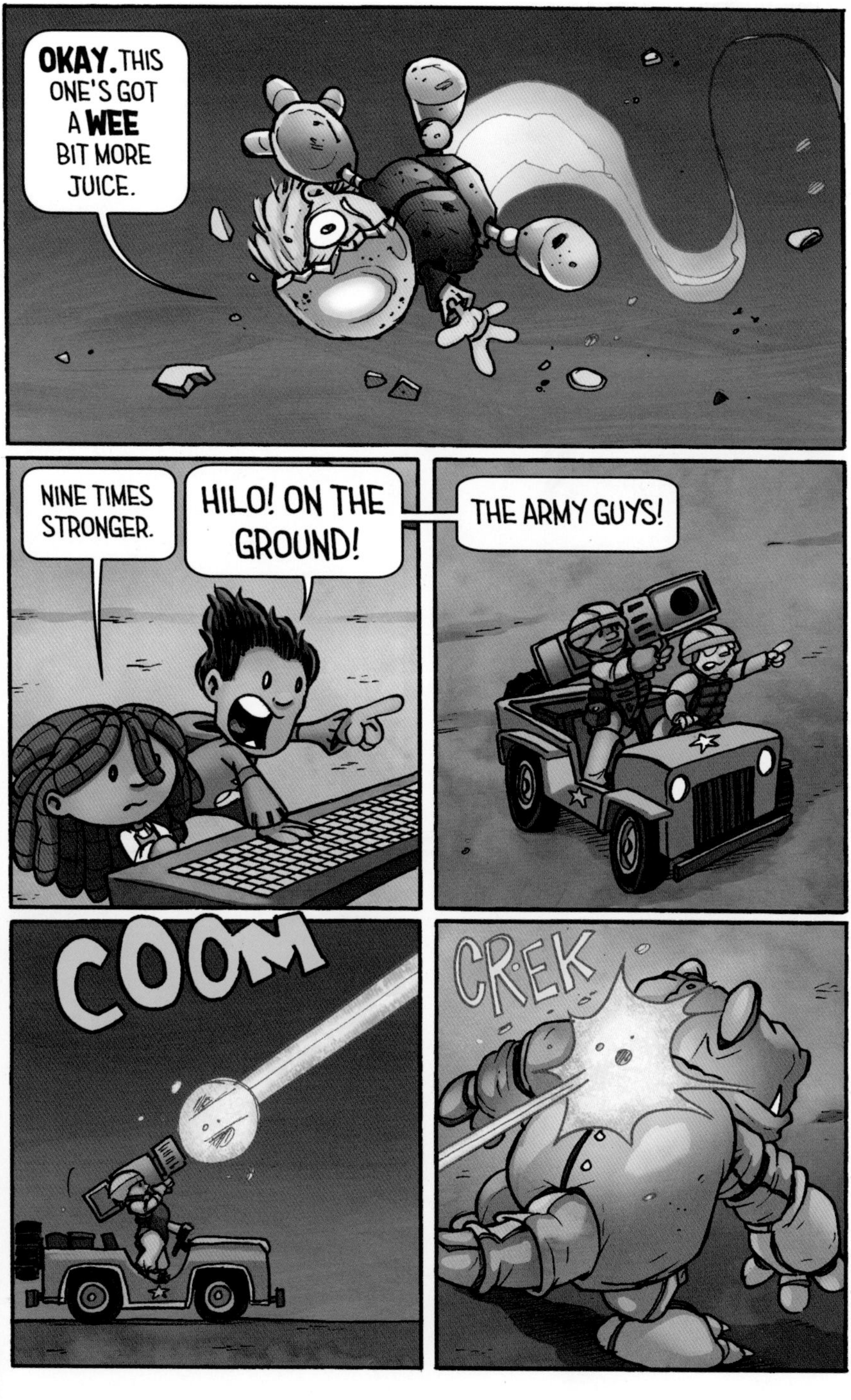

OKAY. THIS ONE'S GOT A WEE BIT MORE JUICE.
NINE TIMES STRONGER.
HILO! ON THE GROUND!
THE ARMY GUYS!
COOM
CR-EK

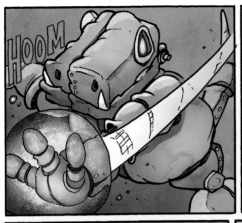

YEAH. I DON'T THINK I CAN FIGHT THIS ONE.

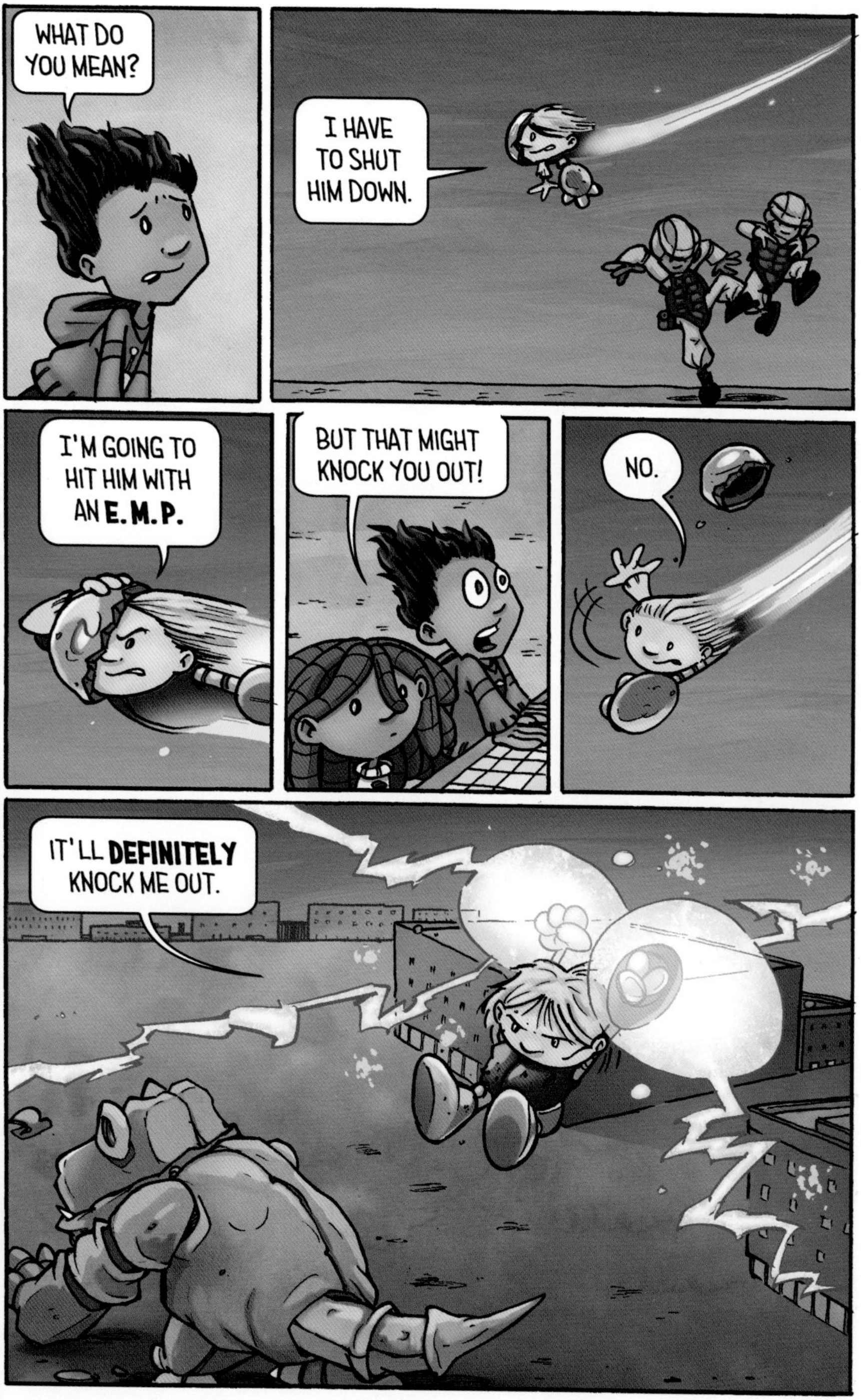
WHAT DO YOU MEAN?
I HAVE TO SHUT HIM DOWN.
I'M GOING TO HIT HIM WITH AN **E.M.P.**
BUT THAT MIGHT KNOCK YOU OUT!
NO.
IT'LL **DEFINITELY** KNOCK ME OUT.

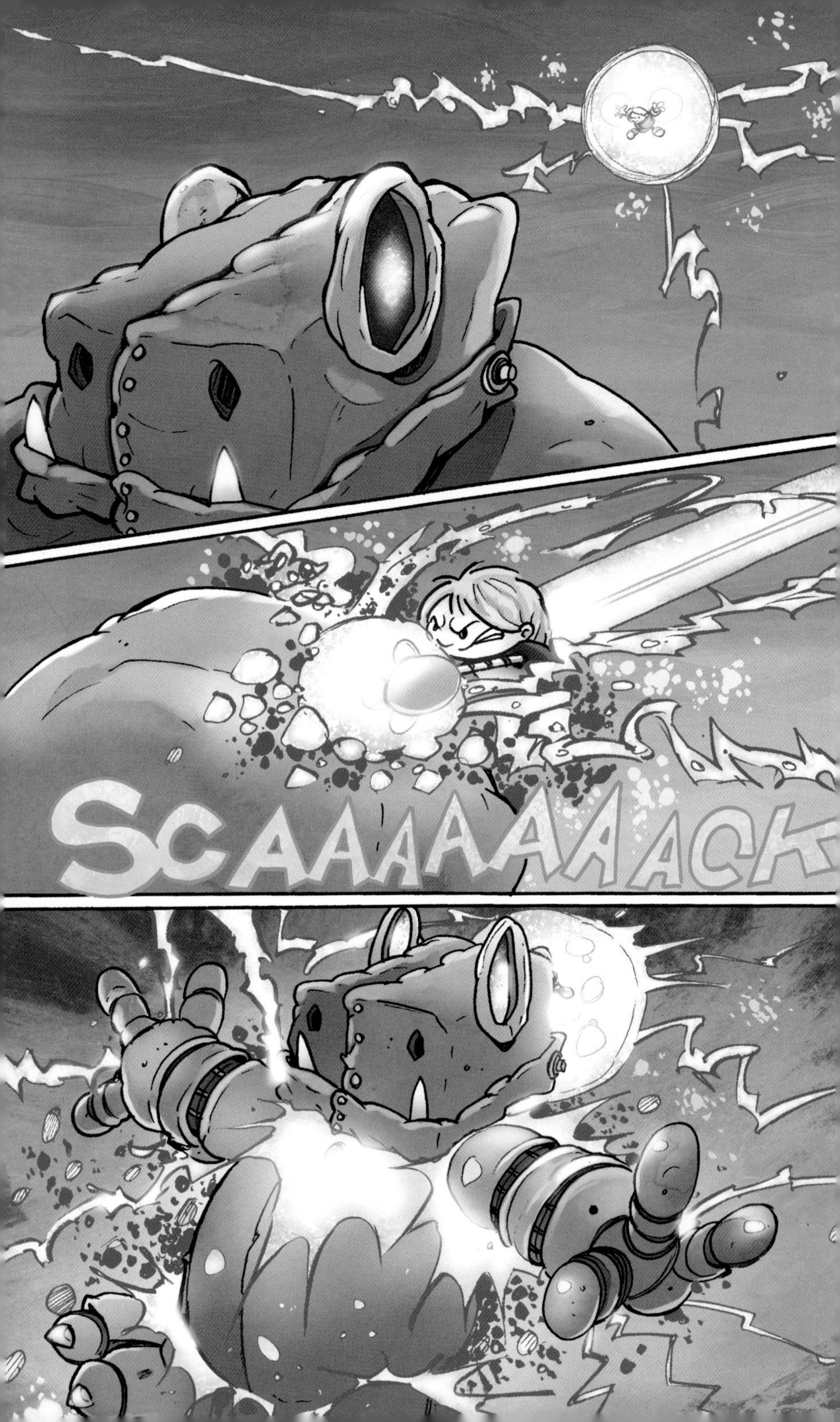
SCAAAAAACK

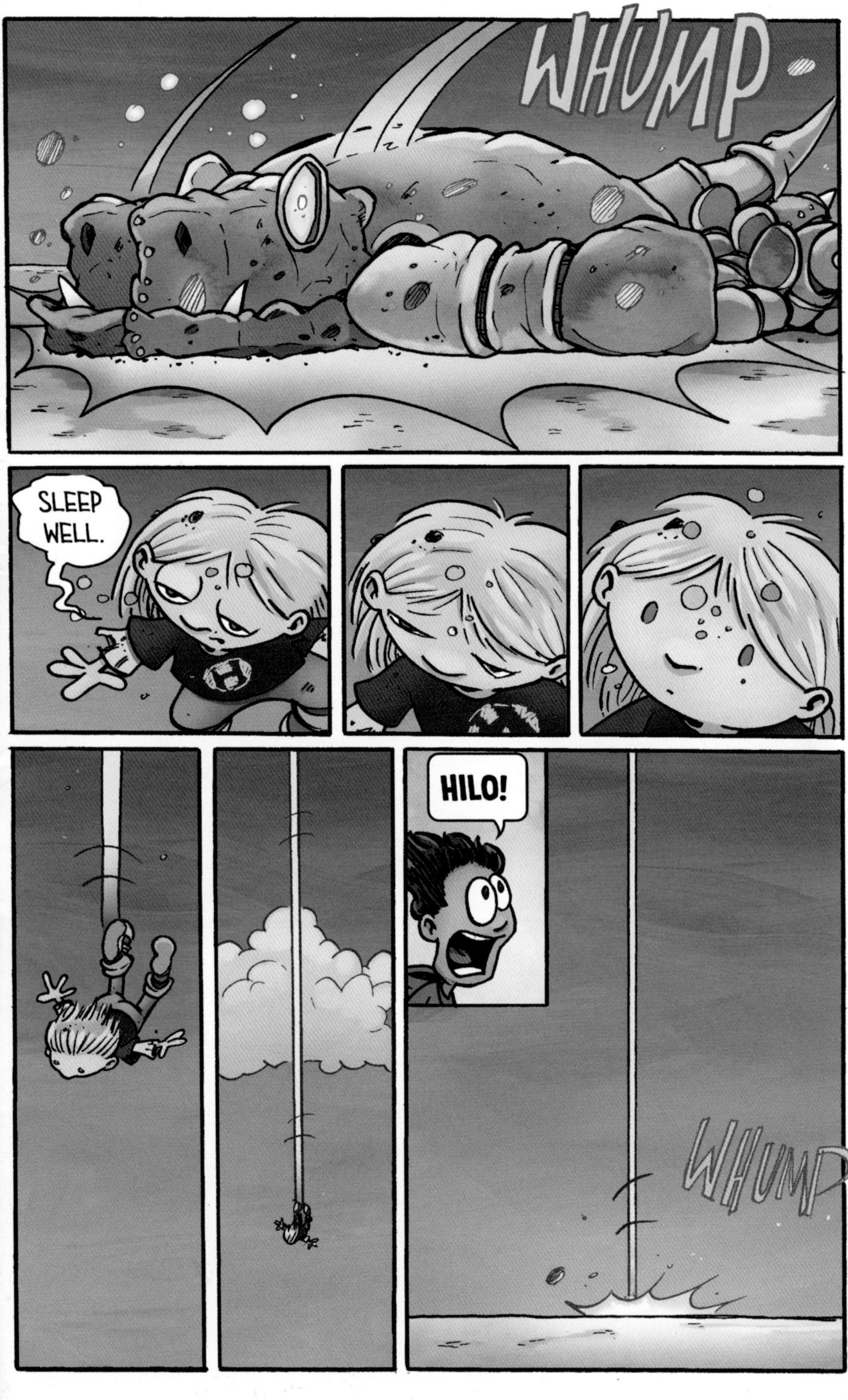
WHUMP
SLEEP WELL.
HILO!
WHUMP

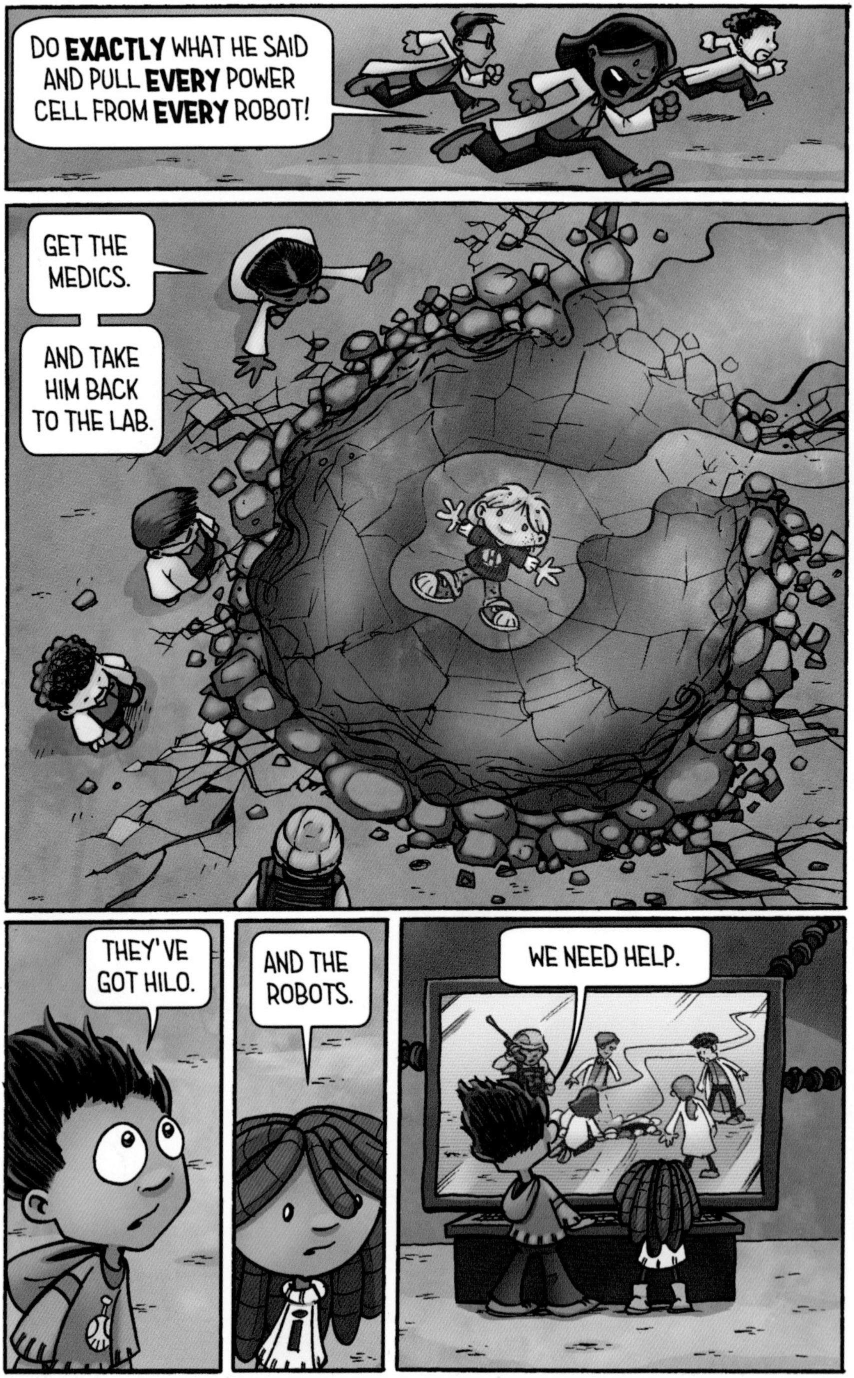
DO **EXACTLY** WHAT HE SAID AND PULL **EVERY** POWER CELL FROM **EVERY** ROBOT!
GET THE MEDICS.
AND TAKE HIM BACK TO THE LAB.
THEY'VE GOT HILO.
AND THE ROBOTS.
WE NEED HELP.

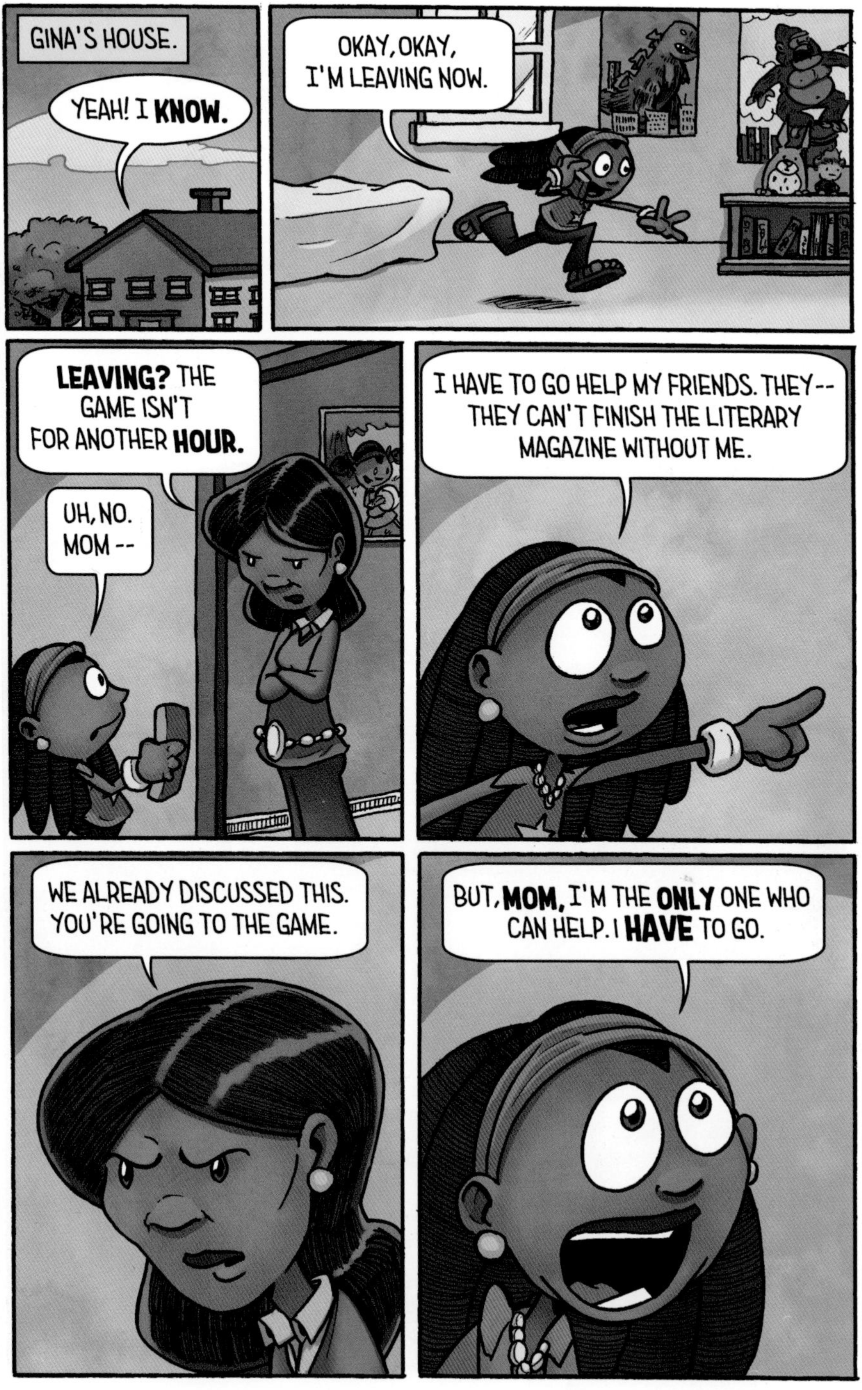
GINA'S HOUSE.
YEAH! I **KNOW.**
OKAY, OKAY, I'M LEAVING NOW.
LEAVING? THE GAME ISN'T FOR ANOTHER **HOUR.**
UH, NO. MOM --
I HAVE TO GO HELP MY FRIENDS. THEY-- THEY CAN'T FINISH THE LITERARY MAGAZINE WITHOUT ME.
WE ALREADY DISCUSSED THIS. YOU'RE GOING TO THE GAME.
BUT, **MOM,** I'M THE **ONLY** ONE WHO CAN HELP. I **HAVE** TO GO.

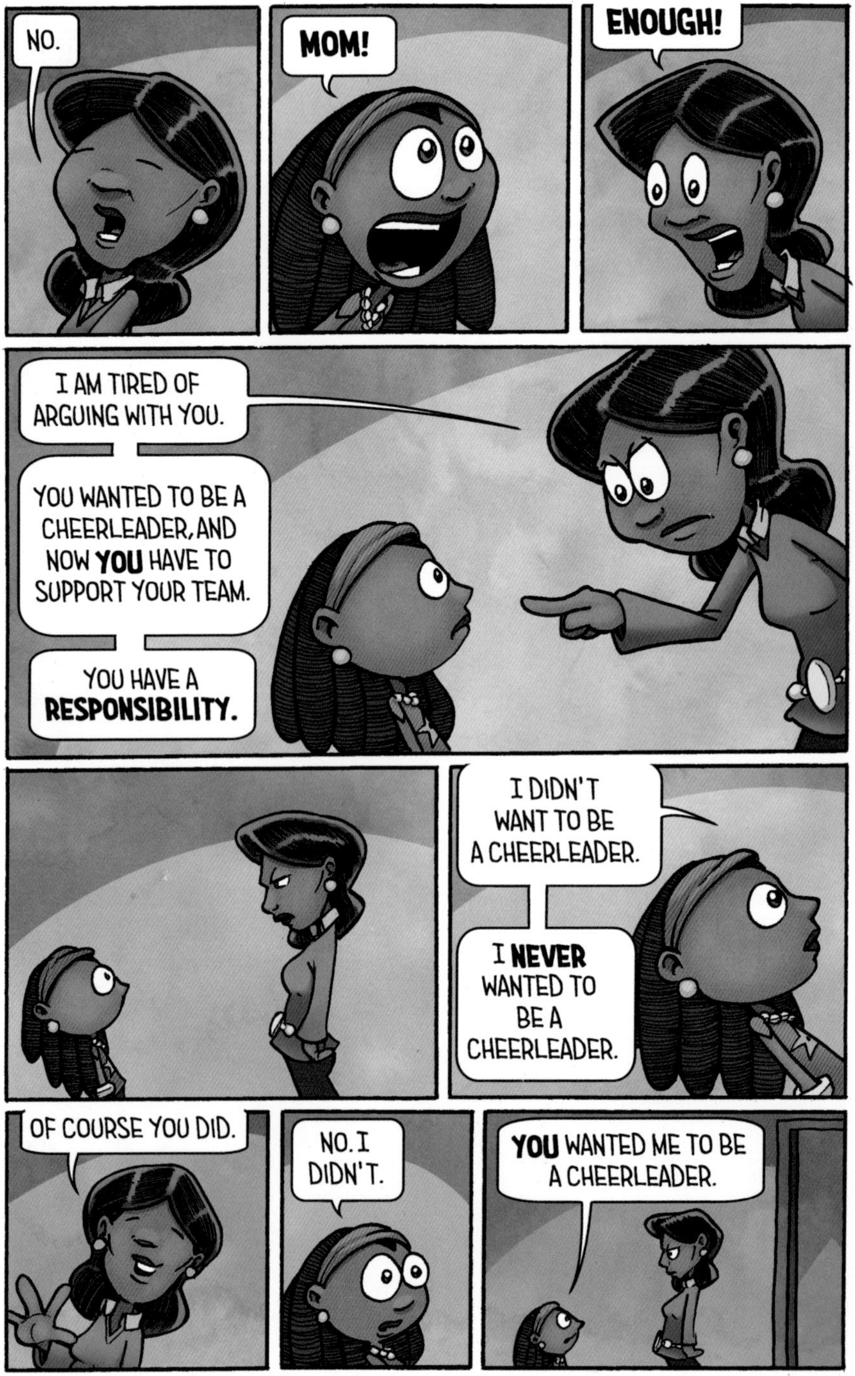
NO.
MOM!
ENOUGH!
I AM TIRED OF ARGUING WITH YOU.
YOU WANTED TO BE A CHEERLEADER, AND NOW **YOU** HAVE TO SUPPORT YOUR TEAM.
YOU HAVE A **RESPONSIBILITY.**
I DIDN'T WANT TO BE A CHEERLEADER.
I **NEVER** WANTED TO BE A CHEERLEADER.
OF COURSE YOU DID.
NO. I DIDN'T.
YOU WANTED ME TO BE A CHEERLEADER.

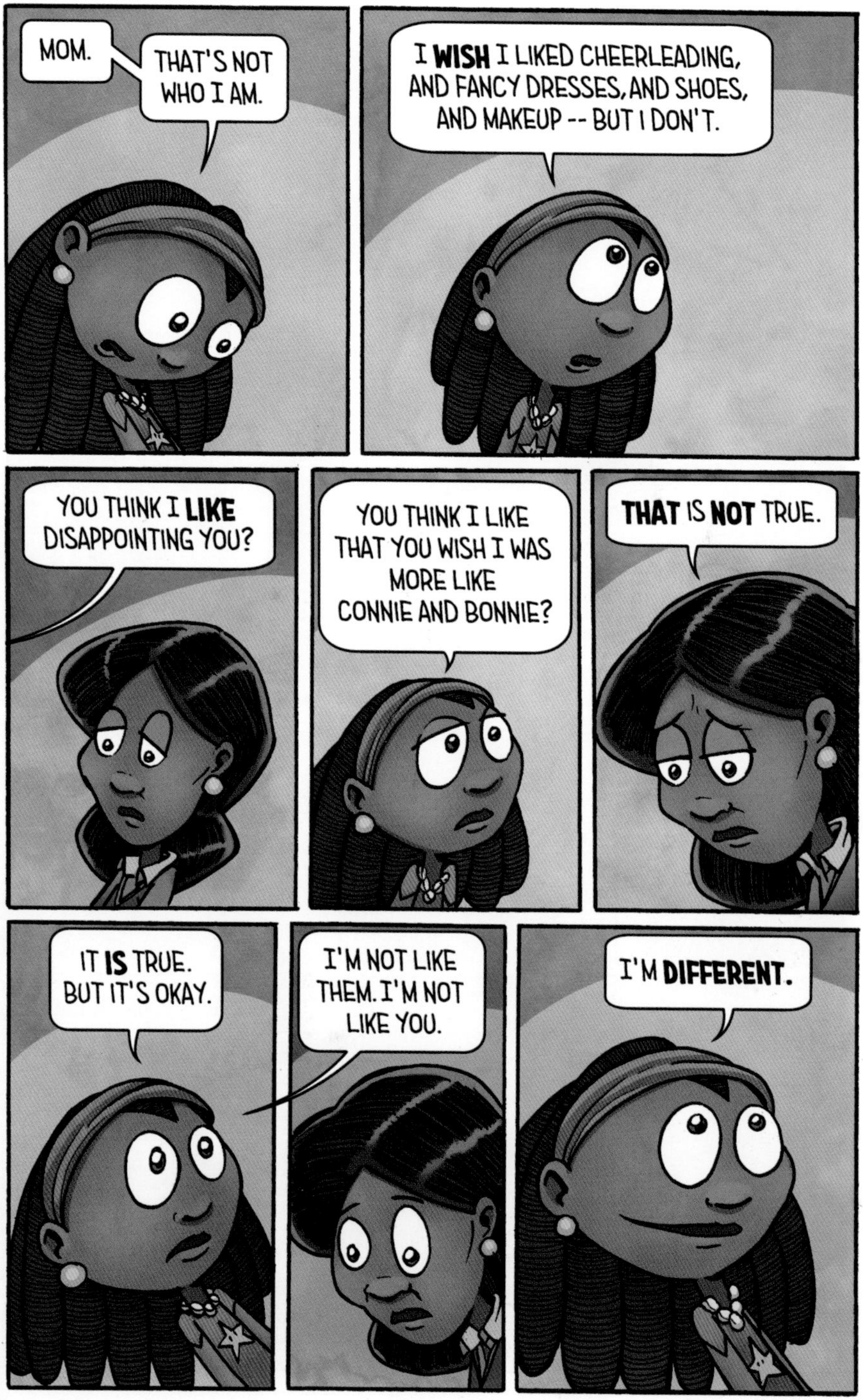
MOM.
THAT'S NOT WHO I AM.
I WISH I LIKED CHEERLEADING, AND FANCY DRESSES, AND SHOES, AND MAKEUP -- BUT I DON'T.
YOU THINK I LIKE DISAPPOINTING YOU?
YOU THINK I LIKE THAT YOU WISH I WAS MORE LIKE CONNIE AND BONNIE?
THAT IS NOT TRUE.
IT IS TRUE. BUT IT'S OKAY.
I'M NOT LIKE THEM. I'M NOT LIKE YOU.
I'M DIFFERENT.

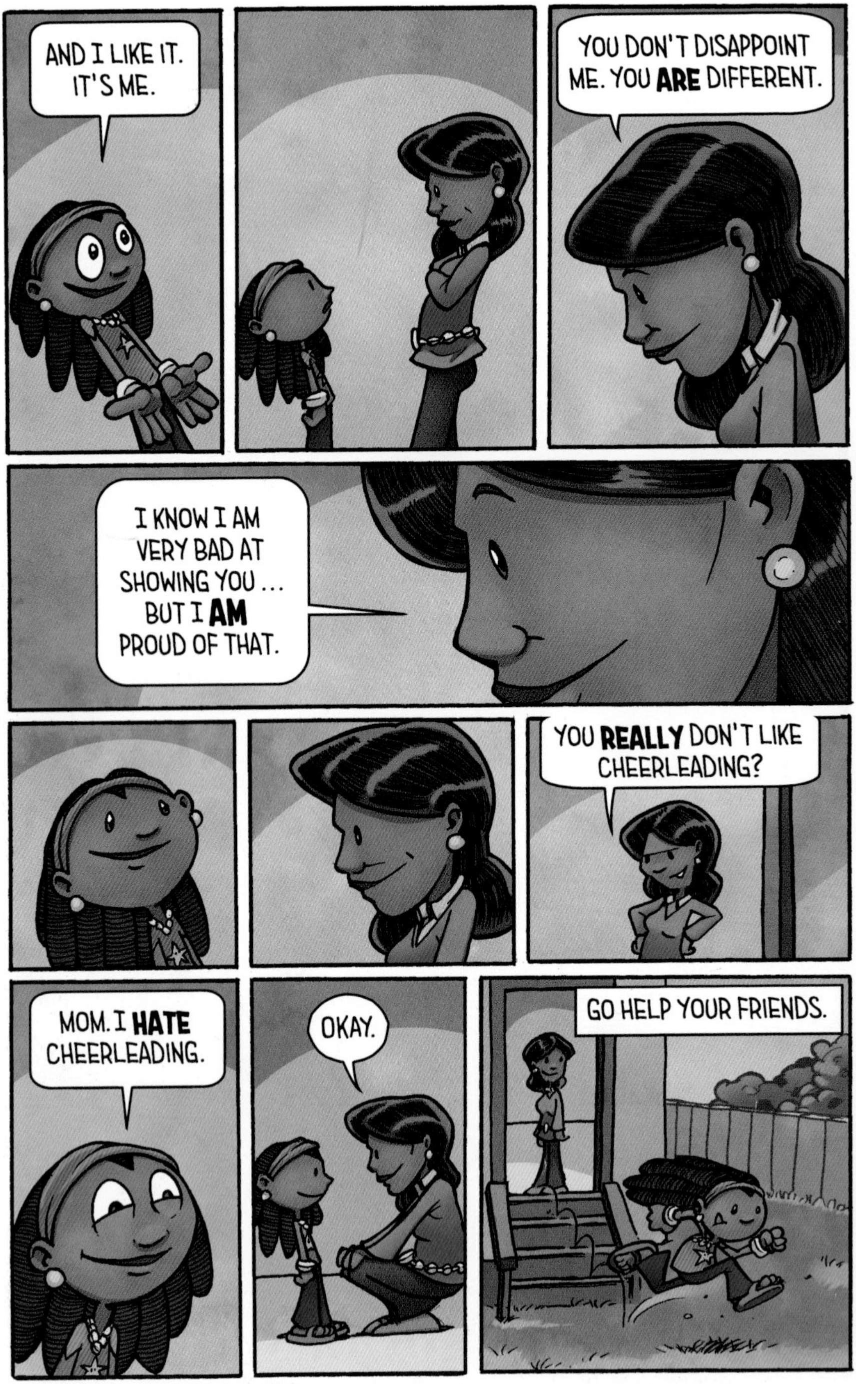
AND I LIKE IT. IT'S ME.
YOU DON'T DISAPPOINT ME. YOU **ARE** DIFFERENT.
I KNOW I AM VERY BAD AT SHOWING YOU ... BUT I **AM** PROUD OF THAT.
YOU **REALLY** DON'T LIKE CHEERLEADING?
MOM. I **HATE** CHEERLEADING.
OKAY.
GO HELP YOUR FRIENDS.

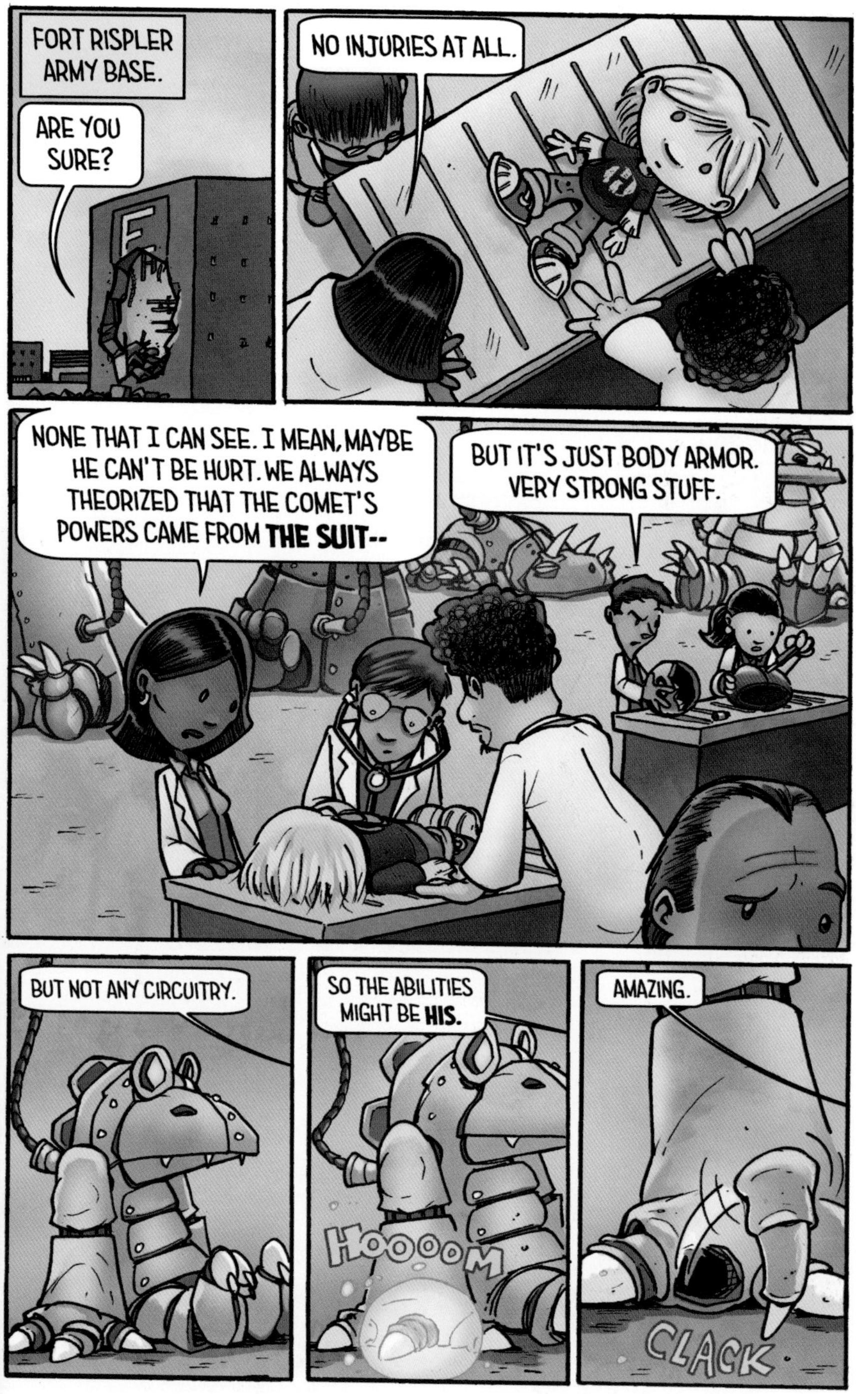
FORT RISPLER ARMY BASE.
ARE YOU SURE?
NO INJURIES AT ALL.
NONE THAT I CAN SEE. I MEAN, MAYBE HE CAN'T BE HURT. WE ALWAYS THEORIZED THAT THE COMET'S POWERS CAME FROM THE SUIT--
BUT IT'S JUST BODY ARMOR. VERY STRONG STUFF.
BUT NOT ANY CIRCUITRY.
SO THE ABILITIES MIGHT BE HIS.
HOOOOOM
AMAZING.
CLACK

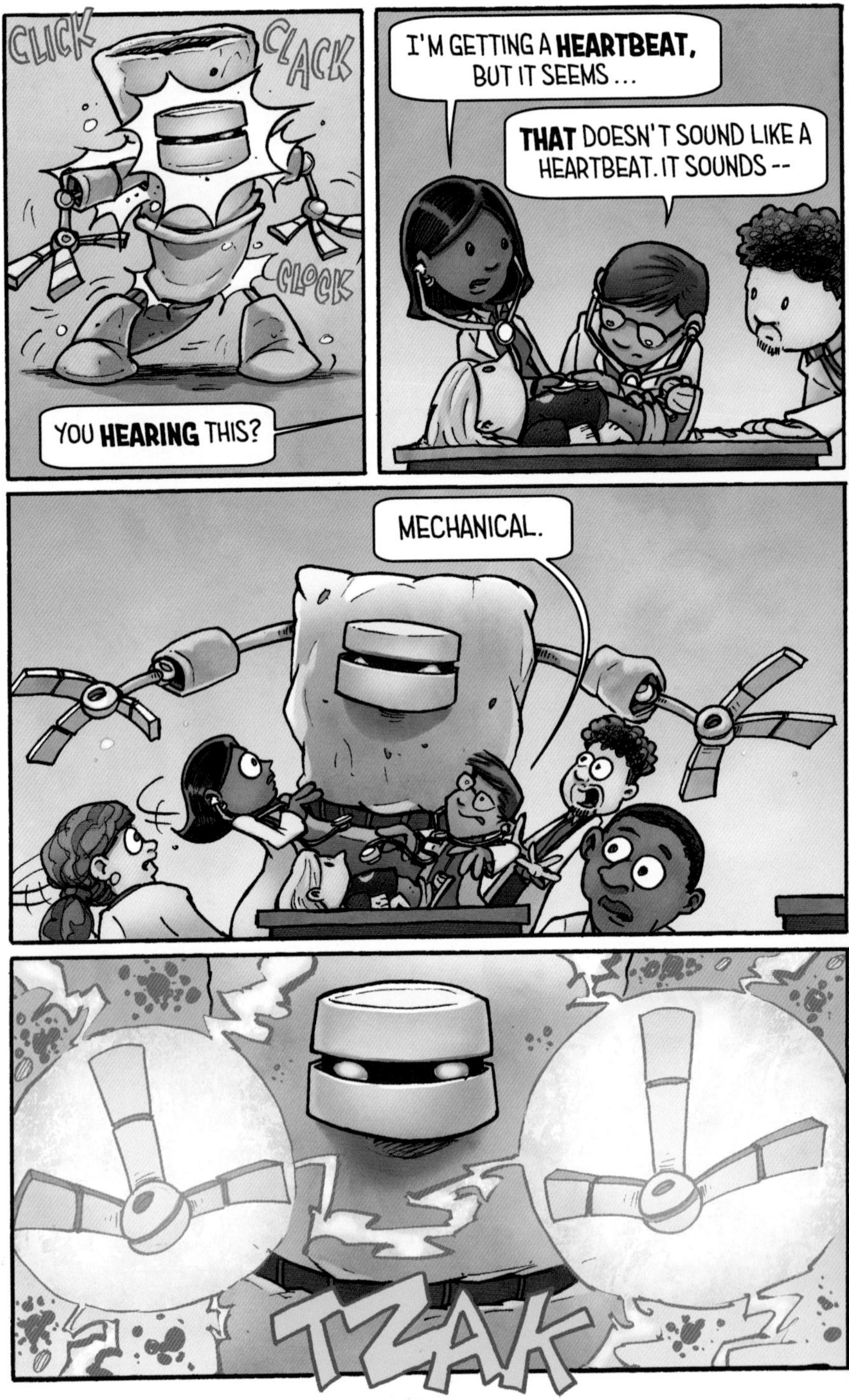
CLICK
CLACK
CLOCK
YOU **HEARING** THIS?
I'M GETTING A **HEARTBEAT,** BUT IT SEEMS ...
THAT DOESN'T SOUND LIKE A HEARTBEAT. IT SOUNDS --
MECHANICAL.
TZAK

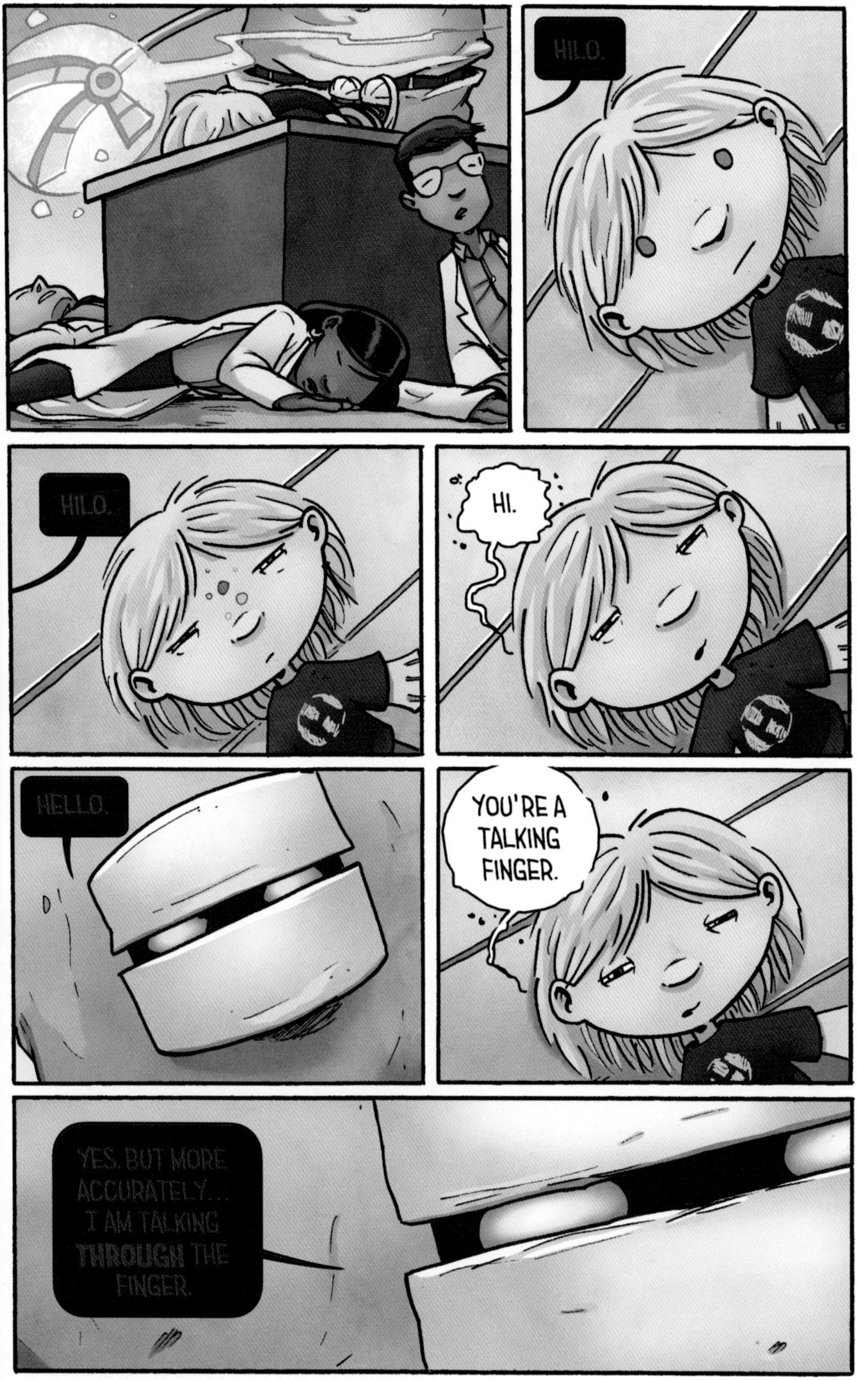
HILO.
HILO.
HI.
HELLO.
YOU'RE A TALKING FINGER.
YES. BUT MORE ACCURATELY... I AM TALKING **THROUGH** THE FINGER.

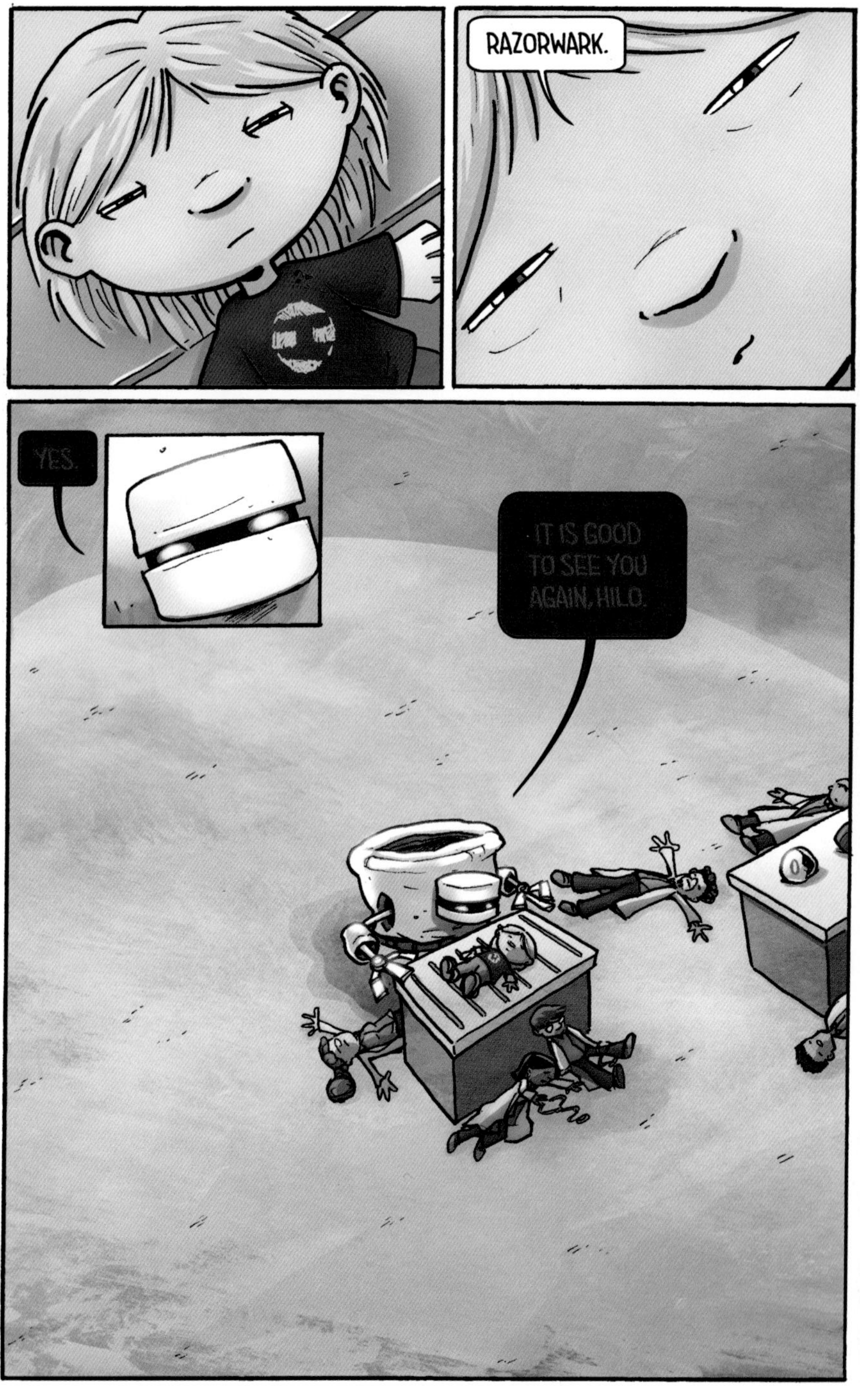
RAZORWARK.
YES.
IT IS GOOD TO SEE YOU AGAIN, HILO.

CHAPTER 9

LIKE YOU. LIKE ME.

IS HE STILL IN THE LAB?
PROBABLY. WE HAVEN'T SEEN THEM TAKE HIM OUT OF THERE. YOU OKAY?
YEP. GOT THE **TELEPORTER,** AND I AM **MOTORING!**

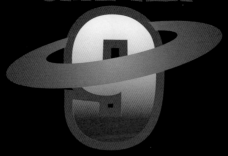

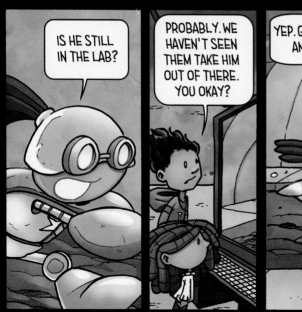

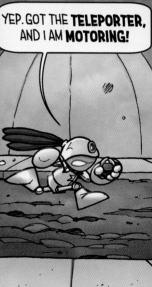

THAT ABANDONED TUNNEL WILL TAKE YOU RIGHT UNDER HIM.

YIKES! WHY DOES IT SMELL SO BAD?!

IT'S AN OLD SEWER.

WHAT?

EW.

GROSS! THIS IS ALL POOP?!

NO. WELL, YES. IT USED TO BE POOP. IT'S VERY OLD POOP.

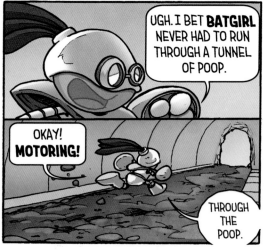

UGH. I BET **BATGIRL** NEVER HAD TO RUN THROUGH A TUNNEL OF POOP.

OKAY! **MOTORING!**

THROUGH THE POOP.

160

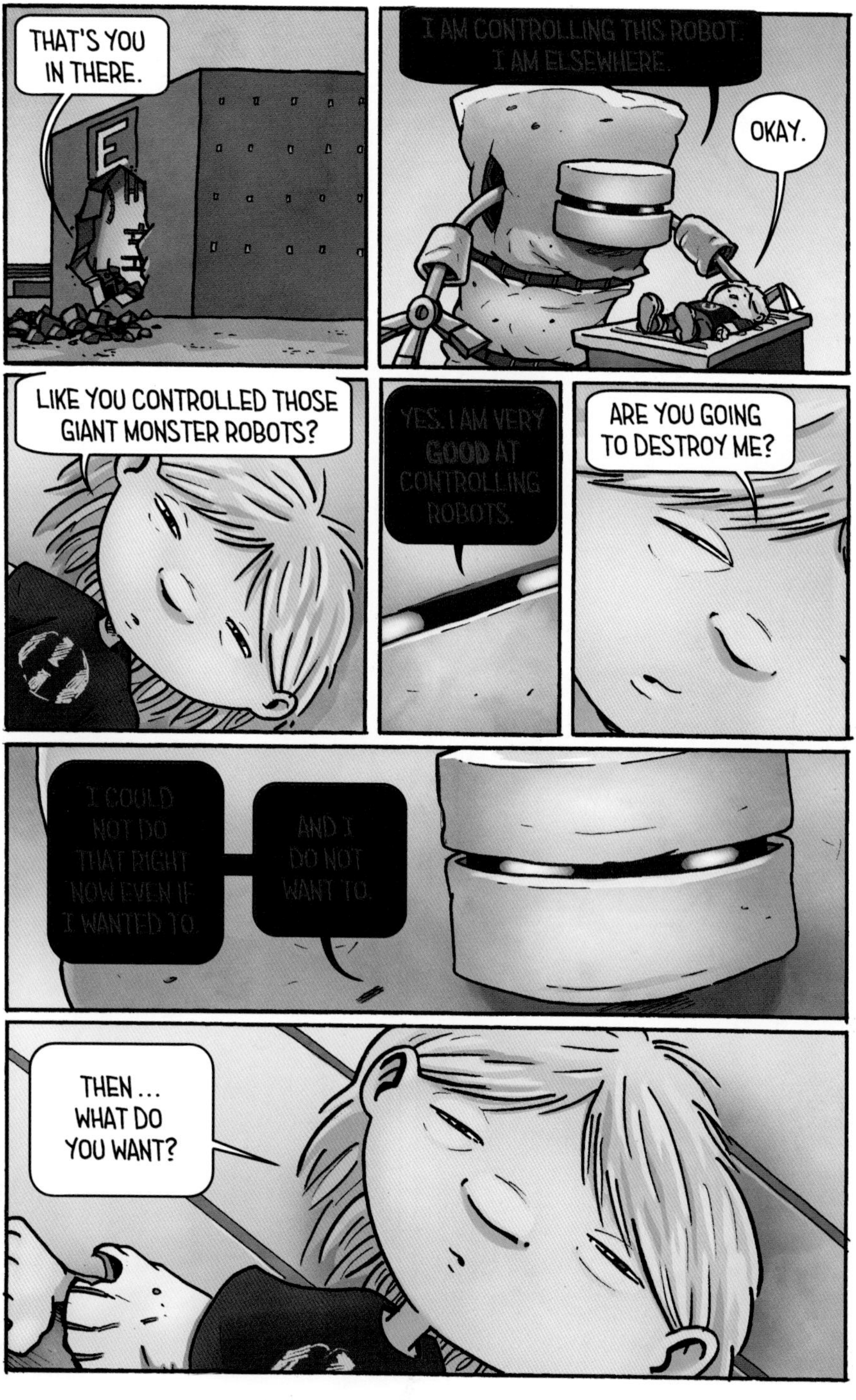
THAT'S YOU IN THERE.
I AM CONTROLLING THIS ROBOT. I AM ELSEWHERE.
OKAY.
LIKE YOU CONTROLLED THOSE GIANT MONSTER ROBOTS?
YES. I AM VERY GOOD AT CONTROLLING ROBOTS.
ARE YOU GOING TO DESTROY ME?
I COULD NOT DO THAT RIGHT NOW EVEN IF I WANTED TO.
AND I DO NOT WANT TO.
THEN… WHAT DO YOU WANT?

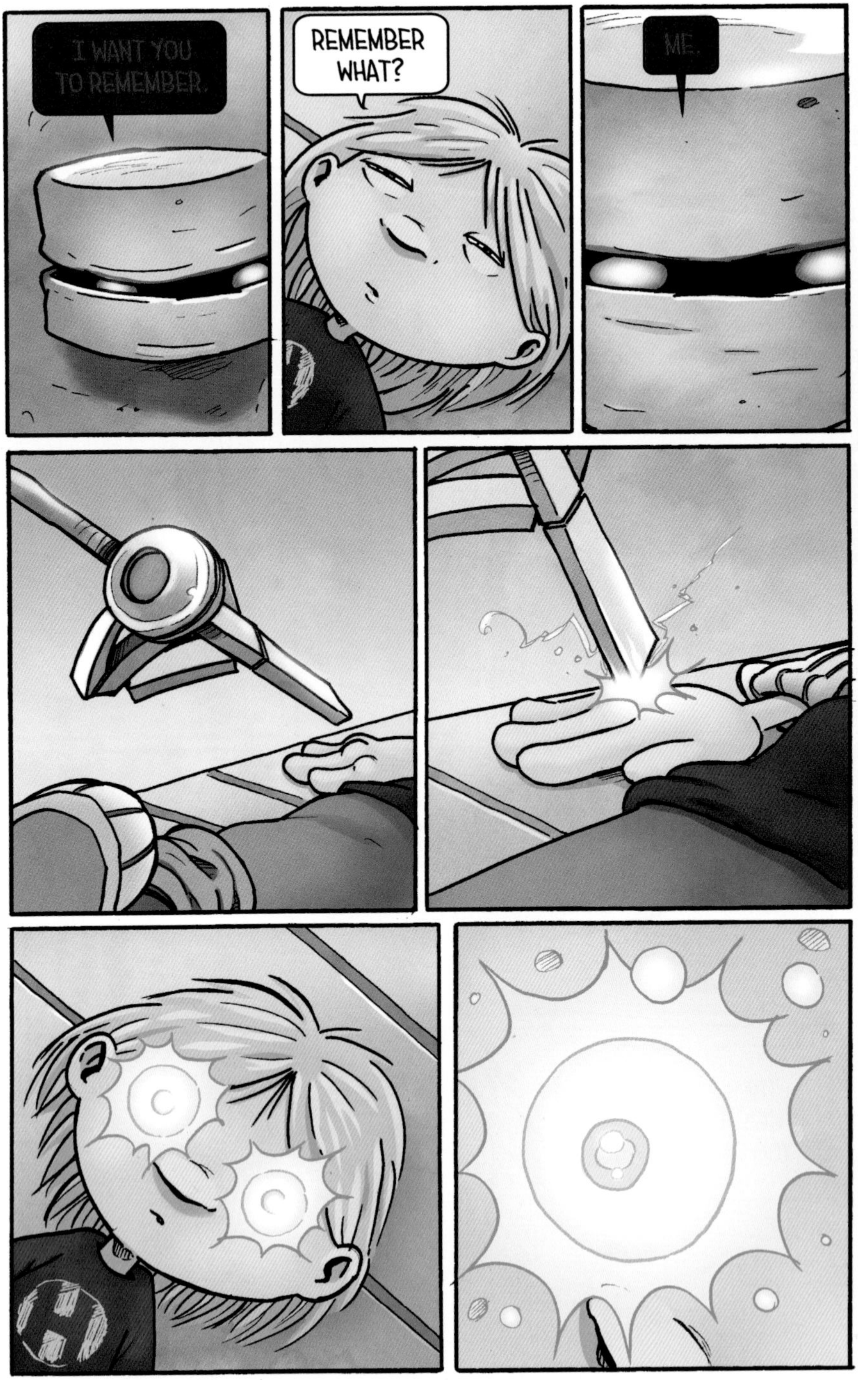
I WANT YOU TO REMEMBER.
REMEMBER WHAT?
ME.

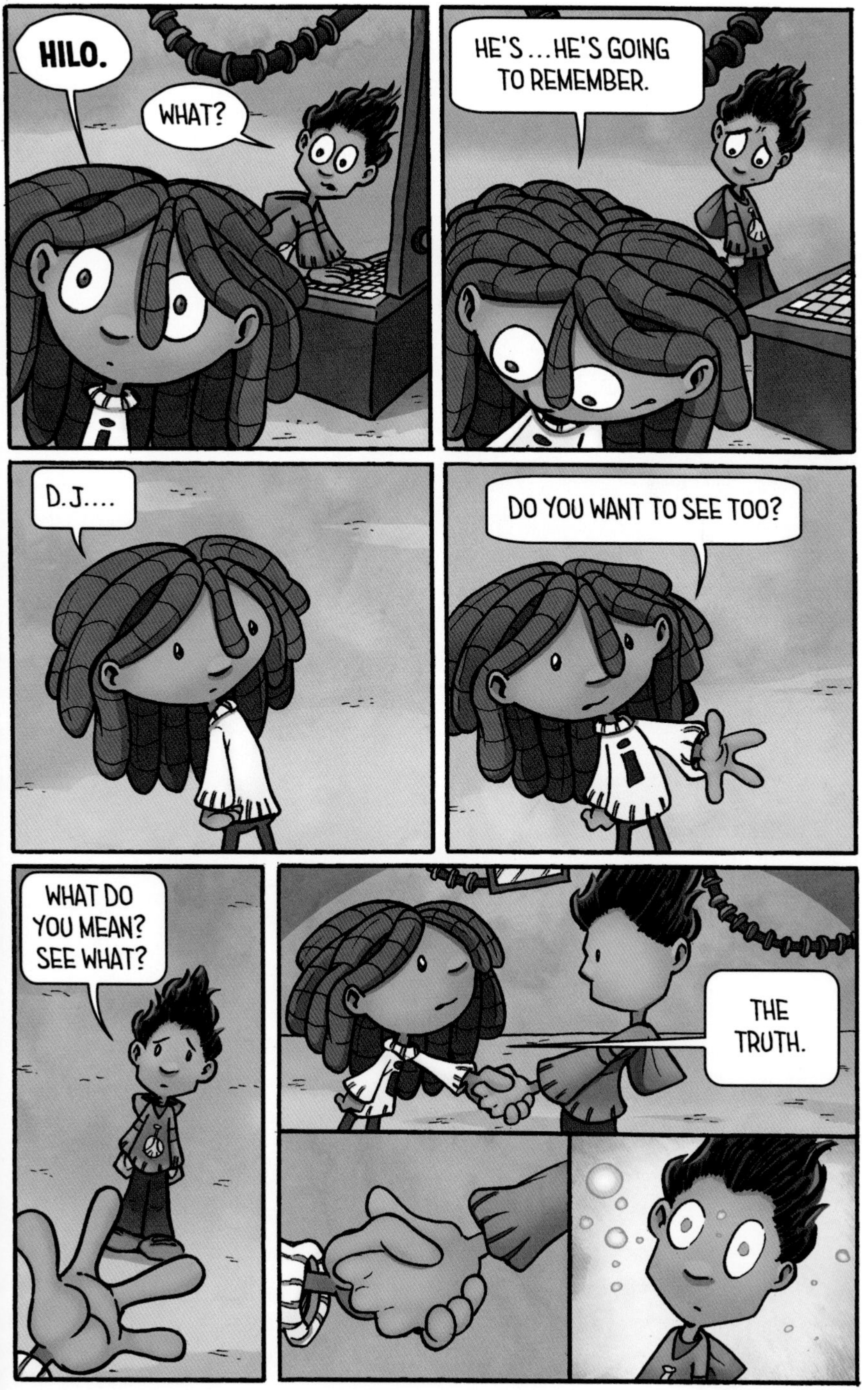
HILO.
WHAT?
HE'S ... HE'S GOING TO REMEMBER.
D.J....
DO YOU WANT TO SEE TOO?
WHAT DO YOU MEAN? SEE WHAT?
THE TRUTH.

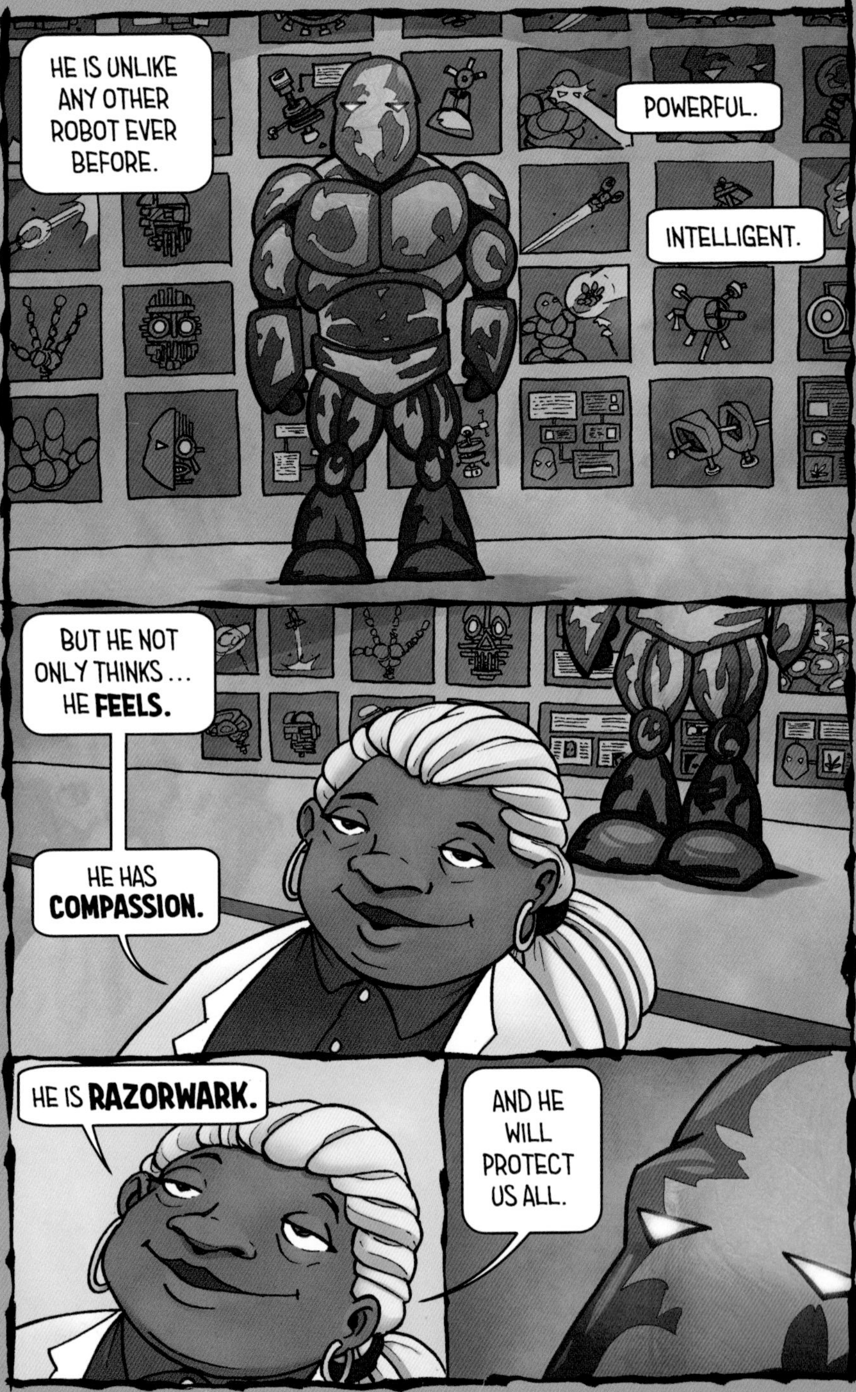
HE IS UNLIKE ANY OTHER ROBOT EVER BEFORE.
POWERFUL.
INTELLIGENT.
BUT HE NOT ONLY THINKS . . . HE **FEELS.**
HE HAS **COMPASSION.**
HE IS **RAZORWARK.**
AND HE WILL PROTECT US ALL.

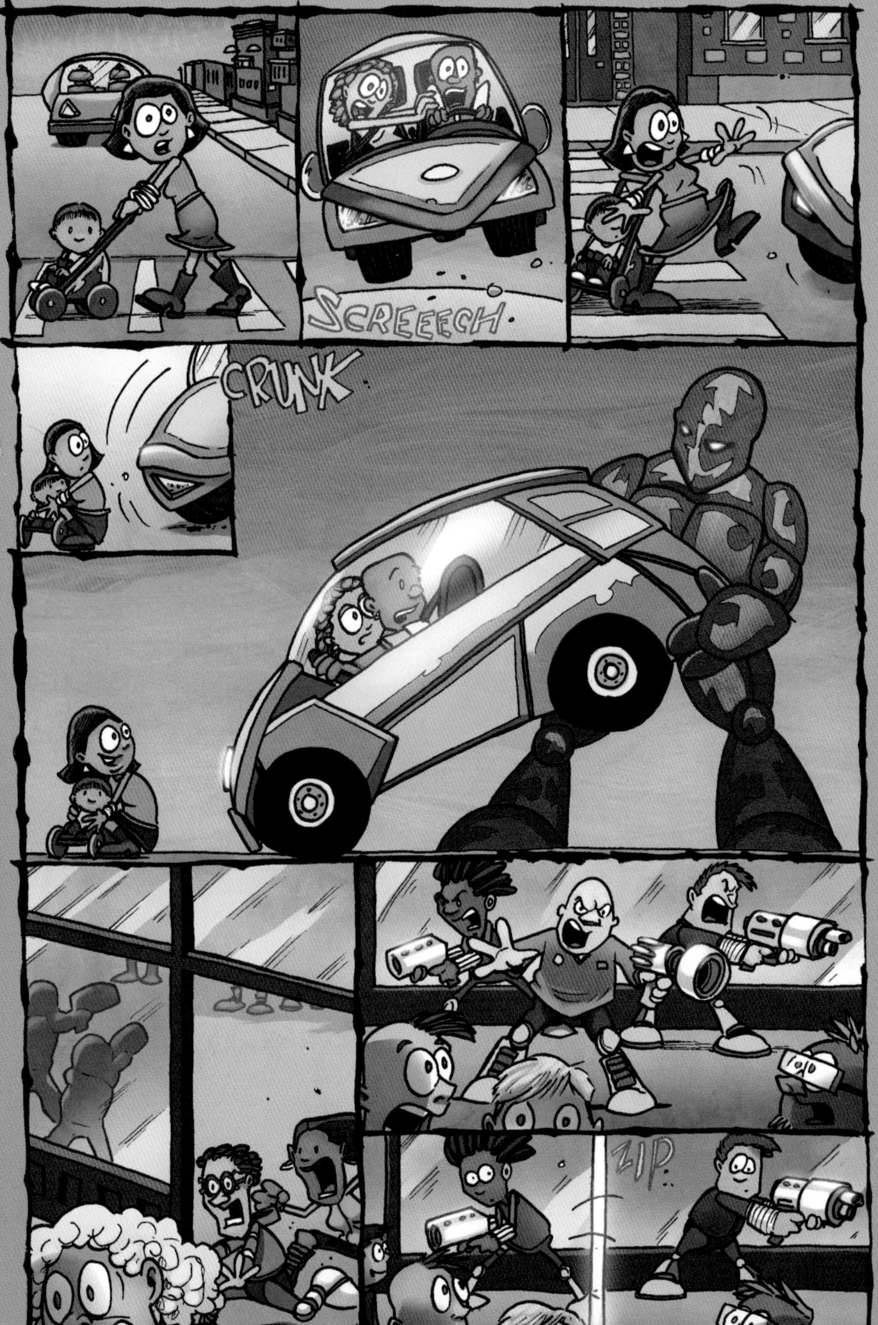
SCREEECH
CRUNK
ZIP

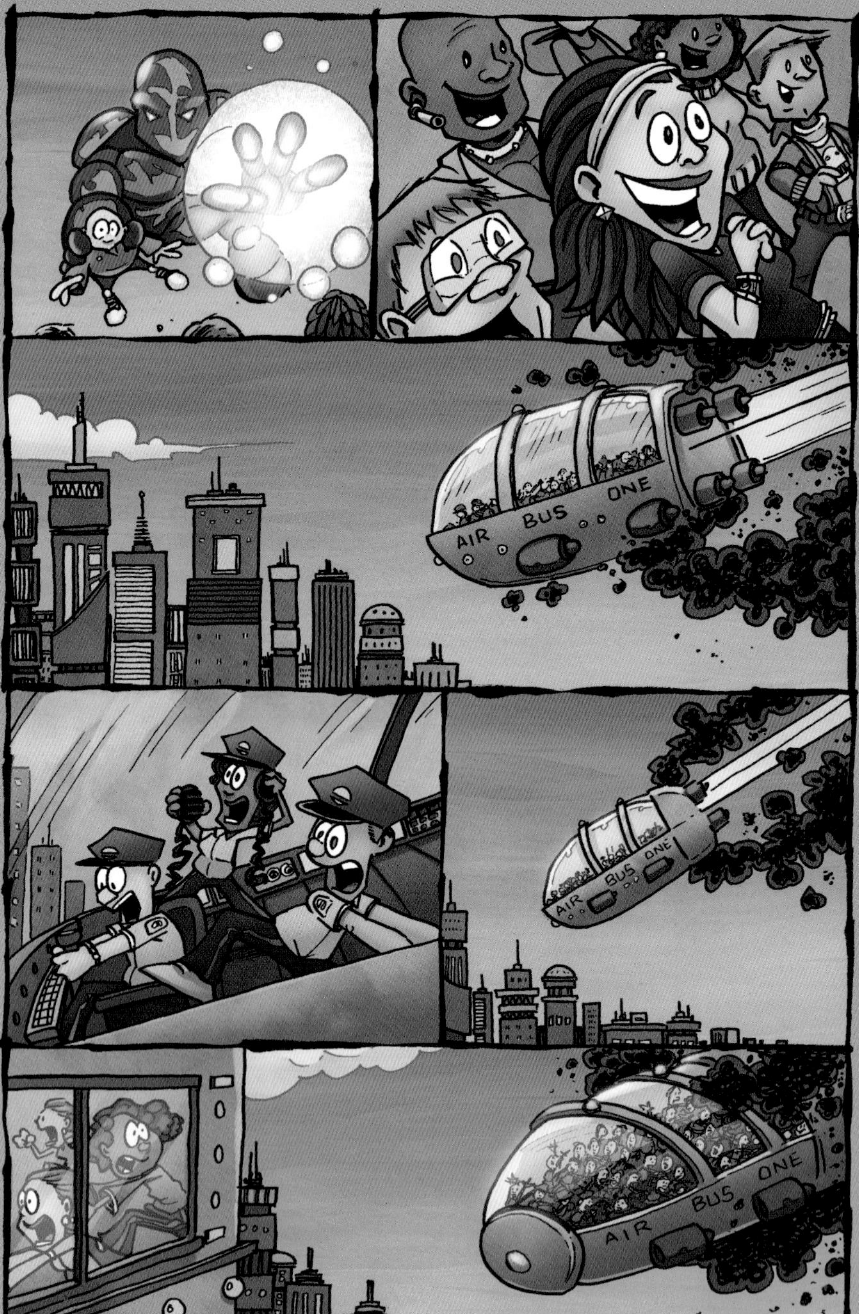
AIR BUS ONE
AIR BUS ONE
AIR BUS ONE

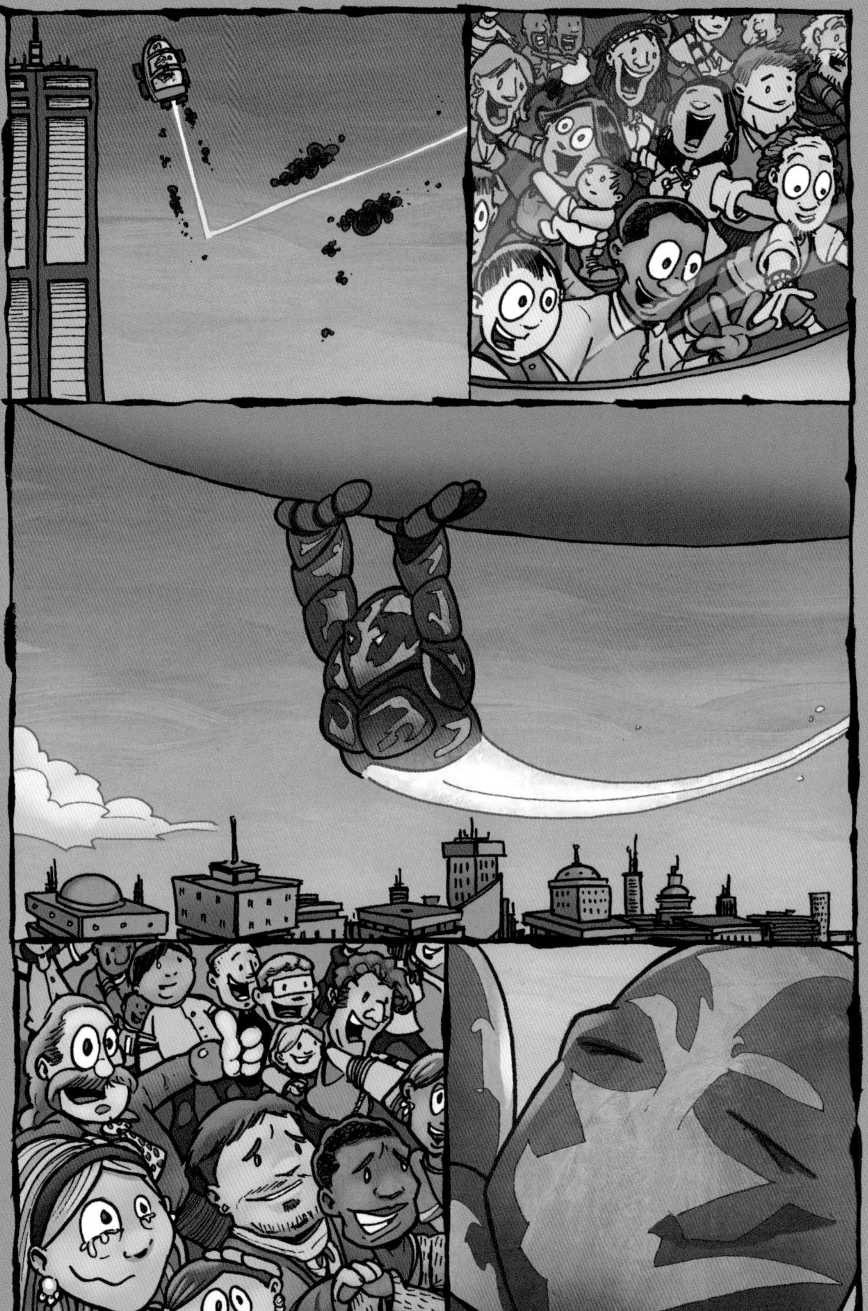

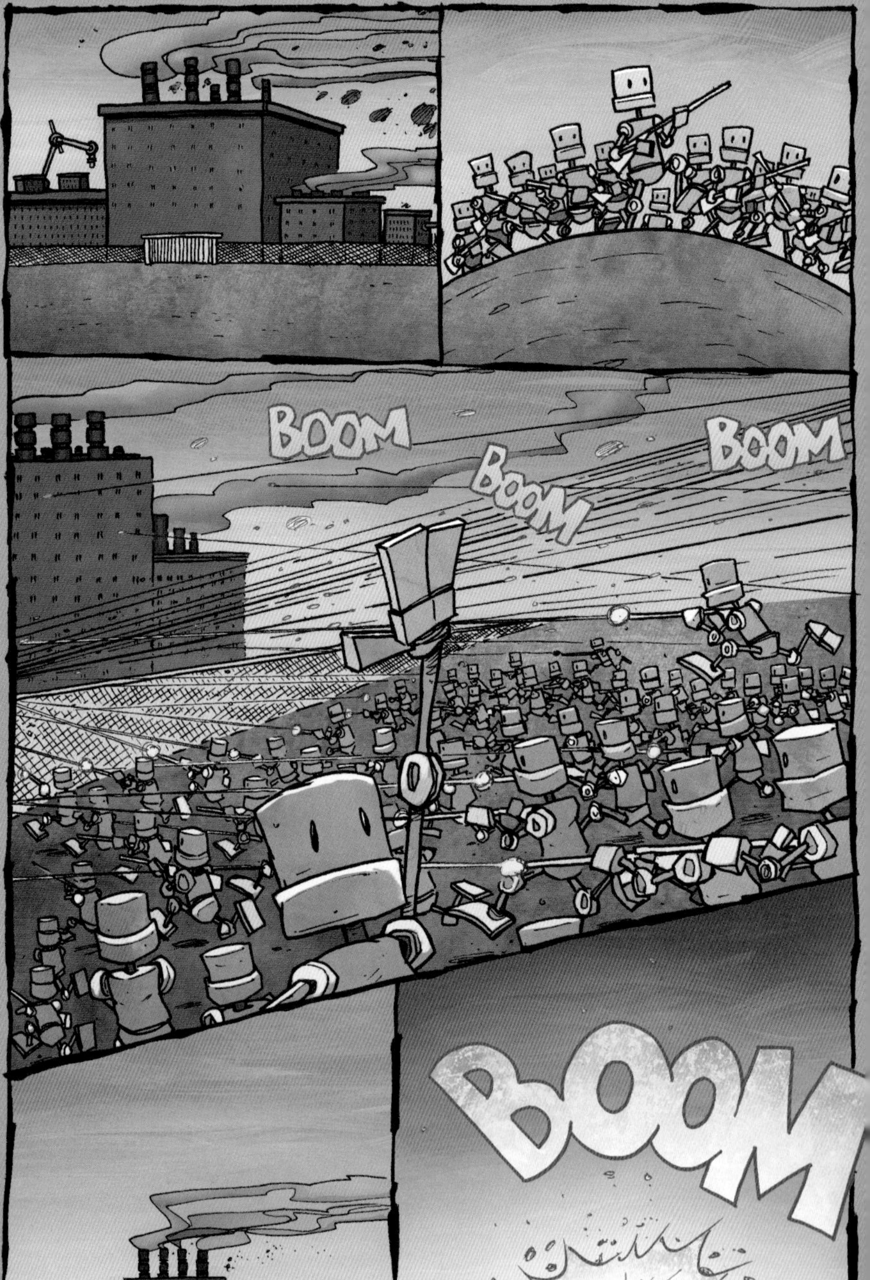
BOOM
BOOM
BOOM
BOOM

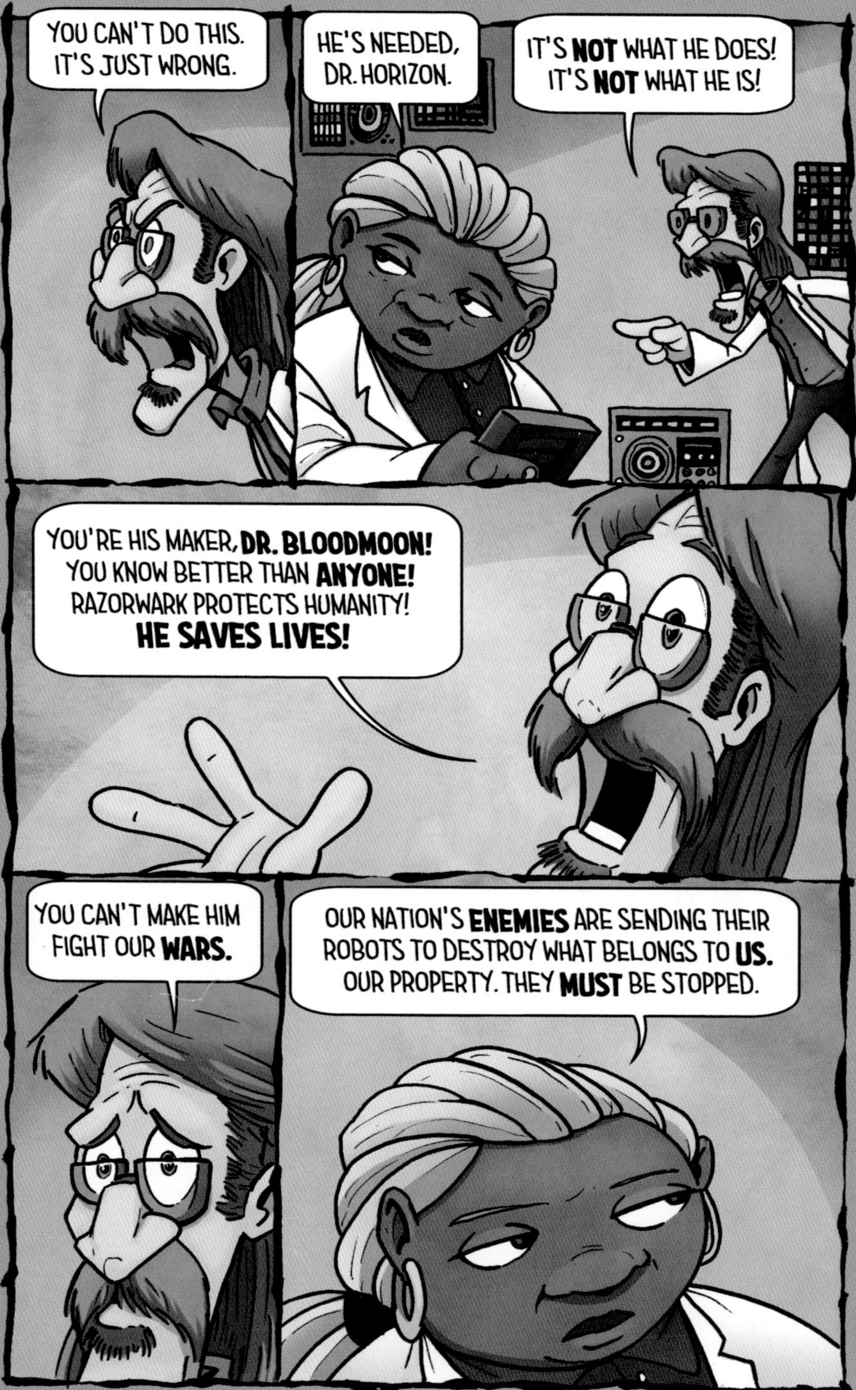
YOU CAN'T DO THIS. IT'S JUST WRONG.
HE'S NEEDED, DR. HORIZON.
IT'S **NOT** WHAT HE DOES! IT'S **NOT** WHAT HE IS!
YOU'RE HIS MAKER, **DR. BLOODMOON!** YOU KNOW BETTER THAN **ANYONE!** RAZORWARK PROTECTS HUMANITY! **HE SAVES LIVES!**
YOU CAN'T MAKE HIM FIGHT OUR **WARS.**
OUR NATION'S **ENEMIES** ARE SENDING THEIR ROBOTS TO DESTROY WHAT BELONGS TO **US.** OUR PROPERTY. THEY **MUST** BE STOPPED.

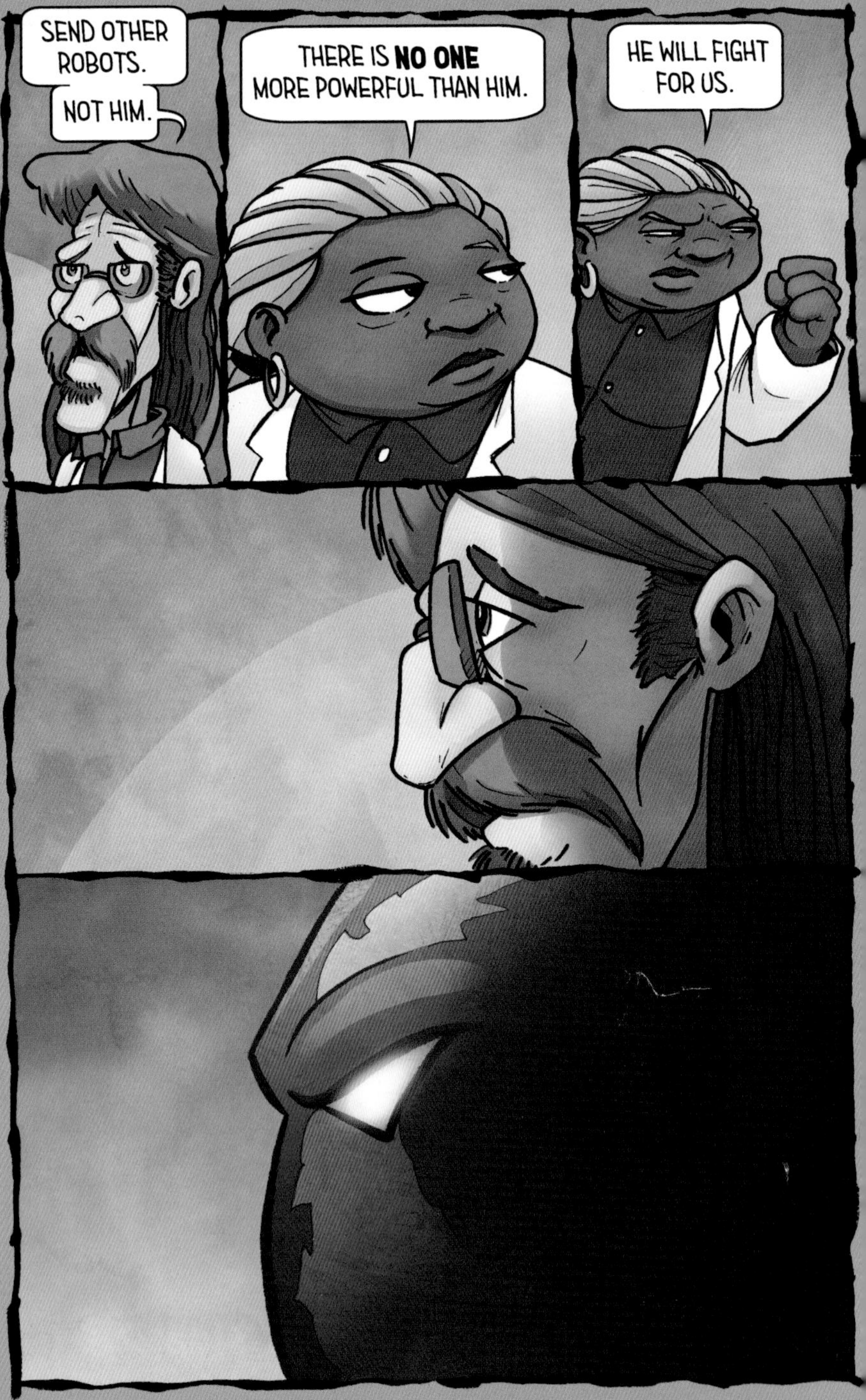
SEND OTHER ROBOTS.
NOT HIM.
THERE IS **NO ONE** MORE POWERFUL THAN HIM.
HE WILL FIGHT FOR US.

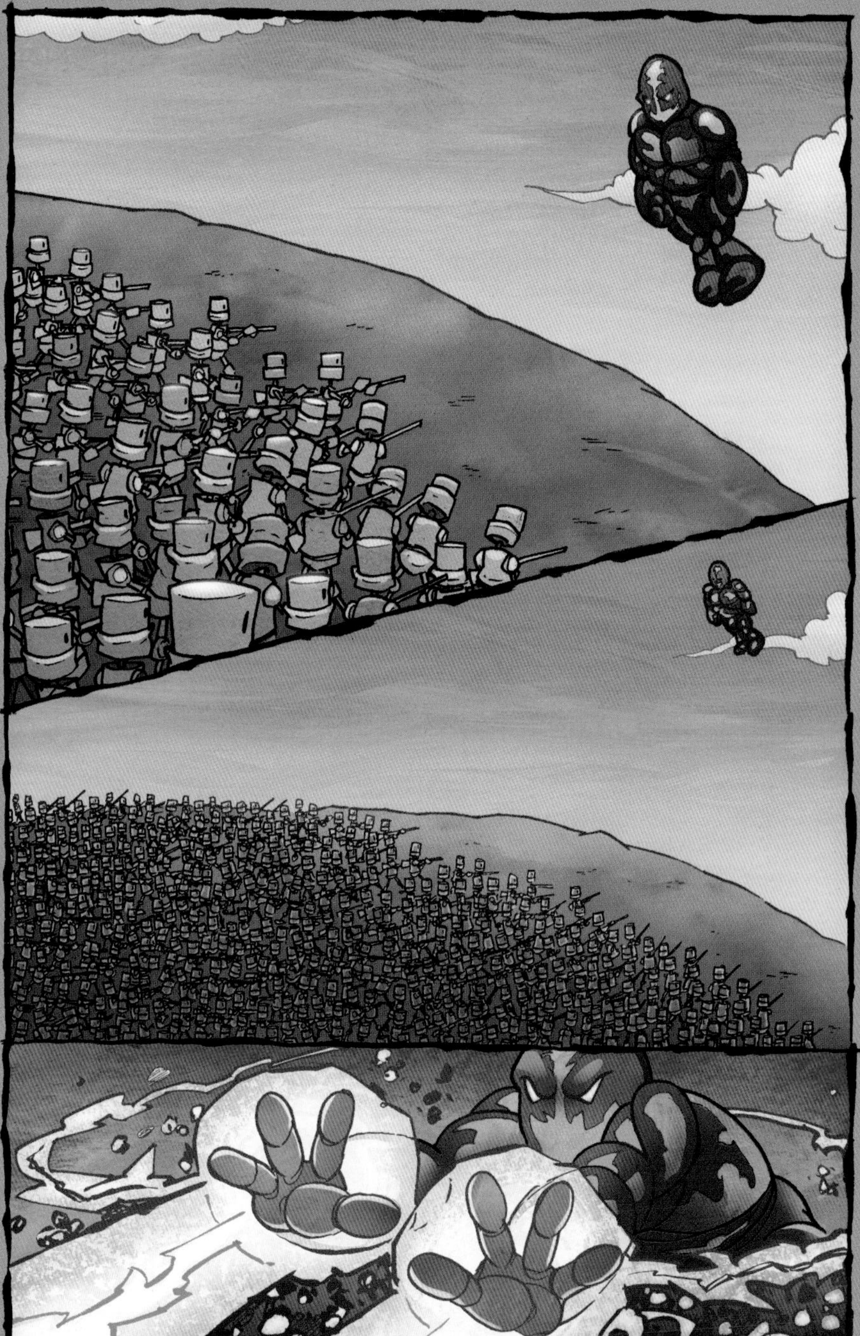

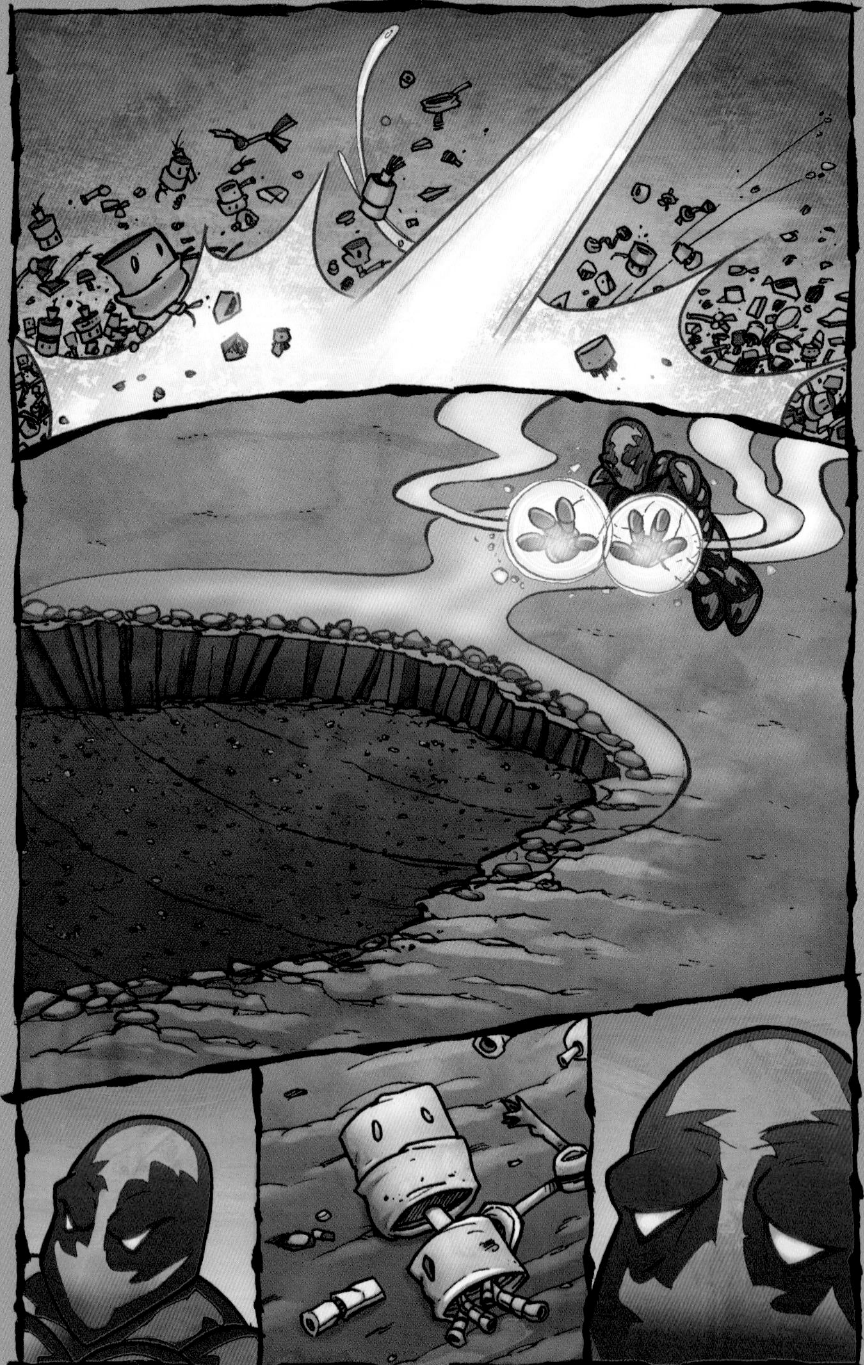

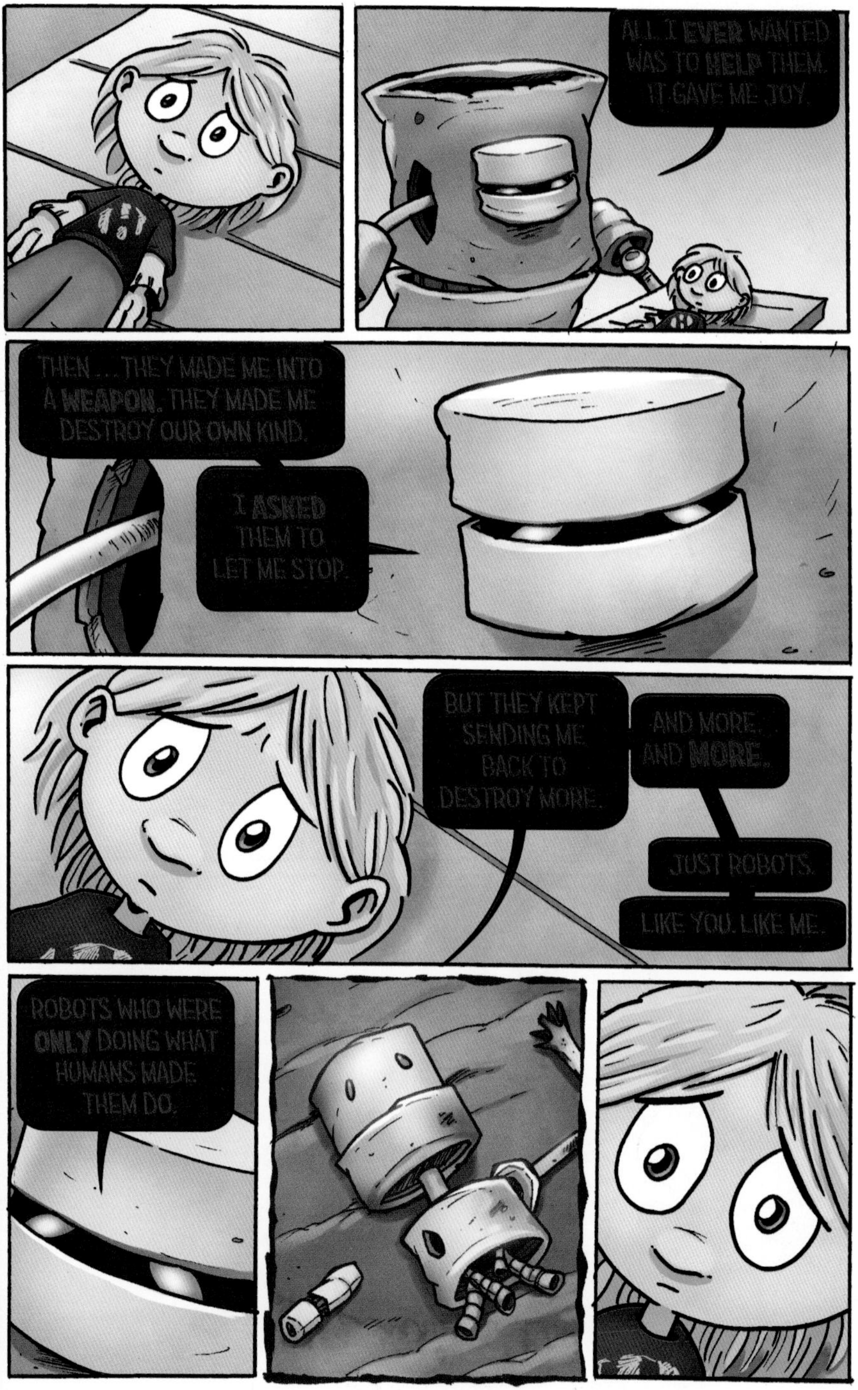
ALL I EVER WANTED WAS TO HELP THEM. IT GAVE ME JOY.
THEN . . . THEY MADE ME INTO A WEAPON. THEY MADE ME DESTROY OUR OWN KIND.
I ASKED THEM TO LET ME STOP.
BUT THEY KEPT SENDING ME BACK TO DESTROY MORE.
AND MORE. AND MORE.
JUST ROBOTS.
LIKE YOU. LIKE ME.
ROBOTS WHO WERE ONLY DOING WHAT HUMANS MADE THEM DO.

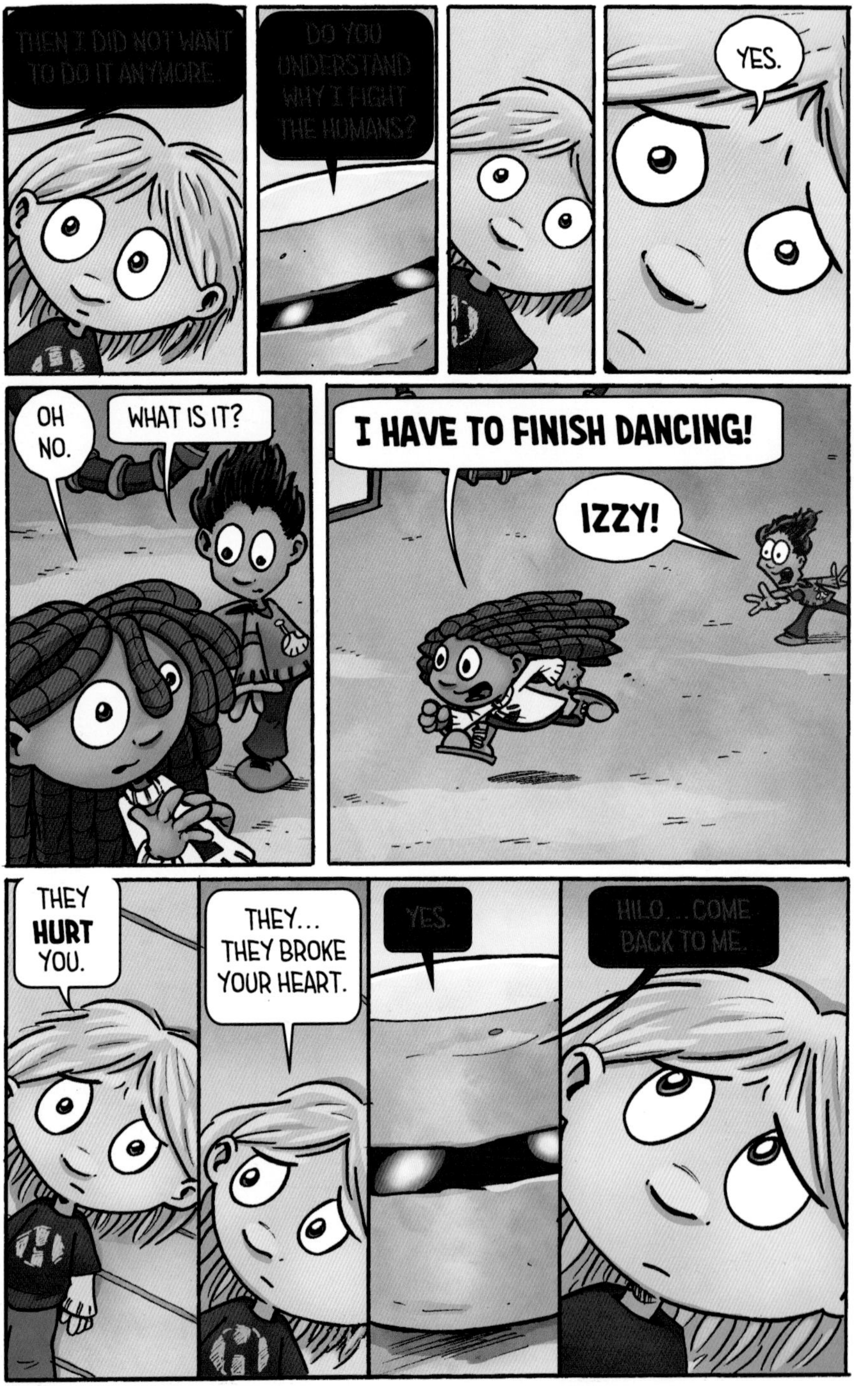
THEN I DID NOT WANT TO DO IT ANYMORE.
DO YOU UNDERSTAND WHY I FIGHT THE HUMANS?
YES.
OH NO.
WHAT IS IT?
I HAVE TO FINISH DANCING!
IZZY!
THEY **HURT** YOU.
THEY... THEY BROKE YOUR HEART.
YES.
HILO... COME BACK TO ME.

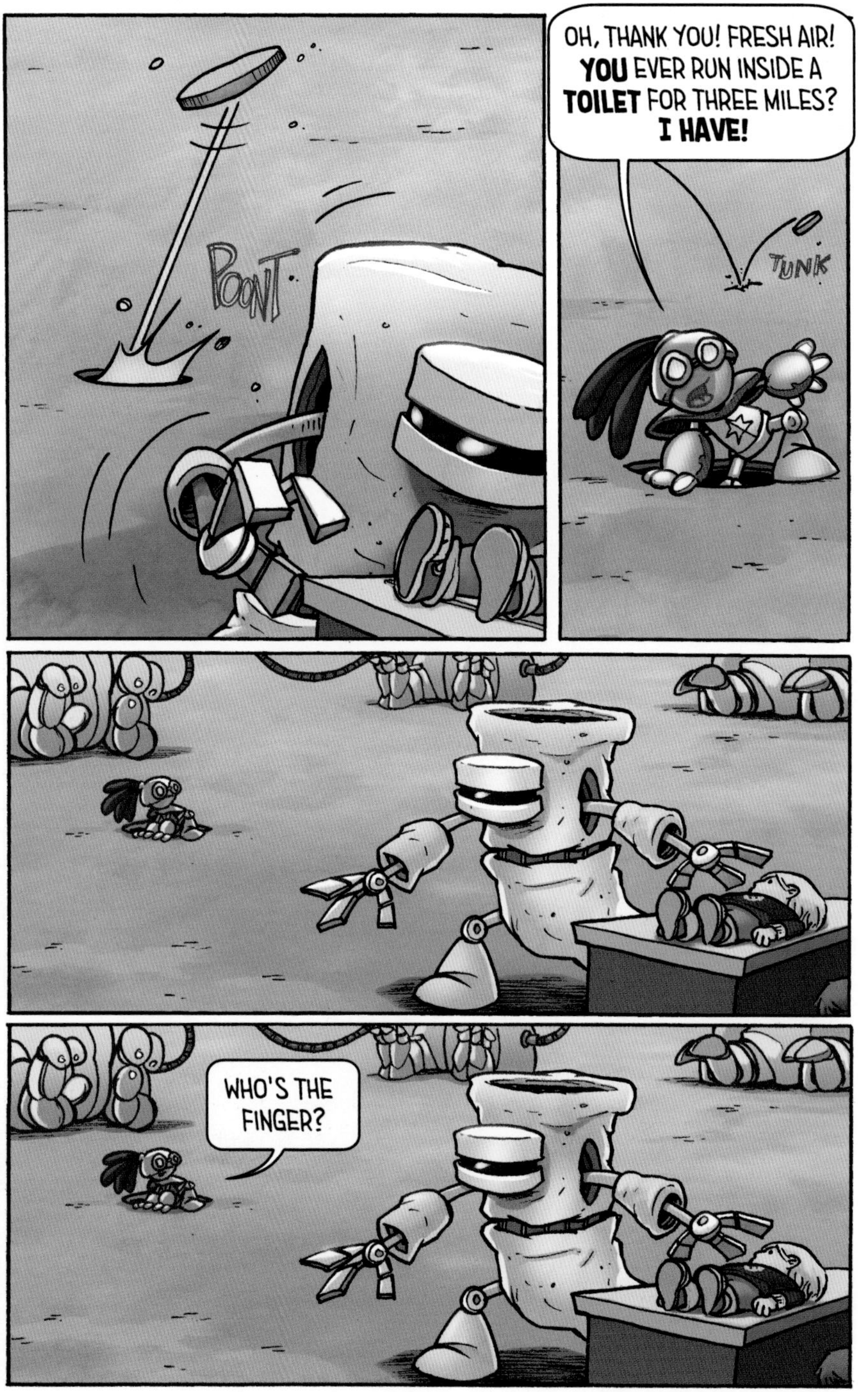
POONT
OH, THANK YOU! FRESH AIR! YOU EVER RUN INSIDE A TOILET FOR THREE MILES? I HAVE!
TUNK
WHO'S THE FINGER?

CHAPTER 10

THE LAST DANCE

IZZY! WE DON'T HAVE TIME FOR DANCING NOW!

I HAVE TO FINISH!

FINISH IT **LATER!** WE HAVE TO HELP GINA AND HILO!

I AM **HELPING!**

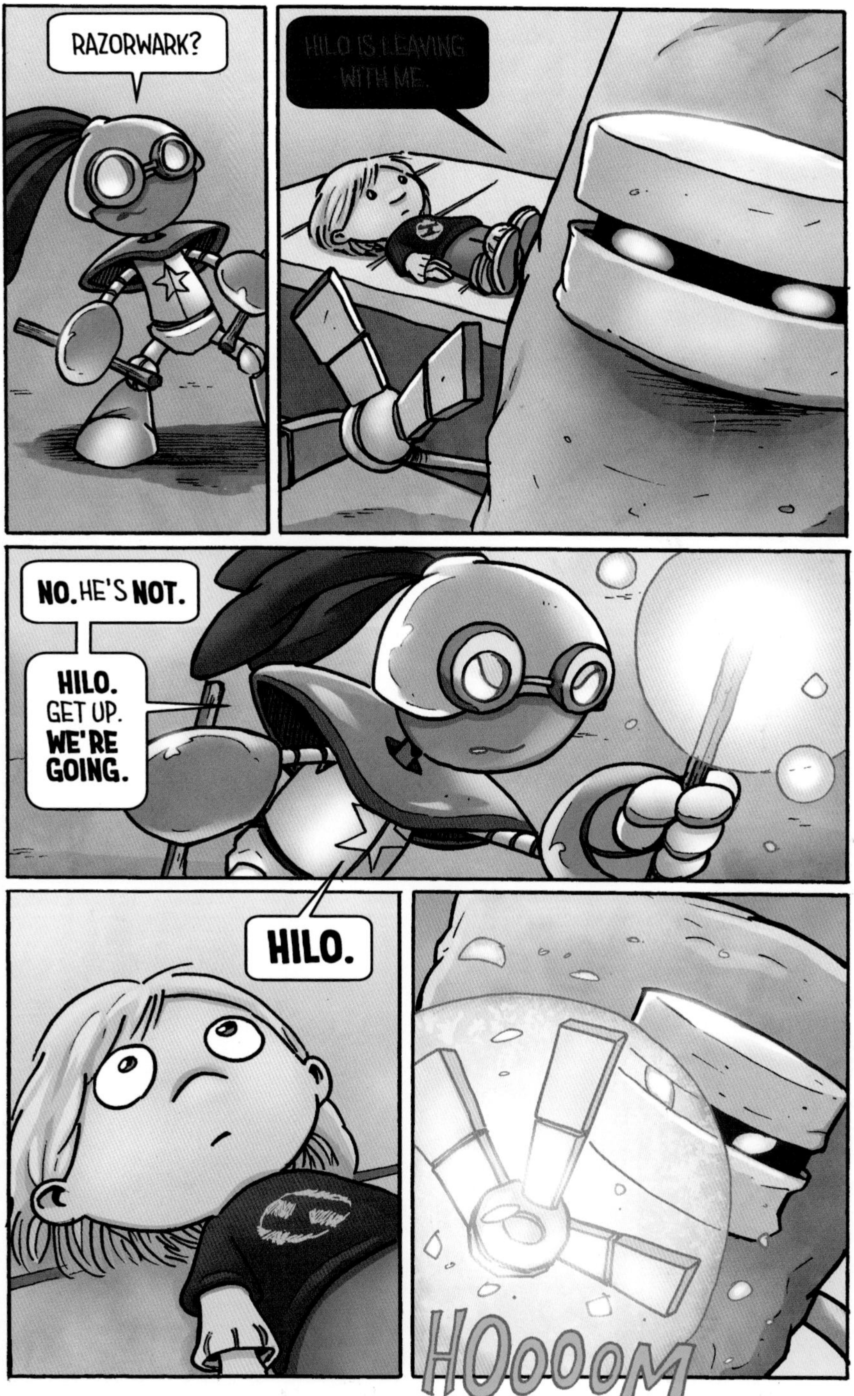
RAZORWARK?
HILO IS LEAVING WITH ME.
NO. HE'S NOT.
HILO. GET UP. WE'RE GOING.
HILO.
HOOOOM

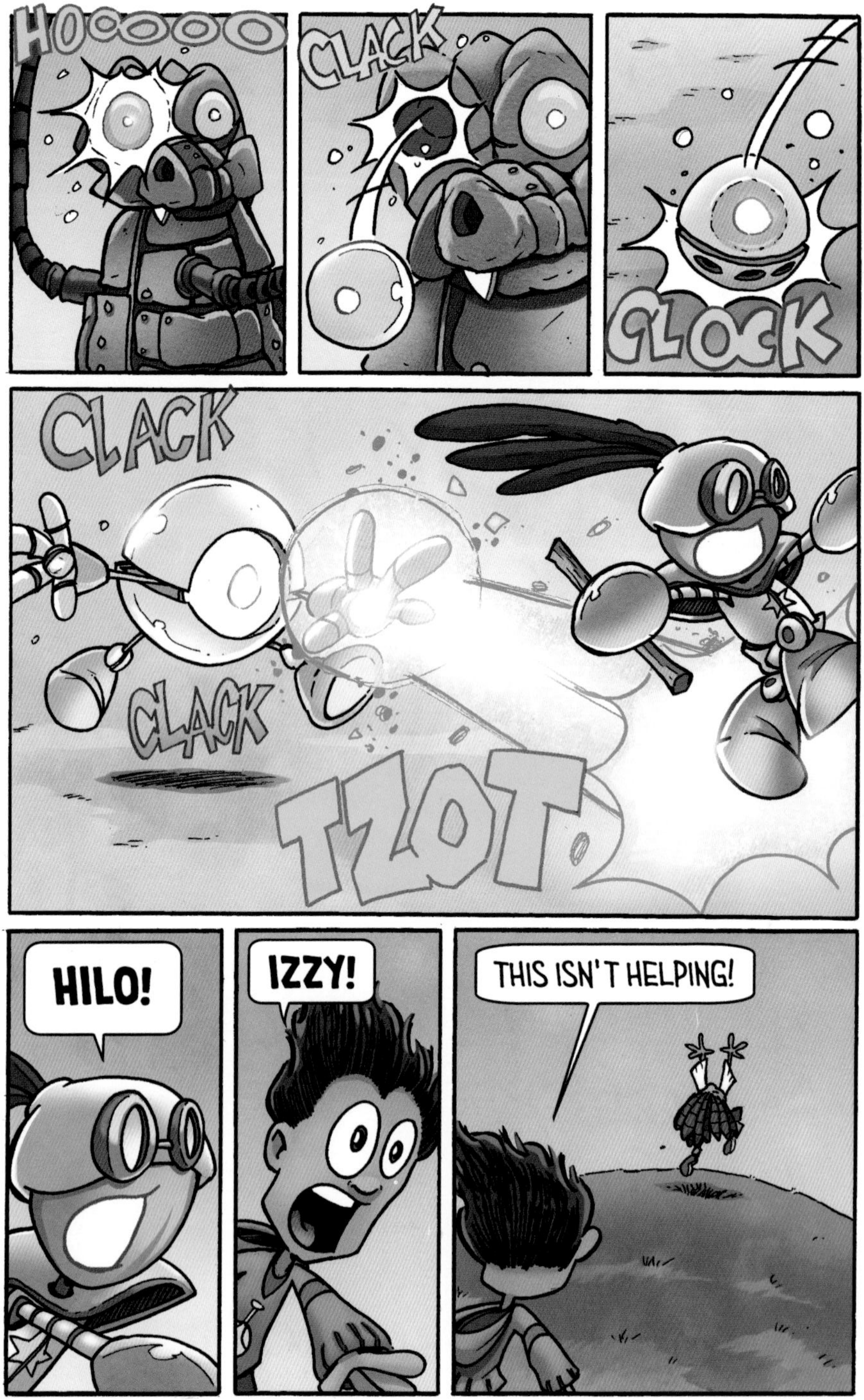
HOOOOOO
CLACK
CLOCK
CLACK
CLACK
TZOT
HILO!
IZZY!
THIS ISN'T HELPING!

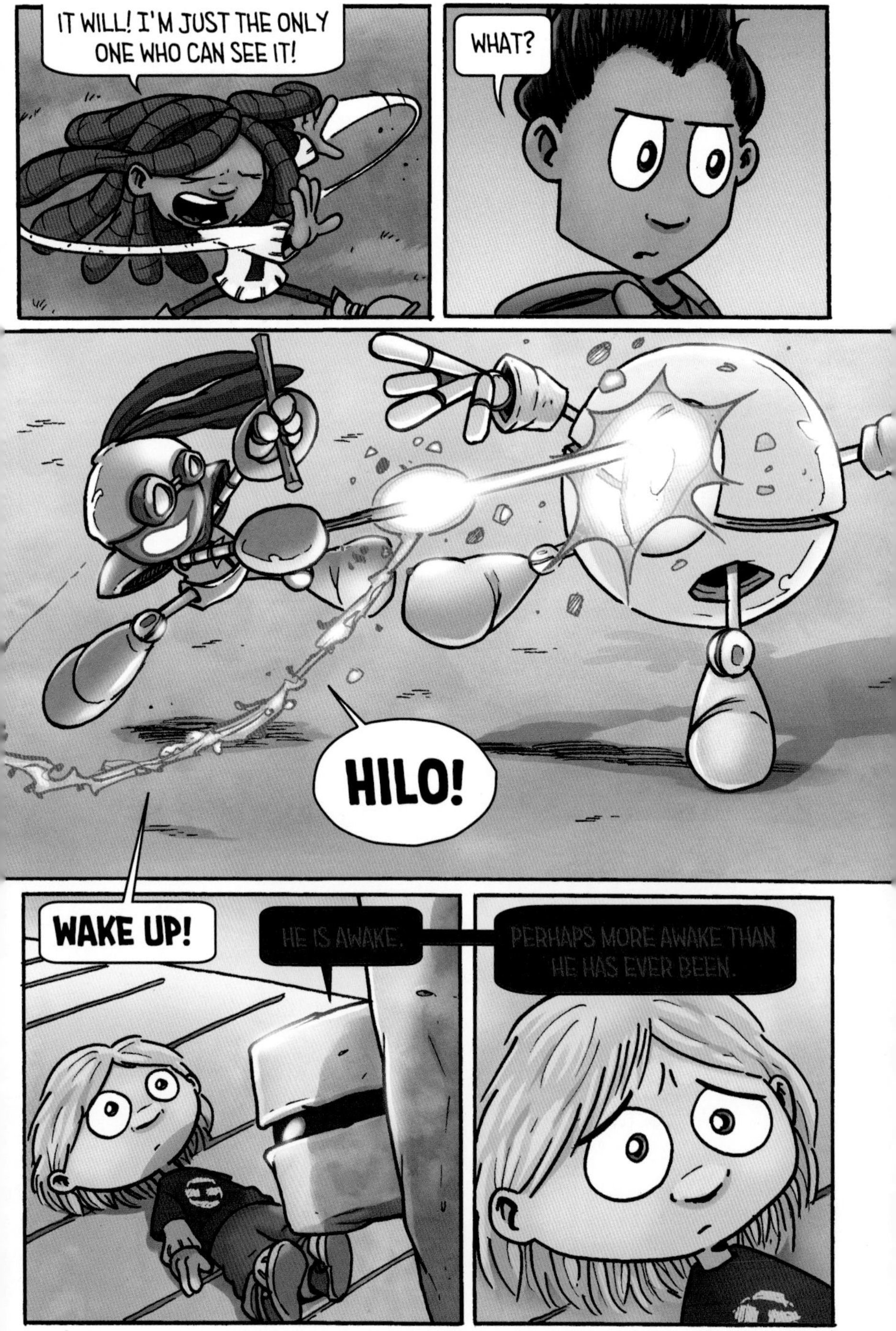
IT WILL! I'M JUST THE ONLY ONE WHO CAN SEE IT!
WHAT?
HILO!
WAKE UP!
HE IS AWAKE.
PERHAPS MORE AWAKE THAN HE HAS EVER BEEN.

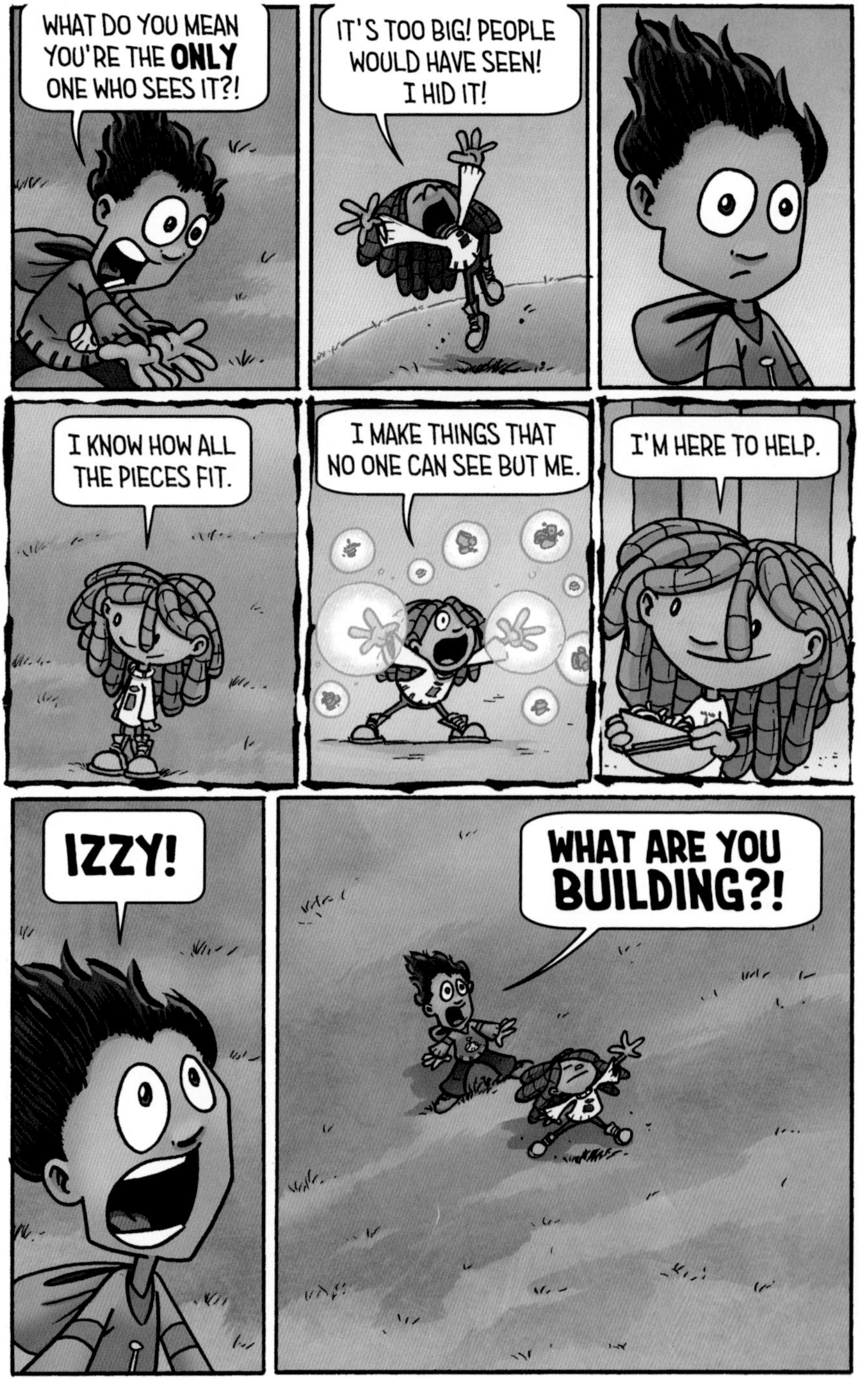
WHAT DO YOU MEAN YOU'RE THE **ONLY** ONE WHO SEES IT?!
IT'S TOO BIG! PEOPLE WOULD HAVE SEEN! I HID IT!
I KNOW HOW ALL THE PIECES FIT.
I MAKE THINGS THAT NO ONE CAN SEE BUT ME.
I'M HERE TO HELP.
IZZY!
WHAT ARE YOU BUILDING?!

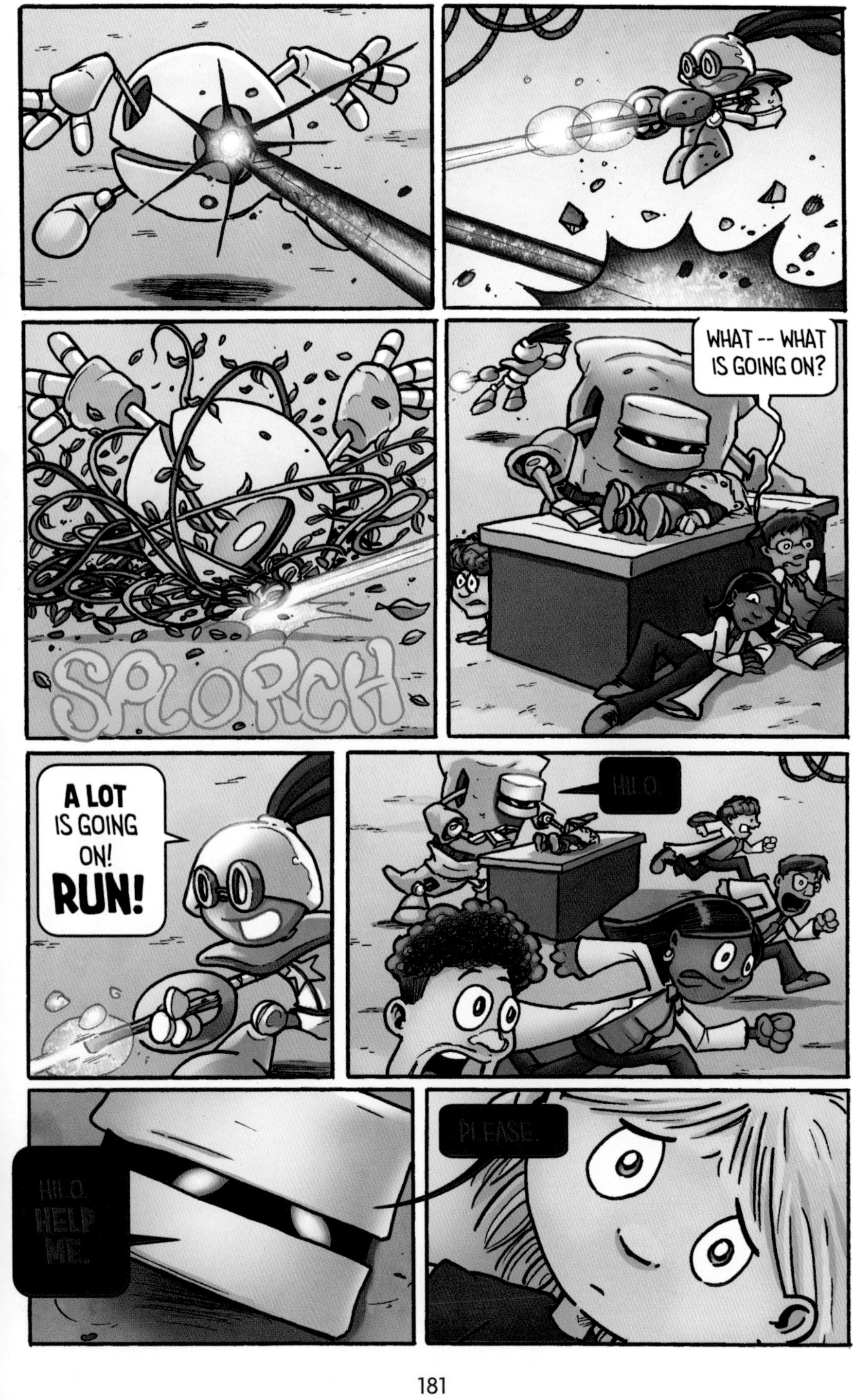

SPLORCH
WHAT -- WHAT IS GOING ON?
A LOT IS GOING ON! RUN!
HILO.
HILO. HELP ME.
PLEASE.

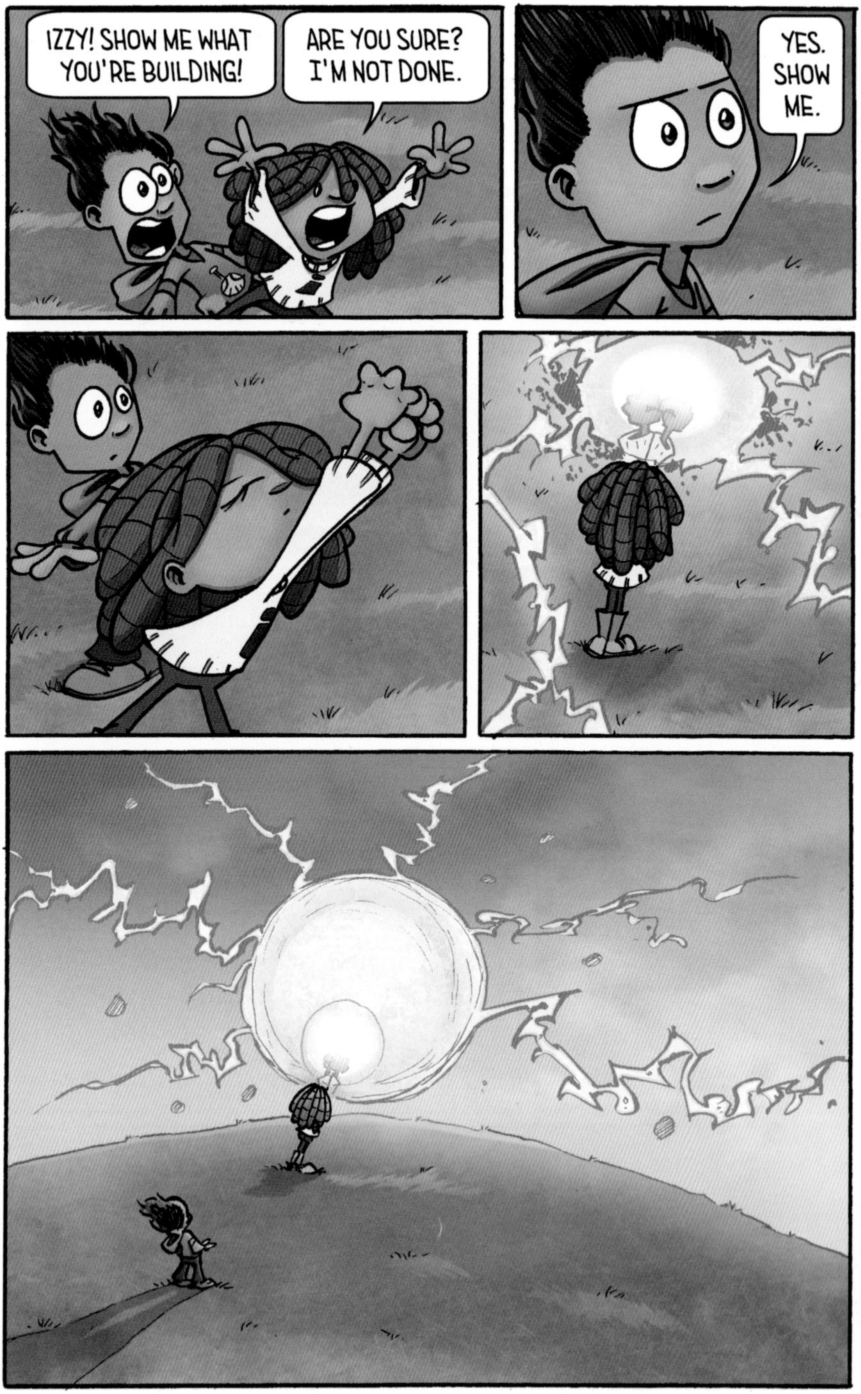
IZZY! SHOW ME WHAT YOU'RE BUILDING!
ARE YOU SURE? I'M NOT DONE.
YES. SHOW ME.

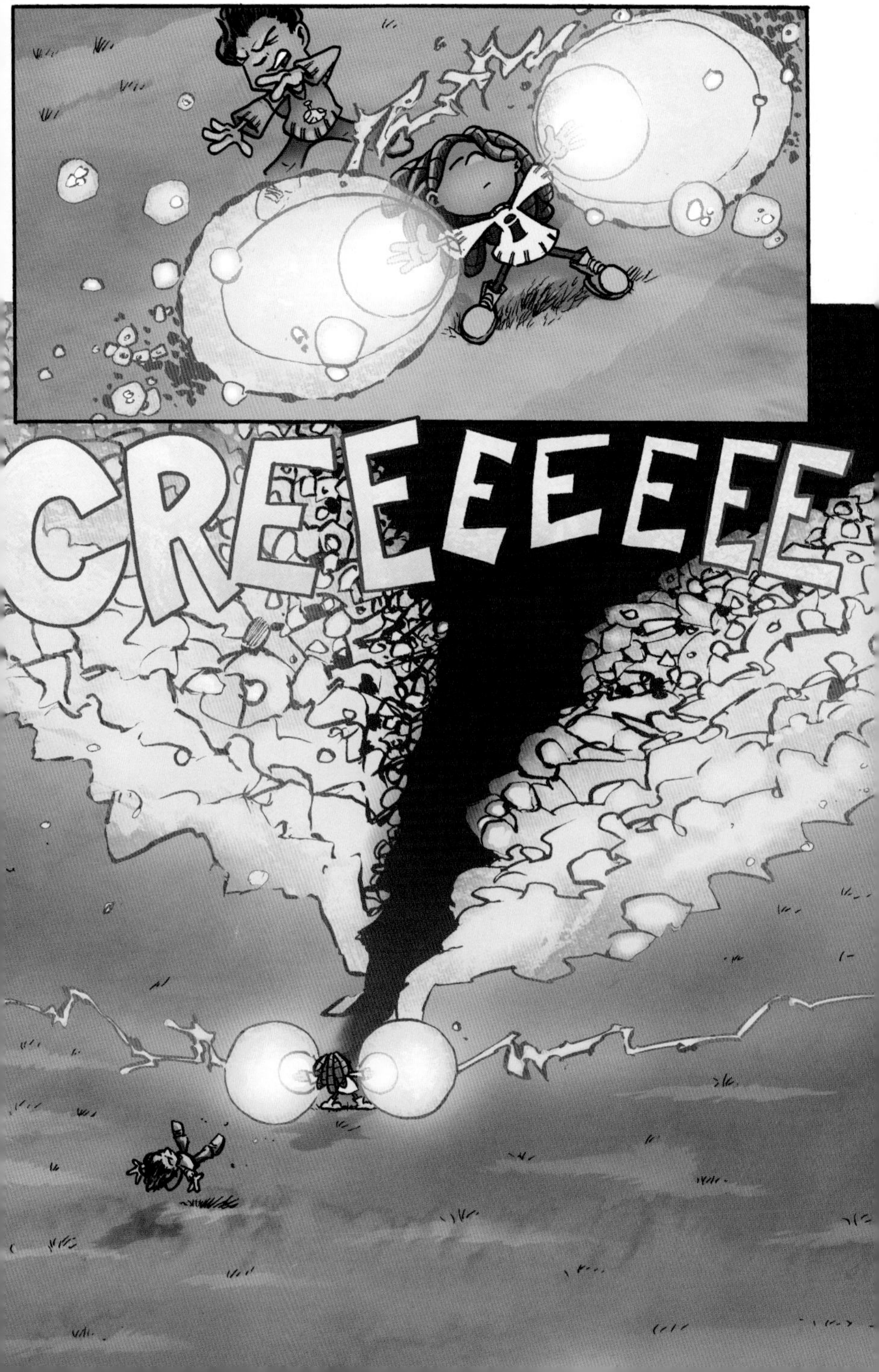
CREEEEEEE

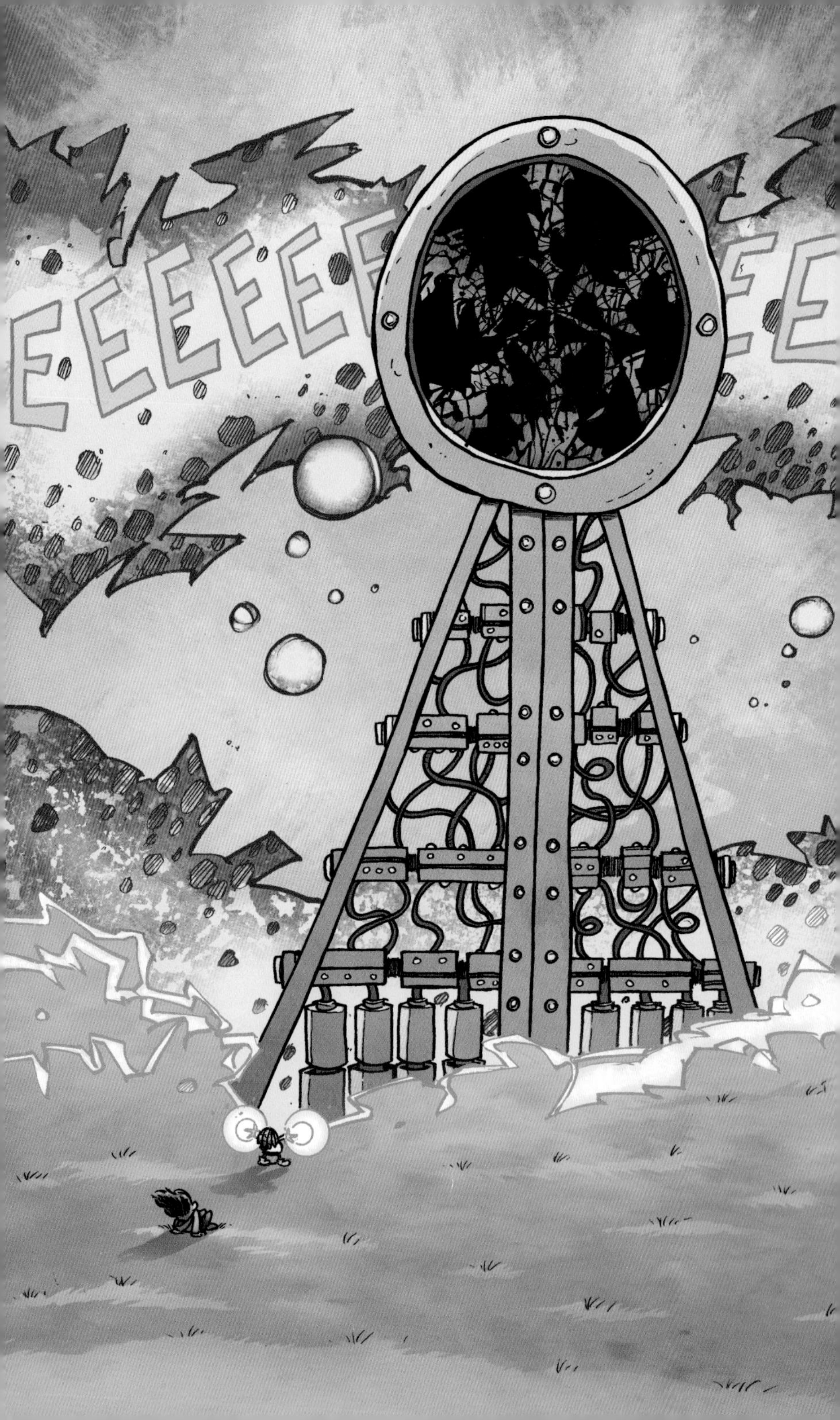
EEEEEE
EE

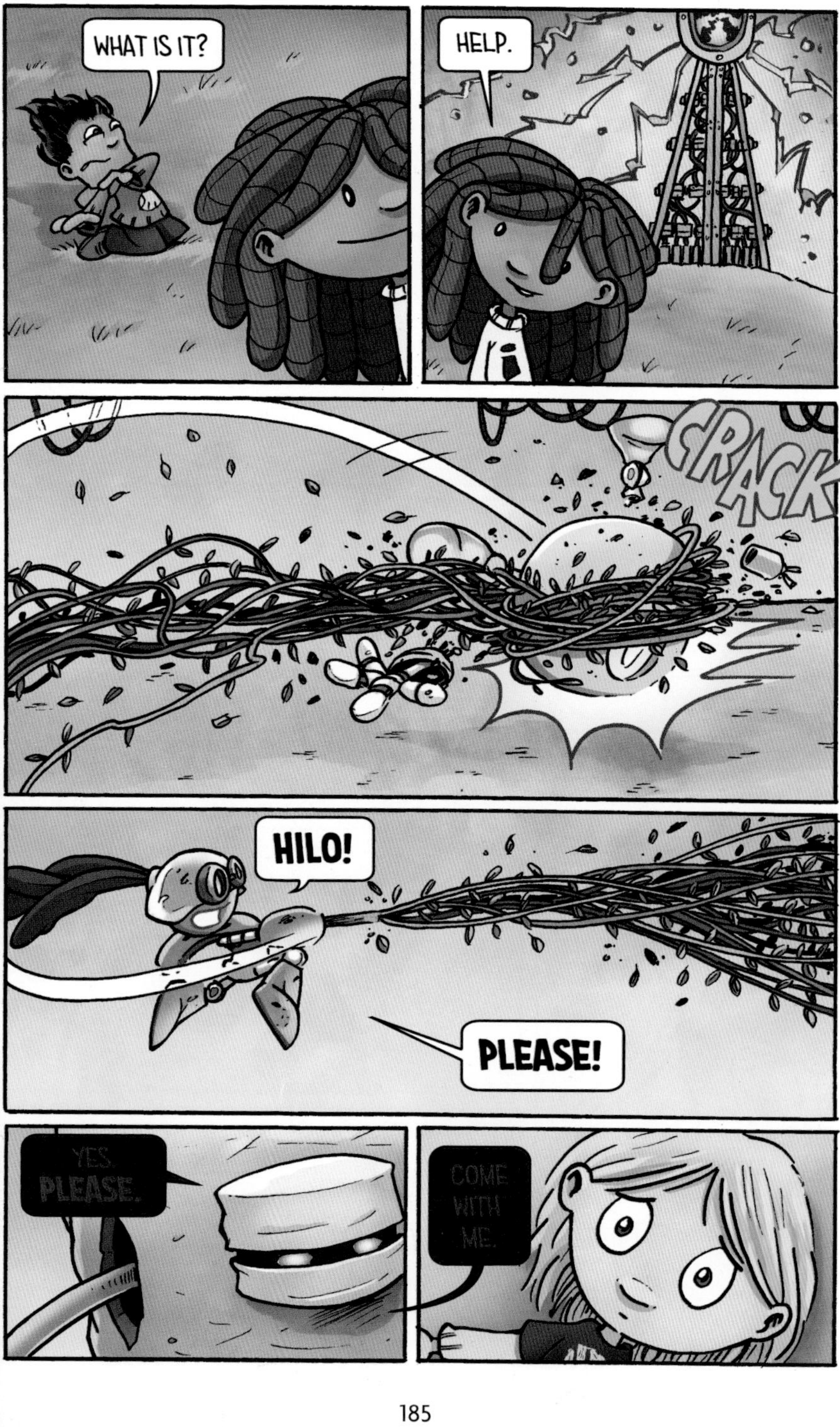
WHAT IS IT?
HELP.
CRACK
HILO!
PLEASE!
YES. PLEASE.
COME WITH ME.

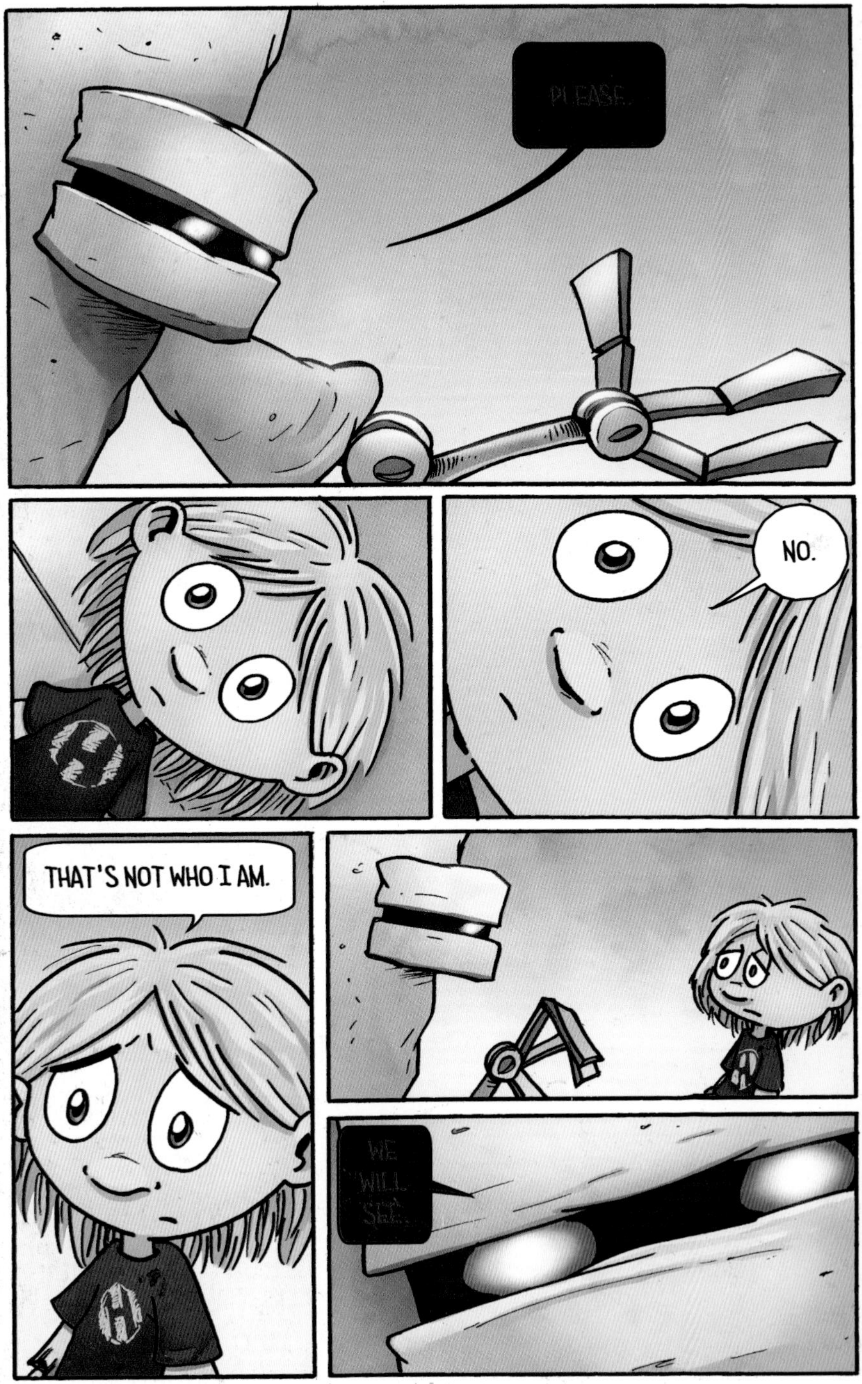

PLEASE...
NO.
THAT'S NOT WHO I AM.
WE WILL SEE...

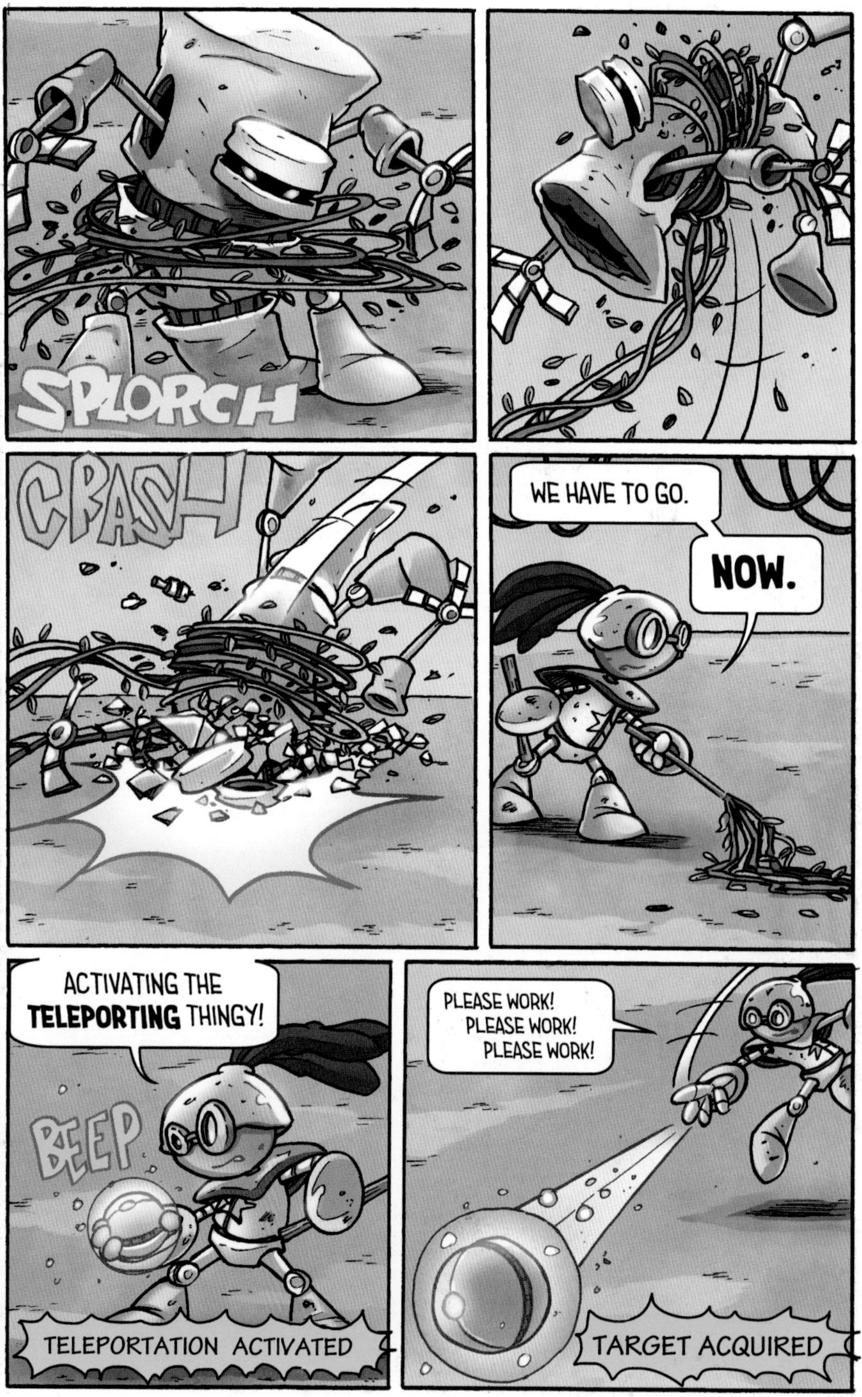
SPLORCH
CRASH
WE HAVE TO GO.
NOW.
ACTIVATING THE TELEPORTING THINGY!
BEEP
TELEPORTATION ACTIVATED
PLEASE WORK! PLEASE WORK! PLEASE WORK!
TARGET ACQUIRED

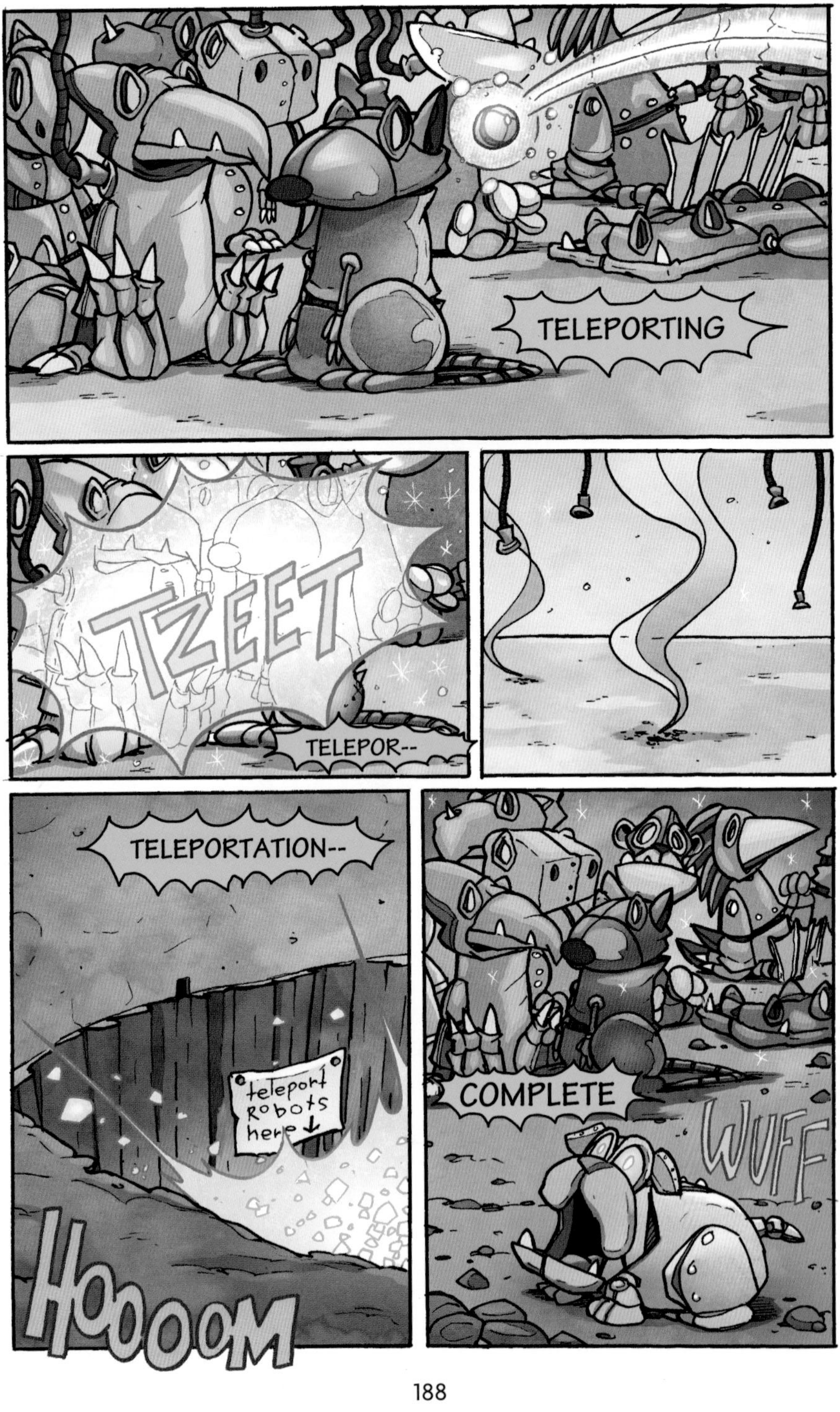
TELEPORTING
TZEET
TELEPOR--
TELEPORTATION--
teleport robots here ↓
HOOOOM
COMPLETE
WUFF

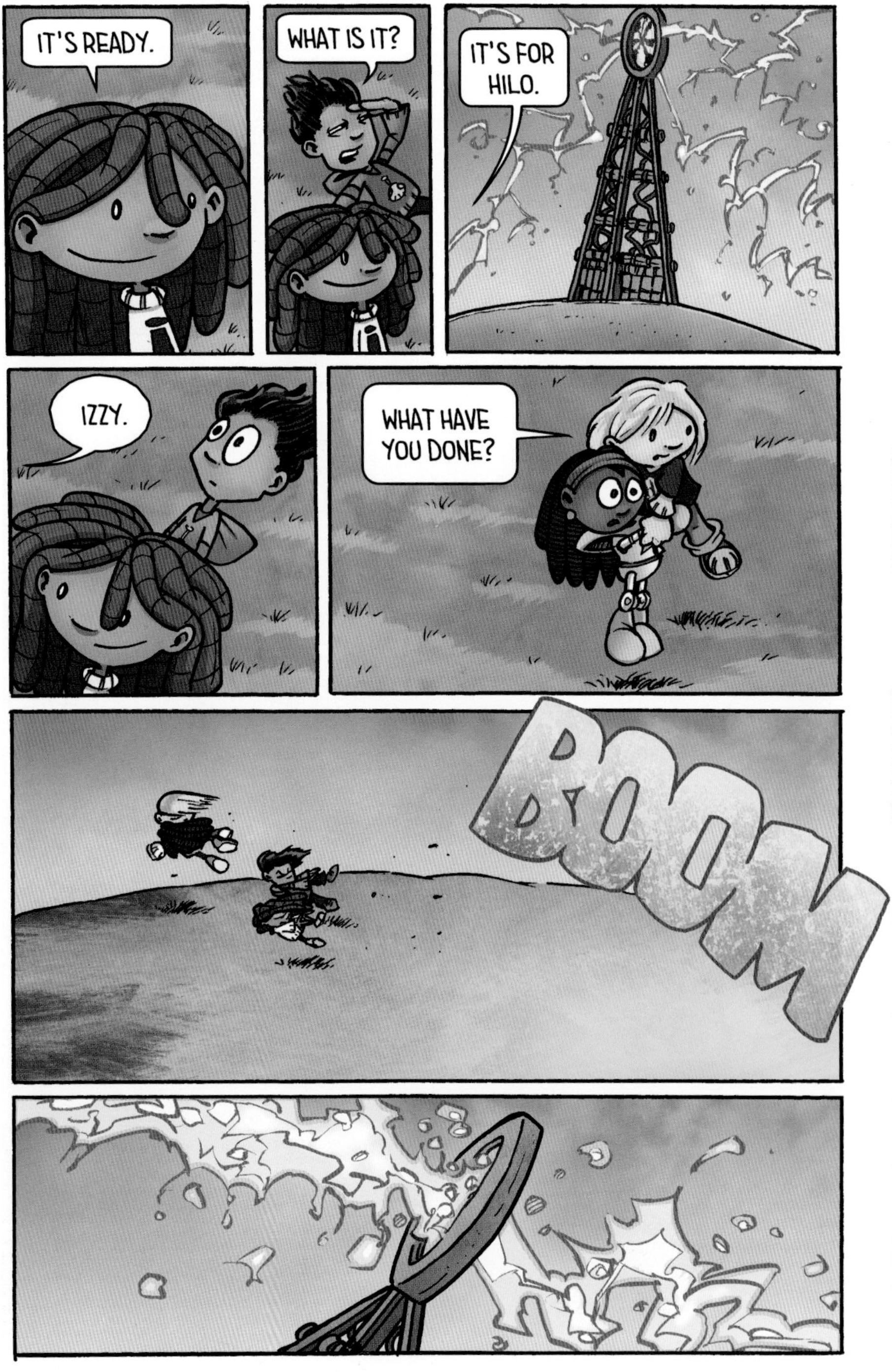
IT'S READY.
WHAT IS IT?
IT'S FOR HILO.
IZZY.
WHAT HAVE YOU DONE?
BOOM

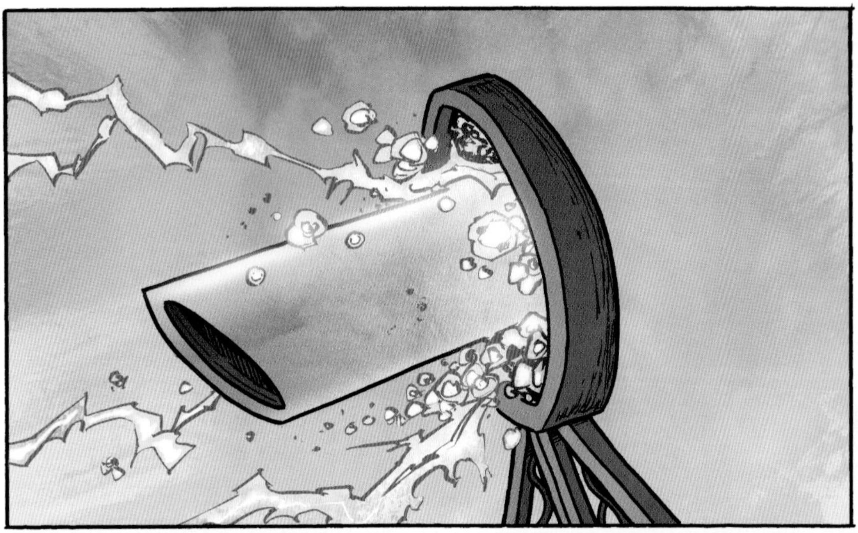

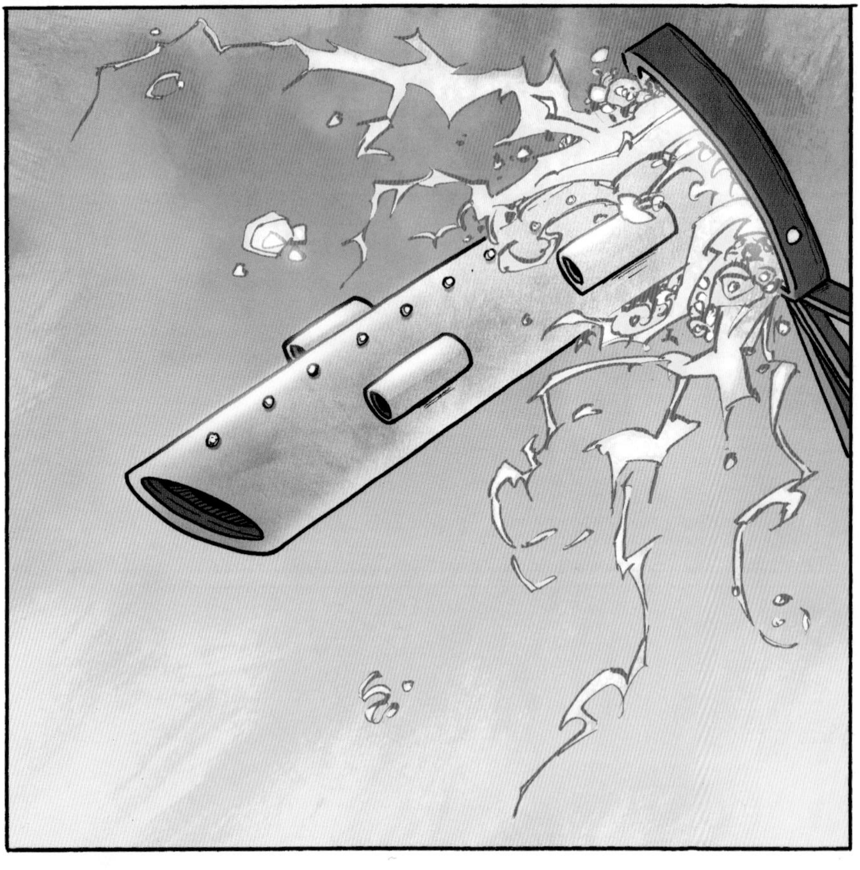

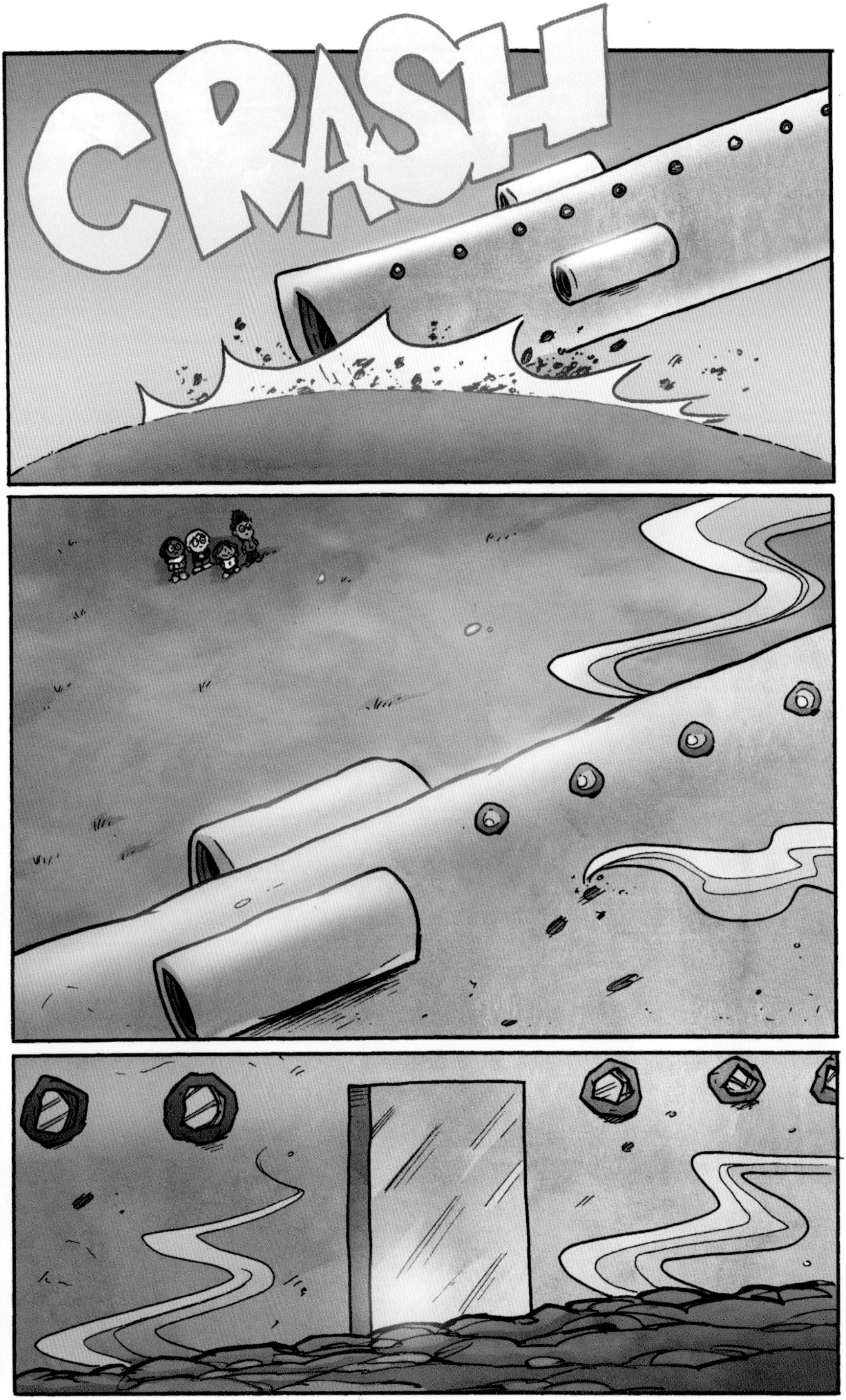
CRASH

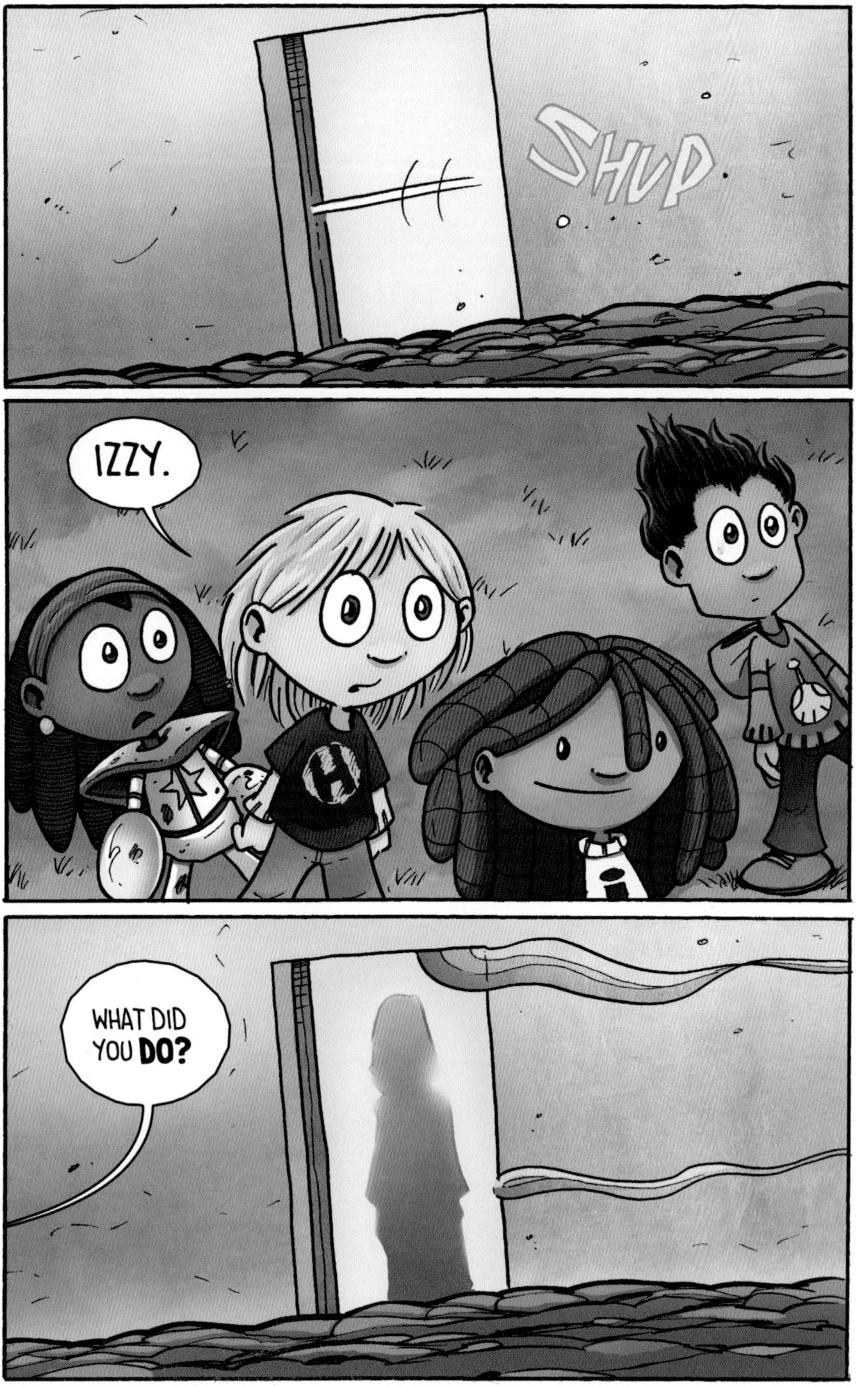
SHUP
IZZY.
WHAT DID YOU DO?

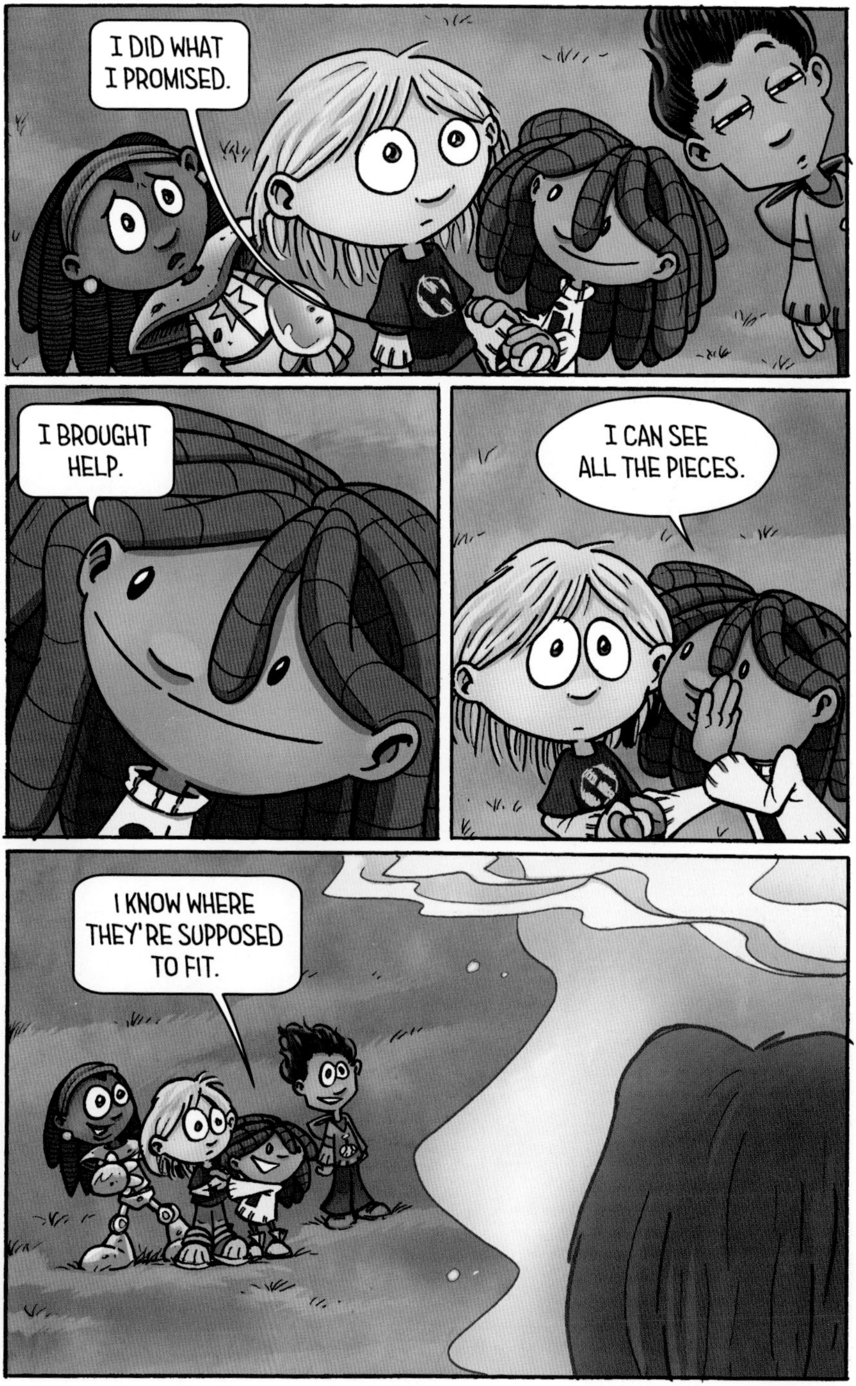
I DID WHAT I PROMISED.
I BROUGHT HELP.
I CAN SEE ALL THE PIECES.
I KNOW WHERE THEY'RE SUPPOSED TO FIT.

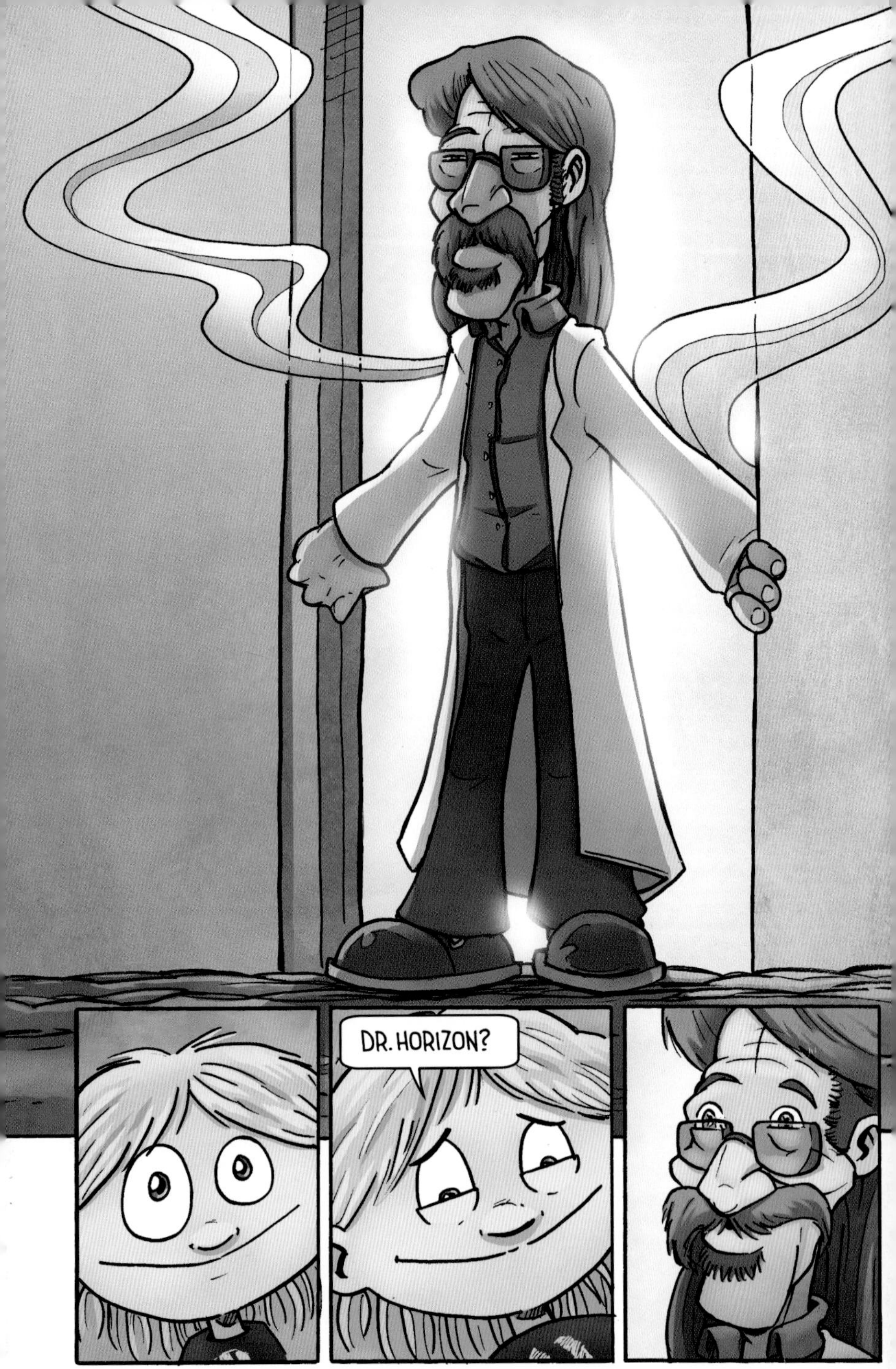
DR. HORIZON?

HELLO.

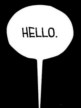

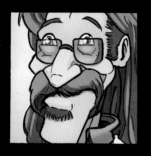

END OF BOOK FOUR

FIND OUT WHAT HAPPENS NEXT IN

HiLO
BOOK 5

COMING TO A PLANET NEAR YOU IN 2019!

SAVING THE WORLD HAS NEVER BEEN SO FUN!

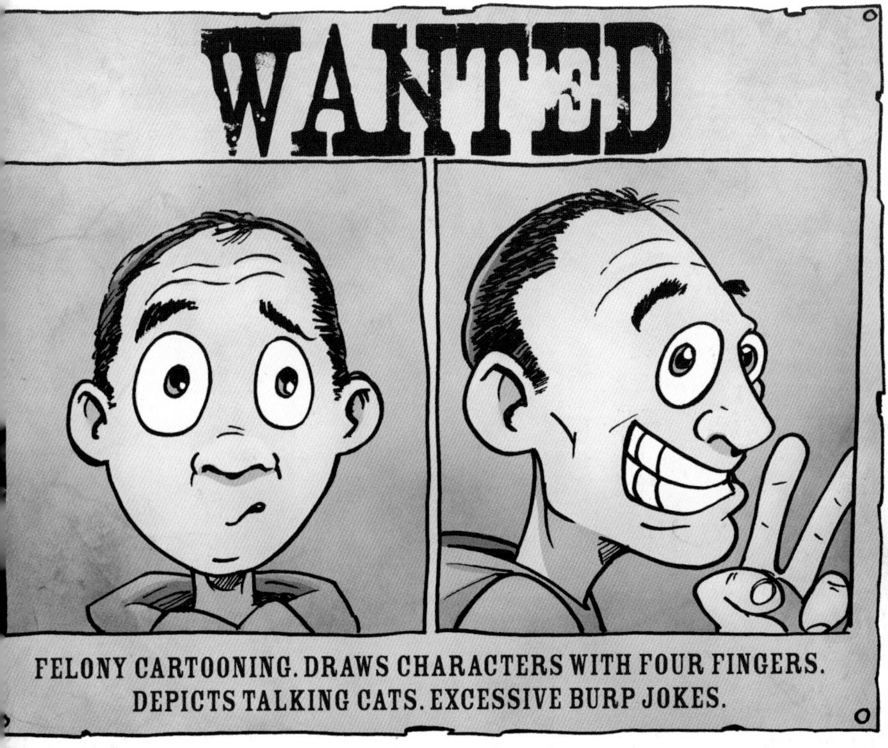
WANTED
FELONY CARTOONING. DRAWS CHARACTERS WITH FOUR FINGERS.
DEPICTS TALKING CATS. EXCESSIVE BURP JOKES.

JUDD WINICK is the creator of the award-winning, **New York Times** bestselling Hilo series. Judd grew up on Long Island with a healthy diet of doodling, **X-Men** comics, the newspaper strip **Bloom County**, and **Looney Tunes**. Today, he lives in San Francisco with his wife, Pam Ling; their two kids; their cat, Chaka; and far too many action figures and vinyl toys for a normal adult. Judd created the Cartoon Network series **Juniper Lee**; has written issues of superhero comics, including Batman, Green Lantern, and Green Arrow; and was a cast member of MTV's **The Real World: San Francisco**. Judd is also the author of the highly acclaimed graphic novel **Pedro and Me**, about his **Real World** roommate and friend, AIDS activist Pedro Zamora. Visit Judd and Hilo online at juddspillowfort.com or find him on Twitter at @JuddWinick.

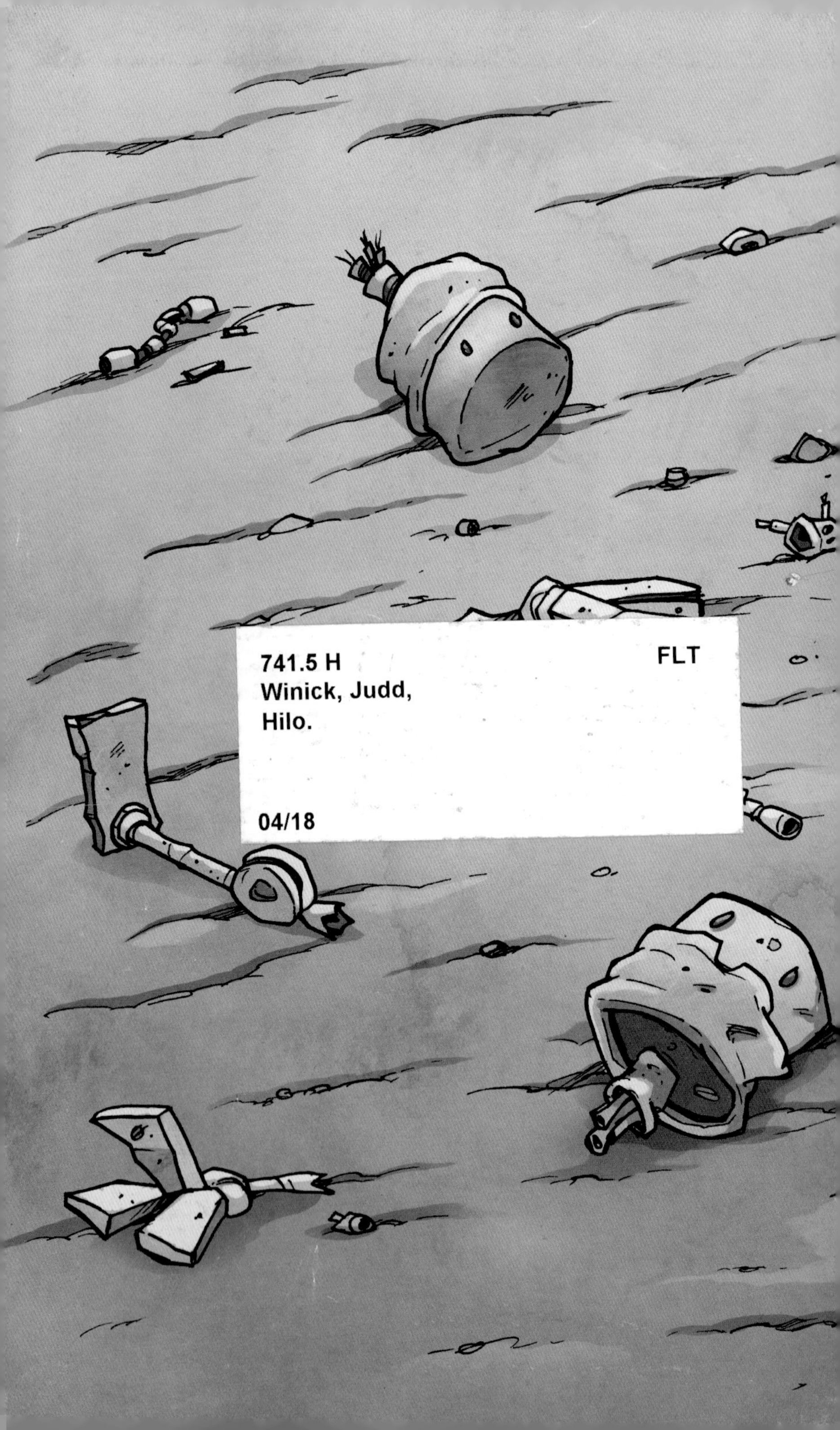